BRONX
JUSTICE

Also by

JOSEPH TELLER

THE TENTH CASE

Watch for

DEPRAVED INDIFFERENCE

Available November 2009

JOSEPH TELLER

BRONX JUSTICE

MIRA®

Recycling programs
for this product may
not exist in your area.

ISBN-13: 978-0-7783-2635-9
ISBN-10:   0-7783-2635-7

BRONX JUSTICE

www.MIRABooks.com

Printed in U.S.A.

To Sheila, who put up with me back then, at a time
when I'm sure I was impossible to put up with.
And to my children, Wendy, Ron and Tracy,
who must have suffered mightily by having a father
absent in more ways than one, but never complained
about it, then or since.

1

IN THE MIDDLE OF THE NIGHT

Jaywalker is dreaming when the ringing of his phone jars him awake. Something about hiking with his wife in the Canadian Rockies. He understands right away it has to have been a dream, because his wife has been dead for nearly ten years now, and he hasn't hiked the Rockies in twice that long.

Groping in the darkness for the phone, his first fear is for his daughter. Is she out driving? Riding with some pimply-faced boyfriend who's had his learner's permit for two weeks now and thinks of driving as some sort of video game? Then he remembers. His daughter is in her early thirties. She has a husband with no pimples, a child of her own, a career, and a house in New Jersey.

"Hello?" Jaywalker says into the phone, then holds his breath and readies himself for the worst. The clock radio next to the phone glows 3:17.

"Pete?" says an unfamiliar male voice.

"I think," says Jaywalker, "that you may have dialed the wrong number. What number were you trying to—"

The line goes dead. No "Sorry," no "Oops." Just a click, followed by silence and eventually a dial tone.

Jaywalker recradles the phone. He lies on his back in the dark, feeling his pulse pounding in his temples. Relief and annoyance duel for his attention, but only briefly. For already, Jaywalker is elsewhere. He's lying in bed in the dark, to be sure, but somehow his hair is brown instead of gray, his face less lined, his body more muscular. And his wife lies beside him, her warm body pressed against his back.

"Who was it?" she asks him.

"A mother," he says. "A mother whose son has just been arrested. A rape case. And it sounds like a bad one."

"For them," says Jaywalker's wife. "But that means a good one for you, right?"

"Right," agrees Jaywalker. He's not yet thirty, this younger version of him. He's been out of Legal Aid for a little over a year now, struggling to build a practice on his own. And *struggling* is definitely the operative word here. So he knows his wife is right: what's bad for the young man and his family is at the same time good for the lawyer and his. One of the strange paradoxes of criminal law that Jaywalker will never quite get comfortable with: that his earning a living is dependent upon the suffering of others.

What this younger Jaywalker doesn't know, what he has absolutely no way of knowing at this point, as he lies in the dark, is that this new case will be different, that it will mark a crossroads in his career and in his life. Should he live to be a hundred, no case that will ever come his way will end up affecting him as this one will. Before he's done with it, and it with him, it will change him in ways that will be as profound as they are unimaginable. It will transform him, molding him and pounding him and shaping him into the lawyer and the man he is today, almost thirty years later. So this is more than just the case he'll forever wake up to when the phone rings in the middle of the night. This is the case that he'll retry in his mind over and over again for the rest of his days, changing a phrase here, adding a word there, tweaking his summation for the hundredth—no, the thousandth—time. And long after he's grown old and senile and has forgotten the names and faces and details of other cases, this is the one that Jaywalker will remember on his deathbed, as clearly and as vividly as if it began yesterday.

2

NO DOUBT WHATSOEVER

That the case had come Jaywalker's way at 3:17 in the morning, while unusual, was not entirely unprecedented. That it had come by way of his home telephone was actually rather typical. Jaywalker had early on developed the habit of giving out his home number liberally. It was but one of many things that distinguished him from his colleagues, who never would have thought of doing such a thing, the functional equivalent of a physician's house call. Moreover, as technology advanced, with the advent of beepers, pagers, car phones, cell phones and BlackBerries, Jaywalker stuck to the practice with characteristic stubbornness, continuing to invite clients and their families to call him at home whenever the need arose. As it had apparently arisen for Inez Kingston on that particular night in September of 1979.

Then, as now, Jaywalker had answered with a fearful "Hello?" notwithstanding the fact that he knew his daughter was safely in bed upstairs and wouldn't even be of driving age for another twelve or thirteen years. Whatever the circumstance, there seems to be something about the midnight phone call that inspires instant dread.

"Mr. Jaywalker?" the woman had said.

"Yes."

"This is Inez Kingston. You represented my son Darren last year. Maybe you remember."

"Sure," said Jaywalker. "I remember." The name did sound familiar, though if pressed, he would have had trouble attaching a face to it, or recalling what the charges had been and how the case had turned out.

"I'm afraid it's Darren again," she said. "They've got him at the precinct. They say he raped some women. They won't tell me any more."

"What precinct?"

"The Forty-third."

Jaywalker jotted down Inez's number in the dark, something he'd learned to do. Otherwise, brilliant ideas that came to him in the middle of the night had a way of vanishing before morning. Written down on paper, they tended to lose some of their brilliance, but at least they survived.

He found the number for the 43rd Precinct. He knew from the precinct number that it had to be somewhere in the Bronx, but other than that, he didn't have a clue. Ninety percent of his practice was in Manhattan, which he liked to think of in sports language as his home court. Of course, at this particular stage of his career, the math wasn't all that hard to do: it didn't exactly require a calculator to convert nine out of ten cases into a percentage.

He reached the precinct and had the desk officer transfer his call to the squad room. There a detective confirmed that they did indeed have a Darren Kingston locked up. He'd been booked for five separate rapes and would be making court in the morning.

Jaywalker thanked the detective and called Inez back. He told her what he'd been able to find out, and offered to meet her in court at nine o'clock. Before hanging up, he told her not to worry. Like most people, if you woke Jaywalker up in the middle of the night, he could be pretty stupid.

It took him an hour or so, and the continued warmth of his wife's body pressed up against his own, but he eventually managed to fall back to sleep. He was sure Inez Kingston didn't.

He had a car back in those days, Jaywalker did. Or sort of. It was an ancient Volkswagen Beetle, its exterior equal parts blue paint and orange rust. The running boards had fallen off, the heater was history, the wipers stuck when they weren't busy scratching the windshield, and the horn worked if you were lucky enough to happen upon the "sweet spot" of the rim.

But it was transportation, something that came in handy when you'd been forced to flee the city's rich rents and poor public schools, and move to the suburbs. If Bergenfield, New Jersey, qualified as a suburb. What it was, was a blue-collar, working-class community, where Jaywalker could mow his own lawn, rake his own leaves and shovel his own driveway without being mistaken for a hired man. Even if his wife hoped for better things, it suited him just fine.

Aiming the VW toward the Bronx that following morning, Jaywalker tried to remember what he could about Darren Kingston. He'd been one of Jaywalker's first clients after he'd left Legal Aid. His mother, Inez, worked at what today is referred to as the Department of Social Services. Back then it was the Welfare Department. Progress, no doubt. One of Inez's coworkers there was Jaywalker's sister-in-law. It had been at her suggestion that Inez had called Jaywalker when Darren had gotten into trouble. Along with two other young black men, he'd been arrested for robbing an elderly white man. Although the case had sounded bad at first, it turned out to be pretty harmless. One of the other defendants had done some work for the man and had had a dispute over how much money was owed him. When he went to collect, he brought his friends along. One of his friends being a knife. Seeing as Darren himself hadn't possessed it, had had very little involvement in the matter and had never been in any sort of trouble before, the charges against him had eventually been dropped.

This time, Jaywalker thought as he maneuvered around the potholes, trash and broken glass of the South Bronx, he was pretty sure things weren't going to be quite so easy.

Arraignments took place in a dark gray building at 161st Street and Washington Avenue, half a block from the abandoned elevated tracks above Third Avenue. It was one of two buildings that together made up the Bronx Criminal Court. Rumor had it that both had been condemned as unsafe since the early 1950s, and in fact they would finally be abandoned a few years later, replaced by a large modern structure closer to the Grand Concourse.

At the time, however, the decaying building was, for most people, their first encounter with what passed for Bronx justice. The floors were stained and uneven. Where they were supposed to be tiled, whole sections of tiles had been removed. Where they were wood, they were splintered and suffering from years of dry rot. The walls were cracked and paint-chipped, and covered with graffiti that was anti-police, anti-white, anti-black, anti-Hispanic, anti-gay, anti-just about everything. The two elevators took turns being out of order. Rather than guessing, Jaywalker headed for the stairwell. Just before entering, he took a deep gulp of air, then breathed through his mouth as he climbed, in order to block out as much of the stench of old urine as he could.

Reaching the second floor, he recognized Inez Kingston and her husband, Marlin. She was a short, heavyset woman whose pleasant smile and soft West Indian accent masked an inner nervousness and chronic high blood pressure. He was an equally short, wiry man with a face that wore the two-day-old stubble of a nightshift worker for the Transit Department. As accustomed as Inez was to hiding her feelings, Marlin was not, and his face that Wednesday morning was tense and unsmiling.

Jaywalker headed over and greeted them. Inez introduced him to her younger brother, who'd come along for support. Jaywalker asked if anything was new since the night before.

"No," said Inez, "but the detective's here. Rendell. He

won't tell us anything, but he did say he'd talk to you. I told him we had a lawyer coming. Was that all right?"

"Yes," said Jaywalker. "Where is he now?"

"In there." She pointed to a door. A sign on it warned passersby to keep out.

COMPLAINT ROOM
POLICE OFFICERS ONLY

"Point him out to me when he comes out, okay?"

It didn't take long. Robert Rendell, all six foot three of him, opened the door and strode out. He was young for a detective, and handsome, with a shock of graying black hair that fell across his forehead. Jaywalker immediately sized him up as a formidable witness. Then he moved to intercept him before he made it to the courtroom.

"Detective Rendell?"

"Yup."

"My name is Jaywalker. I'm going to be representing Darren Kingston. The family said you might be able to give me a little information. They seem pretty confused."

"What can I tell you, counselor? I've got five CWs—" *complaining witnesses,* Jaywalker translated mentally "—and everything they say points to your man."

"Lineups?" Jaywalker probed.

"You're going to have to talk to the D.A."

"Jesus," said Jaywalker, a seriously lapsed Jew. "I've known this kid for years." It was an exaggeration, but a modest one. "Shocks the shit outta you. When did these rapes take place?"

"August, mostly. But I've been looking for him for a couple of weeks."

"Statements?"

"No, nothing really," said the detective. "Says he's innocent. Tell you what, counselor. I got one of the girls coming down this morning. She IDs him, or she doesn't." He shrugged. "If he's not the guy, I don't want him." With that, he excused himself and walked into the courtroom.

Jaywalker looked at his watch. It was a few minutes after ten. Court was supposed to begin at 9:30 a.m., but the judge hadn't taken the bench yet. Nothing new there.

Jaywalker took a minute to consider what he had. Rendell hadn't given him much, but at least he'd added a few more facts to piece into the picture. There were five victims. At least one of them—the one who was on her way to court—apparently hadn't seen Darren since the incident. Assuming it *was* Darren. Most of the rapes had occurred in August, a month ago. That could be good. But Rendell's comment that he'd been looking for Darren sounded bad. It meant that Darren had been positively identified as the result of some sort of investigation. It also suggested that Darren might have been hiding out, trying to avoid arrest. Consciousness of guilt? That there were no admissions was good. If he was guilty, at least Darren had been smart enough to keep his mouth shut.

Already Jaywalker could sense things shaping up as a classic identification case. Five women had been raped. Was Darren Kingston the man who had raped them?

He reported his findings to the family. Then he went into the clerk's office, filled out a Notice of Appearance and traded it for a copy of the complaint. Computers not yet having arrived in the courthouse, the complaint consisted of a preprinted form with the blanks filled in by someone using an ancient typewriter and a generous supply of carbon paper.

Criminal Court of the City of New York

Part A, County of <u>The Bronx</u>

STATE OF NEW YORK
   ss.:   FELONY COMPLAINT
COUNTY OF <u>The Bronx</u>

  <u>Joanne Kenarden</u>, being duly sworn, deposes and says that on <u>August 16, 1979</u>, in the County of <u>The Bronx</u>, City and State of New York, the defendant(s) <u>Darren Kingston</u> committed the offense(s) of <u>rape in the first degree and sodomy in the first degree</u> under the following circumstances:

Deponent states that at the above time and place defendant forcibly at knifepoint committed an act of sexual intercourse upon her without her consent, and also forced her to commit an act of oral sodomy. Knife not recovered.

Sworn to before me
....
................, 19.....   Deponent

....
Judge

Jaywalker was reading it through for a second time when Inez Kingston walked up to him. "The detective just took Darren across the hall," she said.

Jaywalker followed her out of the clerk's office. She pointed to a door, one without a sign. Jaywalker knocked on it. When there was no answer, he pushed it open. After all, he reasoned, there was no sign saying not to. Inside were Detective Rendell, Darren Kingston and a third man, who looked up and said, "Yes?"

"I'm his lawyer," said Jaywalker. "May I know what's going on?"

"Oh, sure." The third man was young, thin and, when he stood up, closer to Jaywalker's height than Rendell's. His face was dominated by a black mustache. "My name is Jacob Pope," he said. "I'm an assistant district attorney in the Mob."

"The Mob?" echoed Jaywalker. It struck him as a curious affiliation.

"The Major Offense Bureau. I was just about to ask Mr. Kingston some questions regarding pedigree, for bail purposes. I didn't realize he had an attorney."

Jaywalker looked back and forth from Pope to Rendell. One of them was playing dirty here—Pope, if Rendell had told him about Jaywalker, Rendell if he'd neglected to. A prosecutor was strictly forbidden from speaking with a defendant who had a lawyer unless the lawyer was present or gave his express permission. And *pedigree* was just a fancy way of describing a series of questions that began with name and address and ended with, "Where'd you hide the body?"

Darren was seated, his wrists handcuffed in his lap. Jaywalker had forgotten how good-looking he was. *Model* good-looking, almost. "How're you doing, Darren?" he asked him.

"N-n-n-not so good."

The stutter. Jaywalker had forgotten *that*, too. Darren had a severe stutter that grew worse when he became nervous. Jaywalker turned to Pope. "Can you give me a moment with my client?" he asked. "Then maybe we'll talk to you."

"Sure," said Pope. "Go right ahead." But neither he nor Rendell made any move to give them privacy.

"Can we take the cuffs off?" Jaywalker asked.

Pope nodded at the detective, who produced a key and removed the handcuffs. Darren rubbed each wrist in turn. Jaywalker waited until Pope and Rendell had walked to the far end of the room. Then he positioned himself between Darren and them, giving them his back. It wasn't much, but it was as good as it was going to get.

As quietly as he could, he asked Darren what was going on.

"I don't know. They say I r-r-r-raped a bunch of women. I didn't do anything like that. I don't know anything about it."

"Darren, they've got five women who say you're the guy. I'm here to help you, a hundred percent. I can help you if you're innocent. But understand this—I can also help you if you're guilty. There are hospitals, there are sexual offender programs." There were; it wasn't a complete lie. "The only way I *can't* help you," Jaywalker went on, "is if you don't tell me. So you've got to try to trust me." He wanted to add "and start telling me the truth." But he didn't. Not yet, anyway.

Darren's eyes met Jaywalker's. "I do trust you, Jay." His

use of the name brought a smile to Jaywalker's face. A year ago, it had taken him a long time to get Darren to stop calling him *Mr. Jaywalker.* But Jaywalker had insisted. If he was going to address his clients by their first names—and he did, always—then they were going to do the same with him. Not that Jay was really his first name. But when your parents hang *Harrison Jason Walker* on you, you're happy to settle for Jay. Or, as a few of his Hispanic clients pronounced it, *Yay.*

"Good," said Jaywalker.

"But you gotta trust me, too, Jay. I d-d-didn't do this."

Jaywalker nodded. He knew it was useless to push at this point. He decided to let Darren answer Pope's questions in his presence. It was his hope to learn a few things, while giving up nothing in return. At the same time, he was looking for any edge he could get. He knew that Pope's recommendation on bail would carry a lot of weight with the judge.

After learning that Darren was twenty-two, married, living with his wife, the father of one child and expecting another, Pope moved on to Darren's employment.

"You work for the post office, right?"

"Right."

"The night shift?"

"Right."

It was obvious that Pope, or perhaps Rendell, had done his homework.

"Were you working the last two weeks of August, or was that your vacation time?"

Jaywalker held up a hand. "I'm not sure that's pedigree," he said. He didn't want Pope fishing around and testing an alibi defense before Jaywalker had had a chance to explore it himself.

"Okay," said Pope, realizing he wasn't going to get

anything else. "Is there any statement you want to make, Mr. Kingston?"

"Yes, there is." The voice was loud and clear. It was also Jaywalker's. "He says he's innocent, and you've got the wrong guy."

Pope nodded dismissively. It was clear that he doubted the words as much as Jaywalker himself did.

Detective Rendell put the handcuffs back on Darren before he led him out of the room. Jaywalker followed them, reminding Darren to say nothing further. Then he walked over to the Kingstons and brought them up-to-date on what he knew, holding back nothing. He told them that one of the women was coming down to court, and that unless she said their son wasn't the right man, he would be charged with threatening her with a knife, raping her, and forcing her to take his penis in her mouth.

Inez Kingston didn't seem to react. It was as though she already understood and had accepted the gravity of the situation. Marlin said, "Oh, God," and started to cry, then put his arms around his wife, right there in the corridor, with total strangers streaming by. They stood like that for several minutes, he crying quietly and she making no attempt to escape his embrace. Finally Marlin let go of his wife. He looked straight at Jaywalker, his eyes red but fixed.

"Jay, that's my son, you see? You got to do what you can for him. He didn't rape anybody. I don't care what it costs, I'll get the money somehow. But you got to help him."

"I'll help him," said Jaywalker.

They spent the next hour and a half in the courtroom, waiting for the arrival of Joanne Kenarden, the victim who was named in the complaint. Jaywalker passed the time watching the parade of arraignments, people who'd been arrested the previous night. An assault, his own head bandaged. A gypsy cab stickup. Four for possession of heroin. A gun. A homicide, a man who'd beaten his two-year-old stepson to death. Almost all were black or Hispanic. In almost every case the judge set high bail and the defendant was walked back into the pen area, out of sight. Family members, who'd moved forward to the railing to hear better and perhaps be noticed, straggled out of the courtroom, sometimes sobbing, sometimes angry, always confused.

It was a quarter past twelve when Joanne Kenarden showed up. She poked her thin face into the courtroom and looked around uncertainly. Something in Jaywalker told him it was her even before Detective Rendell spotted her, stood up and walked over to her. Jaywalker watched them as they spoke briefly at the door. Then Rendell found her a place to sit, had her sign some papers, motioned her to wait and left the room.

Jaywalker moved his own seat in order to get a better look at her. She was pretty, if a bit hard-looking. The thinness of her face and body made guessing her age difficult. Thirty, maybe. She was dressed in inexpensive clothes, jeans and a black top, but carefully. And she was white.

When Rendell came back into the courtroom, Jacob Pope was with him. While Pope took a seat up front, Rendell disappeared into the pen area. When he emerged several minutes later, he was leading Darren by the arm. Today that act itself would be called a suggestive identification procedure; back then, it was simply how things were done. In any event, as soon as she saw Darren, Joanne

Kenarden stiffened visibly in her seat and nodded almost reflexively. To Jaywalker's eye, her response seemed involuntary and genuine. He wondered if Pope had caught it.

"Docket number X974513, Darren Kingston," called the bridgeman, his title derived from his position between the judge and the rest of the courtroom. "Charged with rape, on the complaint of Joanne Kenarden. Detective Rendell." Shielding rape victims' identities didn't happen back then, either.

Jaywalker rose, made his way forward and took his place at the center of a long wooden table in front of the judge's bench. To his left stood Darren, hands cuffed in front of him, a uniformed court officer immediately behind him. To Jaywalker's right stood Jacob Pope, Detective Rendell and Joanne Kenarden.

"Miss Kenarden," said the bridgeman, "do you swear to the truth and contents of your affidavit?" In 1979, there was no such thing as a Ms. You were Miss, or you were Mrs.

"I do."

"Counselor, do you waive the reading of the rights and charges?"

"Yes," said Jaywalker, "we do."

The judge, a fairly recent appointee named Howard Goldman, turned to Pope, waiting for his bail recommendation. Pope responded by describing the Kenarden rape and sodomy, emphasizing the knife. He pointed out that there were four additional rape victims, and added that it had taken the police several weeks to locate the defendant once he'd been identified. The clear implication was that Darren would be likely to flee if released. "Accordingly,"

Pope concluded, "the People request that bail be set in the amount of fifty thousand dollars."

It was Jaywalker's turn. He pointed to Darren's family in the courtroom, described Darren's job and theirs, and mentioned the lack of any prior convictions. He stressed Darren's wife, their child and her pregnancy. He said that he'd known the family for almost two years and felt privileged to have done so.

"I consider these very serious charges," said Judge Goldman.

"So do I," Jaywalker agreed. "I also consider it very possible that this is the wrong man."

Goldman turned toward Joanne Kenarden. "Young lady," he said, "I want you to answer me truthfully. Is there any doubt in your mind, any doubt whatsoever, that this is the man who attacked you? Take a good look at him before you answer me."

Jaywalker took a step back so that she could get a better look at Darren. But even as he did so, he knew it was a futile gesture. They were enacting a charade, after all. Not twenty minutes earlier, having seen Darren led into the courtroom by Detective Rendell, she'd put her signature on an affidavit, swearing that this was the man who'd raped and orally sodomized her. What was she supposed to say now, that she'd changed her mind?

"No doubt whatsoever," she said.

"Bail is fifty thousand dollars," said the judge.

Out of the corner of his eye, Jaywalker could see Darren's shoulders sag, notice him shake his head slowly from side to side. The case was adjourned one week, for a preliminary hearing. But Jaywalker knew there would be no hearing. Pope would present his case directly to a grand jury, who would listen to Joanne Kenarden, and perhaps the other victims as well, and vote an indictment. Jaywalker toyed briefly with the idea of having Darren testify at the grand jury, but quickly rejected it. All Darren could say was that he was innocent. Having him do so, and then exposing him to cross-examination at this early stage, would accomplish little and risk much.

"Anything else?" asked the judge.

"No," said Jaywalker.

"Next case."

Less than ten minutes after it had begun, the arraignment was over. Darren was led back into the pen from which he'd come.

Outside on the sidewalk, Jaywalker explained the bail to Darren's parents. In order to get their son out of jail, they would either have to come up with fifty thousand dollars in cash or go to a bondsman, who would require maybe half that much, as well as the balance in property—bankbooks, jewelry, deeds to buildings or similar collateral. Marlin Kingston shook his head in disbelief, or maybe despair. Jaywalker told him they had an option, to let a few days pass and then go over to the Supreme Court building on the Grand Concourse, where they could make an application to get the figure reduced.

He kissed Inez goodbye, something he didn't ordinarily do. Perhaps it was her own warmth, radiating outward, that compelled him to do so. When he went to shake Marlin's hand, he felt something pressed against his palm.

"What's this?" he asked.

"A hundred dollars," said Marlin. "For today."

"No," said Jaywalker. "You save it. You're going to

need every penny to try to get Darren out." But he realized he was only getting to know this little man, who could cry unashamedly one minute and fight like a warrior the next, when Marlin spoke again.

"This is yours, Jay," he said. "Darren is my son. I'll get him out somehow. Don't you worry."

Jaywalker pocketed the money. It was 1979, and he couldn't afford to sneeze at a hundred dollars. Not with a wife, a child of his own, a mortgage and a stack of bills. But he did worry. If a hundred dollars was nothing to sneeze at, what did that say about fifty thousand?

3

EIGHTY YEARS

On Friday, Jaywalker got another call from Inez Kingston. "We bailed Darren out," she said, "and I was wondering if you wanted to talk to him or anything."

"You're kidding!" Jaywalker couldn't believe it.

"I'm not kidding. Marlin went out to Rikers Island last
night to get him. They didn't get back till three this morning, and I didn't want to wake you. But he's here now, if
you want to talk to him."

"Of course I do. Put him on."

There was a pause, followed by Darren's voice.
"Hello, J-J-Jay."

"Hey! How the hell are you?"

"P-p-pretty good, Jay."

They spoke for a few minutes. Jaywalker told Darren he
didn't want him to be alone at all, whether he was indoors
or out, that some responsible adult should be with him at
all times. That way, if any more rapes were to occur, they
would have an alibi, proof that it couldn't be him. Darren
said he would make sure of that. They made an appointment

to meet at Jaywalker's office on Monday. Jaywalker ended the conversation by telling Darren how happy he was.

"M-me, too, Jay."

Jaywalker hung up the phone absolutely elated. He marveled at the way the Kingstons must have scraped together every cent they had, borrowed what they didn't and put up their small house as collateral. But as happy as he was for them and Darren, he also had a selfish reason to be pleased. A defendant who can't make bail has two strikes against him. His opportunities to sit down and discuss his case with his lawyer are limited in terms of time, place and privacy. He's unable to assist in the legwork of investigating and preparing his case—visiting the scene of the crime, locating and rounding up witnesses, and helping out with a bunch of other details about which he, as the accused, may have the greatest knowledge. He loses his job or drops out of school, or both. As a result, he becomes a less compelling witness in front of the jury, and a less likely candidate for a lenient sentence in the eyes of the judge. Bail, and having the resources to post it, may not be the most obvious way the system discriminates between the rich and the poor, but it often becomes one of the most significant.

So Darren's getting bailed out was as crucial as it was surprising. It was also, Jaywalker dared to hope, something of a good omen. The case had started out badly. The arrest, the disclosure of multiple rapes, the certainty of Joanne Kenarden's identification and the setting of high bail had been one blow after another. Maybe the tide was beginning to turn. Maybe something else good would happen.

Nothing happened.

Had Jaywalker simply been deluding himself when

he'd told Darren he wanted his movements monitored round-the-clock by a responsible adult? Had he been engaging in nothing but wishful thinking by pretending that Darren wasn't the rapist, and that somehow five victims could all have misidentified him?

Or had he simply been doing what defense lawyers do, willingly playing along with a client's insistence upon his innocence until the time was ripe to get real and face the unpleasant truth? In quiet moments that weekend, it surely seemed so.

On Monday afternoon, Darren showed up at Jaywalker's office, accompanied by his father. They spent two hours together, a good part of it with Marlin banished to the waiting room. Admitting you were a rapist was hard enough, Jaywalker reasoned; admitting it in front of your father might border on the impossible. But to Darren, it seemed to make no difference. He continued to deny any knowledge of the rapes.

Jaywalker did his best to hide his disbelief. One victim could certainly be mistaken. Two, perhaps. Even three, however unlikely, was possible. But *five?*

Yet throughout the session, Darren never once wavered in his denials. Nor did he avoid making and holding eye contact, or lapse into any of the other familiar *tells* Jaywalker had seen so often in his Legal Aid days—the barely noticeable facial tics, the collar tugs, the hand involuntarily rising to cover the mouth, the sudden interest in one's shoes or the pencils on the desk or the pictures on the wall. He did stutter from time to time, but—or so it seemed to Jaywalker—no more or less than usual when pressed about his claim of innocence. And every so often, in spite of himself, Jaywalker would find himself wondering if perhaps Darren might be telling the truth after all. But then he would remember that there were five women, each of them prepared to point Darren out as her attacker. As much as he liked this young man—and he was terribly easy to like—and wanted to believe him, Jaywalker kept reminding himself that Darren was lying. He had to be.

Marlin asked what the fee was going to be. Jaywalker started to explain that it looked as though they were in this for the long haul, that there was going to be a trial, maybe even several.

"I understand, Jay. You tell me how much, and I'll pay it. It may take me some time, but I'll pay it."

Up to that point, the most that Jaywalker had ever charged for a case had been twenty-five hundred dollars. It had been a drug dealer, who'd probably been pocketing that much in a week. Jaywalker had gotten him a plea bargain, five years probation. For Darren, there wasn't going to be a plea bargain, and there certainly wasn't going to be any probation.

"Five thousand dollars," said Jaywalker, and held his breath.

Marlin squinted skeptically. "Are you sure that's enough?" he asked.

"I'm sure," said Jaywalker, and they shook hands on it. *Enough?* Jaywalker felt like he'd broken the bank.

Wednesday came. Jaywalker met Darren outside the courtroom known as Part 1-D. Both his parents were with him, as well as his wife, Charlene. She'd missed the arraignment and the office appointment because she'd been home caring for their son, and because she'd feared the experience might prove too much for her. Or maybe it was the thought that her husband was a rapist. In any event, on this day Darren's sister Janie had been enlisted to babysit, freeing Charlene to come. She was short and a bit on the heavy side, not so unlike her mother-in-law. Perhaps it was her pregnancy beginning to show, perhaps not. Although she had a pleasant enough smile, she wasn't nearly as pretty as Darren was handsome. Jaywalker found himself wondering if Charlene's physical shortcomings might not have contributed to her husband's having become a rapist.

Inez reported that Darren's name didn't seem to be listed on the calendar posted outside the courtroom. Jaywalker looked and couldn't find it, either. A check with the clerk's office revealed the reason.

KINGSTON, Darren
Docket No. X974513
Off Calendar—Indicted
Part 12, 9/21

Jaywalker explained to the Kingstons that their trip had been a wasted one. As expected, Jacob Pope had gone directly to the grand jury. There would be no preliminary hearing. Instead, Darren would be arraigned on an indictment in Supreme Court that Friday. Not that anyone had called Jaywalker to alert him and save them the trip. To the system, defendants, their families and their lawyers were pretty much chopped liver.

Downstairs, Jaywalker ushered Darren away from his family. He had a question for him, and he not only wanted to hear Darren's answer, but he also wanted to see his

reaction. And he didn't want Darren posturing for the
benefit of his family, or looking to them for advice. He
watched the young man closely as he spoke to him.

"Darren," he said, "how would you feel about taking a
lie detector test?" He used the phrase *lie detector test,*
instead of the more technically correct *polygraph examination,* because he wanted to make sure Darren understood the question the first time he asked him and wouldn't
be able to buy time by asking, "What's that?"

Darren's answer came without hesitation. "I'd love to,
Jay, if it'll help."

"Well," said Jaywalker, "I can't promise it'll help. But
it will show if you're telling the truth. The problem is, it'll
also show if you're lying. I can guarantee that."

"I'm not lying, Jay."

"I know that, Darren." It was Jaywalker's second lie in
as many statements. "But I'm prejudiced. I'm your lawyer.
Besides that, I like you. So as much as I believe you, I have
to remind myself that I could be wrong. And you have to
understand that if you *did* commit the rapes, the worst
possible thing you could do now would be to take the
test."

Darren started to say something, but Jaywalker held up
a hand and cut him off in mid-stutter. He wanted Darren
to hear him out.

"Look," he said, "if you *did* do those things, if something happened to make you snap, if it *is* you these women
are talking about, it's not the end of the world. There are
doctors, psychiatrists, programs. There are ways to get you
help. Believe it or not, there are even ways to keep you out
of prison." It was yet another lie. "So take a moment to
think before you decide."

Jaywalker's little speech finished, he looked Darren hard in the eye. And as he waited for a response, he realized that just as he was torn between wanting to believe Darren and not being able to, so, too, was he torn between wanting him to be innocent and wanting him to be guilty. What he really wanted was for Darren to tell him, "I can't take a lie detector, Jay. I did those things." Together they could break the news to his parents, to his wife. There would be some initial shock and disbelief, followed by a lot of crying all around. But the rest would be simple and straightforward. Psychiatrists, psychologists. Perhaps even an insanity defense, but more likely a guilty plea. But the worst would be over, the nagging uncertainty gone, and the terrible burden of representing a man who seemed to be guilty but claimed to be innocent lifted from his shoulders. Oh, how Jaywalker wanted Darren to break down and come clean at that moment!

But he didn't. *Break down? Come clean?* He didn't flinch. He didn't even stutter, for once. Instead he looked directly into Jaywalker's eyes and said, "I want the test."

On Friday morning Jaywalker drove to the Bronx County Courthouse, which housed all of the Supreme Court parts. It covered then, as it covers now, an entire city block, from the Grand Concourse on the east to Walton Avenue on the west, and from 160th Street to 161st. From its upper floors you could see then, as you can still see today, the elevated train tracks above Jerome Avenue, and Yankee Stadium just beyond.

Jaywalker took one of the elevators to the sixth floor. The building was laid out around a square center courtyard, and no matter how many times he'd been there, he always found himself disoriented as soon as he stepped off the elevator. As usual, he walked three-quarters of the way around just to get to a courtroom that would have been right around the corner, had only he chosen to walk the other way.

Darren, Charlene, Inez and Marlin Kingston were waiting for him outside Part 12. They exchanged greetings and went inside. Jacob Pope was already there. He handed Jaywalker a copy of the indictment.

SUPREME COURT OF THE STATE OF NEW YORK COUNTY OF BRONX

————————————————————————————-x
THE PEOPLE OF THE STATE OF NEW YORK
    x

    x INDICTMENT
 —against—
    x 5476/79

DARREN KINGSTON,   x
   Defendant.

————————————————————————————-x

THE GRAND JURY OF THE COUNTY OF BRONX, by this indictment, accuse the defendant of the crime of RAPE IN THE FIRST DE-GREE, committed as follows:

The defendant, in the County of Bronx, on or about August 16, 1979, being a male, engaged in sexual intercourse with Eleanor Cerami, a female, by forcible compulsion.

SECOND COUNT:

AND THE GRAND JURY AFORESAID, by this indictment, further accuse the defendant of the crime of RAPE IN THE FIRST DEGREE, committed as follows:

The defendant, in the County of Bronx, on or about August 16, 1979, being a male, engaged in sexual intercourse with Joanne Kenarden, a female, by forcible compulsion.

THIRD COUNT:

AND THE GRAND JURY AFORESAID, by this indictment, further accuse the defendant of the crime of AN ATTEMPT TO COMMIT THE CRIME OF RAPE IN THE FIRST DEGREE, committed as follows:

The defendant, in the County of Bronx, on or about August 17, 1979, being a male, attempted to engage in sexual intercourse with Tania Maldonado, a female, by forcible compulsion.

FOURTH COUNT:

AND THE GRAND JURY AFORESAID, by this indictment, further accuse the defendant of the crime of AN ATTEMPT TO COMMIT THE CRIME OF RAPE IN THE FIRST DEGREE, committed as follows:

The defendant, in the County of Bronx, on or about September 5, 1979, being a male, attempted to engage in sexual intercourse with Elvira Caldwell, a female, by forcible compulsion.

And that was only page one. The indictment went on to charge Darren with additional counts of first-degree sodomy, sexual misconduct, sexual abuse, assault against two of the victims, and criminal possession of a weapon—a knife—on each occasion. In all, there were twenty-three separate crimes charged. The only pieces of good news, if they could be called that, were that from the original five victims, it seemed now they were down to four who were willing to testify, and of those only two had apparently been actually raped; the other two counts were of attempted rape. Still, Jaywalker could do the math in his head: two completed rapes, each carrying a maximum sentence of twenty-five years, plus two attempts, worth fifteen each. Add them all up, and Darren was facing eighty years in prison.

The case was called in its turn, and Jaywalker accompanied Darren to the podium. The clerk asked how the defendant pleaded, and Darren answered, "Not guilty." His voice was soft, but he didn't stutter. Perhaps he'd been practicing the words, having been told ahead of time by Jaywalker that he would be required to say them. Bail was ordered continued, and the case was adjourned for three weeks, to give the defense time to submit written motions.

Outside the courtroom, Jaywalker cornered Pope and asked him if he would consider giving Darren a polygraph examination. Pope raised an eyebrow as he seemed to think about it, but Jaywalker could see *Why rock the boat?* written all over his face.

Finally he said, "Let me run it by my boss." Passing the buck, no doubt, not wanting to be the one to say no. "Oh, one other thing," he added. "Tell your man he'd better keep out of the area up there."

"What do you mean?" Jaywalker was puzzled.

"I mean this," said Pope, in a tone even more serious than his usual humorless one. "I got a call from Detective Rendell the other day. He said one of the girls phoned him and said she'd seen the guy again, in her lobby. Rendell figured shit, maybe we've got the wrong guy locked up. He called me. I did some checking and found out your client had made bail."

"When was this?"

"I don't know," said Pope. "Beginning of the week, maybe. He was out before the weekend, right?"

"Right," Jaywalker had to agree. It was true.

"Now understand me," said Pope, his eyes narrowing. "This is a free country. I'm not telling your man where he's allowed to go and where he's not. But he starts intimidating my witnesses, I'll have him back in jail in an hour, and his family can see if they can make fifty *million* dollars. I suggest you tell him that."

"I will," Jaywalker said soberly. "She's sure it was him?"

"She's sure."

Jaywalker didn't know whether to hate Pope for threatening them or thank him for the warning. Before he had a chance to do either, Pope turned and walked away.

Jaywalker lost no time in confronting Darren with what he'd just been told. He was about to read him the riot act for disobeying explicit instructions when Darren interrupted him. "Jay, you know that's not m-m-me she's talking about. I haven't been out of the house alone for one minute since I got out."

Darren's family jumped to his defense, backing him up completely and persuasively. So Jaywalker sent them off with homework assignments. Each of them was to take paper and pencil and write out everything they could remember about Darren's movements since his release on bail, as well as his whereabouts on the three days listed in the indictment, August 16th and 17th, and September 5th. Jaywalker instructed Darren to buy a pocket calendar and begin making detailed entries of his comings and goings each day, cursing himself for not thinking of it earlier. Then they set up an appointment at his office for Monday and parted ways.

Jaywalker headed for his car buoyed by a feeling of excitement. Admittedly, the indictment had been bad. Of the five victims, Pope had succeeded in getting four of them before the grand jury on short notice, and if he got the fifth, he could always go back in, have her testify and get a superseding indictment. Jaywalker's suggestion of a polygraph examination had met with fairly predictable skepticism, but at least Pope hadn't quite responded with a flat-out no. But by far the most interesting development had been the business about one of the victims claiming to have seen Darren in the lobby of her building since his release. For starters, Darren and the rest of the Kingston family insisted that he hadn't been out alone since Marlin had brought him home from Rikers Island. But even beyond that, it just didn't make sense. In the movies and on TV, the perpetrator invariably returns to the scene of the crime, blending into the crowd or lurking around furtively to watch the investigators at work. But in real life, having been unlucky enough to be arrested but lucky enough to have gotten out on bail, wouldn't he want to stay as far away as he possibly could?

It sure seemed that way to Jaywalker.

* * *

Monday's meeting produced very little. While Darren's recollection of his whereabouts since being released from jail was detailed and complete, mid-August was another matter. He'd been working nights at the post office, midnight to 8:00 a.m., to be exact. During the daytime, he was generally home alone, either sleeping or attending to chores. Charlene had been working days, and their son—whose name was Philip, but whom everyone called "Pooh"—was left in the care of Darren's sister, Janie, at their parents' house, the same house that was now the collateral on Darren's bail bond. Nobody had any specific recollection regarding the first two dates in the indictment, August 16th—when two of the incidents had occurred—and August 17th. But September 5th stood out a bit. That was the day after Labor Day, and therefore the day Janie's classes at school had resumed after summer vacation. So on that day, for the first time, Pooh had been left with a neighbor. Darren recalled having come home from work as usual, about 9:30 in the morning, and hearing Pooh crying next door. He'd called his mother and asked her if she thought he should go knock on the door. Inez had said no, that if he did that the woman would feel they didn't trust her, and that anyway, the child would have to get used to the new arrangement. Darren had reluctantly accepted the advice, stayed in his apartment and gone to bed.

"But it was *h-h-hard*," he remembered.

It wasn't much to go on, but it was something. Jaywalker jotted a note to himself to include a request for the precise time of each of the attacks in his motion papers.

The meeting broke up. By that time, Jaywalker had fully succumbed to the Kingstons' habit of embracing at each greeting and parting. He particularly enjoyed hugging Marlin. Each time he felt the rough stubble of the older man's beard against his face, Jaywalker was reminded of his grandfather, his father's father, whose whiskers had felt like sandpaper and left his young cheeks glowing bright red. So Marlin's hugs were extra-special.

God, these were good people! Born black in a country that too often tended to be kinder by far to whites, living in a borough that in those days got commonly compared to a war zone, often unfavorably, they'd managed to carve out a life for themselves. They got up and went to work or school, or sometimes both. They took care of their children. From modest salaries, they somehow saved enough to buy a home. They didn't seem to drink, use drugs, gamble, curse, get angry or do any of the other things that used to get so many of Jaywalker's Legal Aid clients into trouble so often. In many ways, the Kingstons epitomized that most overworked of all clichés, the American Dream. They lived honest, hardworking and productive lives, day in and day out. They didn't look to others to take care of them; they took care of themselves, and of each other. Now something terrible had happened to one of their number. Some outside force, not fully comprehensible in its awfulness and randomness, had suddenly reared up and threatened to destroy everything. Their reaction was as simple as it was immediate. Even as they'd reached out to Jaywalker for outside help, they'd drawn together even more tightly. They'd mustered their collective strengths, pooled their resources and drawn on their faith. That faith was not so much in a higher power as it was in the system itself. They trusted that the system, which they'd always believed in and lived by, would now protect them.

But the system, Jaywalker knew only too well, protected no one. The system was cold and impersonal. The system was all about budgets and payrolls, statistics and seniority, politics and patronage. When it came right down to it, in an adversarial contest that pitted a professional prosecutor against a designated defender, a person could be protected only by another person. And for better or for worse, because of the absurd accident that Inez Kingston happened to work in the same Welfare Department office as Jaywalker's sister-in-law, he had become the person charged with the responsibility of protecting a young man and, with him, the rest of his family, born and unborn. It was a responsibility that Jaywalker both wanted and didn't want, one that he relished even as he loathed it, and one that was already waking him up each morning and accompanying him to bed each night.

In the short space of a month's time, it had become a responsibility that scared the living shit out of him.

4

HEDGING BETS

Jaywalker busied himself preparing motions.

The days of the computer had not yet arrived, at least for a seat-of-the-pants solo practitioner like Jaywalker. That meant typing out a set of papers the old-fashioned way, on a trusty Remington, the kind that fit into a square black box and came without a cord, much less a battery. He moved for suppression of any statements that might be attributed to Darren as admissions or confessions, exclusion of any identifications of him that might have been tainted by suggestive police procedures, and a severance that would divide the case into four separate trials instead of one. He asked for court-ordered discovery of police reports, medical records, photographs, artists' sketches and the like. He demanded particulars regarding the precise date, time and place of each of the crimes charged. He made copies, served and filed them, and waited for Pope's written response.

Next Jaywalker contacted a private investigator. He called John McCarthy, a former NYPD detective who would go on to do work for F. Lee Bailey, among others. McCarthy was bright, capable, and would make a good appearance on the witness stand, if his testimony were needed. Jaywalker had him come to the office to meet Darren, and the three of them went over the facts of the case in as much detail as they knew them. He instructed McCarthy to use his contacts in the department to gain access to whatever police and housing authority records he could. He told him there would come a time when he'd want him to see if the victims would talk with him. Finally, Jaywalker asked him to spend some time in the Castle Hill area of the Bronx, where the attacks had taken place, on the outside chance that he might be able to locate the real rapist, assuming it wasn't Darren. At that suggestion, McCarthy looked up from his notepad and stared at Jaywalker as though he were on drugs.

Jaywalker looked away.

Things slowed down. And Jaywalker had no complaint about that. A speedy trial, which is a defendant's constitutional right—and these days his statutory right, as well—is in fact a defendant's worst enemy. Time is his ally. Time for his lawyer and his investigator to do their jobs; time for the victims to grow less vindictive and more forgetful; time even for another attack to occur while the defendant's presence elsewhere could be documented. And with Darren out on bail, time also brought the opportunity for him to get back to work, family and normalcy—if there was such a thing as normalcy for a young man facing eighty years in prison.

On a more practical note, time also allowed Jaywalker to attend to the rest of his practice, which he'd begun to neglect as he became immersed in Darren's case. He tried a forgery case in federal court and came away with a lucky acquittal. A robbery defendant, whose victim had leaped out of a fourth-story window in order to escape his captors, pleaded guilty and accepted a five-year prison term. The victim had somehow survived a broken back and was now walking with a cane. Had he not, it would have become a murder case.

And on the personal front, time also gave Jaywalker an opportunity to get reacquainted with his own family, who'd seen precious little of him over the past few weeks. He prided himself on being an active, if not quite equal, partner in the raising of his daughter. Lately, however, his wife had begun to comment that he seemed to be distracted and complained about his growing habit of being absent even when he was present. If their daughter noticed, she didn't say anything. Of course, she was only four. But kids didn't miss much, he knew.

Jacob Pope's response to Jaywalker's motions arrived in the mail. First off, he supplied the locations and times of the crimes. As Jaywalker read the numbers and transposed them from military time to civilian, he could see that each of the attacks had taken place in the early afternoon hours. Even though he'd been expecting as much, seeing it in black and white came as a major blow. It meant Darren had no alibi. He hadn't been at work during any of the incidents.

Jaywalker reacted almost viscerally. During those early weeks and months, his belief in Darren's innocence had swung back and forth like an unseen but ever-present pendulum. One day Darren would look him in the eye and swear he knew nothing of the rapes, and Jaywalker would believe him with all his heart. The next day would bring some new fact or development that would point directly and inexorably at Darren, and Jaywalker would be filled with doubt all over again. The realization that he wasn't going to be able to call a single witness to account for Darren's presence on any of three separate days was a perfect example. And with each such setback, Jaywalker had to contend once again with the distinct possibility—indeed, the overwhelming probability—that maybe they had the right guy after all.

Pope's response continued. He stated that he had no admission or confession of Darren's to offer at the trial. He conceded that a pretrial identification hearing would be necessary, because a photographic lineup had been conducted, and a judge would have to decide if it had been fair or overly suggestive. He resisted supplying the defense with police reports the law didn't require him to turn over yet. And he opposed the request for a severance, contending that all four attacks should be tried together, as one case.

The severance issue was one that bothered Jaywalker. Did he really want one grand roll of the dice, a single trial including all of the victims, winner take all? Or would it truly be better if the case were split up into four, so that a jury trying one part of it wouldn't even learn of the other three attacks? The advantage to such an approach was obvious: they would avoid the prejudice that would flow from the sheer number of incidents and wouldn't have to contend with a jury's falling into a *where-there's-smoke-there's-fire* mindset. But there was an equally obvious downside, too: severance would give Pope multiple opportunities to convict Darren. They were looking at as many as four separate trials—five, if the remaining victim surfaced. He could win three or even four times, only to lose the last one, and still have Darren end up with a fifteen- or twenty-five-year prison sentence.

As the defense lawyer, Jaywalker had had no choice but to make the motion. Failure to have done so would have risen to the level of ineffective assistance of counsel, maybe even malpractice. More to the point, it was the right thing to do. But now, as he thought about it, he began to wonder if they shouldn't be careful about what they asked for, on the chance that they might just get it.

He opted to postpone making a decision on the matter. It could wait, he knew, until such time as he and Pope had to argue the question in front of a trial judge. By that time, though, he would have to decide if he really wanted separate trials or would prefer for the judge to turn him down. There was a way to argue forcefully, after all, and a way to just go through the motions. Besides which, if his motion was turned down and they were forced to defend against all the charges in front of a single jury, and convictions resulted on all counts—as they almost surely would—the issue would have been preserved, and the judgment might well be reversed on appeal. Then, with retrials ordered, they would get a second bite at the apple—or four or five bites, to be more accurate.

The phone rang. It was John McCarthy, calling with the initial results of some legwork. By checking NYPD and Housing Authority records, he'd confirmed that a fifth victim, Maria Sanchez, had been attacked. But she'd been only fourteen, and her parents had refused to let her view photos, testify at the grand jury or otherwise cooperate with the investigation. About all McCarthy had been able to find out about her was that she'd lied about her age to her attacker, telling him she was only twelve, and he'd let her go. McCarthy had also gotten hold of the various descriptions of the perpetrator given by the victims following the attacks. To McCarthy, it seemed there were more than the usual discrepancies that invariably arose. All the victims had described a man slightly heavier and a bit older-looking than the twenty-two-year-old Darren. And although all of them had reported things the attacker had said to them, none of the reports included any mention of a stutter. He was anxious to take a shot at interviewing the victims himself.

Jaywalker thought about it, but only for a moment. "No," he said. "I want you to hold off. I want Pope's answer on the polygraph first."

"These witnesses don't belong to him, you know."

It was true. Despite the common perception that someone is a prosecution witness or a defense witness, those labels only attach at trial and are determined by which side calls the individual to the stand. Unlike expert or character witnesses, "fact witnesses," as they're called, are the exclusive province of neither side; their only allegiance is to the facts themselves. Or so the theory goes.

"You're right," Jaywalker told McCarthy. "But I can't afford to make waves right now. You reach out to the victims, the first thing they're going to do is pick up the phone and call Pope or Rendell. They may even have been instructed to do so. That could sour Pope on the polygraph. And the way I look at it, John, that little black box may be the only real chance this kid has. So I need you to hold off for now."

"Hey," said McCarthy, "it's your show, Jay."

They went over a few other things before hanging up.

McCarthy was right on both counts, Jaywalker knew. They needed to interview the victims, and it was Jaywalker's show. And when it came down to the tough calls, he had to make them and hope he was right. On this one, he had to play it safe.

Which didn't stop him from wondering if maybe his biggest mistake hadn't been deciding against becoming a doctor.

October came. The motions Jaywalker had made and Pope had opposed were formally submitted to the Part 12 judge for consideration, a process that would take several weeks. This was a bail case, after all, and there was no particular urgency on anyone's part to put it on a fast track. The fact that there were motions outstanding meant they would be looking at another postponement on the next date, as well, the 18th.

Again Jaywalker played catch-up with the rest of his cases, and reintroduced himself to his wife and daughter. They made it to a museum and a movie, and he even created a pizza from scratch, managing not to burn the bottom of the crust too badly. They paid a visit to a farm stand and bought the biggest pumpkin they could find. It took up the entire backseat of the Volkswagen, weighed about a ton, required all three of them to lug it into the house and cost Jaywalker half the retainer that Marlin Kingston had pressed into his hand a month earlier.

Not that Marlin hadn't been as good as his word, following up with small sums every time they met at court or at Jaywalker's office. And to a lawyer accustomed to getting most of his income in the form of small checks, smaller money orders, bail receipts conditioned upon a defendant's return to court or hand-scribbled IOUs, cash was always a delight, even as it had a way of burning a hole in Jaywalker's pocket. But no matter. As his daughter assured him, it was a great pumpkin, Charlie Brown.

The 18th came, and with it the first court appearance before the man who would become Darren Kingston's trial judge.

Even though it's a jury that renders the verdict, the judge can affect that verdict in many ways—some major, others minor; some obvious, others subtle; some entirely legitimate, others highly inappropriate. The judge decides if the defendant remains out on bail or is returned to custody once the trial commences. He rules on motions, acting as both judge and jury at pretrial hearings. He decides which items of evidence will be allowed in and which will be kept from the jury. A judge can shape the outcome of a trial by sustaining or overruling a single objection, or by the way in which he treats one lawyer or the other in front of the jurors, or by something so seemingly insignificant as the inflection of his voice when he reaches a key word or phrase during his charge to the jury. So it not only matters who the trial judge is, it matters a lot. Any lawyer who doubts that ought to think seriously about another career.

Max Davidoff was in his mid- to late-sixties, but his face was deeply lined and his hair nearly white. To Jaywalker, he looked like what a judge was supposed to look like. Prior to being appointed and then elected to the bench, he'd been the District Attorney of Bronx County. In other words, Jacob Pope's boss. Jaywalker did his best to assure the Kingstons that that fact alone was no cause for either disqualification or concern. Indeed, he told them, it was former defense lawyers who often turned into the toughest judges, having learned over the years that defendants weren't always to be believed. Former prosecutors, who had spent those same years realizing that cops weren't, either, occasionally became the defense's best friends.

Wherever the truth really lay, the fact was that Max Davidoff had proved himself a pretty good judge. The book on him—and Jaywalker sought out a handful of Bronx Legal Aid lawyers to compile an oral scouting report—was that Davidoff ran a reasonably relaxed courtroom, tended to be fair to both sides, was reasonably knowledgeable when it came to matters of law, and treated attorneys with respect and defendants with compassion. Above all, he had a reputation for letting a lawyer try his case his way. Jaywalker could have asked for more, but not much more.

The case was called. Jacob Pope rose and explained that there were motions pending back in Part 12. Jaywalker suggested a date two weeks off. The case was adjourned.

Outside the courtroom, Darren's family didn't seem to know whether to be amused or irritated that they'd missed a day's work and traipsed halfway across the Bronx just to witness the sixty-second performance they'd been treated to. Jaywalker was in the midst of explaining how over time the family's presence could influence the judge's attitude toward Darren when Pope came out of the courtroom and got his attention.

"Could I talk to you a minute, Mr. Jaywalker?"

"Sure. But it's not Mr. Jaywalker, it's Jay."

"Jay."

He excused himself to the Kingstons and followed Pope over to the large window that overlooked the building's center courtyard. He wondered if he was about to hear that Darren had once again been spotted by one of the victims.

"I spoke to my boss," Pope said. "We're willing to give your man a polygraph."

"Wonderful!" said Jaywalker, making no attempt to hide either his surprise or his pleasure.

"It'll be with the usual stipulation," Pope continued. "I don't know if you're familiar with that or not."

"Vaguely," Jaywalker lied. *Stipulation?*

"If he passes, we D.O.R. the case. If he flunks, the jury gets to hear that he did. I'll go ahead and set up a date with Detective Paulson, who'll administer the test. I suggest you call him in a day or two and get the date. I know he's pretty backed up right now, so it's likely to be a month, at the least."

"Good enough. And I appreciate this," Jaywalker felt compelled to add. Because he really did.

"Let me put it this way," said Pope, all business all the time. "I've got four girls who say they're sure of their identifications. I believe them. But who knows? I could be wrong." And with that, he shrugged, turned and walked away.

Jaywalker lost no time in sharing the news with the Kingstons, who seemed every bit as elated as he was. And if Darren was secretly apprehensive about the sudden reality of undergoing a lie detector test, he never once showed it.

Jaywalker went over the ground rules, explained that a "D.O.R." meant a discharge on one's own recognizance, the functional equivalent of a dismissal of all charges. He added that the flip side, the defense's agreement to let the jury know if Darren flunked the test, was unenforceable. Pope no doubt knew that, and had to assume that Jaywalker did, too. But as a practical matter, the bargain generally served its purpose. Defendants who flunked polygraph exams tended to fold their cards soon afterward and plead guilty.

"Next," said Jaywalker, "we've got to decide whether we want to go into the test cold, or schedule our own private one beforehand."

Marlin was the first to speak. "We leave it up to you, Jay," he said.

"You can't leave it up to me. It's not my money. And it could cost anywhere from three hundred to five hundred dollars."

Marlin took a moment to ponder that. In addition to the strain of having posted Darren's bail, he had Jaywalker's fee to contend with and was also responsible for paying John McCarthy, the investigator. The burden had to be enormous for him.

None of the other family members spoke. Inez may have been the ranking expert on child rearing, and Jaywalker had the sense that she ran a pretty tight ship at home, but on matters of money, they all deferred to Marlin.

"Let's take the private test first," he said finally.

Jaywalker caught himself wondering if that amounted to a hedge of sorts. Did Marlin, too, harbor second thoughts about his son's innocence? But it was a question that went unasked and, therefore, unanswered.

"Fine," said Jaywalker. "I'll set it up as soon as I can. Okay with you, Darren?"

"Okay with me, Jay." His broad smile completely trumped his father's hesitancy, and with it, Jaywalker's own doubts. Once again, it was as though the case was shadowed by a giant overhead pendulum, which would swing one moment in the direction of guilt and the next moment back to innocence.

In a year and half of private practice, and in two before that with Legal Aid, Jaywalker had never had a client take a polygraph examination. There was a reason for that. Polygraph results—unlike fingerprint evidence, blood typing (and now DNA tests), ballistics comparisons, hair and fiber analyses, and even handwriting and voice comparisons—were then, and continue to be, inadmissible at trial. The rule that excludes them is a sound one. Controlled studies have demonstrated their accuracy rate to be anywhere from fifty to ninety percent. Even a ninety-percent certainty leaves much to be desired in a system that prides itself on requiring proof of guilt beyond a reasonable doubt before there can be a conviction. As for a fifty-percent accuracy rate, that's the equivalent of a coin toss.

That said, polygraphs can still be useful tools. For one thing, it's always interesting, and occasionally quite revealing, to watch a suspect's reaction to the suggestion that he submit to a test, particularly when he's been told that the test is guaranteed to reveal deception. Some suspects will hem and haw, make up excuses, or even admit their guilt at that point. Jaywalker had tried the tactic several times already with Darren, warning him that failure would bring disaster. Each time, Darren had, without flinching, reaffirmed his eagerness to take the test.

Secondly, the exam by its nature includes an in-depth interview of the subject, something that law enforcement personnel are always eager to conduct. Many a suspect has been coaxed or tricked into a revealing admission during the interview, occasionally even into an outright confession.

Finally, whatever its intrinsic worth or evidentiary value, a favorable polygraph result becomes something to hang one's hat on. A defense lawyer will leak it to a newspaper reporter; a prosecutor will cite it as a reason to recommend dismissal of a case; and a judge will refer to it in granting that dismissal.

Hypocrisy? Junk science elevated to mainstream thinking? Perhaps. But Jaywalker wasn't going to let such philosophical considerations deter him. Jacob Pope had offered them a way out, and they were going to do their best to take advantage of it.

Over the next few days, Jaywalker asked around about polygraph operators and came up with a handful of names. The one he kept hearing was Dick Arledge, a man who taught and trained other examiners, and who'd refined the technology to the point of developing and designing his own machines. Jaywalker called his office, set up an appointment, and notified Darren of the date and time, and the fee he would have to bring. He also phoned the district attorney's office and learned that they'd scheduled their exam for early December. That was good; it gave the defense ample time to get their own test done and evaluate the results.

Jaywalker didn't bother telling either Pope or Detective Paulson, the polygraphist he'd chosen, that he was having Darren examined on his own. Just as Marlin had hedged his bet by opting for the private test, so was Jaywalker hedging by his silence. That way, if Darren were to pass, great; he would go into the D.A.'s test more confident than ever. And if he were to flunk, they could always pull out of the second one. "I've done a little checking," he could always tell Pope. "I never knew how unreliable these things are. We'll take our chances at trial."

Looking back later, Jaywalker would come to realize that the week waiting for that first exam was a strange time, an interlude during which he fantasized that his role in the case was drawing to an end. In spite of everything he knew about polygraphs and their shortcomings, he gradually put that knowledge aside. Instead, he began to engage in a bit of magical thinking. He became convinced that the test would solve everything. After all, this wasn't a case involving nuances. There was no claim of self-defense, for example, or of an innocent mistake; there were no state-of-mind issues to be debated. No, Darren was either completely innocent or he was just as completely guilty. Now a little black box with a bunch of wires attached to it was going to tell them, for once and for all.

Which made it only natural to wonder just which answer the box was going to spit out.

Jaywalker had begun by assuming Darren's guilt. Three years of lawyering, and two before that with the DEA, had taught him to doubt everyone he encountered, whether it was on the street, across a desk or through the bars of a jail cell. They were all innocent, every last one of them. The junkie with heroin in his pocket had mistakenly put on his roommate's pants. The shoplifter had simply been taking the leather bomber jacket to another department to see how it looked with a white scarf. The burglar was just trying to find his cousin's apartment. The cocaine dealer had all that cash in his sock to buy a stroller for his baby's mama. And the murderer hadn't meant to stab anyone;

he'd simply been cleaning his knife when the victim had accidentally backed into it—thirty-three times.

Learning the morning of Darren's first court appearance that no less than five victims had identified him as their attacker, Jaywalker had drawn the obvious conclusion. They couldn't all be wrong. Darren had to be guilty.

Since then, however, things had begun to happen. Little things. Nothing dramatic, nothing earthshaking. Darren's unflagging insistence on his innocence; his eagerness to take a lie detector test, even after hearing it was guaranteed to reveal the truth; the claim by one of the victims that she'd seen him again in her building when his whole family insisted he hadn't been there; the discrepancies between the victims' descriptions and Darren; and the fact that not one of them had reported that her attacker spoke with a stutter. Not that any one of those things, standing by itself, convinced Jaywalker of Darren's innocence. But combined, they'd gradually begun to take on an undeniable weight. Each new revelation had forced Jaywalker to rethink his initial knee-jerk reaction that Darren had to be the rapist. As the time for the polygraph exam approached, the truth was, he didn't know what to think.

By far the most frequently asked question put to any criminal defense lawyer is "How can you represent someone you know is guilty?" Three years into practice, Jaywalker had developed his response, which he dusted off and repeated whenever asked. Phrases like "Everyone deserves someone in his corner," "I believe in the system" and "Even society's most despised members deserve representation" were met with approving nods or bewildered stares. But what Jaywalker was rarely called on to expound upon was the darker half of the equation. The truth was, as he'd quickly learned, that representing a guilty client brings enormous comfort. The lawyer's job is simple and straightforward: listen to the client patiently, explain the system to him and get him a decent plea offer. If the client accepts it, the case is over. If he doesn't, he takes his chances at trial. If that trial should somehow result in an acquittal, it would mean that Jaywalker had managed to defy the odds. If it should result in a conviction, as expected, it was because the defendant was guilty all along.

So it wasn't the notion of representing a guilty defendant that bothered Jaywalker. It didn't, not at all. What bothered him, what scared the life out of him, was the specter of representing an *innocent* defendant. Suddenly, none of the usual rules applied. To an innocent man, no plea bargain is acceptable. No amount of patient listening will placate him. No explanation of how the system works will suffice. A trial becomes inevitable, and the need to win at that trial becomes nothing less than essential. And whose responsibility is it to win? The defense lawyer's, that's who.

For Jaywalker, that responsibility, that need to win, was as unwelcome as it was awesome. The trial suddenly changes from an exercise in due process to a horror show. Every utterance by the prosecutor, every piece of evidence that suggests guilt, every look of disapproval from the jury box, becomes a gut-wrenching outrage. If the trial somehow ends with an acquittal, it's no thanks to the lawyer: after all, the defendant was innocent, and the system simply worked as it was supposed to. But suppose for a moment that the trial ends with a conviction. What then? For Jaywalker, that was unthinkable; that was the stuff of nightmares.

Which was the beauty of the polygraph, the wonderful lure of the magical thinking in which he now lost himself. It was all so simple. Darren was guilty, or he was innocent. If he was innocent, Jacob Pope would do the right thing and D.O.R. the case. And now they were about to find out.

The little black box was going to tell them.

5

THE LITTLE BLACK BOX

CERTIFIED
LIE DETECTION
INSTITUTE

read the sign on the door. Jaywalker rang the bell and waited, afraid he was too early. Eventually a shadow appeared beyond the frosted glass and the door swung open.

"Mr. Jaywalker?"

"Yes."

"Come on in. I'm Gene Sandusky."

Sandusky was Dick Arledge's assistant. He was young, meticulously groomed, and polished. His black hair was precisely combed to cover a bald spot that vanity prevented him from yielding to.

While they waited for Darren to arrive, Sandusky and Jaywalker went over the facts of the case in detail. Sandusky drew up releases from liability that Darren would have to sign. He explained the procedure that he would be following in this particular case: picking one of

the rapes and concentrating on it. He would compose his
test questions after beginning his interview of Darren, and
sprinkle in some control questions. Jaywalker could observe the test if he wanted to, but because his presence
might interfere with Darren's concentration, he would
have to do so through a special mirror from another room,
without Darren's knowledge. To this day, Jaywalker can't
remember if Sandusky referred to it as a two-way or a one-
way mirror, and has no idea which term is correct. But he
got the idea.

Darren showed up promptly at 9:30 a.m., accompanied by his cousin Delroid. Jaywalker was glad to see
Darren was still following his instructions to have another adult with him at all times. He introduced them to
Sandusky.

"Pl-pl-pl-pleased to meet you," Darren managed to say.

Jaywalker wondered if the stutter was a bad omen.

Leaving Delroid in the waiting area, Jaywalker and
Darren followed Sandusky to a small conference room.
There they spent ten minutes on preliminaries—the
payment of the fee, the executing of the releases and a discussion of the case in general terms. Then Sandusky announced that Jaywalker would have to leave. Jaywalker
rose, shook hands with Darren, wished him luck and said
he would call him later. He felt a little bit as though he
were abandoning him. He didn't know what Darren felt.

Sandusky led Jaywalker out of the room, then out of the
office altogether. Once in the corridor, he unlocked a second
door and ushered Jaywalker into a small room, closing the
door behind them. The room was dark, the only light coming through a two-way—or perhaps a one-way—mirror,
which looked into the testing room. The glass was adorned

with shelves on the other side, which in turn held small fig-urines, in order to give the test subject the impression that the mirror was purely decorative. The testing room itself was also small. It contained only a table, a couple of straight-backed chairs and the polygraph machine.

Sandusky motioned to a chair directly in front of the glass, and while Jaywalker seated himself, Sandusky ad-justed the knobs on some audio equipment.

"Keep the lights off," he cautioned, "and try to make as little noise as possible. And don't smoke. A match or even a lit cigarette can be seen from the other side. Okay?"

"Okay."

Sandusky closed the door tightly behind him. A minute or two later, he appeared in the testing room, followed by Darren. Jaywalker's instinctive reaction was to lean back, away from the glass, certain he could be seen. But Darren's gaze paused only momentarily at the mirror, without any sign of recognition.

"All right, Darren," said Sandusky. "Why don't you have a seat right here." His voice was loud and clear through the speaker. If Jaywalker had earlier felt he was abandoning his client, he now had the sense that he was spying on him. But it didn't occur to him to look away or cover his ears. Instead, he watched and listened intently as Darren sat down. He took his eyes off him only long enough to glance at his watch. It was 9:44.

"Now," said Sandusky, "this is the machine we've all been talking about." He patted the polygraph affection-ately. It was about the size of a large phonograph or old reel-to-reel tape recorder, and had wires that led to various attachments. At one end of the machine was a roll of graph paper, with needles balanced on it.

Sandusky flicked a switch on the side of the machine. The paper began to move slowly. The needles didn't.

"You see what it's doing?" he asked.

"It's dr-dr-drawing straight lines," said Darren.

"Right. How come a straight line?"

"It's not turned on?" Darren guessed.

"No, it's turned on," said Sandusky. "See, the paper's moving. But how come the lines aren't moving up and down?"

"It's not attached to anything?"

"Exactly. This machine does one thing, and only one thing." Here Sandusky paused for effect. "It moves paper. You do the rest."

Sandusky began making adjustments to the machine, continuing to speak as he did so. "Darren," he said, "put your right hand out in front of you and wiggle your fingers."

Darren obeyed.

"Very good. Now your left hand."

Darren obeyed again.

"Good. You've just used part of your nervous system. We have two types of nerves," Sandusky explained, "voluntary nerves and involuntary nerves. By moving your fingers, you just controlled certain nerves in your hands. Because you can control them, we call them voluntary. Now," he continued, attaching a blood pressure cuff to Darren's forearm and inflating it, "notice that our machine works after all."

Indeed, one of the needles had come to life and was dancing up and down on the paper.

"Okay, Darren, I want you to make your heart stop pumping for thirty seconds."

Darren smiled uncertainly.

"What's so funny?" Sandusky asked.

"I c-c-can't."

"Why not?"

"You can't stop your heart."

"Precisely," Sandusky agreed. "That's because your heart is run by *involuntary* nerves. You can't control them. And that's all that this test is about, involuntary nerves. Things that happen inside your body that you can't control."

Jaywalker couldn't help but smile. It was mesmerizing. This guy could have been a terrific car salesman, he decided, or an awesome preacher. Or both. He could sell used Chevys all week and salvation come Sunday.

Even as he'd been talking, Sandusky had attached a second strap to Darren's other wrist, and two to his torso— one around his chest, the other around his midsection. "By the way," he assured Darren, "none of this is going to hurt at all." He taped a final strap to the palm of one of Darren's hands. Each attachment—and there were now five of them—was connected by a wire to one of the needles, which moved visibly up and down on the graph paper and recorded Darren's blood pressure, pulse, upper and lower respiration, and galvanic skin response...the electrical conductivity of the skin, which increases with sweating.

"Now, Darren," said Sandusky, "I've got three cards here." He held them up so that not only Darren, but also Jaywalker, could see that the first was blue, the second pink and the third blue except for a pink border along the top. "I'm going to ask you some questions about them. I want you to answer 'Yes' to each of my questions. No matter what, just answer 'Yes.' Understand?"

"Yes," said Darren.

Sandusky held up the blue card. "Is this card blue?" he asked.

"Yes," Darren answered.

Sandusky held up the pink card. "Is this card blue?"

"Yes," Darren answered.

Sandusky held up the blue card with the pink border. "Is this card blue?"

"Yes."

After each response, Sandusky had marked the graph paper for later reference. Now he stopped the machine and deflated the blood pressure cuff. While Darren stretched and rubbed his forearm, Sandusky studied the paper.

"Wow!" he exclaimed. "We're not going to have any trouble, not a bit. I'd say you're a very sensitive young man, Darren. Has anyone ever told you that? That you're sensitive?"

"Yes," said Darren. "I've heard people say that."

"I'm not surprised," said Sandusky, still studying the paper. "These responses are very sharp. On the first question, about the blue card, you showed a definite truth. On the second question, the pink card, you showed a definite lie, no question about it. What do you think you showed on the third question?" He held up the blue card with the pink border.

"I d-d-d-don't know," said Darren. "Half and half?"

"Nope, not according to this. On the third question, you showed a lie, just as strong as the second. See, this card really isn't blue, is it?" He held it up again. "Now you may think that's not fair, that you were being *mostly* truthful when you said it was blue. But I'm afraid you can't get away with *mostly* here. It's sort of like the kind of *white lie* we sometimes tell people, like saying 'I love you,' or

'I feel fine,' or 'You look terrific,' when it's not completely true. You see, it may be okay to tell white lies to people, to spare their feelings, say. But not to the machine. The machine has no feelings. To the machine, a white lie is like any other lie.

"Let me give you an example, Darren, one actually not too different from your case. I tested a guy last year on a rape. Girl claimed the guy had followed her home, forced his way into her apartment and raped her. He denied it, claimed he'd never seen the girl in his life. His lawyer asked him if he'd be willing to take a polygraph test. He said okay, and he came to see me. I tested him, and he flunked. It was only months later that I found out the real story. Seems he'd picked the girl up in a bar, and she'd invited him back to her apartment. They started to get real friendly, know what I mean?"

Darren nodded.

"Right at the last minute, she gets cold feet. But he figures she's only being cute, playing hard to get. And he's not about to stop by that time, anyway. So he goes through with it. Was it really a rape? Who knows? She must have thought so, 'cause right after he leaves, she calls the police. When they bring him in for questioning, he denies knowing the girl or having been in her apartment, everything. And he had the police believing him, figuring they had the wrong guy. But not the machine. The machine—" and here Sandusky patted it affectionately "—showed only that he was lying. It didn't understand *mostly.*

"The result was," Sandusky continued, "the guy got jammed up real bad. Much worse than if he'd come clean in the first place. I'm only sorry he didn't tell me up front." He began reinflating the blood pressure cuff. "Or his lawyer. I like to think that the lawyer and I are part of the same team. After all, we're both working for the guy that's paying us, right?"

"Right," Darren agreed.

Sandusky started up the machine again. "Tell me," he said, "before you were arrested on this case, had you ever seen Joanne Kenarden?"

"No," said Darren, without hesitation.

Sandusky marked the paper.

"Is there any chance your fingerprints might have been found on her clothing or things?"

"No."

Sandusky made another mark and shut off the machine. He stood up, came around to Darren, and removed the blood pressure cuff and other straps. Darren stretched.

"Seeing as this is your test," Sandusky said, "are there any questions you'd like me to include?"

Darren seemed to think for a moment. Then he said, "Yes. Ask me if I've even been up in that area the past couple of years."

"The Castle Hill Project area?"

"Yes."

"Fair enough. Now, are there any questions you'd like me to stay away from, for any reason?"

Darren thought again before saying no.

"Okay," said Sandusky. "Why don't you relax. I'll be back in a few minutes." With that, he left the room, closing the door behind him. Jaywalker got up and moved back away from the mirror in anticipation of Sandusky's coming into the observation room, fearful that the light from the opening door might reveal him to Darren.

When Sandusky did enter, the first thing he did was

study Darren through the glass. Darren continued to stretch, humming softly to himself. Sandusky motioned Jaywalker to follow him out of the room. When they reached the conference room, he lit a cigarette.

"He's very nervous," he said.

"I would be, too." As soon as Jaywalker had said the words, he realized he was being overly defensive of his client. But that was his job, wasn't it? Besides, there was something about Sandusky's observation he didn't like.

Sandusky ignored the comment. He sat down at his desk and searched through a drawer until he found the form he was looking for. Then he used it to write out the questions he was going to ask Darren. He inserted them in the blanks for questions 2, 3, 6, 7 and 9. Questions 1, 4, 5 and 8 he left open. He stubbed out his cigarette and stood up.

Jaywalker resumed his post in the observation room. Darren was singing softly when Sandusky reappeared in the testing room. Jaywalker didn't recognize the tune.

"All right," said Sandusky. "These are going to be the questions I'll be asking you. Who raped Joanne Kenarden? Do you know who did it? Did you rape her? Did you see her blow you? Did you threaten her with a knife?"

Sitting in the observation room, Jaywalker was a bit surprised that Sandusky would telegraph the test questions to Darren that way. Wouldn't springing them on him be a more effective tactic? But the more he thought about it, the more he came around to understanding Sandusky's strategy. By letting Darren know exactly what questions were coming, he was giving him a chance to build up additional anxiety over the fact that he was going to be lying in his responses.

"How ab-b-b-bout the question I suggested?" Darren asked.

"I'm afraid I can't use it," said Sandusky, without further explanation.

Darren looked disappointed by the answer, and perhaps by Sandusky's dismissive tone, as well. Jaywalker wondered if Sandusky was deliberately trying to agitate Darren by first requesting his input and then rejecting it. But hadn't he just commented on how nervous Darren already was?

"Now," Sandusky was saying, "before we begin the actual test, let's talk about guilt for a moment."

"G-g-guilt?"

"Yes. Darren, when you were growing up, which of your parents would you say was stricter, was more concerned with teaching you right from wrong?"

"They were both pretty strict."

Jaywalker could believe that.

"Which one would more likely have told you it was wrong to hurt people?"

Darren seemed to think a moment before saying, "My dad, I guess."

"How about sex education? Which one took more of a role in teaching you about sex?"

Darren thought again. "I don't know," he said finally. "I—I—I learned that pretty much on my own." Then, when Sandusky didn't react, he added, "I guess it would have b-been my dad again."

"Okay," said Sandusky. "Psychologists and psychiatrists tell us that hurting values and sexual values are taught to us by our parents when we're very young, and that deviance from these values is what produces guilt feelings."

This struck Jaywalker as mumbo jumbo, double-talk. He had the feeling that Sandusky was deliberately trying to lose Darren here, though he didn't know why.

"The problem is," Sandusky explained, "guilt feelings can interfere with the test." To Jaywalker, that sounded counterintuitive. Wasn't the test *premised* upon the existence of feelings of guilt and designed to ferret them out?

"So," Sandusky continued, "when we get started, I'm going to include a couple of questions to eliminate them. One will be about hurting, the other about sex. And by the way, these two questions will be between you and me. I won't report them to anyone, not even your lawyer. Okay?"

Darren nodded.

"Do you know what masturbation is, Darren?"

"Yes."

"What is it?" Evidently Sandusky wanted to be certain.

"It's when you p-p-p-play with yourself."

"Right," said Sandusky. "Have you ever masturbated, Darren?"

"Yes," Darren admitted.

Jaywalker found himself feeling more like a voyeur than ever. But it was riveting stuff, and he was beginning to see where Sandusky was going with it.

"When was the last time?"

"I c-c-can't recall."

"How old are you now?"

"Twenty-two."

"Well," said Sandusky, "that makes you pretty old. I guess it would have had to have been when you were ten or eleven, huh?"

"I g-g-guess so," Darren agreed.

Jaywalker's hunch had been right. Sandusky was building a lie into the test, deliberately coaching Darren to be deceitful when the time came. That way, he would have a control response to a lie, against which he could measure the real responses.

"Well," said Sandusky, "you can't remember masturbating in the last ten years, can you?"

"No," said Darren, swallowing the bait.

"Good. Now, have you ever hurt anybody?"

"Yes," said Darren. "I guess so."

"Who?"

"I've hurt Charlene, my wife, by saying things."

"Can you remember anyone else you've hurt?"

Darren hesitated for a moment. "No," he said.

"Okay," said Sandusky. Once again he attached the straps to Darren's body and inflated the blood pressure cuff. "Now," he said, "put your hands on the arms of the chair. Feet flat on the floor. I want you to face forward and close your eyes. As I ask you questions, you just answer 'Yes' or 'No.'" He turned on the machine.

Jaywalker had to remind himself to breathe.

"Do you live in the United States?" asked Sandusky.

"Yes," answered Darren.

"Did you rape Joanne Kenarden?"

"No."

"Do you know who did rape Joanne Kenarden?"

"No."

"Is your name Darren Kingston?"

"Yes."

"Since you were twelve years old, can you remember masturbating even one time?"

Darren opened his eyes, turned to Sandusky and raised

his hand, as though signaling for a time-out. "I remembered," he said. "I think I did it once since then."

Sandusky stopped the machine, walked over and undid the straps. "How old were you at that time?" he asked. "Thirteen?"

"I m-m-must have been."

"Okay," said Sandusky. "Let's take a break."

Sandusky and Jaywalker met in the conference room again. Sandusky smoked nervously. Jaywalker feared the worst.

"Doesn't look good?" he asked.

"He's just so damn tight. I'm going to have to try to get him to believe in the test a little more."

Jaywalker resumed his observation post as Sandusky returned to the test room. "All right," he told Darren, "we've been going quite a while. I want to check the machine." He hooked it up to Darren again. Then he produced seven oversized playing cards. Jaywalker could see that each one had a different number printed on its face. Sandusky shuffled them and fanned them out in front of Darren, facedown. "Take one," he said, "without letting me see the other side of it."

Darren did as he was told. When he lifted the card to look at it, Jaywalker could see the number thirteen on it. He wondered if he was the only one who'd associated the choice with bad luck.

"Look at it," said Sandusky, "remember it and put it back. Don't tell me what it is."

Darren complied.

"Now," said Sandusky, turning on the machine, "I want you to listen carefully to my questions, but answer 'No' to each one. No 'Yeses,' just 'Noes.' Understand?"

"Yes," said Darren.

"Did you pick the number three?"

"No."

"Did you pick the number five?"

"No."

"Did you pick the number seven?"

"No."

"Did you pick the number eight?"

"No."

"Did you pick the number ten?"

"No."

"Did you pick the number thirteen?"

"No."

"Did you pick the number fifteen?"

"No."

Sandusky had marked the graph paper following each response. Now he shut off the machine and studied the paper. "Okay," he said after a moment. "You picked thirteen."

Jaywalker exhaled. Still, he had the feeling that Sandusky had said it a bit tentatively and was more pleased than he should have been when Darren confirmed that he was right.

"Great," said Sandusky, once again removing the straps. "Let's take one more break. The machine's working perfectly. When I come back in, we'll do the actual test."

In the conference room, Sandusky underscored his uncertainty by asking Jaywalker if Darren had in fact picked number thirteen. But neither of them mentioned the problem that was by this time evident to both of them.

ACTUAL TEST QUESTIONS AND SUBJECT'S RESPONSES POLYGRAPH EXAMINATION OF Darren Kingston, **ADMINISTERED BY** Gene Sandusky **ON** October 25, 1979.

1. Q: Do you live in the United States?
   A: Yes.

2. Q: Last August 16th, did you rape Joanne Kenarden?
   A: No.

3. Q: Do you know for sure who did rape Joanne Kenarden?
   A: No.

4. Q: Is your name Darren Kingston?
   A: Yes.

5. Q: Since the age of thirteen, can you remember masturbating even one time?
   A: No.

6. Q: Last August 16th, did you force Joanne Kenarden to blow you?
   A: No.

7. Q: Last August 16th, did you threaten Joanne Kenarden with a knife?
   A: No.

8. Q: Can you remember hurting one person in your
       life besides your wife?
   A: No.

9. Q: Have you told me the entire truth regarding what
       you know about the Joanne Kenarden rape?
   A: Yes.

The test was over. Sandusky turned off the machine and
removed the straps from Darren. He made one final mark
on the graph paper before tearing it from the roll and heading to the conference room. Jaywalker met him there.

"All right," said Sandusky, lighting another cigarette. "I
was afraid of this. We've got a problem here."

Jaywalker waited for the worst, the news that Darren
had flunked cold. In his mind, he was already rehearsing
his *Okay-it's-time-to-plead-guilty* speech. The problem
was, he was still thinking black and white, winner take all.
And he was wrong.

"I want Dick to take a look at these charts," said
Sandusky, referring to his mentor and senior partner, Dick
Arledge. "But I'm already certain he's going to want to run
a retest. So if it's okay with you, I'm going to go ahead
and schedule it for some time next week."

Jaywalker hesitated. Uncertainty was better than failure, but the test had cost five hundred dollars. He couldn't
be spending more of Marlin Kingston's money without
checking with him first. "The fee—"

"Don't worry," said Sandusky. "There's no additional
charge."

"Okay," Jaywalker agreed. "What do you think the
problem is?"

Sandusky shook his head. "I'm not sure," he said. "He's nervous, he's very tight. Some of it's wearing off. A lot of times they're calmer the second time around. They know what to expect, and the general anxiety is less. That way, the *specific* anxieties show up more. The lies."

Jaywalker said nothing, but he found himself wondering if Sandusky wasn't betraying a bias here. Had he been expecting lies from Darren? Was he surprised they hadn't shown up clearly? And was he implying that a retest was needed in order to better expose them? Or was Jaywalker simply being paranoid?

Not that that would be a first.

Sandusky had Jaywalker leave the office before he went back in to break the news to Darren. Riding down in the elevator, Jaywalker could feel the fascination of the experience beginning to give way to depression. It was already dawning on him that what had seemed the defense's best hope was proving worthless. He suddenly felt exhausted, totally drained.

He drove his VW downtown in silence. Even the radio, his sometimes companion, managed to irritate him. If only Darren could have passed, he thought. It would have been a reprieve from the governor, a rescue by the cavalry. No, he realized, it would have been a deus ex machina, in the most literal sense: god from the machine.

Or if only he'd flunked, Jaywalker admitted to himself grimly. If the test had established his guilt, it would have put an end to any notion of a trial. More importantly, it would have gotten Jaywalker off the hook. Darren and the rest of the Kingston family would have stopped expecting him to perform magic. The case would have become manageable, predictable. Safe. An exercise in damage control.

Instead, this. This nonanswer, the worst of all possible results. Sure, there'd be a retest. But already Jaywalker had begun to steel himself, to accept the inevitable. The result would be the same. The little black box simply wasn't going to decide things. How ridiculous to have expected anything else.

He gave Darren an hour to get home before phoning him from the office. Not knowing that Jaywalker had observed the test, Darren explained what had happened in some detail. He concluded by saying that Mr. Sandusky wanted him to come back on Friday because he hadn't had time to finish the questioning.

"I know," Jaywalker lied. "I spoke with him a little while ago."

"D-d-did he give you any idea of how I was doing?" Darren asked.

"No," Jaywalker lied again. "He said he hadn't had a chance to study the charts yet. Why, you worried?"

"No, Jay, I'm not worried. You know that."

Jaywalker bit his tongue, sorry he'd said it. The truth was, as worried as he himself was, Darren seemed supremely confident. Either he was completely innocent, one hell of an actor—or a total psychopath.

Friday came, and with it the retest.

Jaywalker couldn't go. He had a trial, a non-jury case involving a taxi driver charged with leaving the scene of an accident. The guy had pulled away from the curb without realizing—or so he said—that there was an elderly woman holding on to the handle of the cab's rear door. She'd lost her balance, fallen and broken a hip. Jaywalker argued to the judge that there was no evidence that the driver had been aware of what had happened. The judge looked skeptical, but was forced to agree on the law. Not guilty. Jaywalker gathered up his papers, snapped his briefcase closed and strode out of the courtroom. The victory was a small one, but satisfying. If only they could all be so easy, he thought.

He reached Sandusky at 5:30 p.m. Dick Arledge had run the retest on Darren. Like Sandusky, he'd come up with an indefinite. But they wanted one final try, and had asked Darren to come back on Monday, at which time they would run him through it once more, together. Jaywalker said okay.

He hung up the phone, and settled back into his chair and his depression. The flush from the earlier acquittal was long gone. The weekend, with time to spend with his wife and daughter, took on a bittersweet quality.

Two strikes.

One to go.

Strike three came on Monday.

Dick Arledge called at noon to report that he and Sandusky had tested Darren once more, with the same result: indefinite. "It's unusual," he added, "but it happens."

"Did you tell Darren?" Jaywalker asked.

"No," said Arledge. "I figured I'd let you do that."

Like a doctor afraid to tell his patient he's got cancer and is going to die. Let the nurse do it, or maybe the receptionist.

"Strictly off the record," said Jaywalker. "If you had to make a guess, would you say he's lying or telling the truth?"

"On the basis of the tests?"

"Yes."

"I couldn't even take a guess," Arledge confessed. "For some reason, we simply couldn't get a pattern on him. The truth controls look the same as the lie controls. We start getting what looks like a meaningful set of responses, and then, *wham!* No response where there's got to be one. Or a response to his own name. No, on the basis of the tests, I can't tell you it so much as leans an inch one way or the other."

"And on the basis of anything else?"

"On the basis of anything else…" Arledge repeated Jaywalker's words and paused for a moment. "I like the kid. Gene and I both like him. He sure as hell doesn't *seem* like a rapist."

Jaywalker said he agreed. He accepted Dick Arledge's apology, thanked him for his efforts, and hung up the phone. The strikeout was complete.

So they liked Darren. Great. Jaywalker liked Darren, too. Maybe that was half the problem right there. Nobody could imagine this good-looking, quiet, sensitive, stuttering kid as a vicious rapist with a knife in his hand. But what did rapists look like, anyway? Would you recognize one if you passed him on the street? Sat next to him on the Number 6 train? Did he have a perpetual leer in his eye? Did he drool? Walk around with a giant hard-on?

Or did he look like Darren Kingston? Average height, normal weight, medium complexion. Soft-spoken, well-liked, absolutely ordinary on the outside. Yet deep inside was a whole different person that emerged like some werewolf in the full moon. Only in Darren's case, the full moon was times of stress and sexual frustration. His wife pregnant, his child crying, he himself home alone in the midday un-air-conditioned heat of August in the Bronx.

And what kind of person would get no meaningful responses to a lie detector test? A psychopath, that was who, someone for whom the line between fantasy and reality was blurred to the point of being unrecognizable. Someone who didn't know what was true and what was false. Someone who could look you straight in the eye and tell you that in his entire life he'd never hurt a soul, other than perhaps his wife's feelings, because in his mind he honestly believed that to be so.

Or better yet, suppose Darren was some kind of dual personality, a real-life Jekyll and Hyde. There was the normal, likeable Darren—good husband, loving father and son, responsible provider. And there was Darren the rapist. Perhaps the two were strangers to one another. Darren the good guy didn't even know that Darren the rapist existed. So he could sit there with all sorts of wires attached to him and tell you that he never raped Joanne Kenarden or anyone else, and believe he was speaking the absolute truth. And so believing, he would have no reason to hesitate or flinch or contradict himself. His blood pressure would have no reason to rise, his pulse no reason to quicken, his breathing no reason to labor, his palms no reason to sweat….

Jaywalker took his half-eaten tuna-fish sandwich and threw it into the wastepaper basket. He picked up the phone and dialed Darren's number, and told him to come down to the office. Not asked him. Told him.

Jaywalker was on the phone when Darren arrived. He motioned for him to take a seat. He continued the phone conversation, which wasn't an important one, for another five minutes, making a point of forcing Darren to wait. Only when Jaywalker sensed the young man's uneasiness did he finally hang up.

"Sorry," he said offhandedly.

"That's okay," said Darren. "Wh-wh-what's up?"

"Bad news, that's what."

"B-b-bad news? Wh-what kind of bad news, Jay?" He literally squirmed in his chair.

Jaywalker reached for a file on his desk. It happened to be the one from the taxi driver case, but Darren couldn't see that. Jaywalker opened the file and pretended to study the first page or two.

"A messenger brought these over from Dick Arledge's office," he said. "I'm afraid you didn't do so well after all." He raised his eyes to study Darren's. "These guys are friends of mine," he said. "They did everything they possibly could to make it come out like you were telling the truth. But even with three separate tests, they couldn't do it. Every time they ran you through it, you lied on questions two, five, seven and eight. The ones about the rapes." Jaywalker held up the sheets. "It's all here," he said, shaking his head.

The reaction swept through Darren like a wave. There was no hesitation, no time to plan it. His confused frown disappeared, giving way first to a look of open astonishment and finally to one of frank disbelief.

"Jay," he said, "that can't be. I—I—I didn't rape those women. There's a mistake. The test has got to be wrong." Tears welled up in his eyes and overflowed, running freely down both cheeks. He made no attempt to either wipe them away or avert his eyes.

"There's no mistake," Jaywalker forced himself to say.

"I think we'd better start at the beginning, Darren. Don't you?"

"Jay," he pleaded, "I didn't do it, I didn't do it, I didn't do it, I—"

Jaywalker was the first to break eye contact. His gaze dropped to Darren's hands. Where he might have expected to see fists clenched to maintain control of a performance, he saw instead palms open and extended.

"—didn't do it," Darren finished softly, almost to himself.

"I know," said Jaywalker. "I know."

It had taken a truly cruel stunt on his part. He'd taken a young man—a young man whom he liked immensely, and whose family was not only putting their trust in him, but also backing up that trust with hard-earned money—and compelled him to make an hour's trip each way, then lied to his face and explicitly accused him of being guilty and, worse yet, of refusing to acknowledge his guilt. But as bad as Jaywalker felt about the ordeal he'd put Darren through, he could live with it, because now he knew.

He knew.

6

LAST CHANCE

At the same time as he'd said "I know" to Darren, Jay-walker had taken the file he'd been looking at and slid it across the desk. Darren had picked it up, opened it and begun to read. It took him several moments of total confusion before he began to get it. Then he'd looked up tentatively, the way a boy who thinks just maybe he's got the answer might look up at his teacher. But only when he'd seen Jaywalker's smile had he taken permission to smile in return.

"I'm a shit," Jaywalker confessed, rising and coming around the desk. "And you owe me a punch in the mouth. The tests didn't show anything one way or the other. I did that because I needed to be sure." He withdrew a paper towel from his back pocket, his version of a handkerchief, and offered it to Darren.

Darren dried his tears unselfconsciously. "That's okay," he said. "I just didn't see how I could've flunked it."

"You couldn't have. I'm just sorry I lied to you."

"That's all right, Jay. I won't even p-p-punch you in the mouth."

"You'd better not," said Jaywalker. "It looks like we may be needing it."

* * *

With the private polygraph lost as a weapon in the defense's, arsenal, and the realization that the district attorney's test was likely to prove every bit as worthless, Jaywalker turned his efforts to other aspects of the case. He phoned his investigator, John McCarthy, who reported that he'd located all the victims and was ready to move in and interview them in rapid succession. Jaywalker gave him the go-ahead.

Earlier, Jaywalker had instructed Darren and the other members of the Kingston family to write down everything they could recall about Darren's whereabouts during August, early September, and the week following Darren being bailed out. Now he collected the notes and studied them, searching desperately for some clue, some tiny lead, to jump from the pages in front of him.

Nothing did.

He began spending time in the Castle Hill area. He would change into old clothes before leaving his office at the end of the workday, and instead of heading home to New Jersey, he would aim his Volkswagen for the Bronx. Once up in the projects, he would walk through the lobbies or sit on a park bench or lean idly against a trash can, trying his best to blend in to the landscape. It wasn't easy, because whites in the area were greatly outnumbered by blacks and Hispanics. Still, Jaywalker's face was by no means the only white one in sight. And, he reminded himself, Joanne Kenarden and Eleanor Cerami were white, and so were Tania Maldonado and Elvira Caldwell and Maria Sanchez. At least they *looked* white. So Jaywalker pretended he was one of them. He hung around, waiting for Darren's double to show up. In his mind's eye, he saw

himself spotting him, following him, jumping him, sub-
duing him and dragging him off to the nearest precinct.

No double showed up.

He would get home past dark, in time to eat cold left-
overs over the kitchen sink. If he was lucky, he'd get to
kiss his daughter good-night before she was asleep. His
wife put up with his behavior, but only because by that
time she knew him well enough to know he couldn't help
himself.

In mid-November, the mail brought an envelope from
the judge in Part 12, containing his decision on Jaywalker's pretrial motions. As expected, he'd granted the
defense a hearing on the propriety of the identification procedures the police had used. He'd left the question of a severance—whether there would be one trial or four—up to
the discretion of the trial judge.

They went back to court at the end of the month. Again
the appearance was a brief one. Pope told Justice Davidoff
that there was a polygraph examination scheduled at his
office the first week of December, and the case was adjourned.

Out in the corridor, Jaywalker huddled with the Kingston family. Despite the fact that he'd assured them that
there would be a postponement, they'd all showed up.
Now, while they were talking, Jacob Pope walked over and
motioned Jaywalker aside. Pope wore his trademark dark
suit, white shirt and red tie. As always, he was all business.
He never once smiled, cracked a joke or allowed himself
to chuckle at one of Jaywalker's feeble attempts at humor.

"So," he said, "we're on for the sixth, right?"

"Right," said Jaywalker. "I just hope we get an answer, one way or another."

"We should," said Pope. "Lou Paulson is good. Any reason you anticipate a problem?"

"No," Jaywalker lied, something that was becoming a bit of a habit lately. "Only that he's a pretty nervous kid. I don't know if you're aware of it or not, but he's got a noticeable stutter, and—"

"I'm aware of it."

He said it softly, calmly, but with deadly force. Jaywalker felt the wind knocked out of him. Pope turned and walked away, leaving Jaywalker standing there, dazed. How many of the victims had described the stutter? All of them? What was the difference, really? One would be more than enough to destroy Darren. A physical description was one thing. Height, weight, hair color and complexion were seldom enough to convince a jury. And John McCarthy had already reported finding some discrepancies there.

But a *stutter!*

Jaywalker headed back over to the Kingstons. They looked at him expectantly, too polite to ask what Pope and he had talked about, but obviously wanting to know. Cards on the table, Jaywalker decided. It was how he'd always operated, and how he always would. You told your people everything, even the worst news. *Especially* the worst news. That was the only way they would ever trust you when the time came to tell them something good. If ever it did. So he told them about the stutter.

"The detective, R-R-R-Rendell," said Darren. "He knows I stutter, from arresting me. He c-c-could have told Pope."

"Maybe," Jaywalker agreed. "McCarthy's out interviewing the victims. We'll find out soon enough."

Still, Jaywalker didn't like the sound of it. And unlike Darren, he wasn't prepared to assume that a detective would coach a witness on something like this, not with so much at stake. Sure, cops lied. Jaywalker had learned that early in his DEA days. So did detectives, federal agents, state troopers, and just about everyone else who wore a badge and carried a gun. But they lied selectively. They lied about their own conduct, where they'd cut corners to make a collar stick or a search hold up, or where a case came down to a defendant's word against one of their own. In those instances, an *us-against-them* mentality immediately kicked in, and truth became an early casualty. But in cases involving civilian complainants, where the role of law enforcement was more peripheral, lying on the part of the police was the exception, not the rule. Besides, Detective Rendell had impressed Jaywalker as being fair. "She IDs him or she doesn't," he'd said the morning they were waiting in court for Joanna Kenarden to show up and have a look at Darren. "If he's not the guy, I don't want him."

No, if the victims were saying the rapist had stuttered, Jaywalker was willing to believe them. Which could mean only one thing, he knew.

Again, the pendulum had swung. Jaywalker had done it again. He'd allowed himself to be taken in, to be completely won over by Darren's *I didn't do it,* by his tears and open palms. Would he never learn? Just when he thought himself too hardened and cynical to be conned, along comes this twenty-two-year-old kid who can't even pass a polygraph, and he turns Jaywalker into the easiest mark in town.

He felt like a total jerk.

* * *

John McCarthy called three days later. He'd succeeded in interviewing two of the victims, Eleanor Cerami and Elvira Caldwell. He'd been refused by one, Joanne Kenarden. Tania Maldonado was out of town, but would be back in a day or two. As for the fourteen-year-old, Maria Sanchez, her parents wouldn't let her talk to anybody.

"Both of these girls, Cerami and Caldwell, identify Darren from the photo I showed them," said McCarthy. "Although they both say he looks like he's lost weight since they saw him."

"Independently?"

"Independently. I interviewed them separately. Of course, I told each of them that the other one had already talked to me. Old police habits die hard, if you know what I mean."

"What else did they say?" Jaywalker asked.

"Well," said McCarthy, "the M.O. is identical. He follows them onto an elevator, presses a floor and, on the way up, pulls a knife, takes them off the elevator and up to a landing. There he first makes them blow him, and then he rapes them. He succeeded with Cerami. With Caldwell, there was a noise, and he split."

"Were there conversations?"

"Yeah, both times. He seems to be quite a talker."

Jaywalker took a deep breath and asked The Question. "Either one pick up a stutter?"

"No," McCarthy replied. "That is, I didn't come right out and use the word. But I asked them if they remembered anything unusual about his voice, and both said negative. And get this," he added. "Caldwell's got a kid with a speech impediment, so you'd expect her to be tuned in to that kinda thing."

"Beautiful," said Jaywalker, able to breathe again.

"So I'll go after Maldonado as soon as she gets back."

"Good," said Jaywalker. "No dice with Kenarden, huh?"

"No, she's a pisser, that one. Wants Darren in jail, you in jail, me in jail. Says she's got plenty to say, but she's saving it for the trial."

"Okay, she's entitled. Stay away from her. We'll get her at the hearing. Talk to Maldonado, John, and get back to me."

"You got it."

Two down, two to go, and so far no stutter. But as soon as Jaywalker found himself daring to hope all over again, Jacob Pope's comment came back to him. *"I'm aware of it."* And an icy chill went up his back, just as it had when first he'd heard the words.

During the last week of November, Jaywalker received an envelope from the Bronx County District Attorney's Office, with Pope's name typed beneath the return address. Inside was a form entitled REQUEST FOR ALIBI BILL OF PARTICULARS. Under New York law, a prosecutor had the right to demand the name, address and place of employment of any witness whom the defense intends to call at trial to testify that, at the time of the crime, the defendant was elsewhere, with them. As much as he disliked the law, Jaywalker had no choice but to comply. The penalty for failing to do so was that the trial judge could bar such a witness from testifying.

So he typed out a single-page bill of particulars. On it he listed Darren's wife, Charlene, and his mother, Inez. He also listed Darlene Thombs, the next-door neighbor who'd been babysitting for Darren's son on September 5th, the date of the Caldwell rape. Then he phoned the Kingstons to warn them that an investigator from the D.A.'s office might try to contact them or Miss Thombs, and told them they had a right to decline to talk about the case, if they wished.

John McCarthy called the following day. He'd interviewed Tania Maldonado. Her story was pretty much the same as that of the other victims he'd spoken with. The most interesting fact was that she'd put up a struggle, causing the man to cut his own finger with his knife. When it had begun to bleed rather heavily, he'd panicked and fled.

Good for her, thought Jaywalker, making a mental note to ask Darren and his family about any cut fingers he might have sustained.

According to McCarthy, Maldonado had identified Darren from his photo and remained convinced that he was her attacker. Asked about his voice, she remembered it as normal and unremarkable. She never mentioned a stutter.

Three victims, and still no report of a stutter. That left only Joanne Kenarden. She was certainly the bitterest, the most vengeful. Not that Jaywalker could blame her. Had the rapist stuttered only for her? Or had Detective Rendell trusted only her with the knowledge that Darren stuttered? He could easily have done it that first day, in court, shortly after he had learned it from arresting and processing Darren. There was simply no way of knowing yet. With Miss Kenarden refusing to talk with McCarthy, Jaywalker would have to wait for the pretrial identification hearing to find out.

* * *

The first week of December brought a thin, freezing rain to the city. It also brought the district attorney's polygraph test.

Jaywalker met Darren at Jacob Pope's office, on the sixth floor of the Bronx County Courthouse. While Darren waited outside in the reception area, Pope and Jaywalker signed the stipulation governing the test. Officially, both the prosecution and the defense were agreeing in writing that the results of the exam, if conclusive, could be used as evidence at trial by either side. In reality, Pope was giving his word that, were Darren to pass, his office would move to D.O.R. the case and eventually dismiss it. And Jaywalker was giving his that if Darren flunked, he would do everything he could to get Darren to plead guilty. From the defense's side of the table, it was a good bargain.

"Well," said Pope, as soon as Jaywalker's signature was dry, "maybe he'll do better on this one. I understand Dick Arledge tested him three times and came up indefinite each time."

Jaywalker tried his best to hide his surprise that Pope knew, but his best wasn't good enough. "Let's hope your man is better," was the most he could come up with.

"Lou Paulson's good, though he prefers to get first crack at a subject. But he's willing to give it a shot."

Jaywalker nodded, still feeling like a schoolboy caught cheating. He followed Pope out to the reception area where they'd left Darren. Detective Paulson had arrived, and Pope introduced him to Darren and Jaywalker. Paulson told Darren to come with him, and they left. Jaywalker called out, "Good luck," but had the feeling he was wishing luck to a man being led to his death. The enormity of the fact that he was turning his client over to the enemy hit him with full force. Lou Paulson worked for the D.A.'s office. They gave him a check every two weeks. Suppose he simply decided to report back that Darren had flunked. Would Jaywalker have any meaningful way of disputing his claim? Would he be allowed access to his charts, so he could have Dick Arledge and Gene Sandusky analyze them? And how would they know they were really Darren's charts?

"I'll know what's what in a couple of hours," Pope was saying. "Why don't you give me a ring?"

The cold rain outside felt refreshing. Jaywalker tried to convince himself that Pope and Paulson could be trusted. Anyway, he told himself, what choice did he have? If Darren somehow managed to pass the test, how could they not let him know? The notion that they might suppress the result was simply too obscene to contemplate.

But suppose it came down to a close call? Jaywalker could hardly expect them to give Darren the benefit of any doubt. And what if Paulson were to claim that Darren made some sort of admission during the pretest interview, some damaging statement that Pope could then use at trial? It would be Paulson's word against Darren's, a contest in which Paulson's gold shield would surely tip the balance. The possibilities for disaster seemed endless.

And how, he wondered, had Pope known about the private tests they'd put Darren through? Jaywalker hadn't told him, and Darren certainly hadn't. That left Arledge and Sandusky. Maybe they'd talked to Paulson, mentioned the case because of its academic interest. But why would they have identified Darren as the subject without first asking Jaywalker's permission?

It was a question to which Jaywalker would never learn the answer. But when it came right down to it, what difference did it make? For better or for worse, Pope was still willing to give Darren the test. So what if Jaywalker had been personally embarrassed, caught doing something behind Pope's back? It had been his right to do it, probably even his duty. He would have been a damn fool, letting them test his client without first running a test of his own.

He found his Volkswagen, climbed in and headed downtown. At the first red light that stopped him, the taste of his own blood told him that he'd been biting the inside of his cheek. "Relax," he told himself, drawing a deep breath. "Relax," he repeated, this time for Darren. But Darren was already twenty blocks away by now, nowhere in view in the VW's rearview mirror.

He phoned Pope at one o'clock.

"What's the story?" he asked.

"The story is actually interesting," said Pope. "Paulson didn't test him. During the preliminary interview, Kingston said he's been taking Librium. Now that's not a strong drug, but it *is* a tranquilizer. Paulson's feeling is that it may have been responsible for the results of the previous tests."

"That *is* interesting," Jaywalker agreed.

"So he told Kingston to cut out the Librium, and we've set up another test for Thursday. Paulson's agreed to stay late and do it on his own time. Sound all right to you?"

"Sounds great." It did.

"Okay. And by the way," he added, "has that private investigator of yours come up with anything?"

Caught again. "Not too much, I'm afraid."

"You're really working overtime on this one, Mr. Jay-walker."

"Jay," Jaywalker reminded him.

"Jay."

"I guess so," said Jaywalker. "Wouldn't you be?"

So one of the victims had reported John McCarthy's movements to Pope, or perhaps to Detective Rendell. Jay-walker wasn't too surprised. Probably Joanne Kenarden, he decided.

That was all right. McCarthy had gotten the job done, at least with three of the four victims. And Pope's reaction had been less disapproval than admiration. No damage done, and even a minor boost for the ego, which was always welcome.

What interested Jaywalker more was the Librium busi-ness. Paulson's analysis made a certain amount of sense. A tranquilizer was intended to calm you down, after all, to the point where you wouldn't worry so much—about scary things, depressing things, *all* things. Including lying. The inevitable result would be a smoothing out, a literal flattening out, of one's responses. Which would make it harder for the needles to pick up those responses. Take away the tranquilizer and the test might well turn out dif-ferently. It might show, for example, that Darren was lying on the questions about masturbation and hurting people, but telling the truth about the rapes.

It was more than just interesting. Jaywalker felt a new surge of hope begin to well up. This guy Paulson, whom he'd been so quick to distrust, had homed in on the problem that Arledge and Sandusky had missed. The test was going to work after all, and Darren was going to pass it. Jaywalker stood up from behind his desk, threw a clenched fist into the air above his head and barely suppressed a whoop.

And then he caught himself.

This was crazy. Who did he think he was kidding? Did he really think that this test was going to come out any differently from the first three? And why did he have this burning need to have the case *solved,* figured out by the magic inside the little black box? Why couldn't he just look at it like he did any other case? You plead guilty, or you roll the dice and go to trial. You win or you lose. The answer crept up from somewhere deep inside him, until he not only knew it was true but could even give it a name.

And the name was fear.

Fear, because he knew if he had to try this case, the overwhelming odds were that he was going to lose it. Fear, because Darren and his family had put their complete faith in him, had trusted him to be able to do whatever it took to reverse a hideous wrong. Fear, because the terrible pendulum had swung once again, this time in the direction of innocence.

As much as Jaywalker loved the strange work he'd been drawn to, which pitted prosecutor against defender in a fight to the finish, as much as he wanted to be the hero, the savior to the Kingston family, more than anything else he wanted out of this one. He wanted this one last chance at the polygraph test to work, one way or the other.

He prayed for Lou Paulson to be right.

7

THE BRICK WALL

Lou Paulson was wrong.

Jaywalker reached Jacob Pope Friday morning. "Well?" he asked. By this time, holding his breath had become second nature.

To Pope's credit, he didn't play it cute or mince words. "No good," he said. "Paulson says it's like hooking up the machine to a brick wall. Kingston is simply untestable."

It was mid-December by the time of the next court appearance. The last two obstacles standing between them and trial had been removed. The pretrial motions had been resolved, and the polygraph exams were a memory.

Still, there was no thought of an immediate trial. The holidays made it a hard time to compete with the vacation schedules of judges, witnesses and even prospective jurors. And Darren's being out on bail lowered the priority of his trial. The case was put over to the second week of January.

Jaywalker wanted to drive his wife and daughter up to Massachusetts or Vermont to go skiing. His wife, reading him bleak snow reports from the *Times,* reminded him that they had open-ended plane tickets to Florida and had promised her parents that they would be down to visit soon. They argued, longer and louder than usual. Jaywalker's anxiety over the case, aggravated by his recent realization that it would have to be tried after all, had taken its toll on both of them.

In the end, they flipped a coin.

On Christmas day, it was sunny and eighty-five degrees by the pool.

8

NIGHTS ON THE COUCH

January was a time of cold, wet days, of rain that froze into slick sheets overnight, and of snow that fell wet and heavy, and turned to slush before refreezing and collecting black soot from passing cars.

January was also a time to get ready. Not for the trial, not quite yet, but for the hearing that would precede it. The Part 12 judge who'd ruled on Jaywalker's motions had ordered an evidentiary hearing on the admissibility of the identification testimony. In legal jargon, this is referred to as a Wade hearing, named after one of the U.S. Supreme Court cases that had given birth to the procedure.

The district attorney's office had notified the defense that photographs had been used in the identification of Darren as the perpetrator of the crimes. Unlike lineup results, which a jury may hear about, or "show-ups," which occur when a witness confirms or denies that a single suspect displayed to him is in fact the perpetrator, New York statutory law specifically prohibits the prosecution from eliciting photo "hits" in front of the jury. In spite of that law, Bronx district attorneys stubbornly persisted in showing photos, rather than real people, to witnesses.

But Jaywalker wasn't satisfied with knowing that Jacob Pope wouldn't be able to let a jury know that the victims had picked out Darren from photographs. Indeed, he knew the time might come when he himself might be forced to reveal that they had, so the jurors wouldn't speculate that some other piece of information, something even more compelling, had led to Darren's arrest. So Jaywalker wanted to explore, wanted to find out just how suggestive the procedures had been. For starters, had the victims been shown a whole bunch of photos or just Darren's? If there'd been others, were they of the same approximate age, skin tone and hair length? Had the victims been separated when they picked out Darren's photo, or had they been together? And had the police done anything to coach them, in either obvious or subtle ways? If Jaywalker could demonstrate that the methods used had been unduly suggestive, then the hearing judge might be compelled to conclude that, come trial, the victims would be pointing out Darren not on the basis of what they remembered from their attacks but from their recollections of the photographs, or at least some inseparable combination of the two. If that proved to be the case, the judge could bar such a witness from making an identification of Darren at trial.

Or so the theory went.

In practice, courts—operating at these hearings as both judge and jury—almost always come to the aid of prosecutors. Where conflicts arise between the officers' versions of the facts and the defendants' versions, the overwhelming majority of judges rule in favor of the police, so much so that few defense lawyers will even put their clients on the stand to offer a competing narrative. Even in those cases where the facts *undisputedly* reveal police improprieties, the same judges rule that the witnesses' trial identifications will be based upon the original crime-scene confrontation, untainted by any suggestiveness that may have corrupted the police-arranged identification procedure. Accordingly, they'll permit the trial identifications, even in those cases. It's the rare judge who will come right out and say that a witness's opportunity to observe the perpetrator was so fleeting, and the later identification procedure so suggestive, that the only solution is to bar the witness altogether from pointing out the defendant at trial.

That judicial bias aside, Jaywalker already knew that in this case, the victims' encounters with their attacker had in fact been quite substantial. He knew from John McCarthy's interviews that each of them had gotten a good look at her rapist or would-be rapist. Each had not only had the opportunity to see him "up close and personal" for an extended period of time—fifteen to twenty minutes—but had also heard him speak at some length, as well. Nothing fleeting about that.

Still, Jaywalker wanted the hearing. He needed to know just how suggestive the photo identification procedures had been, in order to be able to make an informed decision as to whether or not *he* wanted to go into the matter in front of the jury. The same rule that barred the prosecution from eliciting testimony about the photo identifications left the defense free to do so if it chose, albeit at its peril.

Even beyond that, Jaywalker wanted a crack at the witnesses before trial, a free look. He wanted the opportunity to size them up, to test their certainty or tentativeness. He wanted to be able to gauge their reactions to different types of cross-examination, and to probe their accounts in more detail than McCarthy had been able to. Best yet, a court stenographer would be taking down every word that came out of their mouths, so that if they varied what they said later on at the trial, he would have their hearing testimony to confront them with. Added to what they'd initially reported to the police and later told McCarthy, it would give Jaywalker a solid bank of material for impeachment.

Finally, in addition to the photo identifications, there'd been at least one live, or "corporeal," identification in the case, one that Jaywalker himself had witnessed. That had taken place the day of Darren's very first court appearance, when Joanne Kenarden had been summoned to court. There she'd watched as Detective Rendell, no stranger to her, had led Darren into court. Minutes later, she'd been asked if she could identify him, and if she was certain. Talk about *suggestiveness*… And unlike the photo identifications, this corporeal identification wasn't barred by the law. If it passed muster at the hearing—and Jaywalker had little doubt that it would, even if it shouldn't—Pope would be free to elicit it at trial.

In short, if nothing else, the hearing would provide a preview for the defense, an advance look at what the trial testimony would be. Jaywalker would have little to lose and much to gain from it. And since he figured he was pretty far behind the prosecution at this stage, gaining took on added importance.

So January, for the defense, was a time to get ready for the Wade hearing. Jaywalker reviewed McCarthy's notes and his own files. He went over every piece of paper he had, over and over again, hoping that one of them would reveal some secret, some clue to Darren's innocence, that he'd missed before. He made copious notes, reducing pages to paragraphs, paragraphs to sentences, sentences to key words. He drew up long lists of questions to ask witnesses. He fell asleep with his head on his desk more than once, and spent several nights on the couch of his office. He missed meals, lost weight he didn't have to lose in the first place, and occasionally appeared in court unshowered and unshaved. Never mistaken for a paragon of fashion, he now began to be noticed for his rumpled hair, wrinkled shirts, and same-as-yesterday suits and ties. He saw little of his wife, and less of their daughter.

But he got ready.

9

THE FREE LOOK

The case was called, and both Pope and Jaywalker answered that they were ready for the hearing. Justice Davidoff marked it for a second call, announcing that he'd begin the hearing as soon as he got through the rest of the matters on his calendar.

Jaywalker stepped outside the courtroom with the Kingstons. He went over the Wade hearing procedures with them once more. For some reason he felt a compulsion to explain everything to them. Again he reminded them that they stood no chance of "winning" anything at the hearing, that for them it represented a vehicle to get more information to use at the trial. A free look.

It was eleven o'clock by the time the case was recalled. Justice Davidoff, squinting at Jaywalker's motion papers in front of him, remarked that there seemed to be two issues before him, the Wade hearing and the defense's motion to sever the cases into four separate trials.

"How is this severance question going to affect our hearing?" he asked.

"It isn't," Jaywalker replied, jumping up to beat Pope to the punch. "I suggest we hold off on the severance issue until after the hearing. Once Your Honor has heard the testimony, you'll be in a much better position to rule on severance."

But Pope wasn't about to be outmaneuvered. "I disagree," he said, rising to his feet. "How many witnesses I call at the hearing depends entirely upon how Your Honor rules on the severance motion. Should you decide, for example, that there must be separate trials, then it would be ridiculous for me to have had to call all four victims to the stand, when it turns out only one was needed."

Between the lines, of course, Pope was offering Justice Davidoff a quick hearing in place of a protracted one. Always an effective strategy.

"Yes," said the judge, "I agree. I think it makes more sense to take up the severance motion first. Do you wish to be heard on it, Mr. Jaywalker?"

"Yes, I do," said Jaywalker, rising again as Pope resumed his seat.

So a moment of truth had arrived even earlier than Jaywalker had expected, or feared. In his motion, he'd formally requested that the case be split up into four trials. Now, as he was about to begin his oral argument in support of that position, he had a decision to make. Did he want to argue forcefully enough to persuade Davidoff, or merely well enough to protect the record, thereby allowing the judge to rule against him, and hopefully be reversed on appeal, in the event of a conviction?

"As I pointed out in my papers," Jaywalker began, "this is not one case, but four. Stacked together in this indictment are four separate sets of criminal acts, each described in a number of counts. There are four victims, four times, and four places of occurrence." The more he spoke, the more convinced he became that he was right, that they truly needed separate trials. And without ever making a specific, conscious decision, he found himself going all out, doing his best to convince Davidoff.

"The district attorney's office," he continued, "has joined these cases into a single indictment. I have to guess that they've done that for two reasons. First, it would save us all—the D.A.'s office, the court, the defendant, and certainly me—a lot of time and effort if we have to try only one case, instead of four. Second, it's a surefire way for the prosecution to win a conviction that they otherwise might not be able to.

"Well," Jaywalker went on, "the answer to the first concern is simple. No amount of time or effort we save is justification to abridge the rights of this young man. If it takes us *ten* trials to insure him his rights under the Constitution, then ten trials we must give him.

"The answer to the second concern is a bit more complicated, but only a bit." He paused for effect. "Each of these four cases involves, if I'm correct, a single-witness identification. In separate trials, the prosecution would be barred from bringing in the other victims. The jury would be considering one attack, one victim, one issue—is Darren Kingston the man who attacked that victim? Both sides would get a fair trial.

"But in a joint trial, in spite of any instructions to the contrary that you might give them, the jury is going to apply the old 'Where there's smoke, there's fire' adage. Forgive my bluntness, but there's simply no way in hell they're going to acquit a man charged with four rapes, whatever the evidence. We might as well sentence him right now.

"Finally," Jaywalker added, "there's yet another problem involved here. Your Honor is going to have to instruct the jury regarding the corroboration requirement required in a rape case. That's a difficult enough matter in a one-victim case. Throw in a second victim, and you're going to have jurors impermissibly bootstrapping one victim's account with the other's. Add two more victims, and you may as well kiss the corroboration requirement goodbye."

It had been a valid argument then, even if it was one that Jaywalker wouldn't be able to make today. The legislature has since seen fit to eliminate the requirement, and rightly so. Even Jaywalker, a defense lawyer, would admit it had been high time for the change.

"I'm afraid," he concluded, "that there's only one way we're going to be able to give this man a fair trial. And that's to give him four trials."

Pope rose as Jaywalker sat down. "Your Honor," he began, "the Criminal Procedure Law gives the court discretion to try cases jointly where it would serve the interest of justice, and where they are similar in time, place and manner.

"In time, two of these crimes occurred an hour apart. The third occurred the following day, the fourth several weeks later. In place, all four occurred in the area known as the Castle Hill Housing Project. In manner, the four could hardly be closer. In each instance, the defendant followed his victim onto an elevator, pulled a knife, took his victim off the elevator, led her into a stairwell or onto a landing, and attempted to rape her. In two instances he succeeded, in two he failed.

"I have faith in Your Honor's ability to instruct the jury

properly, and in the jury's ability to follow your instructions conscientiously."

With that, he sat down.

Justice Davidoff, who'd taken notes throughout the argument, continued to write in silence for several minutes. Finally he straightened up and cleared his throat. "The court," he began to read, "having heard argument of counsel, grants the defendant's motion for a severance to the following extent—the two rapes, involving the victims Cerami and Kenarden, which occurred on the same date and only hours apart, will be tried together. The two attempted rapes, involving the victims Maldonado and Caldwell, which occurred on subsequent dates, are severed."

Jaywalker tried to cover his surprise at what he'd just heard. Already he knew this much: he didn't like it. Somehow the defense had ended up with the worst of all possible worlds. Pope would be permitted to try two of the cases at once, giving him all the edge he would need. But at the same time, holding the remaining two cases in abeyance would deprive Jaywalker of a winner-take-all trial, leaving the prosecution an insurance policy in case it failed to win the first time around. Finally, by basing his decision on the times of the incidents, Davidoff might well have come up with a rationale acceptable to an appellate court.

Jaywalker had certainly lost round one.

"So," the judge was asking, "are we ready to proceed with the Wade hearing as to the two rape victims?"

"Yes, Your Honor," said Pope.

"Yes." Jaywalker nodded weakly.

"Call your first witness, Mr. Pope."

* * *

"The People call Detective Robert Rendell."

Pope motioned to a uniformed court officer, who opened the courtroom door. A moment later, Detective Rendell entered. Jaywalker was struck by the detective's height and good looks, just as he had been upon seeing him that first day in court. He'd known then, as he knew today, that Rendell would make a compelling witness. Although right now, with no jury present, the advantage was somewhat minimized.

Rendell was sworn in by the court clerk and seated. Pope began his direct examination with a few preliminary questions about Rendell's rank, experience and assignments in the police department. Then he moved on to August 24th, 1979.

POPE: Would you tell us what you did on that date, with respect to this investigation.

RENDELL: On August 24th I picked up three females, Eleanor Cerami, Joanne Kenarden, and Tania Maldonado, and drove them down to B.C.I., the Bureau of Criminal Identification.

POPE: Where was that located?

RENDELL: In Manhattan, 400 Broome Street.

POPE: What was your purpose in going there?

RENDELL: I had an appointment with the police artist, to draw a composite.

POPE: What happened when you got there?

RENDELL: I had a one-o'clock appointment, but the artist was late. While we were waiting, I had the girls look through DD-5 files, to see if they could find someone who looked like the perpetrator, so they could show it to the artist when he came.

POPE: Could you describe the files?

RENDELL: There's a filing cabinet, with drawers full of photographs on cards, three-by-five cards, I believe.

POPE: Would you please describe for us what occurred with Mrs. Cerami, Miss Kenarden and Mrs. Maldonado, as they were looking through these photographs.

RENDELL: They were viewing photographs of known residents of the Forty-third Precinct. They'd gone through about fifty photographs, when the three of them yelled out simultaneously that this was the man.

Jaywalker looked up from his note-taking. McCarthy had reported back to him that all three had identified photos of Darren, but none of the details. This was a devastating bit of testimony. Jaywalker listened carefully as Pope pursued it.

POPE: Did you say all three of them?

RENDELL: Yes.

POPE: Were they all looking at the photographs at the same time?

RENDELL: That's right. They were standing by the file cabinet, going through the cards. I'd pulled out the drawer of the Forty-third Precinct, and I'd asked them to look through the black male file. They were looking through it, turning the cards one by one.

POPE: Were you present while they were looking through the file?

RENDELL: Yes, I was approximately five feet away.

POPE: Would you describe what occurred at the time they called out?

RENDELL: I heard one of the girls yell out, "That's him!" And the Maldonado girl, she started walking toward the door, and Miss Kenarden, she turned to me and said, "That's the man." At that point I removed the picture that they'd picked out, that they were on. I placed it with a series of other photographs, and I waited about ten minutes. Then I brought each girl into another room, individually, and I showed them the photographs. And each one made a positive identification of the photograph they'd picked out together.

POPE: And who was that photograph of?

RENDELL: Darren Kingston.

Jaywalker sat back heavily, knowing they were in deep trouble. Pope continued. He had Rendell produce the photograph of Darren. It was a front-and-profile mug shot, bearing a 1977 date, obviously taken at the time of Darren's previous arrest, back when he and Charlene had been living with his parents, in the 43rd Precinct. And although it was more than two years old, it was still a pretty good likeness.

Rendell produced the other photos he'd used. After being marked into evidence, they were placed on the defense table. Jaywalker spread them out in front of him and studied them. There were eighteen in all. All were mug shots of young black males; some even resembled Darren rather closely. Rendell had been fair in his selection. As Jaywalker looked at them, he could see that Pope was watching him, waiting for his reaction. Jaywalker did his best to avoid looking dejected, but it was hard. The simultaneous emotional responses of the victims, the certainty of their exclamations, the fairness of the other photos, and the success of all three victims in picking out Darren's photo from the others—all those elements, when combined, spelled absolute disaster for the defense. Not just at the Wade hearing, which Jaywalker had never had illusions of winning, but at the trial itself.

Pope continued with his direct examination of Rendell, but the remainder was anticlimactic. The damage had been done. When Pope was finished, Justice Davidoff turned toward Jaywalker.

"Cross-examination?"

"Yes, Your Honor."

But Jaywalker had little to ask the detective. He established that there had never been an actual corporeal lineup, just the photo array. He got Rendell to be more specific regarding who had said what upon first seeing Darren's photo. He questioned him about certain details in his reports. After twenty minutes or so, he let the detective off the stand, before Justice Davidoff began to show annoyance. He knew he would have to save the judge's patience for the two victims, whose testimony he needed far more than the detective's.

They broke at one o'clock. Jaywalker politely declined the Kingstons' invitation to join them at lunch. He never ate breakfast, and whenever he was on trial he worked straight through the recess, fueled by adrenaline in place of food. It was a diet not to be recommended to the general public. Good for eliminating five pounds a week, it was also guaranteed to bring its share of blinding headaches.

As he reviewed his list of questions for the victims, it occurred to Jaywalker that much of the responsibility for Darren's arrest was Jaywalker's own. Following the dismissal of the 1977 case, Darren's record was supposed to have been sealed, and all the photographs and fingerprint cards the police had of him should have been destroyed. Jaywalker had dutifully sent off a letter to the NYPD, including with it a copy of the disposition slip. But he'd never followed up on it, never checked to see if in fact the files had been purged. Now it was clear that they hadn't been.

Today the system is self-activated and far more efficient. Back then, it was hit or miss. The truth was, though, that he wouldn't even have known how to go about checking up on something like that. What could he have done, gone to the local precinct house and asked them to go through all their mug-shot files? They would have thrown him out on his ear, or worse. But none of that stopped him from feeling that had he been more thorough, Darren's photo wouldn't have been there, waiting for someone to pick it out.

After the break, Pope called Eleanor Cerami to the stand. She'd been the first of the victims to be attacked. She was a small white woman who spoke timidly and was obviously frightened. Pope had her describe the incident, bringing out the fact that she'd been with her attacker for somewhere between fifteen and twenty minutes, certainly long enough to get a good look at him. Then he shifted to the day at the precinct, eliciting her version of the excitement that had occurred when the three young women had first spotted the photo of Darren. He concluded by asking her if she now saw the man in the courtroom. She nodded and pointed directly at Darren. Jaywalker had the distinct impression that as much as anything else, Pope was running her through a dress rehearsal for the trial. In response to his final question, she said there was no doubt in her mind.

Jaywalker began his cross-examination as gently as he could. He wanted Mrs. Cerami to relax a bit, if possible, to trust him, to treat the proceeding as a search for the facts, rather than a contest between lawyer and witness. He also didn't want to give Justice Davidoff cause to step in and protect her.

He got her to admit that at first she'd paid no particular attention to the man who'd gotten onto the elevator after she had. He was black, but so were lots of the project residents. It had only been when he suddenly displayed the knife that she'd taken real notice of him. Even then, her attention had been divided between the man himself and the knife. And when he'd marched her off the elevator, he'd been alongside her, rather than facing her.

Jaywalker began to feel he was doing all right. He had Mrs. Cerami describe the unscrewing of the overhead lightbulb and the sex acts themselves. Then he decided to go for broke. After all, there was no jury present, and he needed to know.

JAYWALKER: Now, would it be fair to say that you did your best to look away from him?

CERAMI: I was looking at his face.

Jaywalker winced. So much for his clever question. Still, it was better to hear the bad news now than to bring it out in front of a jury. He asked Mrs. Cerami about the lighting, once the man had unscrewed the lightbulb. She said it had still been pretty good. Jaywalker winced again. He pushed on, questioning her in detail about the opportunity she'd had to see the man and the description of him she'd later given to the police. He concluded by bringing out that, according to her recollection, there had been nothing unusual about her attacker in the way of scars, marks, deformities or speech mannerisms. Then he thanked her and sat down.

Next Pope called Joanne Kenarden. Jaywalker recognized her from Darren's first court appearance, back in

September. He was struck again by her hardness, particularly in contrast to the timidity of Eleanor Cerami. Pope asked her about the day of the incident. She answered each of his questions directly, without hesitation. He got to the moment of the sex acts.

POPE: What did he do at that point?

KENARDEN: He made me commit oral sodomy, and he raped me.

Pope continued, bringing out the fact that she'd spent about twenty minutes with her assailant, during which time she'd had ample opportunity to observe and remember him.

On cross-examination, Jaywalker questioned Miss Kenarden in detail about everything that had taken place. She, too, said that her attacker had spoken at some length. Jaywalker brought out as much of the actual conversation as he could. He was mindful of the fact that she was the only one of the four victims John McCarthy had been unable to interview. He needed her answer on the question of whether the man who'd raped her had spoken with a stutter.

JAYWALKER: Now, other than the description you gave Detective Rendell, is there anything else you can now recall telling him about the man?

KENARDEN: No, other than he, you know, spoke softly.

JAYWALKER: Did you tell Rendell that?

KENARDEN: Yes.

JAYWALKER: Anything else?

KENARDEN: He spoke evenly, not abusively. He spoke to me a lot.

JAYWALKER: Anything unusual about his speech?

KENARDEN: No.

Jaywalker exhaled. This was good stuff, but he wanted more. In addition to his stutter, Darren had a chipped front tooth, and a small scar that interrupted one of his eyebrows.

JAYWALKER: Did your attacker have any scars that you noticed?

KENARDEN: No.

JAYWALKER: Any deformities of any sort?

KENARDEN: No.

JAYWALKER: Any unusual mannerisms?

KENARDEN: No.

Jaywalker sat down. The testimony was over; all that remained were legal arguments. He asked Justice Davidoff to rule the photo array impermissibly suggestive, and tainted by the earlier events at the station house. He urged him to hold that a "lineup by photograph" was inherently improper when an actual lineup could have been held instead. The judge interrupted him several times during his argument, though never rudely. But he made it clear that he thought the procedures used were proper. At one point he commented rather gratuitously that "there was no question in the officer's mind, or the witnesses' minds, who the individual was who was responsible."

Even before Pope rose to speak, Jaywalker knew the defense had no chance. His motion to suppress the courtroom identifications was denied, and the case was put over until February 20th.

For trial.

10

A STUBBORN FOG

Be wary of the lawyer who's afraid to go to trial. But be just as wary of the one with no fear at all. The lawyer you want, it turns out, is the one who has a love-hate relationship with the trial process. One who, even as he readies himself to do battle, at the same time knows that it's going to take place because he's failed to deliver for his client. Failed to deliver a dismissal, a desirable plea bargain, whatever. In the final analysis, a trial is a last resort, a roll of the dice that trades compromise for either complete deliverance or complete disaster. Getting ready for trial, therefore, takes on all the seriousness of getting ready for war, and war is as serious a business as there is. The lawyer who doesn't understand this and isn't humbled by it is no lawyer at all.

Jaywalker understood it.

He spent the final three weeks organizing his notes for the hundredth time, all but memorizing the testimony from the Wade hearing, tying up every conceivable loose end and planning what would become his trial strategy, his battle plan.

Some lawyers will tell you that they win their cases by doing exhaustive pretrial investigation, others by conducting withering cross-examinations, still others by delivering brilliant summations. All of these skills are important, to be sure, as are those associated with jury selection, opening statements, direct examination, legal research and a dozen or more other items.

With his own DEA background and John McCarthy's help, Jaywalker was more than competent when it came to the art of investigating. His acquittal rate at Legal Aid, and in the year and a half since, was impressive. But as the trial of Darren Kingston approached, he was only four years into trying cases, and most of those had been non-jury misdemeanors. He still considered himself only an average examiner of witnesses, whether on direct or cross. His summations, while good, were hardly outstanding. Jury selection was still something of a mystery to him. Over time, he would learn how to win a case during the opening statement, but back in 1980, he would have scoffed at the notion that such a thing was even possible. And he would never become a legal scholar.

But even then, even in his infancy as a trial lawyer, Jaywalker loved strategy and—though he would never have admitted it out loud—in private moments he dared to think of himself as a master tactician.

Strategy and tactics are all but invisible to the casual observer of a criminal trial. But to Jaywalker's way of thinking, they were absolutely essential to the business of winning. What kind of a jury do you really want on a given case? Do you reveal your defense to them early on or hold off till the prosecution's committed itself? Do you concede that the crime was actually committed, or do you dispute everything? Do you attack a particular witness head-on, or do you treat her gently? Do you present an alibi defense if it depends upon family members? Do you put the defendant on the stand when doing so will reveal his prior criminal record? Or do you keep him off, knowing that your reasonable doubt argument will be stronger? Do you dress your client up in a suit and tie to show respect, or have him wear jeans and work boots, as he does in real life?

If these seem like trivial considerations, they're anything but. These are the things that trials are won or lost on, the stuff upon which a defendant's freedom depends. Every last one of them involves a monumental decision. And the decisions are lonely ones, made in the early morning darkness following a fitful night's sleep.

There are lawyers who make decisions by committee—consulting with partners, colleagues, jury experts, family and friends. There are lawyers who cop out and practice defensively, refraining from making an opening statement lest they tip their hands or from asking a question on cross-examination unless they know the answer in advance. There are lawyers who put their clients on the stand simply because they want to testify and might later complain that they were talked out of doing so. And there are lawyers who decide things by not deciding, and spend their time sitting on their butts and riding the trial out as it takes its course, like a passenger parked in the middle of a canoe, watching the scenery going by and waiting for the destination to arrive.

And then there was Jaywalker.

He knew that, for better or for worse, the decisions were his to make. Not his colleagues, not his family or friends, not some self-professed expert, not even his client. Never mind that the Constitution gave the defendant the right to testify or to remain silent, the option of making an opening statement or waiving it, the choice of contesting some piece of evidence or conceding it. Jaywalker was going to make those decisions, and then he was going to convince his client why he was right. And there was only one guiding principle involved in the calculus, and its name was winning.

The surest way Jaywalker knew of winning was to go into court with a better game plan than his adversary, to make the right tactical decisions and then to execute them properly. But that was easier said than done. In practice, it was often nothing short of gut-wrenching. Over time, he already knew, it would eat his insides out.

Among the decisions Jaywalker was going to have to make during this trial was what to do about the photographic identifications of Darren by Eleanor Cerami and Joanne Kenarden. Because Jacob Pope was prevented by law from bringing them out at trial, he had no real way of letting the jury know what had led to Darren's arrest. They would be left to speculate, something Justice Davidoff would instruct them that they mustn't do but human nature would compel them to do nonetheless.

But unlike Pope, Jaywalker was free to go into the photo identifications if he chose to. The same statute that tied the prosecutor's hands permitted the defense to explore the matter in front of the jury, in order to show that the procedure used had impacted the identifications the witnesses would be making at trial. Justice Davidoff had ruled that any suggestiveness hadn't risen to the level requiring trial identifications to be excluded, but that ruling didn't prevent

Jaywalker from trying to demonstrate to the jurors that the procedure had nonetheless influenced the witnesses to some extent. Darren's constitutional right to have his case decided not by a judge, but by a jury of his peers, still gave Jaywalker the option of bringing up the matter if he chose to.

But did he?

Talk about a double-edged sword. On the one hand, Jaywalker was anxious to show that Mrs. Cerami and Miss Kenarden had been influenced by each other in picking out the photo of Darren. And Detective Rendell's waiting only ten minutes to show them a photo array, no matter how fairly composed, was hardly a meaningful test. Darren's photo was still fresh in their minds; all they had to do was pick it out again. There were definitely some points to be made here.

On the other hand, the certainty and spontaneity with which they'd reacted to the photo were damaging. And the fact that they'd been able to select it from seventeen similar-looking others, no matter how soon thereafter, was impressive. Jaywalker could imagine Pope offering the full set of photos into evidence—something Davidoff would surely let him do, once Jaywalker had opened the door— and the jurors ending up with it in front of them during their deliberations.

Jaywalker kicked the issue around in his mind for the better part of two weeks. In the end, he decided to keep the photos out.

Next was the issue of how to refer to the various individuals the jury would be hearing from and about. Whether or not he decided to put his client on the stand, Jaywalker already knew that he would be "Darren" and not "Mr.

Kingston," as he was sure Pope would call him. But in Jay-walker's mind, Darren was young enough—and would prove likeable enough—to be called by his first name. In proverbs, familiarity may breed contempt; at trial, handled properly, it was far more likely to breed empathy.

The women posed another problem. To refer to them as "victims" conceded that they were, that they'd indeed been attacked. But Jaywalker was fully prepared to do just that. This wasn't a *What happened?* trial; it was a *Whodunnit?* To refer to the victims as "complainants" or "complaining witnesses"—terms that were both techni-cally correct—struck Jaywalker as an obvious attempt to deny their status as victims, a denial that might offend the jurors, particularly the women among them. And there were sure to women among them.

"Victims" it would be.

And what of those women jurors? Even with his limited jury trial experience, Jaywalker was already convinced that not only were women more sympathetic and forgiv-ing than men, but that they also reacted better to him on a personal level than men did. A lot of sexual dynamics play out in a courtroom. Jurors are yanked from their personal and business lives, and dropped into an alternative universe of sorts. In addition to everything else about the experience of sitting on a criminal trial jury, for most people it's new, different and exciting. Jaywalker was young, and good-looking enough to make the older women on the jury want to mother him and the younger ones fall in love with him. Pope, with his dark mustache, dark suits, white shirts, rep ties and buttoned-down seriousness, was no competition. Knowing all that was important, and taking advantage of it was fair play. Equally important was knowing that the men on the jury might resent Jaywalker for upstaging them. They, too, were on a break from their other lives. What hope did any of them have of seducing the pretty woman sitting beside him in the jury box, when forced to compete against the defense lawyer, the solitary defender of the underdog?

So logic seemed to indicate that women were good for his client, men bad.

But this was a rape case. And not some date-rape case, punctuated with flirtations, nuances and *he-said, she-said* competing versions, calling for Solomonic apportionment of blame. No, these were *forcible* rapes, committed at the point of a knife by a total stranger. Worse yet, a *black* stranger. How on earth could Jaywalker choose women jurors on a case that epitomized every woman's worst nightmare?

But he *could* choose them, he decided. Even look for them. He would just have to talk about the reality of the case sufficiently during jury selection. He would have to find women who could deal with it, who could separate the awfulness of the crimes from the only question before them: was Darren Kingston the young man who'd committed them?

But by far the most important tactical decision facing Jaywalker concerned what sort of defense, if any, he wanted to present at trial. Limited experience had taught him that often the best defense was no defense at all. Jurors are aching to know the defendant's side of the story. They want to hear that alibi, that claim of self-defense, that second version of what happened. It was human nature at work. And why not? In our everyday lives, we're accustomed to choosing the version of the facts we like better. It's easier that way.

But Jaywalker's job wasn't to give the jurors what they wanted or to make things easier for them. It was to win. And he knew that putting on a defense and having a defendant himself testify often succeeded in snatching defeat from the jaws of victory.

And not for the reasons someone might think.

It wasn't, for starters, that a defendant's criminal record came out when he testified. It did, to a certain extent, but Jaywalker felt fully capable of dealing with that, even of turning it to his advantage on occasion. Darren's only prior arrest had ended in a dismissal. Even if Pope were permitted to ask him about it, it wasn't a big deal. And Jaywalker would be able to point to the fact that Darren had never before been arrested on a sex charge of any sort, something he wanted the jury to hear.

Nor did he generally hesitate to put a defendant on the stand because he might sound uneducated or stupid, speak poorly, or be forced to admit he was an unemployed illegal alien with a drug habit. Jurors were capable of forgiving stuff like that, as long as they were warned ahead of time.

No, it was none of those things that made him hesitate.

The single strongest thing a criminal defendant has going for him is the burden of proof the law places on the prosecution, that in order to win a conviction, it has to not only prove the defendant's guilt, but also has to do so beyond a reasonable doubt. It's a burden that the judge instructs the jury about at the very outset of the trial and again at the very end. And in between, Jaywalker would remind them every chance he got. By the time a Jaywalker jury was given a case to deliberate and decide, the words were second nature to them. They might forget the judge's name, the crimes charged and their own phone numbers. But they would remember reasonable doubt.

The problem is, all that goes out the window when the defendant—or just about any other defense witness, for that matter—takes the stand. The human mind, it turns out, is utterly incapable of weighing one story against another while at the same time factoring reasonable doubt into the equation. The judge can tell them to do it, the defense lawyer can tell them to do it, but when it comes right down to it, it's asking the impossible.

Already, Jaywalker had learned all this the hard way. He'd begun his trial career by putting defendants on the stand and calling their mothers to account for their whereabouts at the time of the crime. His efforts were rewarded with apologetic convictions and assurances that he'd done a much better job than the prosecutor, but...

So he changed his approach. He began keeping his clients off the stand and stressing reasonable doubt every chance he got. And what he found was that in a close case, a jury forced to put the prosecution's case to the reasonable-doubt test would grudgingly acquit the defendant and save their apologies for the district attorney, explaining that they were *almost* convinced of the defendant's guilt, but not quite. Sometimes they would even ignore Jaywalker on their way out of the courtroom, their way of letting him know that they both knew his client deserved worse.

Was he insulted at such times? Not a chance. In fact, the jurors' snubs were the highest form of praise they could bestow upon him, their silence music to his ears. In a contest that was all about winning, he would take a grudging acquittal over an apologetic conviction any day of the week.

And yet, in spite of all that, Jaywalker knew that in Darren's case, he was going to have to break his rule. The victims were simply too certain in their identifications. If they were wrong—and on this particular arc of the pendulum, Jaywalker was convinced that they were—it was because they were mistaken, not because they were lying. And unlike lying witnesses, mistaken witnesses can't be tripped up on cross-examination. Because they honestly think they're telling the truth, they come off as though they are, and jurors tend to believe them every bit as much as the witnesses believe themselves.

Jaywalker knew, therefore, that he was going to have to present a defense, and it was going to have to include Darren himself. That thought didn't scare him the way it might have. He told himself that Darren would make a pretty good witness. He was young, good-looking, polite, intelligent enough, and ultimately likeable. His stutter wouldn't work against him once it was explained as a lifelong thing and might even generate a certain amount of sympathy. And if the victims persisted in saying they recalled no stutter on the part of their attacker, it could even become a pivotal point. Darren's previous arrest might come out, but balancing that would be his lack of any history of sex offenses. Finally, Pope wouldn't be able to trip up Darren on cross-examination any more than Jaywalker would be able to trip up the victims, because Darren, too, would be telling what he believed to be the truth. Jaywalker shook his head at the irony of that.

In addition to Darren, there were his coworkers at the post office. Although they couldn't account for Darren's whereabouts during the rapes themselves, they might be able to undercut Eleanor Cerami's "second sighting" of

Darren. And if either of the victims departed in her testimony from what she'd told John McCarthy, Jaywalker could call McCarthy to impeach her. In addition, he knew he had to figure out a way to get Darren's mother on the stand, and perhaps other members of his family, as well, though probably not his father. Marlin had already made it clear that sitting still at his son's rape trial would be difficult for him; testifying without losing it altogether would be an impossibility.

Again, as he had going into the Wade hearing, Jaywalker felt ready. John McCarthy's investigation, if not exhaustive, had been pretty thorough. A lot had been learned at the hearing. Darren's being out on bail had enabled him to assist in preparation, and his family had been immensely cooperative. The luck of the draw had given them a decent judge who could be counted on to give them a fair trial.

And yet, despite all his readiness, Jaywalker still couldn't shake that feeling of apprehension that had attached itself to him early one morning in September and had clung to him ever since, like a stubborn fog that refused to lift.

He was ready, but he was afraid.

11

BOARD GAMES

"All rise! Part Sixteen of the Supreme Court, in and for the County of the Bronx, is now in session, the Honorable Max Davidoff presiding. Please be seated."

Jaywalker scanned the rows of prospective jurors that filled the courtroom and immediately knew they were in trouble.

Today the Bronx is what whites refer to as a "minority borough," with blacks and Latinos comprising nearly ninety percent of its population. If that description betrays a certain amount of ethnocentricity, at the same time it fairly characterizes the borough. Its schools are minority; its stores are minority; its churches are minority; its playgrounds are minority; its politicians are minority. Everything about it, in fact, is minority.

But it wasn't always so.

Beautiful parks once dotted the Bronx, with names like Pelham Bay, Bedford and Van Cortlandt. Graceful shade trees, manicured lawns and spotless sidewalks were everywhere. The Grand Concourse, the broad boulevard that passes directly in front of the courthouse and provides its address, was once second only to Manhattan's Park Avenue in terms of the prestige it carried and the rent it commanded.

But all that changed.

By the late 1960s and early 1970s, the Bronx had become a borough in transition, with its older Jewish, Irish, Italian and Polish residents pulling up and heading to Westchester, Queens, Long Island and New Jersey. In their place, younger blacks and Puerto Ricans began moving in in large numbers, soon to be followed by Colombians, Cubans, Jamaicans, Haitians and Dominicans. The phrase *white flight* was on everyone's lips.

The transformation wasn't an easy one. Unemployment soared, welfare rolls swelled, and crime statistics skyrocketed. Front doors, once left unlocked, now sprouted padlocks and chains. Window glass gave way to plywood. And streets that had been safe at night became dangerous by day. The whites who could, responded by fleeing in increasing numbers; those who couldn't, ventured out of their apartments warily, returned quickly and triple-locked themselves in. By the winter of 1980, as Darren Kingston's case came up for trial, the new immigrants outnumbered the old guard they'd replaced.

Jaywalker would have had no complaint if the jury panel had reflected the changing demographic of the borough. As difficult as it might be, he felt he would have a reasonable chance of convincing a racially mixed jury to keep an open mind in the trial of a black man born to West Indian parents and accused of raping two white women.

He wasn't going to get that chance.

At the time, jury panels in Bronx County were drawn exclusively from voter registration rolls. The whites who'd dug in and remained had lived in the borough for years, often generations. They'd emigrated from Europe, seeking not only economic opportunity but also, in many cases, political and religious freedom, as well. They'd lived through a world war, understood the Holocaust and watched the westward march of Communism. They prized their new-found democracy. And they voted.

The newcomers lacked that history. They typically had less education, lower literacy rates and less familiarity with the English language. They'd come not to escape oppression but to find jobs. Voting was nice, but it would be something their children would do one day, or their grand-children.

As a result, of the fifty prospective jurors summoned to Part 16 on the morning of February 21, 1980, five were black and none was Hispanic. And perhaps it was only Jay-walker's imagination working overtime, but the remaining forty-five seemed barely able to hide the palpable fear of a threatened species.

"The People of the State of New York versus Darren Kingston," announced the clerk.

"The People are ready for trial," said Jacob Pope, in a loud and clear voice.

"Is the defendant ready?"

"The defendant is ready," Jaywalker answered. Then he asked to approach the bench. There, in the presence of Justice Davidoff, Pope and the court stenographer, but out of the jury's earshot, he voiced his objection to the disproportionately small number of minority jurors and requested a new panel.

"There are only five blacks," he pointed out, "and not a single Hispanic, as far as I can tell. Combined, that's precisely ten percent of the total, in a county that's eighty-three percent minority."

Nobody picked up on the oxymoron, or the fact that Jaywalker had made up the statistic on the spur of the moment. He'd learned that if you were specific enough with numbers, people tended to defer to you and accept them at face value.

Justice Davidoff peered over his reading glasses at the jurors. "I count twelve blacks," he said.

"That's because you're counting the defendant's family," Jaywalker told him.

It didn't matter. His objection was overruled and his request for a new panel denied. It was, as they say, an inauspicious beginning.

Jury selection began slowly. Before its completion, it would take two full days. Twelve prospective jurors, whose names had been drawn at random from the panel of fifty, filled the jury box. Pope got to address them first, and his questions sought personal information: their employment, marital status, family makeup, geographical background and education. He seemed intent on finding jurors with daughters, Jaywalker noticed. His manner was businesslike and efficient. No surprise there.

When Jaywalker's turn came, he spent little time exploring the jurors' backgrounds. Instead, he used the time allotted him to tell them, as early on as he could, the most troublesome things about the case they were about to hear.

JAYWALKER: Mr. Peterson, knowing that two young women are going to walk into this room and point out my client as the man they say raped them, and knowing that they're going to do so with all the sincerity and certainty that humans are capable of, do you think you can still give Darren Kingston a fair trial?

PETERSON: Yes, I do.

The answer, of course, was meaningless, unless it happened to be a "No." But by the very asking of the question, Jaywalker was attempting to defuse the worst of the prosecution's evidence—to warn the jurors that this was a double rape case, that the victims were young, that they would point out Darren, that they would do so in good faith, and that they would do so without reservation. The effect, Jaywalker hoped, would be to deprive Pope of whatever drama he was looking to create. Beyond that, it would serve to precondition the jurors, so when the time came for the identifications, they wouldn't seem like such a big deal. Over time, Jaywalker would refine his techniques and improve upon them. But this was 1980, and though he was already comfortable with the business of jury selection, he was still very much a work in progress.

In addition to taking the sting out of the facts of the rapes and the self-certainty of the victims, Jaywalker wanted to indoctrinate the jurors on the law, at least those areas where it helped the defense.

JAYWALKER: Mrs. Wilson, you're going to hear the judge tell you over and over again that the prosecution has the burden of proof here. In other words, they're the ones who have to prove this case, and they have to do it *beyond a reasonable doubt.* Now, is there anything about that rule that strikes you as un-fair?

WILSON: No.

JAYWALKER: You understand that since it's the prosecution that's brought this case into court, it stands to reason that they have to prove it?

WILSON: Yes.

JAYWALKER: And prove it to a very strict stan-dard, *beyond* all reasonable doubt?

WILSON: Yes.

In that seemingly innocuous exchange, Jaywalker first made it a point to depersonalize his adversary. He never used grandiose terms like "The People" or "The Govern-ment." Nor did he say "Mr. Pope" or "the prosecutor." By using the less personal form of the word *prosecution,* he hoped to remove Pope from the equation altogether. Ac-quit my client, Jaywalker was telling the jurors, and no one loses, not even that serious guy over there with the mustache. He's just part of an institution. And the fact that the name of that institution happens to sound very much like *per*secution—well, Jaywalker would leave that little coincidence to the experts on subliminal persuasion.

The second thing he'd done was even sneakier. By placing emphasis on the word *beyond* the second time he'd referred to reasonable doubt, he'd managed to change the modifier immediately preceding it from "a" to "all," without drawing an objection from Pope or a rebuke from Justice Davidoff. From that point on, every time he spoke the words—and there would be literally dozens of such times—it would come out "beyond all reasonable doubt." A small thing? Sure. But to Jaywalker's way of thinking, big trials are often won by small things.

> JAYWALKER: So you understand, Mrs. Fisher, that as the defense attorney, I don't have to prove anything?
>
> FISHER: Yes.
>
> JAYWALKER: Or *dis*prove anything?
>
> FISHER: Yes, I understand.

Again, the answers meant nothing. They were an opaque set of responses from a juror who, for all Jaywalker knew, simply wanted to sit on the case and knew what she was supposed to say to make that happen. It was the questions themselves, which were really statements thinly disguised as questions, that accomplished the conditioning. Jaywalker reworded them, shuffled them, repeated them, apologized for repeating them, then repeated them again. Not only was the juror who was being questioned forced to listen to them, so were those waiting to be questioned, those who'd already been questioned, and even—back in 1980—those who'd already been selected. It was Jaywalker's hope that by being forced to listen, they might begin to think about the meaning of the phrases they were hearing. At least to the point of realizing that it would be their job to focus on the issue of reasonable doubt, rather than the specter of their daughters being raped by a black man.

Several jurors came right out and said they couldn't be fair to a defendant accused of rape. One or two acknowledged other prejudices that might prevent them from being impartial. A few voiced personal reasons that would make it difficult or impossible for them to serve. All were excused on the consent of both lawyers, or by the judge for "cause." There was no limit to the number that could be so excused. With respect to "peremptory" challenges—exercised by either side against a juror who was otherwise qualified to serve—each side had fifteen.

Once Jaywalker had completed his questioning of the twelve jurors in the box, the clerk produced a board with the jurors' name cards in slots corresponding to where they were seated. The lawyers were told to indicate their peremptory challenges by turning over the card of any juror they wanted to strike. Pope was able to eliminate blacks, young people and just about anyone else he thought might be sympathetic to the defense. Back in 1980, it was accepted practice to use a juror's color as the basis for a challenge. Not that it still isn't, despite a change in the law. But these days you have to lie, and claim that it was something the particular juror said or didn't say.

Jaywalker, meanwhile, had his hands full with frightened parents of teenaged daughters, older women who couldn't bring themselves to even look at Darren, and those who'd been attacked themselves or had a close friend or relative who had been.

One way of looking at jury selection is to think of it as a fairly intriguing board game. There are two players, a

game board, and a deck of playing cards spread out on it.
Taking turns, the players have to jointly build a hand containing a dozen cards, plus a few extras. Only the players aren't working together; they're opponents. One of them wants the hand to end up with as many high cards in it as possible—kings, queens, jacks, tens and so forth. The other wants the same hand to have nothing but twos, threes and fours. Each player is allotted fifteen moves, which he can use up quickly, spread out over the course of the game, or hoard for later. Each knows it's important to keep track of his opponent's moves as well as his own, because neither wants to be outmaneuvered at the end.

The idea is simple enough, to get rid of those cards you don't want and pass when it comes to ones you like or will at least settle for. Meanwhile, your opponent is doing the same. Part of the strategy therefore lies in figuring out which cards he's likely to get rid of, lest you waste one of your moves on any of those. An example of *advanced* strategy would be making it look like you're going to get rid of a particular card you secretly like, in the hope that your opponent will fall for the ruse and fail to get rid of it himself.

Sounds simple enough, no?

And it would be, but for one minor detail. Instead of being arranged on the board face up, with their numerical values showing, the cards are spread out facedown. The king of spades looks no different from the two of clubs. So in order to calculate the true value of any given card, you're going to have to take the word of a total stranger, a stranger who may be telling you the truth, may not even *know* the card's value, or may know it but is lying through his or her teeth and simply telling you what you want to hear, because he or she wants you to pick that card.

So you're pretty much left to guess, assuring yourself as you do so that if the process isn't exactly science, it's certainly art. Or that if it isn't actually art and is only guesswork, at least it's *informed* guesswork. And finally, that even if it isn't informed at all and is actually totally blind, well, when it comes right down to it, you're a pretty good guesser.

But jurors weren't cards. They were human beings, with all humanity's attendant foibles and frailties. And the jurors that Pope and Jaywalker would settle on would hold Darren Kingston's life in their hands. They would have the power to walk him out the courtroom door, a free man, his nightmare behind him. In as long as it takes to speak two words, they could restore his entire world: his marriage, his job, his good name, his dignity.

Or they could send him to state prison for the next half of a century.

So if it was nothing but guesswork, let the guessing begin, thought Jaywalker. To him, guessing was a concoction of relying upon stereotypes, playing hunches, employing a bit of magical thinking, looking people in the eye, flirting with the women, using sports analogies with the men, making judgments on the scantiest bits of information and hoping for the best. Over the twenty-some years to follow, his questioning of prospective jurors would evolve, but his selection process would pretty much remain the same. If ever you should happen to come across a lawyer who professes to have truly figured it all out—with or without the assistance of high-priced jury selection "experts"—save your money and run like the wind.

Darren Kingston's jury was finally picked on the end of the second day, a Friday. It had taken five rounds, over the course of which twenty-four prospective jurors were peremptorily challenged—fourteen by Jaywalker and ten by Pope. Of the twelve who remained and were sworn in along with two alternates, seven were women, five men. The oldest was sixty-eight, the youngest thirty-nine. The average age was fifty-one. There were eleven whites and one black, a retired New York State parole officer. On a scale of 1 to 10, with 10 being Jaywalker's dream jury and 1 being his worst nightmare, he rated it about a minus 5.

The evidence hadn't even begun yet, but already Darren was in deep trouble.

12

DISCREPANCIES

Monday, February 25th

The jurors were brought into the courtroom and for the first time arranged in what would become their permanent seats for the remainder of the trial. Their numbers had already shrunk from the previous Friday. One of the alternates had called in sick earlier in the morning. The trial would proceed without her.

Justice Davidoff addressed the remainder of the jurors for about ten minutes, outlining their role in the trial, as well as his, giving them a few general instructions and explaining some basic principles of law. *Boilerplate stuff*, lawyers call it. Then he called upon Jacob Pope to make his opening statement.

Pope spoke for an even shorter time than the judge had, and it, too, was standard stuff. He made the usual observation that it was his duty to open on behalf of "the People," a phrase he would use as persistently as Jaywalker would avoid it. He compared his opening to the table of contents of a book, something every prosecutor feels compelled to do. The trial itself he likened to a jigsaw puzzle, with various pieces contributed by different witnesses. At the end, there might be a piece missing here or there. But, he assured them, there would be more than enough for them to recognize the true picture that emerged. Next, Pope read the indictment, at least those counts that hadn't been severed out, word for word. He told the jurors that they would be hearing the testimony of Eleanor Cerami and Joanne Kenarden, as well as that of other witnesses. Then he thanked the jurors and sat down.

Unlike the prosecution, the defense, with no burden to prove or disprove anything, has no obligation to open. Jaywalker's Legal Aid training had taught him to remain silent, or, as one of his more colorful female colleagues was fond of saying, to "waive my opening in front of the jury." The thinking was, don't commit yourself to a particular line of defense before you have to, and never tell the jury you're going to prove anything, lest you fail to deliver on your promise.

Over the years, Jaywalker would come to completely repudiate those bits of wisdom. As he would hone his trial skills, perhaps the biggest change he made would be in his approach to the opening statement. Today, he considers it a major weapon in his arsenal. Dispensing with the usual formalities of "May it please the court," "Ladies and gentlemen of the jury," or even "Good morning," he launches directly into a narrative account of the way things really happened, according to the defendant. "Darren Kingston woke up on the afternoon of September eleventh and went to work, as he always did." The jurors would listen, riveted, as though they were hearing actual testimony. More than any other change he's made in the way he tries a case, Jaywalker credits this one for the dramatic rise in the number of acquittals he's recently won.

But that was the twenty-first-century version, modified and perfected over the years. This was 1980, and he still had much to learn.

He cautioned the jurors not to make their minds up after hearing the first few witnesses. He told them to refrain from drawing conclusions until all the evidence was in, hinting—without coming right out and saying— that there would be a defense case, and they should suspend judgment while they waited to hear it. He sat down barely three minutes after he'd begun.

Looking back at his opening statement years later, Jaywalker would be forced to give it a failing grade, a flat-out F. It was a brief, cautious, ultraconservative opening, calculated not so much to help the defense as to avoid hurting it. And therein lay the fault. Jaywalker finds a good analogy, as he tends to do these days, in the world of sports.

A football team is clinging to a slim lead late in the game. The coach orders his pass defenders to drop back deep. The strategy is to surrender the short gain, while preventing the long one at all costs. There's even a widely used term for it, the *prevent defense.* Its weakness, of course, is obvious. A clever opposing team will exploit it with a rapid series of short gains, marching down the field and into the end zone. Which is why its critics say that the only thing the prevent defense really prevents is winning.

Jaywalker had deliberately chosen to make a *prevent defense* opening statement. In an exercise of caution, he'd passed up a golden opportunity to immediately go on the offensive. That he was simply doing what he'd been taught to do, what ninety-nine percent of his colleagues would have done in his place, was no excuse.

Jacob Pope called his first witness.

Eleanor Cerami's tinyness must have struck the jury as soon as she entered the courtroom. To Jaywalker, she seemed even more frightened than she'd been at the hearing. Her "I do" when sworn in was all but inaudible.

Pope began his direct examination by bringing out that Mrs. Cerami had two children, one six years old, the other seven months, and that she and her husband were separated. What the jury wouldn't learn was that it had been the rape that had led to the separation, a phenomenon that is unfortunately as common as it is disturbing.

Pope then produced a large two-dimensional diagram of the Castle Hill Houses and offered it into evidence. Jaywalker stated that he had no objection. Because he didn't like jurors to get the impression that he was trying to keep things from them, he made it a habit to move to exclude evidence before trial, whenever possible. Once the jury was present, he did his best to welcome whatever was being offered. In so doing, he hoped to leave the impression that he was open and fair-minded, unconcerned about technical rules, and not the least bit threatened by the evidence about to come in. Lastly, the strategy also helped him buy some credibility with the judge, who would learn that on those occasions when Jaywalker *did* object, his points were usually well taken.

Pope had Mrs. Cerami point out her particular building on the diagram. Then he got down to business.

POPE: Mrs. Cerami, were you living in that building on August sixteenth of last year?

CERAMI: Yes, I was.

POPE: I call your attention to approximately twelve o'clock to twelve-thirty on the afternoon of that day. Do you recall that time?

CERAMI: Yes, sir, I do.

With that introduction, in a voice barely above a whisper, Eleanor Cerami began describing what had happened to her that day. She'd been coming back from the cleaners. She'd entered her building and was standing in the lobby, waiting for the self-service elevator. She'd noticed, if only barely, a young black man, who also seemed to be waiting.

When the elevator arrived, she'd stepped on, followed by the man. She'd pressed her floor, twelve. The man had pressed ten. There'd been no one else on the elevator. When they reached ten, the man had stepped off. Then he'd turned around and gotten back on. Only now he'd been holding a knife. He'd told her to be calm, not to panic or scream. The door had closed, and they'd continued up to twelve. But when the door opened there, he wouldn't let her get off. The door had closed again, and they'd ridden back down to ten.

Pope interrupted the narrative and asked Mrs. Cerami to describe the knife. Except for his questions and her answers, the courtroom was utterly silent.

POPE: What did it look like?

CERAMI: It was big. I'd say the blade was eight inches long. Brown handle, silver blade. Thin.

Back down on the tenth floor, the man had led her off the elevator, holding the knife against her back. He'd taken her through a door, into a stairway and up half a flight of steps, stopping between the tenth and eleventh floors. There he'd reached up and unscrewed a bare lightbulb until it had gone out. The stairway had darkened some, but she'd still been able to see the man pretty well.

POPE: And what happened then, Mrs. Cerami? Tell us as best as you can.

CERAMI: The man stood right close to me and held me. He looked at me and told me to stop shaking, calm down, stop being nervous. And then he said, he asked me to go down on him. I said, "Oh, my God, I can't." And he just showed me the knife, and I had to.

She described how the man had unzipped his pants and exposed himself, and forced his penis into her mouth as she'd knelt in front of him. Finally, gagging, she'd stopped and said, "I can't anymore." And he'd said, "Okay, that's enough."

POPE: Now after that happened, Mrs. Cerami, what happened, what occurred next? What did he do?

CERAMI: He told me to take off my panties, and I did. We went down the stairs to the landing. He told me to lie on the floor with my back toward the floor and my legs leaning down on the stairs. He said, "You know what I'm going to do now?" And he got on top of me and he said, he asked me, you know, to put his penis in me, and he said, "I want you to fuck back good."

POPE: Tell us what occurred. Did he say anything else at this point?

CERAMI: He just kept on saying, "Come on, move, move!" He wanted me to move, but I couldn't. I was too nervous.

Pope pushed on with his questioning.

POPE: Tell us as much as you can. What do you remember him saying to you?

CERAMI: He asked me why I was so big inside. I told him I'd just had a baby. And I guess he was having difficulty, you know, with me. And he just kept on telling me, "Fuck back, fuck back!"

POPE: Okay. What happened after that?

CERAMI: Well, then he said to me, "All right, I'm going to do you a favor. I won't shoot in you, because you just had a baby." And he got up and put his pants on.

She went on to describe how the man had left, and how she'd gotten dressed and run to her apartment. Each time she paused to take a breath, the courtroom was stone-cold quiet. Jaywalker shot a sideways glance at the jurors once or twice. Had he been asked to describe their reactions, the word that would have come to mind was *cringing*.

Pope wasn't finished with Eleanor Cerami. He had her back up to repeat that the lighting had been good enough for her to see the man clearly. He brought out that they'd been face-to-face much of the time, only inches apart. He drew from her the fact that she'd been with the man a good fifteen or twenty minutes. He had her describe the clothing he'd been wearing: a knitted, close-fitting, short-sleeved shirt, jeans—*dungarees* was the actual word she used—and dirty gray sneakers.

Then Pope lowered his voice dramatically.

POPE: Mrs. Cerami, do you see that man now in the courtroom?

CERAMI: Yes, I do.

POPE: Point him out, please.

Eleanor Cerami turned toward the defense table and pointed directly at Darren Kingston. "Right there," she said.

Still Pope pushed on. He had his witness look at a full-body photograph taken of Darren at the time of his arrest, so that she could point out the sneakers he was wearing—the same ones, she stated, that he'd worn when he raped her. Asked to compare how the defendant looked in court to how he'd appeared back in August, she said he was thinner now, and neater.

Pope questioned Mrs. Cerami about her actions following the incident. She'd run first to her apartment, then to a neighbor's, where she'd begun screaming and crying. She'd phoned her mother, then a friend, who had called her husband. Later that afternoon, the police had shown up and spoken to her. Then her husband had come and taken her to the hospital to be examined.

Next Pope wanted to know about Mrs. Cerami's recent pregnancy. She testified that she'd given birth at the end of June, some six weeks before she'd been attacked. And she stated that, except for the rape in August, she hadn't had intercourse during the period between then and the trial.

Pope moved on to another area.

POPE: After the date of the rape, August sixteenth, did you have occasion to see the defendant again?

CERAMI: Yes, I did.

POPE: And do you recall when that was?

CERAMI: About a week after, in the lobby of my building. I was going to get my mail, and I saw him coming in from one entrance of the building and crossing through to the other side, to get out.

Jaywalker took notes furiously. This couldn't be the incident Pope had warned them about, shortly after Darren's release on bail. He'd had Darren check that one out, and—if they were right about when it had occurred—it was possible that Darren had been at his job at the post office at the time. But now Pope seemed to be asking about a different occasion, one back in August, prior to Darren's arrest.

POPE: You say a week after. You mean in the same month? August?

CERAMI: The same month.

Had there indeed been another, earlier sighting of Darren, after the rape but before his arrest? Or was Cerami simply mistaken about how soon she thought she'd seen her attacker again? And was Pope as surprised as Jaywalker was? Or was he now trying to take advantage of the situation and move the sighting from September back into August, in order to preempt any alibi Jaywalker might have for it?

POPE: Was it August? Or September?

CERAMI: August.

POPE: Do you recall the date?

CERAMI: No. I just know it was a Monday.

POPE: You don't recall the date exactly. Is that correct?

CERAMI: No, I don't.

POPE: And did you have a conversation with someone with respect to seeing the man again?

CERAMI: Yes.

POPE: And who was that?

CERAMI: I called Detective Rendell.

POPE: And did you call him on the same day that you saw the man again, walking through your lobby?

CERAMI: Yes.

So from momentarily thinking there'd been yet another sighting, or even suspecting Pope of deliberately muddying the waters with his witness's mistake, Jaywalker now saw that Pope was playing it straight. He was obviously every bit as surprised by Mrs. Cerami's error as Jaywalker was. First he'd tried to jog her memory, but since she was his witness, he couldn't do so by leading her or otherwise coaching her. Having failed to get her to correct herself, he'd had to settle for highlighting her slight uncertainty. Finally, he'd tied the sighting to her phone call to Detective Rendell, who would be in a position to clear up the confusion once he took the stand, later on in the trial.

So Pope hadn't been trying to pull a fast one, which was pretty much in character. He was simply being the same old Jacob Pope: thorough, formal, dry, colorless to the point of being stiff. But not dirty.

If anyone had been at fault, it had been Jaywalker himself. As soon as he'd realized Mrs. Cerami's error and Pope's inability to correct it, he should have asked Justice Davidoff's permission to confer with Pope. Together, they could have stipulated to the actual date of Mrs. Cerami's phone call to Detective Rendell and announced it to the jury, quickly putting any confusion to rest. But Jaywalker still had plenty to learn back then, and he'd let it go.

Pope had one final question for his witness. As he had several times earlier on, he lowered his voice dramatically.

POPE: I have no further questions at this time, except one. Let me ask you, Mrs. Cerami. I want you to look at the defendant again. I want you to tell me whether there is any doubt in your mind that this is the man who raped you and orally sodomized you on August sixteenth, nineteen-seventy-nine.

The question was repetitive, and Jaywalker could have objected to it. Maybe he realized a second too late. Maybe he was afraid his objection would be overruled, serving only to draw attention to the point Pope was trying to make. Perhaps he was even entertaining the fantasy that the witness might somehow hedge or stumble in her answer, betraying the slightest bit of hesitancy. If so, it was a foolish fantasy. Again Mrs. Cerami looked directly at Darren.

CERAMI: No, there's no doubt in my mind.

As he had at the Wade hearing, Jaywalker began his cross-examination of Mrs. Cerami gently. The hearing had taught him what *not* to ask her at the trial. He knew better, for example, than to try to shake her certainty that Darren was her attacker. The most he could hope to do was to demonstrate that there'd been obstacles to her observations, lapses in her memory, and discrepancies between how she'd described her rapist to the police and how

Darren Kingston really appeared. The very worst thing Jaywalker could do was to attack her and end up alienating the jury even more against his client. Eleanor Cerami had already been victimized once, after all, and once had been more than enough.

So he began by establishing that Mrs. Cerami had had no reason to pay attention to the man upon first seeing him, and in fact had barely taken notice of him before he'd pulled the knife. He got her to agree that once he did pull the knife, she focused on it, rather than on his face. Therefore, on the elevator—where the lighting had been the best—she'd had little occasion to study her attacker's face.

JAYWALKER: Did he sort of put one hand on you to guide you out?

CERAMI: Sort of.

JAYWALKER: So he sort of followed you off the elevator?

CERAMI: Right.

JAYWALKER: And did he sort of steer you toward the door—

CERAMI: Yes.

JAYWALKER: —to the stairs?

CERAMI: Yes.

JAYWALKER: So he was sort of behind you, and still had the knife somewhere against your back. Is that right?

CERAMI: Right.

JAYWALKER: And he came in behind you?

CERAMI: Yes.

JAYWALKER: And the door then closed behind him. Would that be right?

CERAMI: Yes.

JAYWALKER: Did you then go up the steps? Or down the steps?

CERAMI: Up the steps.

JAYWALKER: And again he was behind you, guiding you or steering you?

CERAMI: Right.

Jaywalker asked her to demonstrate how the man was holding the knife. When she gestured with her right hand, he pressed on.

JAYWALKER: You're indicating with your right hand. Is that your recollection?

CERAMI: Yes.

JAYWALKER: Did he have anything in his left hand?

CERAMI: No.

Jaywalker brought out that at no time had he cut her. He wanted the jury to be certain of that. He also wanted to try to get Mrs. Cerami to relax just a bit, if she could, instead of concentrating so hard on where he was going with his questions. Because there were a couple of important points he needed to develop with her. The exact way in which the man had loosened the overhead lightbulb, for example.

JAYWALKER: Did he do it with his bare hand?

CERAMI: Yes.

JAYWALKER: He wasn't wearing gloves?

They'd found a smudged partial fingerprint of indeterminate age on one of the bulbs, too fragmentary to be classified and used to search databases for a match. But it hadn't been Darren's.

CERAMI: No.

JAYWALKER: Or using a handkerchief?

CERAMI: No.

JAYWALKER: Do you remember which hand he used?

CERAMI: I think it was his right.

Jaywalker took a deep breath before deciding to go for broke.

JAYWALKER: In other words, he switched the knife from his right hand to his left hand—

CERAMI: Right.

JAYWALKER: —and unscrewed the lightbulb. Is that correct?

CERAMI: Yes.

Jaywalker let the breath out. Eleanor Cerami had just described the act of an unmistakably right-handed person. Darren Kingston was left-handed.

He had her concede that, with the bulb unscrewed, the stairwell had become darker than it had been before. He brought out that she'd been terribly frightened and very nervous. He asked her to repeat as many of the man's actual words as she could remember. He had her state, as she had at the Wade hearing, that the man's speech, other than being polite and soft-spoken, was in no way unusual. Jaywalker would have liked to take it one step further. He would have liked to come right out and ask Mrs. Cerami if she remembered the man ever stuttering. But he figured

Rendell had asked her, and Pope had probably asked her half a dozen times. Jaywalker's asking her might finally wake her up to the fact that his client must be a stutterer. All she would have to do would be to say, "Oh, yeah, now that you mention it, I think he did stutter." At that point, Jaywalker might as well walk over to the window, open it, wave goodbye and jump. Though six floors up might not be high enough.

So he moved on to the physical description Mrs. Cerami had given of her attacker. Jaywalker was armed with the police reports, so he knew pretty much what her answers would be and could focus on those items that contrasted with Darren Kingston's appearance. He brought out that she'd described a man twenty-five to thirty years old, weighing 180 pounds and sporting a short Afro. Darren was twenty-two, weighed less than 160, and had medium-length hair.

JAYWALKER: Do you recall describing the man as having red eyes?

CERAMI: Yes, sort of, like maroon.

JAYWALKER: Well, do you recall giving that description?

CERAMI: Yes.

JAYWALKER: By that, did you mean his natural eye color?

CERAMI: Yes, that's what I meant.

JAYWALKER: You didn't mean that his eyes were bloodshot.

CERAMI: No.

Although some African-Americans do indeed have reddish or maroon irises, Darren didn't. His eyes were brown.

Next Jaywalker had Mrs. Cerami describe in greater detail the shirt the man had been wearing, a tight-fitting, short-sleeved beige V-neck. Both Darren and his family had insisted that Darren owned no such shirt and never had. Jaywalker got Mrs. Cerami to specify that her rapist's sneakers had been low-cuts. Darren's were high-cuts. And in spite of the fact that Darren had a chipped front tooth and a noticeable scar through one eyebrow, Mrs. Cerami could recall no scars, deformities or other distinguishing marks on the man.

That brought Jaywalker to the task of trying to establish that it had been September, not August, when Mrs. Cerami claimed she'd seen her attacker again, walking through the lobby of her building. He wanted to show that Darren had already been arrested and released on bail by that time, and would have been unlikely to go anywhere near Castle Hill. But the more Jaywalker questioned her, the more she stuck to her story, that it had been in August, only a week after the rape. It made no sense. She'd phoned Detective Rendell the Monday after Darren had been arrested. Rendell, afraid they had the wrong man, had contacted Pope, who'd checked and found out that Darren had made bail. Several days later, Pope had warned Jaywalker to have Darren keep away from his witnesses.

Then, in the midst of Jaywalker's questions, Mrs. Cerami suddenly offered an explanation for the confusion.

CERAMI: I think I've seen him twice since.

JAYWALKER: Twice, in addition to August sixteenth?

CERAMI: That's right.

JAYWALKER: Okay. Do you know when that third time was?

CERAMI: I think it was right after the arraignment or something. I can't remember very well.

JAYWALKER: Where did you see the man then?

CERAMI: In the lobby of my building again.

JAYWALKER: Same place you'd seen him the second time?

CERAMI: Right.

What had happened, Jaywalker was pretty sure, was that the witness had finally realized her error. No doubt she and Pope had gone over the date of the second sighting during trial preparation, and her transposing it from September back into August had been nothing but an honest mistake. But now that she'd said what she'd said, under oath, she was afraid to change it. Never mind that an honest admission would have cost her nothing in the eyes of the jurors, and would have neither helped nor hindered the prosecution or the defense. So she'd decided to invent an additional sighting a week after the rape, leaving the details of it—which were really the details of the so-called third sighting—intact, because she'd already described them that way.

Well, thought Jaywalker, so be it. He was less concerned with showing that Mrs. Cerami had lied than he was with nailing down the details of the September sighting, the one that had actually occurred. So he concentrated on that one.

JAYWALKER: No question that it was the same man?

CERAMI: It was.

JAYWALKER: Do you know what day of the week that was? Was that also a Monday?

CERAMI: I think so.

JAYWALKER: Isn't it a fact, that on what you say was the third time, which would have been the second time you saw the man after the incident, that you called Detective Rendell? And you learned that he was off that day. Someone else took a message, and Rendell called you back.

CERAMI: Yes.

JAYWALKER: And that was on Monday, September seventeenth.

CERAMI: I don't know the date.

JAYWALKER: You do recall that it was a Monday, though.

CERAMI: Yes.

JAYWALKER: It was early in the morning, right?

CERAMI: Yes.

Jaywalker could have left it at that, but he needed to pinpoint the time, particularly if he was going to try to show later on that it couldn't have been Darren.

JAYWALKER: How early in the morning?

CERAMI: About nine-thirty.

JAYWALKER: Are you certain of that?

CERAMI: Yes.

JAYWALKER: And are you certain it was the same man who'd raped you?

CERAMI: Yes.

JAYWALKER: Are you as certain that it was the same man who'd attacked you as you are that this is in fact the man?

Jaywalker stepped back so she could get a good look at Darren. It was a *win-win* question, he knew. On the one hand, if the witness were to say no, it meant she was now hedging on her earlier testimony, and that she was no longer positive of her identification of the defendant as her rapist. On the other hand, if she were to say yes, that she was just as certain, and Jaywalker could somehow establish a solid alibi for Darren at the time of the sighting, he would be able to argue to the jury that if Mrs. Cerami was wrong about that having been Darren, despite all her certainty, then she could be just as wrong about Darren having been her attacker in the first place.

But if Eleanor Cerami recognized the trap, she gave no sign of it. She answered without hesitation, the way any witness who's convinced she's telling the truth would have answered.

CERAMI: Yes, I'm just as certain.

Jaywalker left it at that. If it turned out that he could really account for Darren's whereabouts at 9:30 on the morning of September 17th, it would look like a coup, a triumph of cross-examination. But if he couldn't, and if the jurors happened to call for a read-back of Mrs. Cerami's testimony during their deliberations—and the chances were they would—the read-back would end right there, on that note of absolute certainty. Jaywalker would have egg all over his face, and Darren Kingston would have the next twenty-five years to wonder what his family had been thinking when they'd hired him.

Pope's second witness was Michael Pacheco, the police officer who'd responded to Eleanor Cerami's apartment on the afternoon of August 16th. On direct examination, Officer Pacheco described Mrs. Cerami as nervous and sometimes in tears. He'd conducted a search of the area for the perpetrator, without success. After that he'd instructed Mrs. Cerami's husband to take her to Jacobi Hospital.

On cross-examination, Jaywalker zeroed in on the description Mrs. Cerami had furnished Pacheco, at a time when her memory of the man was most vivid. She'd told him the man was in his early thirties and weighed approximately 180 pounds. With that, the witness was excused, and Justice Davidoff broke for lunch.

Jaywalker spent a few minutes with the Kingstons, reviewing the morning's events. Eleanor Cerami had been a good witness, they all agreed, and a sympathetic one. But everyone felt Jaywalker had scored a few points with her. Perhaps more importantly, he'd succeeded in pinning her down on several matters that they would be able to explore later, with other witnesses. Officer Pacheco hadn't really hurt them; in fact, Jaywalker had been able to use him to underscore the physical differences between the man she'd first described and Darren.

As the Kingstons headed out for lunch, Jaywalker took refuge in the first-floor library to go over his notes and prepare his cross-examination for the afternoon's witnesses.

Following the lunch break, Pope called Alphonse Guitterez, a friend of Eleanor Cerami. Guitterez testified that he'd gone to her apartment on August 16th, in response to a phone call. He'd found her upset and crying, "nearly hysterical." He'd called her husband for her and waited there until Mr. Cerami arrived, followed shortly by the police.

Jaywalker had no cross-examination for Mr. Guitterez. Other than further reinforcing Mrs. Cerami's mental state—which was already pretty clear to the jury—he hadn't hurt the defense. There are lawyers who've never met a witness they didn't want to question. It's almost as if, even with nothing to ask and no reason to ask it, they're afraid they might be criticized for their silence. Or perhaps they're getting paid by the word. Who knows?

Jaywalker would never be one of them.

Joseph Cerami, the victim's husband, took the stand next. He testified that he and his wife had been married six years, had two children, and had separated three months ago. On August 16th he'd received a phone call at his job and had rushed home in response. He'd found his wife frightened, upset and barely able to speak. Alphonse Guitterez was already there, and the police arrived a short while later. After speaking with the police, Mr. Cerami had taken his wife to Jacobi Hospital. In response to Jacob Pope's final question of him, Mr. Cerami confirmed the fact that between the birth of their second child in June and the rape in August, he and his wife hadn't had intercourse.

Again, Jaywalker asked no questions.

Pope called the second victim to the stand.

In striking contrast to the timidity of Eleanor Cerami, it struck Jaywalker that Joanne Kenarden strode into the courtroom almost belligerently. Much has changed in terms of people's attitudes toward victims of sexual assault. It's entirely possible that Joanne Kenarden was simply ahead of her time, while Eleanor Cerami was a victim twice over—once at the hands of her assailant and once again of the prevailing attitudes of her generation. Her husband's abandonment of her because she'd been raped—just when she needed his love and support the most—stands as a cruel footnote not only to the case but to its time. Would he have preferred her to fight back and risk being maimed, or even stabbed to death? Don't be too quick to answer that one.

How would the jurors respond to this defiant woman? Jaywalker tried to gauge their reactions as she made her way purposefully to the witness stand and took the oath in a loud, clear voice. Eleanor Cerami had averted her eyes from Darren until literally forced to identify him. Joanne Kenarden stared directly at him even as she took her seat.

As he had with the first victim, Jacob Pope began with the diagram. He had Miss Kenarden identify it and mark the location of her building on it. With Justice Davidoff's permission, Pope then held it in front of the jurors, so they could see the proximity of the two buildings. Next he elicited from the witness that she was divorced and the mother of three children. Then he moved on to August 16th.

At about 1:45 that afternoon, Miss Kenarden had returned to her building from a shopping trip. She'd stopped at her mailbox before walking over to the elevator and pressing the button. She'd noticed a man, a black man, standing nearby. When the elevator door opened, she'd stepped on. So had the man. She'd pressed four; he hadn't pressed a button. When the door opened on the fourth floor, the man suddenly grabbed her and slammed her against the elevator wall. Then he put a knife to her ribs and told her not to scream.

POPE: Will you please describe the knife you saw.

KENARDEN: It was like a long kitchen knife, about twelve inches long. Brown handle, long shiny blade.

POPE: Thin shiny blade?

KENARDEN: Yes.

At that point, the man pressed twelve. They rode up in silence. When the door opened again, the man pressed his body against hers and, holding the knife against her side, forced her off the elevator, across the corridor and through a door into the stairwell.

POPE: Once you went into the stairwell, what happened?

KENARDEN: I recall him reaching up with his left hand and turning the lightbulb out.

In his notes, Jaywalker underlined the word *left*. If the man had used his left hand to loosen the bulb, it meant that his right hand had been busy holding the knife. Not quite as persuasive as Mrs. Cerami's having had him switching hands to free up his right, but still a pretty good indication that the rapist, unlike Darren, was right-handed.

Next the man forced Miss Kenarden up the stairs to a landing. When she began pleading with him not to kill her, he assured her that he wasn't going to hurt her. Then he told her to take her pants off.

POPE: He told you what?

KENARDEN: To take my pants off. I had jeans on, and I took them off. And then he told me to take my underwear off, and I did.

POPE: What happened after that? Did he say anything else to you?

KENARDEN: Yes, he did.

POPE: What did he say?

KENARDEN: He told me that he wanted me—he told me what he wanted me to do to him.

POPE: Use the exact words he used.

KENARDEN: He said, "You're going to go down on me, and I want you to—"

POPE: I want you to what?

There was no answer from the witness.

POPE: I know it's difficult, Miss Kenarden, but we have to hear the exact words he said.

KENARDEN: "I want you to suck on me," he said. "And after that, I'm going to fuck you. When I'm ready to come, I'm going to pull out. You're going to take it in your mouth. Do you understand?"

POPE: And after he told you that, what happened?

KENARDEN: He opened up his pants and just lowered them a bit, and exposed himself. And he told me, "Come over here and go down on me."

POPE: What in fact happened?

KENARDEN: I did it. He told me to eat it.

POPE: Did he put his penis in your mouth?

KENARDEN: Yes, he did.

Again Jaywalker was struck by the contrast between the two victims. Eleanor Cerami had seemed absolutely mortified at having to testify about the details of her ordeal. As he listened to Joanne Kenarden now, he had the strange feeling that she was somehow taking a measure of satisfaction from the opportunity to testify. This wasn't her shame; it was her revenge.

Pope asked her what happened next.

KENARDEN: Well, when he felt he was ready, he pushed me down and said, "Lie here." And he got on top of me and put himself inside me.

POPE: Put his penis into your vagina. Is that correct?

The question was leading, and Jaywalker could have objected. But he saw nothing to be gained, other than antagonizing the jurors.

KENARDEN: Yes. And he told me to…told me to wrap my legs around his back.

POPE: All right.

KENARDEN: And then he proceeded to talk to me.

POPE: What did he say?

KENARDEN: Well, he told me that I was very deep, and that it was good for me to be deep. And he asked me, his exact words were, "Have you ever been fucked by a black man?" He said, "Your husband must be very big."

POPE: Was he keeping up this conversation the entire time?

KENARDEN: Yes, he was.

POPE: And how did he speak? What type of voice did he have?

KENARDEN: Very gentle and very soft-spoken. I told him I was scared of him.

POPE: And what happened after that?

KENARDEN: Well, he felt me a little bit. He told me to kiss him, but he didn't kiss me, just put his mouth on mine. He told me to suck on his tongue, and to put my tongue in his mouth, but he didn't do anything.

POPE: All right, Miss Kenarden. After he had intercourse with you, what happened at that time?

KENARDEN: He said he was ready to come. He
said, "You're going to take it in your mouth again, do
you understand?" I said yes. And he pulled out, and
he said, "Okay, now!" And he came in my mouth.

Pope questioned her about the lighting. She said it had
been good. He asked her if she'd been able to see the
man's face during the incident. She said she certainly had.
He asked her how long the entire encounter had taken. She
estimated fifteen to twenty minutes. Then he stepped back.

POPE: Miss Kenarden, do you see that man here
today, in the courtroom?

KENARDEN: Yes, I do.

POPE: Will you point him out?

KENARDEN: The one with the leather jacket. Over
there.

She pointed at Darren, directly and defiantly.
As had Eleanor Cerami, Joanne Kenarden stated that
Darren looked thinner now than he had back in August,
and that his hair seemed to be longer now than then.
Shown the full-body arrest photo of Darren, she, too,
identified the sneakers.
Miss Kenarden, it turned out, hadn't phoned the police

until that night. Pope, anticipating that Jaywalker might try to exploit the delay, asked her to explain why. She testified that she'd been afraid, and had waited for her son to get home from school. Only after she'd fed him and put him to bed had she called the police. At their request, she'd gone to the precinct, and from there to Jacobi Hospital.

Back in 1980, the prosecution had to introduce independent evidence to corroborate each element of a sex crime. In a rape case, that meant proof that force had been used. Mindful of the requirement, Pope turned to the subject of any injuries Miss Kenarden had sustained.

POPE: Miss Kenarden, were you injured at all during this incident?

KENARDEN: Yes, sir. I received back injuries.

POPE: What type of back injuries?

KENARDEN: Swelling on my lower back, and bruises all up my spine and on my shoulders. Swelling and bruises.

POPE: And what caused those injuries, if you know?

KENARDEN: Well, that was from being on the concrete floor, on the landing. With my legs around him, I wasn't able to move. And the friction, you know, was really hurting my back.

Pope finished up by asking Miss Kenarden if the man had stuttered while speaking to her. Jaywalker fought back a surge of total panic. Having made no reference at all to it in her Wade hearing testimony and her trial testimony up to this point, was she suddenly going to remember it now, with Pope's prompting?

But she said no, she hadn't noticed a stutter.

Pope, obviously sensing that Jaywalker would be making a point of it, was simply bringing it out himself first, trying to steal a little thunder from the defense. Taking a page, in other words, from Jaywalker's playbook.

Jaywalker began his cross-examination of Joanne Kenarden as he had with Eleanor Cerami, trying to develop the point that she'd had no occasion to pay attention to the man on the elevator before he turned on her. This time, he didn't get away with it. Miss Kenarden insisted that she'd looked directly at the man at one point early on.

Jaywalker had more success when it came to having her place the knife in the man's right hand.

JAYWALKER: And I think you testified, or if you didn't, let me ask you. Do you remember which hand the man held the knife in?

KENARDEN: His right hand.

JAYWALKER: Are you sure of that?

KENARDEN: Yes, sir, I am.

Again Jaywalker established that on the way from the elevator to the staircase, the man had been behind her. Again he tried to show that once the man had unscrewed the light-bulb, it had become significantly darker in the stairwell.

JAYWALKER: After the man unscrewed the light-bulb, the only light that remained was coming from the door to the roof. Is that correct?

But where Eleanor Cerami had been easy to lead, Joanne Kenarden proved more than a match for him.

KENARDEN: No, sir. There was light coming from a huge window.

Jaywalker moved on to the information Miss Kenarden had given the police. He drew from her that she'd described a man twenty-five to thirty years old, weighing approximately 175 pounds. She'd also characterized his eyes as "hooded," with a large area of the eyelid visible even when his eyes were open, giving him a "sleepy" appearance. And she'd said his breath had an odor of alcohol, specifically wine.

Darren was bright-eyed; there was nothing sleepy-looking about him. And though he drank in moderation on social occasions, his taste ran to Scotch.

Jaywalker knew from the police reports that Miss Kenarden had reported that the man was circumcised. Darren had told Jaywalker that he wasn't. Knowing that the difference in appearance is slight in an erect penis but significant in a flaccid one, Jaywalker wanted to get Miss Kenarden to say that at some point she'd seen her attacker in a nonerect state.

JAYWALKER: After the first part of your conversation with the man, there came a time when he told you he wanted you to go down on him, and he unzipped his pants. Is that correct?

KENARDEN: Yes.

JAYWALKER: Do you recall if he was wearing a belt?

Jaywalker had learned then when dealing with a hostile witness, it sometimes paid to camouflage the important questions. It wasn't so different from the way Dick Arledge or Gene Sandusky had sprinkled in control questions about Darren's age or address. By keeping the witness slightly off guard, he hoped to prevent her from knowing in what direction he was heading.

KENARDEN: No belt.

JAYWALKER: And did he take his penis out?

KENARDEN: He didn't have to. He was exposed.

JAYWALKER: Was it erect at that point?

KENARDEN: No, sir.

JAYWALKER: Are you certain of that?

KENARDEN: Yes, I am.

JAYWALKER: Were you able to determine if the man was circumcised or not?

KENARDEN: He was.

JAYWALKER: He was circumcised. You're certain of that, also?

KENARDEN: Yes, sir.

On direct examination, Miss Kenarden had testified that during intercourse, the man had put the knife down at one point. Jaywalker saw another chance to emphasize his right-handedness.

JAYWALKER: Was he facing you at the time he did this?

KENARDEN: Yes.

JAYWALKER: Where did he put the knife?

KENARDEN: On the stairs, about two steps down.

As she answered, she pointed. And pointed to her left.

JAYWALKER: You're indicating to your left.

KENARDEN: Yes, sir.

JAYWALKER: So the man put it down on his right?

KENARDEN: That's where the stairs were, to his right.

JAYWALKER: So the knife was in his right hand as he put it down?

KENARDEN: Yes, sir. It was in his right hand.

Jaywalker brought out that, like Eleanor Cerami, Joanne Kenarden had noticed no scars or deformities on the man. As had Mrs. Cerami, she recalled dirty gray sneakers, but she couldn't say if they were low-cut or high-cut. And despite all her conversation with the man, she'd never once heard him stutter.

It seemed as good a point as any to quit on.

Pope, on redirect examination, sought to reinforce the certainty of his witness's identification of the defendant as her attacker.

POPE: Is there any doubt in your mind, Miss Kenarden, that this man, Darren Kingston, is the man who raped you on August sixteenth, nineteen-seventy-nine?

KENARDEN: No, sir, there is no doubt.

But Jaywalker managed to get the last word in, on recross.

JAYWALKER: Is there any doubt that he held the knife in his right hand?

KENARDEN: No, sir, there is no doubt.

JAYWALKER: Any doubt that he was circumcised?

KENARDEN: No, sir, no doubt.

Jaywalker took his seat. Joanne Kenarden stepped down from the witness stand and strode out of the courtroom, as defiant as ever. Justice Davidoff recessed the trial until the following morning.

Late that night, Jaywalker found himself unable to fall asleep. Not that there was anything unusual about that. They were finished with the two victims' testimony. Though both had pointed Darren out as their rapist with unflinching certainty, Jaywalker felt he'd nonetheless scored some points. He'd managed to lay the groundwork for demonstrating a number of discrepancies between the man the victims had described and the one who was on trial.

While his wife and daughter slept, Jaywalker sat at the kitchen table, scribbling notes.

	Eleanor Cerami's Rapist	Joanne Kenarden's Rapist	Darren
Age	25-30+	25-30	22
Weight	180	175	145
Eye color	Red	——	Brown
Eyelids	——	Hooded	Normal
Penis	——	Circumcised	Uncircumcised
Speech	Normal	Gentle	Stutter

Shirt	Tan knit	Tan knit	Doesn't own
Sneakers	Low-cut	——	High-cut
Body build	Heavy	Solid	Slender
Hair	Short Afro	Short	Medium Afro
Handedness	Right	Right	Left
Scars	None	None	Eyebrow
Deformities	None	None	Chipped front tooth

While some of the discrepancies were arguably minor, some were truly significant—the stutter, for example, and the circumcision, and the left- or right-handedness. Perhaps even more tellingly, wherever the victims were off the mark in describing the defendant, their versions barely departed from each other. In other words, they were describing the same man; it just didn't happen to be Darren.

But in order to drive this point home, Jaywalker knew, he would have to put Darren on the stand, as well as other members of his family. He would have to prove, for example, that Darren was left-handed, that he hadn't lost weight since last August, and that he'd never owned the shirt or sneakers the witnesses had described. Because judges tend to disapprove of people dropping their pants on the witness stand, Jaywalker would have to find a doctor to examine Darren and testify that he wasn't circumcised. On top of those things, he would need to round up witnesses from the post office to show, if they could, that Darren had been at work at the time Eleanor Cerami claimed she'd seen him again in her lobby, a second—or perhaps a third—time.

And if he did all those things and more, was that going to be enough? Would logic prevail? Or were the jurors simply going to throw all that to the wind and remember only how absolutely certain the two victims had been that Darren Kingston was the man who'd raped them?

It would be a long time before Jaywalker would make it to bed, and an even longer time before anything remotely resembling sleep would come his way.

13

THE CYCLONE

Jacob Pope's first witness Tuesday morning was a gynecologist from Jacobi Hospital named David Blume. Dr. Blume had examined Joanne Kenarden; a Dr. Genovese had examined Eleanor Cerami, but he was currently out of the country. So Dr. Blume was called to describe the findings from both examinations—Miss Kenarden's from his own recollection and Mrs. Cerami's from Dr. Genovese's notes.

Eleanor Cerami had been seen at 3:50 p.m. on August 16th. She'd presented as agitated and nervous. There'd been no sign of external injury, such as bruises or lacerations. A pelvic examination had revealed no obvious evidence of internal injury. A vaginal smear had been taken, and upon microscopic examination it had revealed the presence of one or two sperm.

Today, of course, those one or two sperm might have made all the difference in the world. With DNA testing, it's entirely possible that a technician could have enhanced the sample and typed it, and then provided the jury with a genetic profile of the sperm donor, either establishing beyond astronomical odds that it was indeed Darren Kingston or excluding him with an equal degree of scientific certainty. But this was 1980, and the technique was still in its infancy. Genetic typing had only begun to be seriously studied, and it would be years before it would begin to make the journey from the laboratory to the courtroom.

Joanne Kenarden had been seen at 1:13 a.m. on August 17th. She'd complained of pain to her lower back, and Dr. Blume had found some tenderness in the area. Microscopic examination of a vaginal smear had revealed no sperm.

Jaywalker's cross-examination of Dr. Blume was brief. He established that during intercourse a fertile young male would normally discharge as many as sixty to a hundred million sperm, some of those even prior to ejaculation. But there was little more Jaywalker could do. The fact that the rapist hadn't ejaculated in Mrs. Cerami—or "shot," as he might have phrased it—made the discovery of only one or two sperm in a representative smear seem reasonable. And Miss Kenarden's testimony had left little doubt that ejaculation had taken place in her mouth, rather than in her vagina. That fact, coupled with her delay in going to the hospital, rendered meaningless the absence of sperm in her swab.

Pope next called Dr. Paul Jarakanak, a surgical resident at Jacobi Hospital. Joanne Kenarden had been referred to him by Dr. Blume, and he'd examined her later that same morning, August 17th. Dr. Jarakanak had found tenderness in the lower vertebrae, and had ordered X-rays, which had failed to disclose any fracture or dislocation. Still, according to Dr. Jarakanak, Miss Kenarden's tenderness could have been caused by trauma or physical injury.

All of these findings—with the exception of the one or two sperm found in Mrs. Cerami's swab—added up to almost nothing, in medical terms. But Jaywalker understood the prosecution's interest in nevertheless pursuing them. Pope was concerned about the corroboration requirement. It would be his position that in Mrs. Cerami's case, corroboration could be found in the sperm, which, according to both Mrs. Cerami and her husband, could only have come from her attacker. In Miss Kenarden's case, with the absence of sperm, Pope would argue that the lower back tenderness supplied corroboration.

But to Jaywalker, tenderness was a complaint, not a finding. With no fracture, dislocation, bruising or even redness in the lower back area, the doctors had been essentially taking Miss Kenarden's word that she was in pain. But her word wasn't corroboration at all. Quite the contrary: under the law, it was her word that *required* corroboration.

But that was a legal distinction that would have to be argued later on, before the judge. For now, on cross-examination, Jaywalker had to settle for establishing that neither of the doctors who'd examined Joanne Kenarden had been able to *see* evidence of pain—the bruising and swelling she'd claimed to suffer—either by looking at her back or studying her X-rays. And even if the area was in fact tender, that tenderness could have been the result of infection, arthritis, muscle strain, dysmenorrhea or just about anything else, for that matter.

As his final witness, Pope called Detective Robert Rendell. Jaywalker winced as Rendell entered the courtroom, knowing that the jurors couldn't help but be influenced by his appearance. Tall, good-looking and beginning to gray around the temples, Rendell would be a relaxed and well-spoken witness, Jaywalker knew, one who would impress the jurors as being honest and fair. Looking back on the case twenty-five years after the fact, Jaywalker would have no reason to rethink that assessment.

In response to Pope's background questions, Rendell stated that he'd been with the NYPD for eleven years, five of those as a detective. He gave his current assignment as the Bronx Sex Crime Squad, but indicated that back in August of 1979 he'd been working out of the 8th District Burglary and Larceny Squad. Even then, he'd specialized in rape cases, some of which began as break-ins, and therefore burglaries. Jaywalker couldn't help but wonder if it had been Darren Kingston's arrest that had "made" Rendell and earned him the new assignment.

On August 16th, Rendell had been working an evening tour of duty, from 5:00 p.m. to 1:00 a.m. Around 11:00 or 11:15, an individual named Joanne Kenarden had come into the squad room. Today, chances are she would be assigned a female detective; in 1979, that sort of sensitivity was unheard of. In any event, it was Rendell who had interviewed her, helped her file a complaint report and driven her in his radio car to Jacobi Hospital. After that, he'd gone to the scene of the crime Miss Kenarden had described.

POPE: What did you do there?

RENDELL: I surveyed the scene. I spoke with people in the area. I removed some lightbulbs, which I

dusted for latent fingerprints. But there were none
of any value.

POPE: When you say none of any value, you mean
there were no prints on the bulbs?

RENDELL: No. There were some partial prints on
the bulbs, but none of any value.

Rendell soon inherited another investigation, that of
the Eleanor Cerami rape. Although he himself hadn't conducted the initial survey of the crime scene in that case,
Justice Davidoff permitted Pope to ask Rendell what he
knew about it.

POPE: With respect to the complainant Eleanor Cerami, was any physical inspection done?

RENDELL: Detective Talbot conducted a survey of
the scene and also removed some lightbulbs, which
he had tested for fingerprints but which were also
negative. No latent prints of any value.

Pope's next question must have truly mystified the
jurors. They, of course, knew nothing about the gathering
of three of the original five victims to meet with the sketch
artist. They knew nothing of the intensity of the women's
emotional reactions upon first coming across the mug shot
of Darren Kingston. They would never hear about the
photo array Rendell had subsequently created, or the fact
that Mrs. Cerami and Miss Kenarden, as well as Tania
Maldonado, had succeeded in picking out Darren's photo

from seventeen others. Because Pope was prohibited by the law from bringing out the photo identifications, and because Jaywalker had made a tactical decision to steer clear of the dramatic events that had unfolded that day, the jury would be forever kept in the dark about what it was that had caused the investigation to focus on Darren.

POPE: And did there come a time, Detective Rendell, when, as a result of your investigation, you began to look for one Darren Kingston?

RENDELL: Yes.

POPE: And approximately when was that?

RENDELL: August twenty-fourth.

Rendell testified that it had taken him nearly three weeks to locate and arrest Darren. If he deserved high marks for being honest and fair, Rendell was revealing himself here as being something short of an accomplished investigator. The address on the back of Darren's mug shot was that of his parents, with whom he'd been living a year and a half earlier. Since that time, he and Charlene had found an apartment of their own. A check with the phone company would have netted that address in five minutes' time, as would a simple question to his parents.

According to Rendell, the defendant had spoken softly and clearly at the time of his arrest. But later on, when permitted to make a phone call, he'd begun to stutter noticeably. At the precinct, there were times when he stuttered and times when he didn't.

Lastly, Pope tried to establish through Rendell that the stairwell where Joanne Kenarden was assaulted was well-illuminated by a large window to the outside. But Rendell replied that he'd never visited that particular location during daylight hours. If Pope ended on a note of minor frustration, that fact was more than offset by Rendell's use of the opportunity to impress the jurors with his candor.

As the first business of his cross-examination, Jaywalker wanted to dispel any suggestion that Darren had been hiding out during the three weeks when Rendell had been looking for him. He brought out that the detective had eventually gone to the home of Darren's parents, who'd readily provided him with their son's address. Then, by eliciting from Rendell that both Darren and his parents had telephones in their homes, he laid a foundation for proving later on that, following Rendell's visit, the Kingstons had promptly phoned Darren, who—even when informed that the police were looking for him—hadn't fled. Next Jaywalker established that Rendell had never bothered to obtain a search warrant for Darren's apartment in order to find out if Darren owned a tight-fitting, short-sleeved, tan V-necked shirt, a pair of dirty gray low-cut sneakers or a knife that matched the one described by the victims.

From there, Jaywalker moved on to Rendell's version of the phone call made by Eleanor Cerami after she thought she'd seen Darren in her building again.

JAYWALKER: Now there came a time, did there not, when Mrs. Cerami called your office and reported seeing her attacker again?

RENDELL: That's correct.

JAYWALKER: Did you receive Mrs. Cerami's call when she phoned?

RENDELL: No, I did not receive it.

JAYWALKER: How were you informed of it?

RENDELL: A message was left for me that she had called.

JAYWALKER: How soon did you get the message?

RENDELL: The same day.

JAYWALKER: Did this happen once? Or twice?

RENDELL: Just once.

JAYWALKER: Can you fix a date for us?

RENDELL: September seventeenth, the Monday after Kingston's arrest.

The date matched. Jaywalker was halfway there. Eleanor Cerami had said it was a Monday, about 9:30 in the morning. Now Rendell had supplied the date. If Jaywalker was right, post-office employees could place Darren at his job, literally miles from Castle Hill. And if Eleanor Cerami could be wrong, despite her absolute certainty, that her attacker was back, so, too, could she be wrong about her identification of Darren. And if she *was* wrong, didn't that mean Joanne Kenarden was, too?

Trying hard to conceal his excitement, Jaywalker cemented the date.

JAYWALKER: There's no question in your mind that it was on Monday, September seventeenth, that you received the message?

RENDELL: I'm almost positive. I contacted the district attorney immediately.

JAYWALKER: You contacted Mr. Pope. And you know that Mr. Pope spoke to me about that.

RENDELL: That's correct.

JAYWALKER: And all of that was on Monday, September seventeenth?

RENDELL: That's correct.

JAYWALKER: Thank you, sir.

Jaywalker sat down. He had what he wanted from Rendell. Pope stood and announced that the detective had been his final witness, and that the People's case was concluded. After a brief conference at the bench, Justice Davidoff sent the jury home until the following morning.

At the end of the prosecution's case, the defense gets a chance to ask the judge to have the case dismissed. The motion takes on different names in different jurisdictions, but the theory is the same: that even if every word of the prosecution's case were to be accepted as true by the jury, those words still don't add up to be legally sufficient to support a conviction on the charges.

As Jaywalker rose to make the motion and argue in support of it, he had no illusions. He knew full well that Justice Davidoff would rule against him. Being a good judge doesn't necessarily mean you've got the biggest balls in town. Max Davidoff had come up through the system, running errands, paying clubhouse dues, and learning the art of politics long before he'd become a district attorney and then a judge. Nearing mandatory retirement age now in the final job he would likely ever have, the very last thing in the world he wanted was to wake up in the morning to a headline screaming

SOFT-ON-CRIME JUDGE
FREES RAPIST OF FIVE!

Still, Jaywalker knew that with respect to the corroboration element, the case was a close one, and if there was a conviction, some appellate court was going to have to wrestle with it.

The ancient and archaic rule requiring corroboration in sex cases grew out of a belief—championed in legislatures that were ninety-nine percent male—that accusations of rape were too easily made and were often contrived out of some ulterior motive on the part of the accuser. In order to protect innocent gentlemen from this sort of abuse, the lawmakers enacted a rule requiring that a complainant's testimony be supported by independent evidence with respect to each and every element of the crime. *Elements* are those things the prosecution is required to prove. In a forcible rape prosecution, that meant there had to be additional proof that the defendant was the perpetrator, that his penis actually penetrated the complainant's vagina, and that he accomplished his goal through the use of force.

Over the years, some observers finally began to question the wisdom of the requirement. Were sexual assaults really so different from other crimes? Couldn't one just as easily fabricate a robbery accusation as a rape accusation? Some wondered if the distinction was really a valid one, or simply a vestige of a puritanical, male-dominated heritage.

Today, thanks in large part to the efforts of women's rights groups in educating the world that rape is less about sex than it is about power, and is essentially a crime of assault, the corroboration requirement has gone the way of the dodo, and properly so.

But change comes slowly to the law, and at the time of Darren Kingston's trial, the rule had become endangered but was not quite yet extinct. The standard that Justice Davidoff had to apply was that in order for a forcible rape conviction to be upheld, the victim's account had to be supported by some other evidence on two points. First, that the defendant had used force, and second, that he'd at least attempted to accomplish intercourse.

Had he been asked over dinner for his personal feelings on the wisdom of the corroboration requirement, Jaywalker would have had no trouble condemning it. But he could hardly let his opinion relieve him of arguing that because it was the law, the court was bound to enforce it. Besides which, he told himself, if it turned out to be the corroboration requirement that prevented Darren Kingston from being convicted, the result might be highly ironic, but it would at the same time be highly just.

Jaywalker began by conceding for the purpose of his argument that with respect to Eleanor Cerami, the sperm found in her vagina could be deemed sufficient corroboration of attempted intercourse, particularly when coupled with her and her husband's testimony that she'd had no other intercourse in the weeks preceding the attack. But nowhere in the evidence was there corroboration as to any force used against her.

As for Joanne Kenarden, the exact opposite was true, Jaywalker pointed out. The lower-back tenderness "found" by the doctors at Jacobi Hospital might conceivably be accepted by the jury as evidence of force. But when it came to independent evidence that her attacker had attempted to have intercourse with her, there simply was none.

Pope countered by arguing that each victim corroborated the other. As authority for his position, he cited a pair of proceedings from Family Court. Family Court is the lowest of the low. It's where Judge Judy worked before she got promoted to daytime television. It's where you go if you're twelve and cut school too often, or if you're divorced and fall behind with your alimony payments. If citing a United States Supreme Court decision is worth a ten, they've yet to come up with a decimal small enough to describe the weight of a Family Court ruling.

Jaywalker was no legal scholar and never would be. But he'd done his homework, and he, too, had come across the two cases cited by Jacob Pope. For starters, both had dealt solely with issues of identity, no longer an area where corroboration was required. Beyond that, they'd been concerned not with corroboration, but with the admissibility of evidence of one crime to prove another. To allow Pope to "cross-corroborate" the cases, Jaywalker now argued, would be to permit him to "double bootstrap"—to tie together two legally insufficient prosecutions that couldn't survive on their own. These were two separate cases, he reminded Justice Davidoff, joined for trial solely for reasons of convenience and judicial economy.

If Jaywalker succeeded in convincing himself—and he came pretty close, the further he got into his argument— he had less success with the court. Justice Davidoff denied the motion to dismiss, without comment, and recessed for the day.

Justice Davidoff's ruling made it clearer than ever that the defense was going to have to put on a case of its own. Up to this point, Jaywalker's strategy had pretty much been dictated by the prosecution's evidence. Unable to shake the two victims from their identifications of Darren Kingston as their attacker, he'd all but conceded that they'd been raped and honestly believed it was Darren who'd raped them. So instead of attacking them head-on, he'd tried to draw from them details about the rapist that would distinguish him from Darren—his physical appearance, his lack of a stutter, his right-handedness, his being circumcised, the clothing he wore and the absence of a chipped front tooth or eyebrow scar. Now Jaywalker needed to complete the picture by presenting evidence of his own that would demonstrate the contrast in each of these areas between the actual rapist and the young man who was on trial.

Toward that objective, Jaywalker had been lining up witnesses for several weeks. They included Darren himself, members of his family and fellow employees at the post office. He'd even spoken with several doctors, in the hopes of getting one of them to come to court and establish that Darren wasn't circumcised. Now it was time to put it all together, to orchestrate the defense case.

Jaywalker started with the proposition that he wanted to save Darren for last. Unlike other witnesses, the defendant gets to be present in the courtroom during all of the trial testimony. By putting him on last, Jaywalker would be giving him the benefit of hearing the other defense witnesses testify. Though by this time he was confident that Darren would be telling the truth—the pendulum long ago having come to rest on innocence—this way he wouldn't contradict other defense witnesses on any of the little details that might make it seem as though he were lying. Far more important than that reason was the dramatic aspect. The defendant is the witness jurors want to hear. Jaywalker had worked with Darren enough to know he was unlikely to disappoint them and might even be able to win them over. He therefore wanted everything in the trial to build toward the moment when he stood to announce his final witness.

Back in college, Jaywalker had been a member of the track team. Not that he'd planned on it. Recruited out of high school as a seventeen-year-old pitcher who could throw a baseball at ninety-seven miles an hour, he'd managed to blow his arm out even before arriving on campus. Needing to keep his scholarship, he'd tried out for the track team and found a berth as a middle-distance runner. His favorite event was the mile relay, in which each of four runners ran a quarter of the total, or 440 yards. It was too short a distance to hold back and pace yourself, but at the same time, too long to sprint without tearing your lungs out. So you did so anyway, at full tilt, and collapsed afterward. The only strategy that had come into play, therefore, was how the coach had arranged his runners. He'd saved his strongest runner for last, as Jaywalker was now doing with Darren. But just as it was important to have a good anchorman to finish things up, so, too, was it crucial to get off to a good start, with a runner who was *strong out of the blocks,* as they called it. Jaywalker had become that runner on the track. Now he had to decide who would take that role in court.

Darren's family, however well they might testify, would be regarded with a certain amount of skepticism by the jury, simply because they *were* family. So Jaywalker decided to move them to the middle of his order. He would lead off with the post-office employees, in order to prove Darren's alibi for the morning of September 17th. That was the morning Eleanor Cerami had seen her attacker again, she'd said with certainty. If she could be wrong about that, she could be wrong about everything.

To Jaywalker, a trial has always been something of an emotional roller-coaster ride, punctuated by a series of long climbs and gut-wrenching dives. There's the climb that anticipates jury selection and culminates in addressing the jurors. There's the climb during the prosecutor's opening statement, which leads to the defense's opening. Then there's the long, drawn-out climb of the prosecution's evidence, which suddenly gives way to the defense case.

The thing of it is, Jaywalker has always hated the roller coaster with every fiber of his being. To this day, he holds on to the safety bar with both hands, his knuckles bone-white. He grits his teeth, closes his eyes and screams at the top of his lungs at every dive.

But he always gets back on.

It was well past midnight when he hung up from his last phone call, assured that each of his witnesses knew exactly where to be and when to be there. And it was after two when he finally drifted off to a troubled sleep, dreaming of the Cyclone, that mother of all roller coasters, at the Coney Island of his youth.

14

FAMILY AND FRIENDS

The first defense witness Jaywalker called was Andrew Emmons. Mr. Emmons, a black man, testified that he'd worked at the same branch of the post office since 1965, and had known Darren Kingston since he'd been assigned there a couple years back. Although the two worked different shifts, their schedules were set up so they overlapped by several hours.

JAYWALKER: And what branch is it that both you and Mr. Kingston work at?

EMMONS: That's the Gracie Station branch.

JAYWALKER: Where is that located?

EMMONS: In Manhattan, at East Eighty-fifth Street.

Jaywalker drew from Mr. Emmons that Darren appeared no thinner now than he had back in August. In fact, the witness explained, the workers would occasionally step onto the large parcel scales to weigh themselves. Darren's weight had always been right around 150 to 153 pounds.

Next Jaywalker asked Mr. Emmons about Darren's coming back to work following his arrest. Although he didn't remember the date, he did recall Darren's arriving one morning "off his shift"—in other words, not at his regular starting time—after having been absent about a week. The two had had a brief conversation, during which Darren had explained that he'd been arrested. Then Darren had gone in to speak with his union delegate, a man named George Riley. The time, according to Mr. Emmons, had been 9:00 in the morning.

Pope's cross-examination was brief. He questioned whether the employees really weighed themselves, but Mr. Emmons assured him that they did. Asked if he'd ever been convicted of a crime, Mr. Emmons replied that he hadn't been. Pope was fishing there. Because the post-office employees weren't testifying to Darren's where-abouts at the time of any of the crimes, they weren't alibi witnesses in the strict sense of the term. Therefore Jay-walker hadn't been required to turn over their names in advance. With no chance to check Mr. Emmons out, Pope took a cast anyway and came up empty.

Next Jaywalker called George Riley, a white man. A number of Darren's fellow workers had offered to testify, and Jaywalker had been able to pick from among them. His choice of a biracial sample was no accident. Justice may be color-blind, but the same isn't necessarily true of jurors.

Mr. Riley testified that he'd been working at Gracie Station for twelve years and also served as a shop steward active in union matters. He'd known Darren since Darren had begun working at the post office, and their shifts overlapped. He first learned of the case when Darren came in one morning to see him. Darren explained that he'd been arrested about a week earlier and wanted to know the proper procedure for explaining his absence. Mr. Riley told him to see Mr. Hamilton, the supervisor, and explain exactly what had happened. Shortly thereafter, Darren had indeed gone in to see Mr. Hamilton. According to Mr. Riley, the time was somewhere between 9:00 and 10:00 a.m.

Pope, on cross-examination, tried to cast doubt on whether Darren had actually gone to see Mr. Hamilton. But Mr. Riley stated that he himself had spoken to Mr. Hamilton and told him that Darren was coming in.

In his next line of questioning, however, Pope scored heavily. He drew an admission from Mr. Riley that he was unaware of Darren's stutter. It was a blow, and one that Jaywalker could do nothing about.

Jaywalker called P. G. Hamilton. Asked to spell his first name and last, Mr. Hamilton gave up P-H-I-L-B-E-R-T with obvious reluctance. As for the G., it remains a mystery to this day. Mr. Hamilton made an impressive physical appearance. A bearded and distinguished-looking white man, he could easily have been mistaken for a college professor or a psychiatrist. He testified that he'd been with the post office since 1944, and a supervisor since 1953. He identified Darren as one of his employees. He described him as "slightly built," appearing the same in court as he had back in August.

Jaywalker asked Mr. Hamilton if there'd come a time when he'd learned that Darren had been arrested. He stated that he had, though offhand he couldn't recall the date. But P. G. Hamilton had brought with him something far more persuasive than his own memory. In summoning him to court, Jaywalker had served upon him a subpoena *duces tecum,* ordering him to produce all records the post office had regarding Darren Kingston and the date September 17, 1979. Now, as Mr. Hamilton sat in the witness box, he withdrew from his jacket pocket a piece of paper and unfolded it.

JAYWALKER: And what is that?

HAMILTON: This is a form, an official government form, called a 3971. This is made out by an employee for any type of leave whatsoever—sick leave, annual leave, even jury duty. The employee must make this out for any leave.

Mr. Hamilton related in detail how one morning in September—the 17th, according to the document—Darren Kingston had come into his office to see him, to tell him he'd been arrested, and to discuss the time he'd missed from work. Mr. Hamilton had directed Darren to fill out a Form 3971, to cover emergency leave from September 12th—the date of Darren's arrest and the first day he'd missed work—through September 18th, the following day. That added up to one calendar week, the equivalent of five working days. Mr. Hamilton recalled specifically that in filling out the form, Darren had misunderstood the instructions and dated it September 18, instead of September 17. Mr. Hamilton had caught the error and corrected it. Then he'd approved the form by signing it and dating it himself, and forwarded it to the computer processing unit.

Jaywalker offered the form into evidence. Pope requested a voir dire examination to challenge its admissibility, and Justice Davidoff permitted him to interrupt Jaywalker's examination and ask a series of questions about the document. Pope tried his best to dispute Mr. Hamilton's account, but this time his best wasn't good enough. When he saw that the judge was about to admit the item, he withdrew his objection. Then he completed his about-face by pretending that the exhibit—which only moments earlier he'd fought so hard to keep out of evidence—was insignificant. When Jaywalker asked Justice Davidoff's permission to pass the form among the jurors so that they might decide for themselves, Pope crossed the line for the first time in the trial, committing prosecutorial misconduct by injecting his own opinion into the issue.

POPE: We'll let the jury look at it for what it's worth. I don't think it really makes much difference whether they see it or not.

JAYWALKER: Your Honor, if I may, I'm going to pass this among the jury. Even though Mr. Pope doesn't think it's important.

THE COURT: That remark was uncalled for.

Which only goes to show that at trial, as in sports, it's usually the player who commits the second foul who gets caught.

On cross-examination, Pope stayed away from Form 3971. Instead, he tried to use Mr. Hamilton, as he had so successfully used the previous witness, George Riley, to cast doubt on Darren's stutter. Pope was evidently banking on the fact that none of the post-office witnesses had come to court expecting to be asked about the stutter. And he was right; Jaywalker had completely overlooked the matter in interviewing and preparing them. Furthermore, Pope was aware that they'd gone right from Mr. Riley's testimony to Mr. Hamilton's, providing Jaywalker no opportunity to alert Mr. Hamilton at the last moment.

POPE: What was Darren Kingston's manner of speaking? Describe his voice for us.

HAMILTON: Mr. Kingston's voice is high.

POPE: Well, would you say he's loud when he speaks to you?

HAMILTON: No, Mr. Kingston is usually very soft-spoken.

Pope had scored a point, and he knew it. Sensing his advantage, he couldn't resist the urge to press on.

POPE: Very soft-spoken?

HAMILTON: Yes.

Another point. Jaywalker wondered if Pope would have the good sense to quit while he was ahead, at a point where he could later argue to the jury that Mr. Hamilton's failure to mention anything else unusual about Darren's speech spoke volumes. Jaywalker could tell from Pope's pause that he was wrestling with the idea. But then greed got the better of him.

POPE: Does he stutter at all when he talks to you?

HAMILTON: Once in a while, I would call it. What we would normally call a stutter, once in a while, a word or two. Sometimes he would come on a word and repeat a syllable one or two or three times. Not on all words. Not what I would call normal stuttering.

Bingo. By asking one question too many, Pope had elicited a classic definition of stuttering: occasionally repeating a syllable once or twice, or even three times. What was more, he'd elicited it from a witness who obviously hadn't been coached to say it. With no further questions for Mr. Hamilton, Pope sat down heavily. Jaywalker thought he heard him curse under his breath, but he couldn't be sure.

As Jaywalker watched P. G. Hamilton make his way out of the courtroom, he couldn't help but feel buoyed by his testimony. Here was a man who'd given nearly four decades of his life to the post office. He'd come in, armed with official paperwork, to establish that at the moment Eleanor Cerami was seeing her rapist in the Bronx, Darren

Kingston was at East 85th Street in Manhattan. On top of that, he'd corroborated Darren's stutter.

Jaywalker would only learn much later on that, in one of the many ironic footnotes to the case, Mr. Hamilton had already been reprimanded by his own superior for permitting Darren to return to work without any disciplinary action being taken against him for being absent without authorization.

As the old saying goes, no good deed goes unpunished.

In order to complete the September 17th "alibi," Jaywalker called Darren's cousin, Delroid Kingston, to the stand. Delroid was a witness about whom Jaywalker had great reservations. He was unemployed, separated from his wife and definitely not the sharpest tack in the toolbox. There was no way he was going to be a match for Jacob Pope's cross-examination skills. Yet Jaywalker felt he had little choice in the matter. When Darren had been released on bail, Jaywalker had instructed the family to have someone with him at all times. He'd wanted to be able to have somebody to account for Darren's whereabouts, in case the real rapist were to strike again. Responding to Jaywalker's request, the family had mobilized its personnel. Darren, Charlene and their son had moved back in with Darren's parents, as had Delroid, who was out of work and having trouble making ends meet. Since Marlin and Inez had to work—there was the cost of the bail bond to absorb, as well as Jaywalker's fee and other expenses related to the case—that left only Delroid to shadow Darren. So on the morning of September 17th, when Darren had gone to the post office to explain his recent absence from work, Delroid had gone with him.

JAYWALKER: How did you go there with him?

DELROID: We took the train from his house.

JAYWALKER: And was that the first time Darren went back to work after he came out of jail?

DELROID: I think it was. Yes.

JAYWALKER: Once you got to the post office, did you go upstairs with him?

DELROID: No, I didn't. The only ones that were allowed upstairs were the people that worked there.

JAYWALKER: All right. About what time did you get there? Do you remember?

DELROID: We got there approximately about a quarter to nine, something around that vicinity.

JAYWALKER: And when Darren went upstairs, what did you do?

DELROID: I remained downstairs in the lobby.

JAYWALKER: Do you recall when the next time you saw Darren was?

DELROID: Approximately about two and a half hours later.

JAYWALKER: Two and a half hours later?

DELROID: That's when he came back downstairs.

JAYWALKER: And what did the two of you do then?

DELROID: From there we went back to the train station and took the train back uptown.

JAYWALKER: Back uptown to where?

DELROID: To his parents' house.

JAYWALKER: Do you recall what time you got back there?

DELROID: Well, one-fifteen, one-thirty, somewhere around that.

JAYWALKER: And do you know if Darren went out again until dinnertime?

DELROID: He did not.

Jaywalker concluded by establishing that "home" was not only a lengthy ride from the post office, but also a good mile from the Castle Hill area.

On cross-examination, Pope demonstrated that he'd done his homework. He brought out the fact that Delroid's parents, Darren's aunt and uncle, lived on Olmstead Avenue, which was considerably closer to Castle Hill. But Delroid stated that Darren was at most an infrequent visitor there, and that in fact Delroid had never once seen him there.

Pope next tried to attack Delroid's claim of being able to account for Darren's whereabouts following his cousin's release on bail. But Delroid was firm in his testimony that he'd been with Darren since then, every day, practically all day long. Had the expression "twenty-four/seven" been coined back then, no doubt Delroid would have used it.

From there, Pope went into an incident that had occurred toward the end of September. Darren had an aunt by marriage by the name of Yvette Monroe. Several weeks after Darren's arrest and release, Yvette had been in the Castle Hill area when she'd spotted a young man who resembled Darren so much that at first she'd thought it was him. When she'd realized her mistake, it had occurred to her that the encounter might have significance. She'd immediately phoned the Kingstons, who'd hastily organized a "search party" to rush over to the area. Delroid had been a member of the search party. But by the time they reached Castle Hill, the young man had disappeared.

Jaywalker had told Pope about the incident, in the hope of convincing him that not only was Darren innocent, but also that the real rapist was still at large in the Castle Hill area. Why Pope was now choosing to go into the incident puzzled Jaywalker. Perhaps he anticipated that Jaywalker himself would, and was making a preemptive move to blunt the impact. Actually, Jaywalker had thought about going into it, but doubted that the rules of evidence would permit him to do so. But now, by "opening the door" to the subject, Pope was inadvertently giving Jaywalker an opportunity to explore it in detail. Jaywalker scribbled himself a note to get in touch with Yvette Monroe as soon as he could.

Whatever Pope's true interest in the matter had been, he succeeded in making little of it. He asked Delroid a few questions about it and got nowhere. With that, he gave up. As Delroid stepped down from the witness stand, Jaywalker had to suppress an urge to rush over to him and hug him. This out-of-work man, literally dependent upon others for the food on his plate and a roof over his head, who'd caused Jaywalker such great concern, had come through with flying colors.

Jaywalker called Darren's mother, Inez Kingston, to the stand. She entered the courtroom from the corridor immediately outside, where, as a defense witness, she'd been banished until that moment. As she came in, her husband, Marlin, suddenly sobbed audibly, rose from his seat and rushed out through the same doorway Inez had just entered. He would explain later that the prospect of seeing his wife testifying on behalf of their falsely accused son was simply too much for him to bear.

Inez walked slowly to the witness stand. As she stood and took the oath, her calm, warm voice belied what he knew was the boiling of her blood pressure.

Jaywalker had her identify herself immediately as Darren's mother. He questioned her about the evening of her son's arrest. She recounted how two detectives had come to her home looking for Darren. One of them was named Rendell. She'd given them Darren's address. As soon as they'd left, she'd phoned Darren, to find out what was wrong. What Jaywalker wasn't allowed to bring out was Darren's response, that he had absolutely no idea. That would have been hearsay, and inadmissible. But he'd at least established the existence of the conversation, which he would be able to use later to show that Darren, alerted that the police were looking for him, had made no attempt to flee.

Before his next series of questions, Jaywalker had Darren stand at the defense table.

JAYWALKER: Mrs. Kingston, did you see your son in August of last year?

INEZ: Yes.

JAYWALKER: As you see him now, does he look any different from the way he looked then?

INEZ: No, he doesn't.

JAYWALKER: Does he look any taller?

INEZ: No.

JAYWALKER: Any shorter?

INEZ: No.

JAYWALKER: Any heavier?

INEZ: No.

JAYWALKER: Any thinner?

INEZ: No.

Jaywalker motioned to Darren that he could resume his seat.

JAYWALKER: Mrs. Kingston, is your son right-handed or left-handed?

INEZ: Left-handed.

JAYWALKER: How do you know that?

INEZ: He writes with his left hand. He eats with his left hand. He throws with his left hand. He does everything with his left hand. From the time he was a toddler, everything he did was with his left hand.

Jaywalker asked her whether any attempt had ever been made to convert Darren to being right-handed. She replied that there had indeed been attempts, as had been commonplace years ago, with people trying to "cure" children of their left-handedness, much the way some modern-day do-gooders try to "cure" individuals of their homosexuality. Some evidence had even shown that tampering with left-handedness could produce stuttering, because the portion of the brain responsible for speech is situated in the left hemisphere. In fact, Jaywalker had briefly considered trying to find an expert to bring into court to discuss it, but because the theory was at best a controversial one, he'd decided against it. It was enough that Darren was left-handed, and that he stuttered. Cause and effect, if indeed there was one, was irrelevant.

Jaywalker next brought out that, as far as Inez was aware, Darren neither owned a car nor knew how to drive.

He wanted to dispel any notion the jurors might have that Darren had the mobility to zip around from the post office to his apartment to the Castle Hill area.

Then he moved on to the subject of Darren's speech.

JAYWALKER: Does your son stutter?

INEZ: Yes.

JAYWALKER: And in connection with that stuttering, when he was growing up, did he ever take any special classes?

INEZ: Every year he went, they gave him speech class. Every grade. He had to attend speech class every grade.

JAYWALKER: And when did he stop stuttering?

INEZ: He never stopped. He still does.

It seemed a pretty good note to stop on, so Jaywalker thanked the witness and sat down.

Pope began on a low key, careful not to antagonize the jury by attacking Inez head-on. He established that years earlier the Kingstons had lived some twenty blocks from Castle Hill, that they still had relatives there, and that Darren was familiar with the area. From there he brought out that back in August, Inez had taken care of Darren and Charlene's son while Charlene worked, an arrangement that would have left Darren alone in his apartment when he came home from his job each morning.

Little by little, Pope managed to chip away at Inez Kingston's direct testimony. Darren, though left-handed, could certainly do some things with his right hand. Inez wasn't really familiar with her son's exact weight. In a situation where Darren felt in control, his stutter was less noticeable. And Inez couldn't say where her son had been on the afternoon of August 16th, the date of the two rapes.

POPE: How about August fifteenth, the day before? Could you tell us where he was on that day?

INEZ: No.

POPE: August seventeenth, the day after?

These were standard cross-examination questions for an alibi witness who claimed to recall with specificity a date long ago. By showing that the witness couldn't remember the day before or the day after nearly as well, the questioner could cast doubt on the legitimacy of the alibi.

But something was wrong here. True, as required, Jaywalker had listed Inez as a potential alibi witness. But that had been with regard to the September 5th incident, the one she recalled because Darren had phoned her to say he could hear his son crying next door. That incident had been severed out by the judge and wasn't part of this trial. And Inez had just conceded that she couldn't account for Darren's whereabouts on August 16th, the date of the Cerami and Kenarden rapes. Even as Inez began her answer regarding August 16th, alarm bells were going off in Jaywalker's mind.

INEZ: No. How can I tell you that? How can I go
back that far?

POPE: And how about September fifth?

Jaywalker was on his feet objecting, even as Inez tried
to say she knew Darren had been home that day. Up at the
bench, out of the hearing of the jury, he pointed out to
Justice Davidoff that while Pope might have selected
August 15th and 17th at random, to believe so was actually
giving Pope the benefit of the doubt. The 17th, after all,
was the date of the attack on Tania Maldonado. As to September 5th, there could be no doubt whatsoever. Pope had
obviously picked it purely because it was the date of the
attack on Elvira Caldwell. Pope was doing one of two
things, Jaywalker told the judge. Either he was fishing
around to see if the defense had alibis for the other two incidents, or he was suggesting to the jury that something
of significance had occurred on those dates, and inviting
them to speculate and imagine the worst. Whether it was
the former, the latter or both, Pope's attempts were improper.

Defending himself, Pope pointed out that Jaywalker
had brought out a number of dates during his questioning
of various witnesses, giving him the right to do the same.
Furthermore, he argued, he had every right to test Inez
Kingston's credibility by asking her about her son's whereabouts on September 5th.

Pope was flat-out lying there. The first of his stated
reasons—that he could ask about dates because Jaywalker
had—was utter nonsense. The second—that his question
about September 5th went to the witness's credibility—

was totally dishonest. In fact, what Pope was doing was setting up a "straw man," even as he hid his true intentions with evasive explanations. The full scope of his plan wouldn't become clear until later on in the trial.

In hindsight, Jaywalker should have seen it coming. But you know what they say about hindsight. All he could do at the time was object, and hope the judge would see it his way and sustain the objection. But Justice Davidoff permitted the question. He did suggest to Pope that he ask the witness about September 6th, 7th or 8th, as well, in order to disguise the fact that the 5th was, as he put it, a "red letter day."

Finally given a chance to respond to the question about September 5th, Inez stated that she knew Darren had been home on that date. It had been the first day of school for his son, and consequently the first day Inez no longer had to look after him. She also recalled having spoken with Darren on the phone sometime that morning.

Pope asked her about September 4th. That had been Labor Day, she recalled, and Darren, Charlene and their son had come over to his parents' house to visit. To wind up his cross-examination, Pope succeeded in getting Inez to admit that she couldn't say for a fact whether Darren had been in the Castle Hill Houses during August and September.

There was no way Jaywalker was going to let Pope have the last word with Inez. On redirect, he had her recount an incident in which Darren had once tried to change a light-bulb for her. The fixture was in a hard-to-reach place, and Darren, on a stepladder, had been required to unscrew the burned-out bulb with his right hand. Unable to do it, he'd been forced to call upon his brother for help.

Pope, on recross, sought to show that Inez had fabricated the entire incident.

POPE: Was there a particular reason, Mrs. Kingston, why you watched your son change this lightbulb?

INEZ: Yes. I was looking at him changing the bulb because I thought he was going to break it, or fall off the ladder and hurt himself.

After a few more questions, Pope was finished with Inez, and this time Jaywalker left well enough alone. As she took a seat in the courtroom—where she was now permitted to observe the rest of the trial—Jaywalker had to wonder about the jurors' reactions to her. On the plus side, she'd established Darren's left-handedness, his stutter and several other matters. But underlying her testimony was the fact that she was the defendant's mother. To the jury, that no doubt raised a caution flag over everything she'd said.

Jaywalker called Charlene Kingston, Darren's wife, to the stand. He knew full well that the same caveat attached to Inez's testimony would apply to Charlene's. But Charlene had a few points of her own to contribute. Besides, Jaywalker wanted the jurors to hear her. And as she was entering her ninth month of pregnancy by this time, he wanted them to see her, as well.

He established that Charlene was Darren's wife, that they lived together, and that they already had a three-year-old son. He asked her about Darren's appearance back in August, and she replied that it had been the same as it was now. He asked her if Darren owned or had ever owned a tan V-neck shirt. She replied that he never had, but that she could recall Detective Rendell asking her about such a shirt. He asked her if Darren ever drank, and she said he did, on social occasions. Did he drink wine? No, he drank Seagram's V.O. Did he ever carry a knife? No, never. Did he stutter? Yes, he did. And with that, Jaywalker thanked her and sat down.

In Jaywalker's book, less was often better. If you asked your witness only a few questions, you left your adversary with little to pick apart. If he then chose to open up new areas to explore, he did so at his peril.

As he had with Inez, Pope began gently with Charlene.

POPE: Mrs. Kingston, I apologize for asking you these questions. I know it's difficult for you. I assume you love your husband, do you not?

CHARLENE: Yes, I do.

POPE: You would do everything you could to help him, would you not?

CHARLENE: Yes.

Pope asked Charlene if she knew where Darren had been on August 16th. She replied that he'd been home. But when Pope pressed her to explain how she knew that, Charlene could only say that that was where he always was during the day. Although she'd been in the habit of speaking with Darren on the phone while he was home and she was at work, it was usually her husband who made the calls. On top of that, he usually called in the morning, before falling asleep. So Charlene, too, was unable to specifically account for Darren's whereabouts in the early afternoon hours of August 16th or, for that matter, any other afternoon of that month.

These days, computer technology captures every phone call we make or receive, and it would be possible to subpoena printouts that would show whether calls had been made to or from Darren and Charlene's apartment—as well as the exact times and the length of any conversations—around the times the rapes were being committed. But none of that was possible back in 1980.

As Pope succeeded in chipping away at her testimony, Charlene's frustration grew visibly. Tears welled up in her eyes and ran down her cheeks. When Pope drew from her a concession that her conclusion about Darren's never carrying a knife was based purely upon the fact that she'd never *seen* him carrying one, she sobbed openly. At that point, Darren rose from his seat to move toward her, and Jaywalker had to just about tackle him to hold him back. Moments later, evidently fearful that continuing might turn the jury against him, Pope announced that he had no further questions.

Jaywalker's redirect examination was brief.

JAYWALKER: Charlene, in response to Mr. Pope's questions, you indicated that you love your husband.

CHARLENE: [Sobbing] Yes.

JAYWALKER: And you indicated further that you'd do anything you could to help him. Is that correct?

CHARLENE: Yes.

JAYWALKER: Charlene, would you lie under oath to help your husband?

CHARLENE: No.

Looking back at the exchange, Jaywalker would find fault with his preparation of Charlene Kingston. Had he been able to put words in her mouth, he would have had her answer his final question differently. "I don't honestly know," would have been more effective, quickly followed up by, "All I can say is I'm telling you the truth." Or, "If I thought for a moment that my husband was the one who raped those women, not only wouldn't I lie for him, I'd be the first one in line to testify against him."

Hindsight again. But hindsight that would become foresight as Jaywalker would hone his trial skills over the years to come. For the moment, though, all he could do was thank Charlene for her testimony. By that time, she had to be helped from the witness stand by other members of Darren's family. Justice Davidoff called a recess for lunch.

During his cross-examination of Delroid and Inez, Pope had established that Darren had an uncle living on Olmstead Avenue, just a few blocks from the Castle Hill Houses. Afraid that the jury might buy what was sure to be Pope's argument—that Darren had somehow used that location as a "base of operations" for the Castle Hill attacks—Jaywalker wanted to do what he could to dispel the notion. A phone call brought Samuel Kingston, whom

Jaywalker now interviewed during the recess, down to court, along with Yvette Monroe.

Jaywalker was having little trouble sticking to his no-breakfast, no-lunch diet.

He put Samuel Kingston on the stand as the first witness of the afternoon session. Samuel identified himself as Darren's uncle and gave his address as 435 Olmstead Avenue, acknowledging that it was no more than three or four blocks from the buildings where Eleanor Cerami and Joanne Kenarden lived.

JAYWALKER: When is the last time you can recall your nephew Darren coming over to your house?

SAMUEL: About six years ago. And he only came there because his family did, for Thanksgiving dinner. He never visits us.

JAYWALKER: Does he have a key to your house?

SAMUEL: No.

There was one other subject Jaywalker wanted to address with Darren's uncle.

JAYWALKER: You work at night, don't you?

SAMUEL: Yes.

JAYWALKER: Do you happen to know where you were around noon on August sixteenth of last year?

SAMUEL: Not definitely.

JAYWALKER: Do you have any idea at all as to where you were?

SAMUEL: Somewhere around the house. I know I was home. I'm home during the daytime.

Pope asked no questions.

Jaywalker called Yvette Monroe next. In contrast to the rest of Darren's family, Yvette was white. She was also young and pretty. At the time of the trial, she'd been in the country only four years, and her testimony bore a noticeable French accent.

Yvette identified herself to the jury as being the wife of another of Darren's uncles, making the defendant her nephew by marriage. Jaywalker needed to establish that she'd spent enough time around Darren that the mistaken identity incident would be meaningful to the jurors.

JAYWALKER: How long have you known Darren?

YVETTE: Since I came to this country, in nineteen-seventy-six.

JAYWALKER: Do you have occasion to see him from time to time?

YVETTE: I lived in the same house.

JAYWALKER: Until when?

YVETTE: Until November of nineteen-seventy-nine.

JAYWALKER: So would you say you know him quite well?

YVETTE: Very well. Yes, sir.

JAYWALKER: Yvette, do you remember learning about Darren's arrest in connection with this case?

YVETTE: Yes, sir.

JAYWALKER: And did there come a time when an incident occurred near the Castle Hill housing project that involved you?

YVETTE: Yes, sir.

JAYWALKER: Can you give us an approximate date with respect to that incident?

YVETTE: I would say around the beginning of October of last year.

JAYWALKER: And can you tell us where you were?

YVETTE: I had gone to Nathan's, which is a restaurant in the Bronx, opposite Korvette's. And as I entered Nathan's, there were several people sitting around eating. And I got shook up when I saw this man sitting at a table with this girl, because he had a striking resemblance with Darren. My first impression is that here's Darren, sitting at the table. And so I approached the table where they were sitting, and then I realized it was not Darren.

Yvette explained that she'd just come from the Kingston house, where Darren had been. Logically, therefore, she knew this couldn't be him. Yet the resemblance had been so strong that she'd still thought it was, at least at first.

Realizing the significance of what had happened, Yvette had immediately phoned Inez, only to find her line busy. Next she'd tried to reach her own husband, with the same result. She stayed in Nathan's for fifteen to twenty minutes, dialing both numbers while staring at the man and the girl. Finally she'd gone to the Kingston house and told them she'd seen a man who looked just like Darren.

JAYWALKER: And what did they do?

YVETTE: I was so upset and so sure that I'd seen this man who looked like Darren that I asked them to get the car and go back to Nathan's.

JAYWALKER: And did anyone do anything?

YVETTE: My husband and Delroid went together to Nathan's.

JAYWALKER: Do you know if they were able to find the man?

YVETTE: They came home about thirty, forty-five minutes later, and said they didn't see anybody.

JAYWALKER: You didn't go with them?

YVETTE: No, sir, I didn't. I stayed with the baby.

Pope, on cross-examination, first established that Yvette was fond of Darren and had known he was in trouble at the time of the look-alike incident. Then he set out to reduce it to an everyday occurrence.

POPE: Mrs. Monroe, have you ever walked down the street and seen someone you thought you recognized?

YVETTE: Yes.

POPE: And you've gone up to that person and realized you don't know the person?

YVETTE: Yes.

POPE: It's happened to you a number of times?

YVETTE: A few times, yes.

POPE: And in fact that happened to you sometime in the beginning of October nineteen-seventy-nine, the incident you're talking about. Right?

YVETTE: Right.

Pope was scoring effectively. He drew from Yvette an admission that it had been a matter of only three or four seconds before she'd realized the man wasn't Darren. He asked her if she'd made an attempt to call a police officer. She said she hadn't. Had she attempted to find out who the man was? No. Had she waited around and then attempted to follow the man? She hadn't. Had she mentioned the problem to anyone else in the restaurant? No, she hadn't.

To Jaywalker's way of thinking, the answers to all Pope's questions were self-evident. Wouldn't following a suspected knife-wielding rapist be the last thing in the world a young woman would want to do? Would a police officer really have arrested a man because someone claimed he looked like a defendant on a case? Would innocent bystanders have grabbed him and held him?

But as he looked at the jurors, he saw only blank faces. Weren't they capable of seeing through Pope's cross-examination? Were *any* of the defense witnesses getting through to them? Or had the case ended for them when the victims had pointed to Darren as their rapist? Were they simply too overwhelmed, too frightened by the prospect of a black man on the loose, attacking women like themselves, their wives and their daughters in their own neighborhood, where they lived and worked and tried to cling to a way of life that was vanishing before their eyes?

Finally, Pope showed Yvette a photograph taken of Darren at the time of his arrest on September 12th. Although she was able to identify her nephew, she seemed uncertain. She thought the eyes looked strange, and the body shorter and heavier than Darren's.

At last Yvette Monroe was allowed to step down from

the witness stand. Pope, through an effective piece of cross-examination, had seriously undercut her testimony, and whenever a prosecutor succeeds in doing that, he causes the jury to look with suspicion upon the entire defense. Witnesses are expected to help the side that calls them, and when a witness fails to do that—or inadvertently helps the other side—the damage can be incalculable.

And once again, Jaywalker held only himself to blame. Yvette had come into court armed with nothing but the truth, and sometimes that's not enough. By failing to anticipate where Pope might go with his cross-examination, Jaywalker had left her vulnerable to attack. And in so doing, he'd not only let her down, but he'd also let his client down. And the fact that he would learn how to do things better and never make the same mistake again was of little consolation at the moment.

He nodded a thank-you to Yvette as she walked past him to take a seat in the audience. Then he rose to his feet and announced that he was calling Darren Kingston to the stand.

15

DARREN

Until the actual rendering of the jury's verdict, the moment when a defendant rises to take the stand is second to none in terms of the drama it infuses into a trial. Often, the moment doesn't happen at all. Many defendants never testify. Even when they do, typically the jurors have been forewarned and have spent days—sometimes many of them—anticipating their appearances. This jury, on the other hand, had never been told, one way or the other, whether Darren would testify. Now their eyes turned as one upon this young man who'd sat almost in their midst for more than a week now, had stretched his legs in the same corridor as they had during court recesses, and had even ridden up and down the same elevator as they had, standing inches from their shoulders. And in all that time, they'd yet to hear him utter a single word.

Now, as that young man slowly made his way from the defense table to the witness stand, Jaywalker sat down. This was Darren's moment, after all, and he wanted the jury to focus on him, and him alone.

By this time, Jaywalker had spent hours with Darren—days, if you added up the time, or even weeks—first as an investigator, then as an examiner, finally as a mock interrogator, and throughout as a friend. Most of the sessions had taken place months ago, back at a time when Jaywalker had harbored serious doubts about Darren's claims of innocence and had been more interested in breaking his story then he'd been in presenting it. By the time the moment finally came to call him to the witness stand, Jaywalker had been fully converted. So convinced was he of Darren's innocence now that he literally would have bet everything he owned on it. Not that that would have amounted to all that much: a heavily mortgaged house, furnished largely in early '50s Salvation Army; a rusting Volkswagen, complete with loan payment book; a pair of skis, badly dinged; a bunch of law books, out of date; and a stack of bills, overdue.

But you get the point.

So convinced was Jaywalker, in fact, that once the trial had gotten under way, he'd spent very little time with Darren in terms of actual witness preparation. Was he about to repeat the error he'd just made with Yvette Monroe? The thought certainly occurred to him now. But even as it did, he rejected it. He felt certain that Darren's innocence would cloak him with more protection against whatever Pope might throw his way than all the coaching Jaywalker could ever give him. To be sure, he'd told Darren in broad terms the areas he expected to go into with him, the types of responses he wanted, and the things he could expect from Pope on cross. But he'd stopped short of asking him the actual questions he intended to put to him once the moment finally came. This wouldn't be a reprise of the lie detector test, where the aim had been to get Darren to sweat over questions he'd known were coming his way. This would be about a young man, falsely accused of being nothing less than a monster, finally getting a chance to tell the jury who he really was.

The courtroom grew absolutely silent. Every eye riveted on Darren as he dutifully placed his left hand on the Bible, raised his right arm and faced the court clerk. Today, in a new century of religious tolerance and political correctness, we've grown accustomed to modified oaths. The deity is often omitted, so as to avoid offending those who doubt his existence, and witnesses are even permitted to "affirm" rather than swear. But this was 1980, when every courtroom sprouted an American flag, the words *IN GOD WE TRUST* were as much a part of the décor as a wooden gavel, and an oath was an oath. So, repeating after the clerk, Darren swore to tell the truth, the whole truth and nothing but the truth, so help him God.

The moment was here.

Jaywalker began gently, asking Darren about simple things. His age, his address, his family. Even as Darren answered these preliminary, nonthreatening questions, his stutter was noticeable. Jaywalker suppressed a smile each time he heard it, just as he knew Pope must have been struggling to hide a grimace.

He asked Darren about his past record, figuring that it was better to bring it out than wait for Pope to do it. Today, refinements in the law allow for a pretrial conference to determine what matters a prosecutor may go into when cross-examining a defendant, and Darren's prior arrest would no doubt be ruled off-limits. But back then it was considered fair game. Darren described the arrest and his limited involvement in the incident. He explained that all the charges against him had ultimately been dismissed. Other than that matter and the present case, he'd never been arrested. And he'd never before been charged with a sex crime.

Jaywalker questioned Darren about the extent of his education, and about his employment. Darren talked about his current position at the post office, the specific location where he worked, and how long he'd worked there. Asked about his weight, Darren placed it at 151 or 152 pounds. The last time he weighed himself, he stated, the scale had registered 154, but he'd been fully clothed. When and where had that been? Last night, he said, at his lawyer's house. Jaywalker sneaked a sideways glance at the jurors. He hoped it wouldn't be lost on them that the door of his home was open to this young man. But if it had made any impression on them, they weren't showing it.

JAYWALKER: Now, Darren, are you right-handed or left-handed?

DARREN: I'm l-l-left-handed.

JAYWALKER: Did you ever play football?

DARREN: Yes.

JAYWALKER: What hand do you throw a football with?

DARREN: My left hand.

JAYWALKER: What hand do you sign your name with?

DARREN: Also my left hand.

JAYWALKER: Do you bowl?

DARREN: Yes, I bowl.

JAYWALKER: What hand do you bowl with?

DARREN: My l-left hand.

JAYWALKER: Do you play baseball?

DARREN: Yes.

JAYWALKER: What hand do you throw with?

DARREN: My left.

JAYWALKER: Do you bat?

DARREN: Yes.

JAYWALKER: Do you bat left-handed or right-handed?

DARREN: L-l-left-handed.

Jaywalker removed an item from a paper bag and had Darren identify it. It was a baseball glove, so ancient that the leather was dry and cracked. It was a Phil Rizzuto model, but made to wear on the right hand, freeing the player to throw with his left. It was the only one of its kind that Jaywalker had ever seen, or ever would. He had it received into evidence.

He asked Darren if he drank. Darren replied that he did, occasionally. When he did, he drank Seagram's V.O., a brand of blended whiskey. Never wine.

He asked about any scars or deformities Darren had. Darren pointed to an old scar that ran clear through one eyebrow, where no hair grew. Then he described a front tooth that was noticeably chipped. At that point Jaywalker had him step to the front of the jury box to show the jurors. Jaywalker wanted him close to them. *Look at him,* he wanted to tell them. *Lean forward. He won't hurt you.* He tried willing them to feel free to reach out to Darren, to touch him, to know he was every bit as harmless as they were. But if they were feeling that way, they weren't doing anything to show it.

Jaywalker asked Darren if he owned a car or knew how to drive. He answered no to both questions. How long would it take him to travel from his apartment to Castle Hill, or from the post office to Castle Hill? Either trip, he answered, would involve subway and bus combinations that he estimated would take over an hour, one way. Asked about his uncle Samuel's house on Olmstead Avenue, he said he'd last been there at a family dinner in 1975 or 1976, and that he'd never had a key to the house.

Jaywalker asked about sneakers. Darren said he owned one pair. Jaywalker produced another item from the paper bag and had Darren identify his sneakers, which were received into evidence. They were white and high-cut, with canvas that fully covered the ankles. And although they were worn, they could hardly be called gray.

Jaywalker asked Darren about his stutter. Darren stated that he'd been stuttering for as long as he could remember. He described speech classes he'd been forced to attend at school. He produced a draft card, which was received into evidence. It bore a notation that Jaywalker read aloud: "Other obvious physical characteristics: speech defect."

Jaywalker moved on to September 17th, the day Darren had returned to the post office following his release on bail. He described going there with his cousin Delroid, and seeing Andrew Emmons, George Riley and P. G. Hamilton. He identified his signature on the form he'd had to fill out that morning. He related how he'd left, met up with Delroid again in the lobby, and how the two of them had traveled back home, where they'd stayed the rest of the afternoon.

JAYWALKER: Darren, you heard Eleanor Cerami testify, didn't you?

DARREN: Yes, I did.

JAYWALKER: Are you the man she saw walking through her lobby on the morning of September seventeenth, at about nine-thirty?

DARREN: No. I couldn't have been. I was in M-M-Manhattan, at the post office.

JAYWALKER: Are you the man that raped her on August sixteenth?

DARREN: No, I am not. No.

JAYWALKER: Or any other date?

DARREN: No.

JAYWALKER: You heard Joanne Kenarden testify, didn't you?

DARREN: Yes.

JAYWALKER: Are you the man who raped her?

DARREN: No, I am not.

Jaywalker sat down, turning Darren over to Pope for cross-examination. Pope began with the left-handed issue, drawing from Darren an admission that he could in fact do certain things with his right hand, including unscrewing a lightbulb. Where Jaywalker had made a point of calling Darren by his first name, Pope now carefully avoided the trap. Over and over again, he inserted "Mr. Kingston" into his questions whenever he could, his attempt to depersonalize Darren in the eyes of the jury. Fair was fair, after all.

Next, despite the fact that Jaywalker had already gone into the matter pretty exhaustively on direct examination, Pope asked Darren about his prior arrest.

POPE: Isn't it a fact, Mr. Kingston, that on April tenth, nineteen-seventy-eight, you, with one Marvin Rollins and one John Washington, entered the apartment of a person named Cato Billingsly, and that you, holding a knife, robbed him of some two dollars?

Jaywalker jumped to his feet and objected. At the bench, he explained to Justice Davidoff that he'd represented Darren on the case and had interviewed the complainant, who'd never alleged that Darren had had a knife.

THE COURT: Overruled. He has a right to ask the question.

Jaywalker had no recourse, but he knew for a certainty that the judge was wrong there. Pope was deliberately hiding behind the general acting-in-concert language of the complaint he'd dug up from the old case. Had he looked into the facts at all, he would have quickly realized that he lacked a good-faith basis to suggest that Darren had possessed a knife in connection with the incident. But this case involved knifepoint rapes, and evidently Pope saw mileage to be gained by putting blinders on and implying that the defendant was no stranger to knives.

At the very least, Justice Davidoff should have called a recess and asked for the court papers and the D.A.'s file from the earlier case. It had happened right there in the Bronx, after all, less than two years ago. It couldn't have taken more than half an hour to find out what the complainant had really said. Instead, the judge allowed the question, and Pope took full advantage. Over and over he asked Darren if he hadn't held a knife in the case, changing a phrase here or a word there. Worse yet, each time he posed the question, he made it look as though he were reading from an official paper of some sort. All Darren could do was deny the fact each time he was asked, as emphatically as he could.

But there was a certain genius to Pope's handling of the issue. In his persistence, and particularly in his pretense that he had documentary proof backing up his point, he was able to pit his own credibility against that of the defendant. And with whom could the jurors be rationally expected to side? An assistant district attorney, trusted to try major felonies in Supreme Court? Or an accused rapist with a prior robbery arrest?

Finally Pope zeroed in on the day of the two rapes.

POPE: I believe you stated that on August sixteenth, nineteen-seventy-nine, you were at home asleep. Is that correct?

DARREN: That's true.

POPE: But you don't specifically remember that day, do you?

DARREN: No, I d-d-don't.

POPE: Tell me, were you in the Castle Hill project on that date?

DARREN: No.

POPE: When was the last time you were at the Castle Hill project?

DARREN: Not since nineteen-seventy-five or so.

POPE: And since then, have you at any time, on any date, been in any of the buildings of the Castle Hill project?

DARREN: Ac-ac-actually I have been.

Jaywalker's heart stopped beating. And Pope must have thought for sure he'd struck paydirt.

POPE: And when was that?

DARREN: That was after m-m-m-my arrest, with m-m-my investigator, Mr. McCarthy.

Jaywalker's heart resumed beating. Pope, visibly disappointed, launched into a series of questions about Darren's daily routine as it had been back in August.

POPE: What time do you get off work?

DARREN: At eight-thirty in the morning.

POPE: What do you do when you get off work?

DARREN: I get onto the number five train at Eighty-sixth Street. That t-t-takes me to One Hundred and Forty-ninth Street and the Grand Concourse. And I change to the number two train, to Allerton Avenue.

POPE: When you get off at Allerton Avenue, you walk to your home from there?

DARREN: The m-m-majority of the time I stop at Food City. It's under the train station. I buy groceries.

POPE: And approximately when do you arrive at your home?

DARREN: Between nine-thirty and ten o'clock.

POPE: And when you get home, what do you do?

DARREN: I might look at some TV, eat b-b-breakfast, call my wife to see if she got to work all right, and go to sleep.

POPE: You go to sleep at some point in the morning. Is that right?

DARREN: Yes.

POPE: And you sleep until when? What time do you wake up?

DARREN: About four-thirty, five o'clock.

POPE: And when you wake up, what do you do at that point?

DARREN: I'll take a shower, get c-c-cleaned up and wait until my wife gets home.

Eventually Pope grew tired of questioning Darren about his routine. It seemed to Jaywalker that Darren had handled himself flawlessly, and that Pope had accomplished absolutely nothing in the exchange.

Next Pope took aim at Darren's stutter.

POPE: Now, Mr. Kingston, isn't it a fact that you are under a lot of tension and pressure at the present time?

DARREN: Ever since I was arrested.

POPE: This case is important to you, of course. Isn't it?

DARREN: Definitely.

POPE: And you feel uneasy up there on the stand. Isn't that correct? I mean, it's a tense situation. Isn't that true?

DARREN: You could say that.

POPE: Isn't it a fact, Mr. Kingston, that when you are in a tense situation—when you're talking to Mr. Jaywalker about your suspension, for instance, or when you're on the witness stand, or when you're being told you've just been arrested—in situations like that, that you stutter quite a bit? Isn't that true?

DARREN: M-m-more than usual.

POPE: But usually, Mr. Kingston, isn't it a fact that you don't stutter as much as you're stuttering on the stand today? Isn't that correct?

DARREN: There is a slight d-d-difference, I guess.

POPE: In fact, Mr. Kingston, when you're in control of the situation, as in the case of August sixteenth, when you had the knife in your hand and you were telling Mrs. Cerami and Miss Kenarden what to do, you don't stutter at all, isn't that correct?

DARREN: I wasn't even there.

Bravo, thought Jaywalker. He couldn't have come up with a better answer himself.

POPE: You didn't stutter when you said that, either, Mr. Kingston.

As Jaywalker rose to object to Pope's nonquestion, he could hear Charlene crying in the spectator section of the courtroom. And he couldn't have been the only one to hear her.

DARREN: I stutter when I'm under stress, sure. And you know I'm under g-g-g-great stress now, because I didn't do these things. And I'm going to tell you—

The remainder of Darren's answer was drowned out by his wife's sobs. As Jaywalker objected, Pope complained, and as Justice Davidoff called for order, Marlin and Inez helped Charlene from the courtroom. A ten-minute recess was declared.

Outside in the corridor, Jaywalker found Charlene sobbing uncontrollably, fighting to catch her breath. Someone pulled up a chair for her. George Goddard, a physician who'd arrived a little while earlier to be the final defense witness, finally succeeded in calming Charlene down. He later confided to Jaywalker that his motivation had been at least partly self-serving. An internist with a subspecialty in endocrinology, Dr. Goddard hadn't delivered a baby in many years, and he wasn't particularly anxious to renew his obstetrical training on the sixth floor of the Bronx County Courthouse.

Following the recess, Darren resumed the witness stand. Pope questioned him briefly about his uncle Samuel, who lived near Castle Hill, and about Darren's own residence back in 1975, which had also been close to the area. But Darren continued to deny that he'd been back there since, except for that one time with John McCarthy.

POPE: In other words, Mr. Kingston, what you are testifying to—correct me if I'm wrong—is that Mrs. Cerami and Miss Kenarden are mistaken in their identification of you. Is that correct?

DARREN: That's exactly what I'm testifying.

POPE: No further questions.

Jaywalker thought it a strange way for Pope to conclude, reducing Darren's testimony—and anticipating Jaywalker's summation—so neatly for the defense. He should
have known better, should have figured out that there was
a method to Pope's madness.

Darren stepped down from the witness stand and re-
joined Jaywalker at the defense table. For two hours, he'd
become an active participant in his trial—indeed, the
central player of it. And he'd come through beautifully,
Jaywalker felt. Now Darren's moment was over. As it had
been before, his role was reduced to that of a spectator.

As much as Jaywalker would have liked to rest after
Darren's testimony, he had one more witness to call, and
circumstances beyond his control had dictated the order
of doing so.

For the better part of two weeks, he'd been trying to
locate a doctor willing to come to court and testify to the
fact that unlike the man Joanne Kenarden had described,
Darren wasn't circumcised. What had seemed a simple
enough proposition had taught him just how leery the
medical profession is of the legal profession. Darren's
own doctor refused, as did at least twenty others contacted
by his family or by Jaywalker. Several declined because
the defense couldn't afford to pay them enough for their
time, with some of their demands running well into four
figures. But most stated candidly that no amount of money
could induce them to testify, about any matter. A few
offered to sign letters or even affidavits, but those would
have been inadmissible as hearsay, inasmuch as the doctors themselves wouldn't have been available for cross-
examination. At one point Jaywalker had been ready to

give up and ask Pope to concede the point and stipulate to it. But he much preferred the idea of a live witness, for the impact he felt it would have upon the jury.

In the end, he'd had to impose upon a personal friend. The evening before, in the makeshift examining room of Jaywalker's study, George Goddard had come over and examined Darren. Then he'd managed to cram a full day's schedule into a morning, and driven from his office in Livingston, New Jersey, to the Bronx.

As he now began by asking Dr. Goddard to state his credentials, Jaywalker felt that the jurors couldn't help but be impressed. A graduate of Dartmouth College and Harvard Medical School, Dr. Goddard had interned at Bellevue and Columbia Presbyterian hospitals, completed residencies at both places, and studied under a fellowship at Mount Sinai. He was board certified and licensed in both New York and New Jersey.

The remainder of Jaywalker's examination was predictably brief.

JAYWALKER: Have you had occasion to examine the defendant, Darren Kingston?

GODDARD: Yes, I have.

JAYWALKER: And having conducted that examination, can you tell us, to a degree of medical certainty, whether or not Darren Kingston is circumcised?

GODDARD: He is not circumcised.

JAYWALKER: Is there any doubt in your mind?

GODDARD: None whatsoever.

Jaywalker hadn't expected there to be any cross-examination, but Pope surprised him. He asked Dr. Goddard to describe the difference between a circumcised penis and an uncircumcised one. Then he tried to suggest that although a doctor could distinguish between the two, a layperson might have difficulty.

POPE: If you were a nonmedical person, there would be a greater difficulty in determining whether or not Darren Kingston was circumcised. Is that correct?

GODDARD: I don't think it would be very difficult. He happens to have a long foreskin.

Still Pope pressed on. First he got Dr. Goddard to concede that it might be more difficult for a layperson to make the determination seeing a penis only in its erect state. Never mind that Jaywalker had gotten Joanne Kenarden to say that she'd seen her attacker's penis both erect and flaccid. Then Pope broke new ground in the annals of disguise, by asking if it would be possible for an uncircumcised person to pull back his foreskin, in order to appear circumcised. To this suggestion, Dr. Goddard acknowledged that it might be possible, though rather unlikely, and perhaps even quite painful.

As he stepped down from the stand, Jaywalker stood and announced that Dr. Goddard had been his final witness. The defense rested.

Pope, however, indicated that he had rebuttal witnesses to call, and that they weren't immediately available. Justice Davidoff gave him until the following morning to produce them. Then he recessed.

If Jaywalker's witnesses had come off well enough, not one of them had been able to provide an alibi for Darren. The closest thing to that had been supplied by a single sheet of paper from the post office. As for the witnesses themselves, however well-meaning and earnest they'd been, they'd also been pretty much family and friends, two groups that jurors were often quick to disregard. Even if he'd scored a few points here and there during the defense case, he was painfully aware that the potential for disaster was still there. And now Pope was promising just that.

It would be a long, sleepless night. For a change.

16

THE OTHER MAN

On Thursday morning, just before the jury was brought into the courtroom to resume the trial, Jacob Pope asked to approach the bench for a conference. There, in his usual businesslike voice, he announced that something had come up that might prove beneficial to the defense. He couldn't say what it was until he checked it out, and it would take him the rest of the day to do so. But he assured Jaywalker that whatever it was, at the very least it couldn't hurt the defense. When Jaywalker pressed him for more detail, he wouldn't budge, except to repeat that the defendant had everything to gain and nothing to lose.

"You've found the real rapist," said Jaywalker.

"I can't say anything more yet," was the best Pope would do. But even his refusal to tell Jaywalker that he was way off with his guess seemed pregnant with possibility. And Justice Davidoff was no help. He declined Jaywalker's request that he compel Pope to disclose what was going on.

Jaywalker walked back to the defense table and explained the situation to Darren, who reacted with visible excitement. They agreed to go along with Pope's request. Justice Davidoff called for the jury. He told them that certain legal matters had come up that didn't concern them but required that he excuse them for the day. He instructed them to return the following morning, Friday, at ten o'clock. Whispering among themselves, the jurors filed out of the courtroom. Perhaps they were every bit as intrigued by the latest development as Jaywalker and Darren were. More likely their enthusiasm was over the prospect of a free day to go shopping or sit in front of their television sets.

Out in the corridor, Jaywalker tried to pry some hint out of Pope, without success. The prosecutor did promise to let them know what was going on as soon as he'd had an opportunity to check it out. Then he excused himself, walked away, and joined a cluster of people that included two detective types and a pair of young women in their late teens or early twenties.

Jaywalker tried to contain his excitement as he and Darren discussed the matter with the Kingston family downstairs. Something had obviously happened, or was happening, or was about to happen. Either they'd found the real rapist, or another attack had occurred that bore his signature. And it couldn't have been Darren, because this time Darren had the best alibi of all time: he'd been sitting in court.

Whatever it was, it could only be good. Even in his secrecy, Pope had said enough to hint that he was now on their side. Justice was about to be done. Darren was about to be rescued. And if Darren was about to be rescued, so was Jaywalker.

* * *

Friday.

Jaywalker arrived in court so early that he had to wait for the doors to be unlocked. Fueled by pure adrenaline, he'd slept two hours, if that. And he was only the lawyer; he couldn't begin to fathom what Darren was going through.

But the suspense was to be continued.

Pope informed them that he was still awaiting further developments and asked that the case be put over once more, until Monday morning. Again he gave solemn assurances that the delay was in the interest of justice and could only benefit the defense. Jaywalker said he was prepared to agree to the continuance, but that fundamental fairness required their being told what was going on. *Fundamental* and *fairness* are two words that appellate courts tend to use a lot when reversing convictions, and Jaywalker's use of them was no accident. This time, after thinking about it for a moment, Justice Davidoff agreed.

Reluctantly, Pope complied. Measuring his words carefully, he prefaced his remarks by stating that he himself had no doubts about the case. But Jaywalker's insistence on his client's innocence had prompted the district attorney's office to continue surveillance in the Castle Hill area, even as the trial progressed. Over the past several days, Pope had been receiving reports that a young black man had been seen hanging around the project, acting suspiciously. Preliminary indications were that he closely resembled Darren Kingston. Pope wanted to continue the surveillance a bit longer. If the man made a move, he could be arrested on the spot. If he didn't, he would still be picked up and brought in, so that the defense could see him. Perhaps a lineup could even be arranged for the victims to view.

Jaywalker's heart pounded as he took all this in. He was immediately skeptical about the lineup; the victims were by now convinced it was Darren who'd raped them and would continue to identify him. But as far as having this new suspect watched and brought in, they certainly had nothing to lose from that.

"Have you thought about setting up a decoy operation?" he asked. Why wait for the man to pick out a victim, after all, when a young female officer could be enlisted for the role and sent in, backed up by an undercover surveillance team?

"Why don't we leave it to the professionals?" was Pope's response to the suggestion.

Jaywalker bit his tongue and said nothing. Never mind that he'd *been* one of the professionals not too long ago, making multikilogram undercover purchases of heroin and cocaine for the Drug Enforcement Administration. This was Pope's show, and he didn't want to do anything to derail it. He readily agreed to the requested continuance, and the judge granted it.

If the jurors had been curious about the first postponement, now they looked truly mystified as they were told for the second time in as many days that they would be hearing no testimony. Justice Davidoff instructed them not to speculate about the reason and sent them home for the weekend.

Again Jaywalker huddled with the Kingstons, sharing with them everything Pope had said earlier. They left the courthouse seeming cautiously optimistic. The optimism, of course, came from the news of the "other man." The caution came from Jaywalker and, he guessed, from their own reluctance to trust in something that seemed too good to be true. Perhaps they'd suffered too many disappointments already: the arrest, the arraignment identification, the high bail, the indictment, the many polygraph frustrations, the severance decision, the racial composition of the jury, and the continuing certainty of the victims that it had been Darren who'd attacked them. If their faces wore expressions that translated as "We'll believe it when it happens," Jaywalker could hardly blame them.

As for Jaywalker, he drove home filled with a strange mix of emotions. He took comfort, and even a measure of pride, from the notion that Pope had, at least to a certain extent, made Jaywalker's doubts his own. It renewed his faith in Pope, and in the system. Beyond that, he was thrilled that the detectives might be onto the real rapist. He knew in his heart that the man was still out there somewhere. And more than anything else, he wanted Darren's nightmare to end.

Yet for all that, Jaywalker was also aware that there was a part of him that wanted to be the hero. Not Jacob Pope. Not some detective. *Him,* Jaywalker. *He* wanted to win this. He didn't want his role to be reduced to that of a bystander when the case got solved.

He turned on the AM radio of his old VW. An AM-FM upgrade would have cost him another fifty bucks, and tape decks, CD players and iPods hadn't even been born yet. He gave the thing a hard rap to get it working. He wanted to drown out the voice of his own ego, needed to remind himself that this wasn't about him. When it came right down to it, it didn't matter *how* Darren got off, it only mattered that he *did.* The radio finally warmed up, and the single station that worked on it came to life. Through the static and the whine of the engine, Jaywalker could just make out the throaty voice of Carly Simon.

You're so vain,
I bet you think this song is about you.
You're so vain.

17

LOW BLOWS

Any threat to Jaywalker's ego ended promptly at ten o'clock Monday morning. Pope announced that he had the "suspect" in his office, for Jaywalker to view and interview, if he wished. He added that he was certain the man wasn't the rapist and thought Jaywalker would agree as soon as he saw him. Together they walked down to his office, prosecutor and defender. Allies for a moment, but about to become adversaries again.

The young man did in fact look something like Darren. He was a light- to medium-skinned black man, about Darren's height, and slightly heavier. He'd been told why he was being picked up, and he'd agreed to come in voluntarily, without protest. And the reason was plain to see. On the man's right forearm was a prominent tattoo, an elaborate serpent-and-sword affair that could hardly have been missed by the victims of a man wearing a short-sleeved shirt. Pope said he'd double-checked with his witnesses to make certain, and none of them recalled a tattoo. And it wasn't new, because a check of the man's criminal record had turned up a 1974 arrest, complete with a description that included the tattoo. As to what the man had been doing "acting suspiciously" in the area, he had a logical explanation for that, too. But by that time, Jaywalker was no longer listening.

He felt like he'd been kicked in the gut. Here it was, ten o'clock in the morning, and already he was totally exhausted. He barely heard Pope asking him whether he wanted to pursue the matter further. The second time he was asked, he shook his head slowly, then followed Pope back to the courtroom. Somewhere along the way, he managed to thank him for trying.

Back in the courtroom, Jaywalker's gratitude quickly evaporated when Pope announced that he intended to call the young man as a witness. He wanted to demonstrate to the jury just how hard the district attorney's office had worked to insure that they had put the right man on trial.

Jaywalker all but exploded. Making sure they were trying the right man was one of the duties of a prosecutor, he argued, and Pope deserved no extra credit in the eyes of the jury for doing his job. It was Darren Kingston who was on trial, not the Bronx County District Attorney's office, and calling the young man served no legitimate purpose whatsoever.

For once, Justice Davidoff sided with Jaywalker. Pope seemed so surprised and rebuffed by the ruling that Jaywalker found himself reevaluating his adversary's motives. He began to wonder if Pope had looked upon this "other man" business all along as nothing but an opportunity to do a little grandstanding and win some points with the jury.

To this day, he really doesn't know.

* * *

Finally accepting the judge's ruling, Pope indicated that he was ready to proceed with his rebuttal case. It was close to eleven o'clock by the time the jurors were brought in, no doubt wondering what surprise was in store for them next. But the surprise was to be Jaywalker's.

Pope called Tania Maldonado.

Jaywalker was on his feet asking to approach the bench before the witness made it through the door. There he reminded Justice Davidoff that Tania Maldonado was one of the victims whose case he himself had ordered severed, to be tried separately. Now Pope was trying to bring in Miss Maldonado—and presumably Elvira Caldwell, as well—to rebut Darren's testimony that, except for one visit with John McCarthy, he hadn't been in the Castle Hill area in years. And Pope was seeking to do it by placing Darren there on August 17th and September 5th, the dates of the Maldonado and Caldwell attacks.

Pope argued that Jaywalker had "opened the door" by putting the defendant on the witness stand and having him deny his presence in the area. But it had been *Pope* who'd elicited the denial, Jaywalker told the judge, through his own questions on cross-examination. That amounted to setting up a "straw man" for patently impermissible rebuttal. Jaywalker was shooting from the hip a bit here, making up his argument as he went along. But Pope's tactic struck him as yet another in a series of low blows. If permitted to get away with what he was proposing, Pope was now going to be allowed to parade two more victims in front of the jury—when the judge had already ruled that the unfair prejudice from that would be so great that it would deprive the defendant of a fair trial.

Pope acted as though he was surprised by Jaywalker's objection. All he intended to do, he assured the judge, was to ask each witness in turn if she'd seen the defendant in the area on a particular day. He didn't plan on going into what had happened.

Jaywalker pointed out to Justice Davidoff that permitting Pope to ask these other two victims *anything* would put the defense in an impossible position. If Jaywalker chose to cross-examine them as to their ability to meaningfully identify Darren, all the circumstances of their confrontations with him would come out, including the fact that they, too, claimed to have been among his victims. When the judge had ruled that that was too much for a single jury to handle, what sort of relief had he meant to give the defense? A trial where Jaywalker couldn't possibly put his client on the witness stand to deny his guilt?

Again a sports metaphor came to his mind. Watch a baseball or basketball game for a while. The umpires and referees do a terrific job. But every so often, they blow a call, whether it's a ball versus a strike, or a defensive foul versus an offensive charge. And the fans—and these days the miracle of instant replay—are quick to let them know. So what happens a minute or two later? The *payback call,* that's what. The same official makes an equally bad call, only this time against the team that unfairly benefited from the first one. Moral? It all evens out in the end.

Now, as Jaywalker heard Justice Davidoff ruling against him, *payback* came to mind. Pope would be allowed to ask the two additional victims what he proposed. Jaywalker could cross-examine or not, as he chose. But if he did, the judge explained, then both sides would be free to explore the full circumstances of the incidents.

But if this was indeed payback for the earlier call, in which Justice Davidoff had refused to allow Pope to call the "other man" only minutes ago, didn't the judge realize how different the two matters were? The first had been a no-brainer; *of course* Pope had no right to show how thorough his office was. But this second ruling—allowing Pope to set Darren up during cross-examination, just so he could bring in victims three and four on rebuttal—was nothing short of devastating to Darren's chances of getting a fair trial. It was tantamount to correcting a trivial ball-or-strike call by saying a game-ending home run hit by the other team the following inning had landed in foul territory.

As a last resort, Jaywalker demanded a Wade hearing as to the identifications of the two rebuttal witnesses, reminding Justice Davidoff that he'd been deprived of one only because of the severance. But here again, the judge said no, unless Jaywalker were to commit in advance to cross-examining the witnesses. That caveat struck Jaywalker as bordering on the bizarre. If a witness is going to point out a defendant at trial, that fact alone entitles the defense to explore, in the absence of the jury, any prior identifications—lineups, photographs, whatever—that the witness has previously made of the defendant. Tania Maldonado, Jaywalker knew for a fact, had been one of the three victims who'd come across Darren's photo together and had subsequently selected it from an array. Who knew what prior identification procedures Elvira Caldwell had been put through?

But the judge had made his ruling, and he made it clear that he wasn't about to change it. Jaywalker thought about his options for a moment, but only a moment. There was simply no way he could open up the trial to two more incidents. Better to highlight the impact of Justice Davidoff's ruling by declining to cross-examine the additional victims. That way, at least, there would be a nice, clean issue preserved for appeal, in the event of a conviction. And that event was suddenly looming larger than ever.

Jaywalker told Justice Davidoff that until he'd heard the direct testimony of the rebuttal witnesses, there was no way he could state with honesty whether or not he intended to cross-examine them. With that, the judge denied his request for a Wade hearing and told Pope he would be permitted to proceed as he wished. Jaywalker sat down heavily, feeling as though he'd taken a knee to the gut, or perhaps slightly lower.

Tania Maldonado was finally permitted to enter the courtroom. Jaywalker recognized her as one of the two young women who'd been standing with the detectives last Thursday. The other one, of course, must have been Elvira Caldwell. The jurors, who hadn't seen or heard anything for four days now, swung their heads toward her in heightened anticipation. What they saw was yet another young woman, very young, very pretty—and very white.

Jaywalker sat back, took a deep breath, and steeled himself for the worst. It wouldn't help.

POPE: How old are you, Miss Maldonado?

MALDONADO: Seventeen.

POPE: Do you work, or do you go to school?

MALDONADO: Both. I work, and I go to school.

POPE: What grade are you in?

MALDONADO: I'm in the eleventh grade.

Pope zeroed in on August 17th. He established that the witness had been entering a particular building of the Castle Hill Houses sometime in the early afternoon. He had her point out the building on his chart, for the jurors to see.

POPE: Miss Maldonado, when you were inside that building, did you see anyone else?

MALDONADO: Yes.

POPE: Was that a male or a female?

MALDONADO: Male.

POPE: Miss Maldonado, do you see that person in the courtroom today?

MALDONADO: Yes, I do.

POPE: Would you please point him out.

Without a moment's hesitation, Tania Maldonado pointed directly at Darren.

POPE: Is there any doubt in your mind that this is the person who was with you that day?

MALDONADO: No.

POPE: No further questions, Your Honor.

There didn't have to be. In deliberately using the words *who was with you,* rather than *whom you saw,* Pope had conveyed to the jury the full meaning of his rebuttal case. Now, as Jaywalker stood to question this witness whom he didn't dare question, he felt as though he was carrying an extra five hundred pounds on his shoulders.

JAYWALKER: Miss Maldonado, before August seventeenth, how many times do you say you had seen this man?

MALDONADO: I didn't see him before.

JAYWALKER: And since August seventeenth, when is the last time you say you saw him?

MALDONADO: I didn't see him again.

JAYWALKER: Until today.

MALDONADO: Yes.

JAYWALKER: You haven't seen him between last August seventeenth and today, March fourth?

MALDONADO: That's right.

Jaywalker quit right there, before getting into real trouble. But he knew there was no way the jury could make any sense of her testimony, other than to conclude that she had to have been a third victim.

With a fourth to come.

POPE: How old are you, Miss Caldwell?

CALDWELL: I'm seventeen years old.

POPE: Do you got to school?

CALDWELL: Yes, I do.

As before, Pope had the witness give her address and then locate it on the diagram for the jury. It, too, was in the Castle Hill project.

POPE: Were you in that building on September fifth, nineteen-seventy-nine, at about two or two-thirty in the afternoon?

CALDWELL: Yes.

POPE: Was there anyone else with you at that time?

CALDWELL: Yes.

POPE: Was that a male or a female?

CALDWELL: A male.

POPE: Do you see that male in the courtroom?

CALDWELL: Yes, I do.

POPE: Would you point him out, please?

And just as Eleanor Cerami had, just as Joanne Kenarden had, and just as Tania Maldonado had done only minutes earlier, Elvira Caldwell pointed her finger directly at Darren Kingston.

CALDWELL: He's right there.

POPE: No further questions.

Jaywalker brought out, as he had with the previous witness, that Miss Caldwell hadn't seen the man before or since. Short of questioning her about the incident itself, he simply couldn't think of anything else to ask her. Even an innocuous "And yet you can say you're sure it's him?" would have flung the door open for Pope to come back on redirect and ask her how close she'd been to him, where they'd been, how long they'd been there, what had been going on, and what it was that caused her to remember him so well. That, of course, was the catch-22 of Justice Davidoff's ruling.

So Jaywalker could do nothing but give up at that point and sit down. That, and pick up a stray paper clip, pry it open and dig one end of it beneath his thumbnail until the blood ran bright red.

Pope announced that he had no further rebuttal witnesses and rested once again. The judge swung his gaze to the defense table. Jaywalker leaned over toward Darren and muttered under his breath, "Fuck me if we're going to end on that note." It came out a little louder than he'd planned. Or maybe not. At that point, he didn't much care.

Then he asked for a recess.

Outside the courtroom, Jaywalker told Darren he was going to put him back on the witness stand. He didn't even bother telling him what he was going to ask him. For one thing, he was too angry to talk, too angry to think straight. But there was no need to rehearse. So convinced was Jaywalker of his client's innocence that he knew there was simply no way Darren could screw up. He might not be the smartest witness who ever testified, or the most eloquent. But every last word he'd ever said about the charges against him was true. And nothing Jaywalker or Pope or anyone else might ever ask him could possibly trip him up, because he had nothing to hide, nothing to trip up over.

But if Jaywalker didn't want to talk, Darren did. "It l-l-looks bad, huh, Jay," he said.

"Well," Jaywalker admitted, "I don't like it. But right now, there isn't too much we can do about it."

It was the truth. And Darren's rebuttal testimony a few minutes later would do little to erase the damage that had been done.

JAYWALKER: Darren, the two witnesses who've just testified. Have you ever seen either of them before today?

DARREN: No, I haven't.

JAYWALKER: Except for that one trip with the investigator, when is the last time you were in the Castle Hill project area?

DARREN: N-n-nineteen-seventy-five, nineteen-seventy-six.

JAYWALKER: Did you see Tania Maldonado on August seventeenth of last year?

DARREN: No.

JAYWALKER: Did you see Elvira Caldwell on September fifth of last year?

DARREN: No.

JAYWALKER: Is there any doubt in your mind?

DARREN: No, absolutely no doubt at all.

Pope asked no questions. It was his way of telling the jurors that Darren's denials were so self-serving that they didn't even need to be dealt with.

Jaywalker rose to announce that the defense was resting. He tried his best to sound triumphant, but he knew he wasn't fooling anyone. Justice Davidoff recessed until the afternoon for summations. Jaywalker sent Darren and his family to lunch, and headed for the library.

The summation, or closing argument, is generally considered the single most important part of any trial. As imperfect as Jaywalker's courtroom skills were back at the time of Darren Kingston's trial, he was already accomplished in the art of arguing to the jury at the end of the case. Sure, there were better orators, lawyers with more years of experience in the trenches, more tricks in their bags and more booming voices. But summing up isn't just about emoting or drawing on experience or being clever, or even about which lawyer has the deepest, most resonant voice.

Summing up is about taking everything that happens during the course of a trial and making sense of it for the jury to see, understand and finally be persuaded by. Months before the first prospective juror walked into the courtroom where the case of *The People of the State of New York versus Darren Kingston* would be tried, Jaywalker had already been working on his summation. Even as Darren sat in a cell on Rikers Island, waiting for his father to come and post his bail, Jaywalker was creating a file with two words inked on the jacket. SUMMATION NOTES, it read. It had contained only a scribble or two back then. But as Jaywalker had learned more about the case, paragraphs were added, and then pages. John McCarthy's investigation had contributed facts, and those facts in turn had bred ideas. If called upon to do so, Jaywalker could have delivered his summation long before the trial began. That was how well he knew the case, and how well he knew he would argue it to the jury when the time came.

Then, as actual witnesses had begun taking the stand and testifying, as exhibits were admitted into evidence and stipulations read, the file grew thicker. And in every spare moment, Jaywalker was constantly reading it, reviewing it, tweaking it, until he knew everything that was in it, forward and backward, inside and out. There were times when, driving home from the Bronx at the end of a trial day, he would catch himself trying out a phrase here, an expression there. Sometimes he would arrive home with no memory of the trip at all, save for what he'd been telling the jurors. That he survived the daily commute was more a product of providence or dumb luck than any concentration on his part.

It was the same with every trial, until finally, the evening before he expected to sum up, when his daughter was asleep, his wife smart enough to find someplace to hide, and the house was quiet enough, he would sit himself down at the kitchen table and work into the night, putting it all together. If he got to bed by two or three, he considered himself ahead of the game, knowing that pure adrenaline would get him through the rest of the day.

Although he could deliver an opening statement without notes—and always would, even as his openings grew over the years from perfunctory to protracted—Jaywalker didn't dare sum up without having something on paper in front of him. There was simply too much he needed to say, and the danger of omitting something important was too great to leave to chance. But he would never write out a summation word for word or anything close to it. Instead, he would reduce his notes to topics, and from there to key words. The blanks, which were anything but blank in his mind, he would fill in as he spoke. Jurors want to be persuaded, after all, not read to.

And as much as the process consumed him and drained him, Jaywalker absolutely loved it. For him, summing up was not only the most important part of the trial, it was by far the most exciting. It was every bit as intoxicating as it was exhausting. It was Hamlet's *"To be, or not to be,"* Othello's lament, Lear's rage. It was Clarence Darrow, literally fighting for Leopold and Loeb's lives. It was Gregory Peck's closing prayer to the jury in *To Kill a Mockingbird:* "For God's sake, do your duty."

But most of all, it was Jaywalker himself.

More than any other part of the process, the final argument represented Jaywalker's chance to inject himself into the struggle on a primal level, to stand up and place himself squarely between the jury and the defendant, and to say to them loudly and clearly, "Before you dare convict my client, you must come through me."

So it became intensely personal, this business of summing up, and Jaywalker would have had it no other way. It was about acceptance or rejection. There were those who'd likened a trial to a search for the truth. They were as wrong as wrong could be. The truth was something that had happened long ago and far away, and could never be recreated in a courtroom. Not with all the American flags and In-God-We-Trusts in the world. A trial was a battle, a war, a struggle to the death. One side won, the other lost.

In Darren Kingston's case, that was truer than ever. Here was a young man whom Jaywalker believed—no, *knew*—to be innocent. Yet a quartet of honest witnesses had come into court with absolutely nothing to gain by lying and everything to gain by telling the truth. Each of them in turn had placed one hand on a Bible, then raised the other hand, and in a solemn voice had sworn to tell the truth, the whole truth and nothing but the truth, so help her God. And then they had. *Their* truth. The only thing was, they'd all been wrong. Darren knew that. His family knew that. His lawyer knew that. But there were twelve people who didn't. Not yet, anyway. Now was Jaywalker's last clear chance to make them know that, too.

18

THREE PITIFUL WEAPONS

It was just after three o'clock when Jaywalker rose to address the jury. By the time he would sit down, it would be a little after four. Many, if not most, lawyers would have spoken longer. In the years to follow, Jaywalker himself would deliver many lengthier summations, including a three-and-a-half-hour personal longest in defense of a Korean merchant who set off a boycott in Flatbush. But that was a complicated case. This one, at least in terms of the issue, was a simple one. Either the evidence proved beyond all reasonable doubt that Darren Kingston was the man who'd raped Eleanor Cerami and Joanne Kenarden, or it didn't. And Jaywalker's appraisal of the jurors was that their collective attention span was limited. The last thing he wanted was to see them begin to fidget, yawn, glance at their watches and doze off.

He began in a conversational tone, reminding them of several predictions he'd made to them as early as jury selection, almost two weeks ago. Both victims had indeed been raped, he'd told them, and by the same man. Both had

had lengthy opportunities to observe their rapist. Both would point out Darren. And both would say they were absolutely certain. If the jurors chose to make their job quick and easy, the case could end right there. But the fact was, that was where the case began. Under the American system of justice, deliberations are conducted and verdicts are delivered not by witnesses, but by jurors. Jurors just like them.

Jacob Pope, in his opening statement, had compared a trial to a puzzle and had suggested that as the jurors got toward the end of it, they might discover they were missing a few pieces but that they would have enough to see the whole picture. Now Jaywalker picked up on the metaphor and challenged the jury to take a good hard look at the missing pieces with him, and try to make sense of them.

First, he told them, they needed to recall that both victims had described how the man had unscrewed the overhead lightbulbs. When he'd done so, he hadn't been wearing gloves or using anything else to do it with. Detective Rendell had come along later the same day and had removed a number of bulbs. All of them had been tested for the presence of latent fingerprints. In fact, only prints "of no value" had been found on them. Translated into plain English, that could only mean they'd tried to match them with Darren Kingston's prints and couldn't.

In fact, there was absolutely no physical evidence that pointed at Darren. Not one piece of scientific or medical proof. Not one sperm that could be shown to have come from him. Nothing found on him that connected him to the victims or to the crime scenes. No blood, no hair, no clothing fibers. No knife. Nothing, absolutely nothing.

Each of those things was what the prosecution might—in an attempt to gloss over and minimize their significance—call missing pieces. But there was more, much more. Far more significant than the pieces that were merely *missing* from the puzzle were the pieces left on the table that *didn't fit*.

There was Darren's chipped front tooth. There was the scar that ran clear through one of his eyebrows. The victims spent fifteen to twenty minutes with the man who raped them. He was directly in front of them, *on top of them*. He spoke to them, and they to him, making eye contact. Yet neither of them ever saw a chipped front tooth or a scar clear through an eyebrow. Those weren't just missing pieces. Those were pieces the jurors had in front of them, and they were pieces that simply didn't fit in this puzzle.

Next, he told them, there's the right-handed or left-handed piece. Ordinarily, that wouldn't be a big deal. We all know that whether they're right-handed or left-handed, most people can perform tasks like holding a knife or unscrewing a lightbulb with either hand. So the fact that both witnesses say their rapist used his right hand to do these things is *suggestive* of right-handedness but hardly *conclusive*. But there's more. Mrs. Cerami is absolutely certain and absolutely specific in terms of what she remembers about the man, and here it is. He held the knife against her with his right hand, until it came time to unscrew the overhead lightbulb. And what did he do then? Did he reach up with his free left hand? No! He took the trouble of switching the knife from his right hand to his left, in order to free up his right hand to loosen the bulb. That, members of the jury, is the unmistakable signature of a right-handed person.

And Darren Kingston, this man here? We know for an

absolute fact that he's left-handed. How do we know it? We know it because he tells us, because his mother tells us, because his wife tells us, because his left-handed Phil Rizzuto glove tells us, and because even Mr. Pope tells us when he *stipulates* to the fact, conceding it to be true. So there's another piece of the puzzle that you have in front of you, another piece that *doesn't fit.*

Jaywalker had a couple of bigger pieces that didn't fit, but ever mindful of the relay-race strategy, he wanted to save them for last. So he turned to the descriptions provided by the victims shortly following their attacks, when their memories were most vivid. Both, he said, had described a man five or ten years older than Darren, and twenty-five to thirty-five pounds heavier. Both now tell you that it's Darren, but he must have lost weight since then. But the fact is, he hasn't. He still weighs the same. Those things aren't missing, *they don't fit.*

There was the shirt described by the victims. When the police had gone to Darren's home to arrest him, they'd looked through his clothing. No such shirt. Even his sneakers were of a different cut and color than those described by the victims. And the odor of alcohol on the rapist's breath. Even assuming that Darren had gotten off his shift at the post office and, instead of going home to sleep at nine or ten in the morning, had gone out to drink and rape, he didn't drink wine, the specific odor reported by Miss Kenarden. On those rare occasions when Darren did drink, he drank Seagram's V.O., a blended whiskey that smells nothing like wine.

Jaywalker took a step back. He told the jurors he didn't want them to get the idea that he was attacking the victims. They'd been raped. About that, there could be no doubt.

But they'd been raped by someone other than Darren, someone who wasn't in the courtroom today. "Who knows?" said Jaywalker. "Perhaps it was the man Yvette Monroe saw that day in Nedicks—"

"Nathan's," corrected a juror.

"Nathan's, thank you."

Jaywalker was elated. Not only were they listening to his every word, they were *helping* him. It was every lawyer's dream. *He had them.*

He moved on to the geography of the case, how it would have taken Darren an hour or more to travel to Castle Hill by subway and bus. How Pope had tried to make that piece fit by showing that Darren had an uncle who lived near the project. But the defense had brought that uncle into court, Jaywalker reminded the jurors. Samuel Kingston recalled that the last time Darren had visited him was with the rest of his family, four or five Thanksgivings ago, and that Darren had no key to the place and never had.

It was time for the three biggest pieces of all, the *anchormen* Jaywalker would rely upon for a final kick to the finish line.

First, there was the stutter. The victims had been with their attacker for fifteen or twenty minutes. Both said he'd talked constantly. Yet neither one had reported anything remotely resembling a stutter, either to the police officers who responded to their homes, to Detective Rendell, to Jacob Pope or to the jury.

Darren stuttered. He always had; no doubt he always would. As was the case with his left-handedness, the jurors didn't have to take Jaywalker's word for it, or even Darren's word. "You have his mother's word," he told them, "his wife's word, his boss's word. You have Detective Rendell's word. You have a lifetime of speech classes. You have a draft card, with an official notation on it. But most of all, you know Darren stutters because you heard it with your own ears. And you know it's real." He touched on Pope's theory, that the stutter only showed up during periods of stress and would have been absent during the rapes. "That," said Jaywalker, "is nonsense, pseudopsychology." Today, he would have used the phrase *junk science.* Or, if he was really on a roll, *bullshit.*

The second huge piece that didn't fit into the puzzle was the fact—and it *was* a fact—that the rapist was circumcised. Again, Pope had tried to confuse the issue. He'd tried to get Dr. Goddard to say that it would be hard for an ordinary person to tell in the case of a penis that was erect. He'd even gone so far as to suggest that a man would pull back his foreskin, as some sort of attempt to *disguise* the fact that he wasn't circumcised. This from a man, mind you, who'd made no attempt whatsoever to hide his *face.* But Dr. Goddard had stood firm in his testimony. Not only was Darren *un*circumcised, his foreskin was long. And pulling it back would have been difficult and probably quite painful. "As to the business about the victims' only seeing their attacker's penis when it was erect," said Jaywalker, "check the testimony. Joanne Kenarden said she saw his penis both when it was erect and *before it was erect.* So there's another piece that, no matter how you turn it, no matter how you try to twist it and squeeze it and reshape it, *it just doesn't fit.* Why? Because it's from some other puzzle. It's about some other man."

Jaywalker was now down to the final piece: Eleanor Cerami's claim, no doubt true, that she'd seen her attacker a second time. The jurors could forget about a third time;

she'd been mistaken about that. How did they know? Because Detective Rendell had cleared it up for them, that's how.

Mrs. Cerami had testified that when she'd seen the man again, she'd been absolutely certain it was him. "In fact," said Jaywalker, "she told you she was as certain about that as she was in pointing out Darren Kingston as the man who'd attacked her. Only she was wrong. And you and I now know that for a fact.

"Eleanor Cerami isn't sure exactly when she saw her attacker for a second time. She knows it was about nine-thirty in the morning, and she's pretty sure it was a Monday. What she knows for sure is that she got to a phone and called Detective Rendell right away. It turns out Detective Rendell wasn't in. It happened to be his day off. So all Mrs. Cerami could do was leave a message for him. Well, Detective Rendell got that message, and he got it the very same day. And *he* knows the date. It was September seventeenth, which was indeed a Monday. In fact, after returning Mrs. Cerami's call, Rendell phoned Mr. Pope to tell him about the incident. And when he phoned Mr. Pope, it was *still* Monday, September seventeenth. So there can be absolutely no doubt about the date, the day of the week or the time."

Jaywalker paused for a moment. He liked leaving things for the jurors themselves to figure out. But this one was too important to leave up in the air. Dropping his voice so low that they had to lean forward to hear him, he posed the question that lay at the very heart of the case. "Where," he asked them, "was Darren Kingston at nine-thirty in the morning on Monday, September seventeenth? It turns out he was at the United States Post Office, Gracie Station, on

East Eighty-fifth Street, in Manhattan. Miles away. Hours away.

"Once again, you don't have to take Darren's word for it, although by now you should. But you can take Delroid Kingston's word. You can take Andrew Emmons's word. You can take George Riley's word. You can take P. G. Hamilton's word. And if none of that's good enough for you, you can read the fact from an official United States Post Office document. It's in evidence. And it proves exactly where Darren Kingston was at the moment Eleanor Cerami was watching her rapist walk through her lobby."

Jaywalker reminded the jury that, as defense counsel, he didn't have to prove or disprove anything. That was the job of the prosecution. Yet with that document, and all the circumstances surrounding it, he'd proved—and proved beyond any shadow of a doubt—that as horrible as the rapes had been, the wrong man was on trial.

He asked the jurors to put themselves in Darren's shoes for just a moment. For him, the case had begun the instant his mother had phoned him and told him the police were looking for him. "What does he do?" Jaywalker asked. "He waits right there for them. He accompanies them to the precinct, where, for the first time he hears that he's being accused of committing rapes that happened a month earlier. And his nightmare begins.

"He doesn't concoct some phony alibi for you. He doesn't ask his family to lie for him about where he was back on August sixteenth. He was home in bed, having worked the night shift, just as he did and does, five nights a week. But because he was home in bed alone, his nightmare continues.

"He pleads not guilty, and he asks for a trial. He asks

that twelve fellow citizens from the Bronx be drawn at random to judge him. He comes to court. Not in some fancy suit and tie, to impress you. No, he comes as who he is. A son, a husband, a father, a breadwinner. He brings with him three pitiful weapons and one absolutely magnificent one. The three pitiful weapons are his draft card, his sneakers and his Phil Rizzuto baseball mitt. The magnificent one is the truth.

"He takes the witness stand. And every word he tells you is the truth. On direct examination, on cross-examination, and on rebuttal. And the best the prosecution can do is to question him about a two-dollar larceny case that was dismissed a year and a half ago. And accuse him of stuttering more than usual because he's under stress.

"Yet because of his work schedule, because he was home in bed alone when somebody raped these young women, Darren has no way of ending his nightmare. He simply doesn't have the power. Because his family members weren't with him, they can't end his nightmare for him. Nor," Jaywalker confessed, "can I. In another minute, I'll sit down. My job will be done. There will be nothing else I can do or say. Not even Justice Davidoff can end Darren's nightmare. He's the judge of the law in this case, but not the judge of the facts.

"So who's left to deliver Darren from his nightmare?" Jaywalker asked, his voice cracking, almost gone. "Only you. You are the judges of the facts. You've heard the evidence, seen the exhibits and listened to the stipulations. You've seen the pieces that fit, and you've seen the pieces that don't fit. The power is yours, and yours alone, to deliver this innocent young man from his nightmare. And the duty is yours, as well. Be the jury you promised to be.

Exercise that power. Do that duty. Darren Kingston is every bit as innocent of these crimes as you and I are. Tell us that. Tell us that with your verdict."

Jaywalker wanted to thank them, but his voice had quit on him, and the last drop of adrenaline had been squeezed from his veins. He opened his mouth one last time, but no sound came out. Hoping they understood, he nodded at them, walked back to his chair at the defense table and sat down.

Jaywalker knew only too well that if there was one advantage that outweighs all others at a trial, it was having the last word. Handled properly, that advantage could often tip the scales toward a conviction in a close case. Misused, it can backfire. The inexperienced prosecutor, who devotes his summation to rebutting his adversary's final argument, not only wastes his opportunity, he highlights and reinforces the defense lawyer's points, often leading to an acquittal.

Jacob Pope established right away that he knew what he was doing. "You are not here," he told the jury, "to deliver anyone from a nightmare. You are not here to use sympathy. You are here to decide, from what you heard on the witness stand, whether or not this man, Darren Kingston, raped two women on August sixteenth, nineteen-seventy-nine.

"We are talking about two very vicious, brutal crimes—rape and oral sodomy. They are not like robbery or burglary. They involve a violation of the person, the individual."

From there, Pope launched into a discussion of the corroboration requirement, drawing the jury's attention to the medical testimony: the sperm found on Eleanor Cerami's vaginal smear and the lower back tenderness suffered by Joanne Kenarden. In addition to that, he made the argument that the testimony of each victim corroborated that of the other—the very argument that Jaywalker had failed to persuade Justice Davidoff was improper. "These are two women who didn't know each other," Pope told the jurors. "They have no reason to cook up a story and come into this courtroom and try to frame somebody. Why should they do that? They're telling you the truth. They're telling you that there's absolutely no doubt in their minds that this is the man who raped them on August sixteenth. Mrs. Cerami and Miss Kenarden sat in this courtroom and looked at this man and told you he raped them. *And they know.* For fifteen or twenty minutes, both of these women were with the man who victimized them. The *same* man. *They had to stare into the face of the man who was raping them.*"

Pope discussed the descriptions that the victims had supplied of their attacker. He told the jurors that the defendant looked older than his age and heavier than his weight. He dismissed as meaningless the failure of the police to find the shirt or the knife. Darren's claim that he drank Seagram's, but not wine, he labeled a fabrication. As for the geographical distance between Darren and Castle Hill, Pope argued that it stood to reason that no one would commit these crimes close to home. Yvette Monroe's claim to have seen a "look-alike" was worthless.

When it came to Eleanor Cerami's September 17th sighting of her rapist, Pope seemed to have a bit more difficulty. "Maybe there was a mistake about the time on that day," he suggested. "Perhaps Mrs. Cerami did see Darren

Kingston in her building at nine o'clock, and perhaps an hour later he was at the post office in Manhattan. Perhaps he did see Mr. Hamilton there. But that's not the crucial question. The crucial question is, on August sixteenth, did he rape Mrs. Cerami and Miss Kenarden?

"About the stuttering. Darren Kingston stuttered on the witness stand. He stuttered all through his testimony. But he didn't stutter that morning when he had the knife in his hand, when he was in control of the situation and knew what he wanted. He doesn't have to stutter when he has control.

"Circumcision. Miss Kenarden says the man who raped her was circumcised. There's no question in her mind about that. And the defendant produced Dr. Goddard, who said Darren Kingston is uncircumcised. And I won't dispute that. I am going to take his word. But if the defendant had had an erection with someone else, and then shortly after that attempted intercourse again, the foreskin might not have gone back down, and it would be possible that a layperson—such as Miss Kenarden—might mistake him as being circumcised. And I submit to you that that's exactly what happened on August sixteenth, because Mrs. Cerami had just been raped by this man. And then, an hour or so later, when Miss Kenarden saw him, he appeared to be circumcised. That is what occurred in this instance."

Pope discussed the failure of the defense to prove an alibi for August 16th. "Darren Kingston cannot account for his time on that date," he told the jurors, "because he was in the Castle Hill project raping and orally sodomizing Mrs. Cerami and Miss Kenarden.

"Don't decide this case," he cautioned them, "with your

own imagination of what a rapist is. There is no such animal as a person who looks like a rapist. They come in all shapes, all sizes, all ages. You can't look at Darren Kingston and tell he's a rapist just from looking at him. You can't decide his guilt or innocence based on whether or not he looks gentle and unassuming here at the counsel table.

"If, after listening to Mrs. Cerami and Miss Kenarden, and Miss Maldonado and Miss Caldwell, or any of the other witnesses, you believe that Darren Kingston is innocent and didn't commit these crimes, you must find him not guilty. But, ladies and gentlemen, if you believe beyond a reasonable doubt that Darren Kingston *is* the man who raped and sodomized Mrs. Cerami and Miss Kenarden on the afternoon of August sixteenth, then you must come in here and, unpleasant though it may be, you must find him guilty of having committed those crimes on that day. That also is your sworn duty."

With that, Jacob Pope sat down. Having tried a good case, he had now delivered a good closing argument. Not flashy, not spectacular. But good. Much like Pope himself.

Justice Davidoff recessed for the day, instructing the jurors to return the following morning to hear his charge on the law. He gave them his final admonition to refrain from discussing the case, forming an opinion or visiting the Castle Hill area.

Outside, the Kingstons gave Jaywalker their collective approval of his summation. They seemed genuinely pleased, and their words were nice to hear. Jaywalker thanked them. He'd always been a pushover for praise, and always would be. Then he found his car and drove home, physically and mentally drained, but hopeful. And comforted by the knowledge that there's no night's sleep quite like the sleep after a strong summation.

19

THE SHORTEST DAY

Thursday, March 5th

The jurors filed in and took their seats. The court clerk announced that the judge was about to charge the jury, and that all those wishing to leave should do so now. Then he motioned to one of the uniformed court officers, who locked the doors. They don't do that anymore, but they used to, back then.

Justice Davidoff began his instructions. As do most judges, he read from a prepared text, knowing that any misstatement of the law could provide the basis for an appeal, in the event of a conviction. An acquittal can't be appealed; to permit a retrial after a not-guilty verdict would run afoul of the double jeopardy rule.

The judge told the jurors the same thing Jaywalker had told them earlier: that while he was the judge of the law, they were the judges of the facts. He explained that they were to assess the credibility of the witnesses, cautioning them to consider the interest any witness might have in the outcome of the case. The defendant, he said, had an interest greater than that of any other witness. Today, that comment alone might be grounds for a reversal. Back then, it was a standard part of the charge.

He instructed the jurors about various terms and propositions of law, including the presumption of innocence, the burden of proof and reasonable doubt. "A reasonable doubt," he told them, "isn't just any doubt. It has to be a doubt arising out of the evidence, or the lack of evidence. A doubt you could give a reason for." Next he did his best to explain how the rule requiring corroboration worked.

"You may, if you wish, find that the testimony of each of the two victims corroborates that of the other," he said. It was a reading of the law that Jaywalker disagreed with, and he scribbled a note to himself on the pad in front of him.

He discussed the various counts of the indictment and the elements of each crime charged. He explained that their verdict would have to be unanimous on each count, guilty or not guilty. He concluded by telling them that while it was their duty to express their views and exchange their ideas in an attempt to reach a verdict on each count, they also had a right to stick to their opinions.

Before the jury retired to begin deliberating, the lawyers were invited to approach the bench and place on the record any exception they wanted to take to the charge. Jaywalker took full advantage, starting with Justice Davidoff's having told the jurors that they could consider each rape as corroboration of the other. While the judge noted the exception, he said he was going to adhere to his original instruction. "I think I'm right on this," he added, "though I'm aware that it presents an interesting question."

Cold comfort, thought Jaywalker. He listed half a dozen other exceptions he had, but they were pretty minor. Except for the corroboration issue, the charge had been standard stuff.

Then, to the jury, the judge said simply, "All right, you may go to the jury room and begin your deliberations." And one by one, they filed out of the room, those twelve judges of the facts.

Jaywalker looked up at the clock. It was 11:05 a.m.

Some lawyers work while their juries deliberate. Some read newspapers or novels. Others return to their offices, if they're nearby enough, or retire to local bars if they're not, leaving phone numbers with the court clerk.

Jaywalker sweats.

Always has, always will.

The only life experience he'd ever had that he could meaningfully compare to waiting for a verdict was the time he'd spent waiting for the birth of his daughter. In each instance there was the terrible tension of having no idea how long things would take, or if they would turn out all right. In each instance the news could come at any time. And when it came, it would bring either monumental joy or total disaster. And in each instance the outcome was completely out of Jaywalker's hands. His part in the drama was over. All he could do was wait.

There are juries that begin their deliberations by asking to have the various exhibits sent in to them. There are juries that request extensive read-backs of the trial testimony, both direct and cross-examination. There are juries that want specific portions of the judge's instructions repeated, explained or amplified. There are juries that want all of these things and more.

Darren Kingston's jury seemed interested in none of them. It was almost as though, despite being told they were entitled to them, they didn't quite believe it. Or if they believed it, they didn't care.

Around one o'clock, a delivery boy showed up, balancing a huge carton on one shoulder. It contained the jurors' lunches, which were sent in to them. At that point, Justice Davidoff told the lawyers that they might as well go out and eat, as well, since nothing was likely to happen while the jurors had lunch. Jaywalker stuck to his diet. The Kingstons left, but he couldn't imagine them eating much.

Everyone reassembled around two. Still no word from the jury room, which was close enough to the courtroom that raised voices, even if not intelligible, would have drifted in. Weren't they fighting, Jaywalker wondered, or at least disagreeing about *something?* Hadn't both he and Pope given them plenty to disagree about? Where had they been for the last week and a half?

Five minutes to three.

A buzzer from the jury room.

That could mean one of two things. A verdict, or a note. Jaywalker, his pulse somewhere in the hundreds, listened as a court officer out of his sight knocked loudly on the door to the jury room. "Cease deliberations!" he shouted. There followed an eternity of silence. The door to the jury room was being opened, he knew. The foreman was either telling the officer they had a verdict or handing him a piece of paper. The door closed. Footsteps. The officer appeared in the doorway to the courtroom.

"It's a note," he said.

A *reprieve,* was all Jaywalker could think. They were still alive. The jurors no doubt wanted some testimony read back, or some clarification on a part of the judge's instructions. An exhibit, perhaps. Please let it be Darren's draft card, Jaywalker prayed, or his Phil Rizzuto mitt. Or, better yet, P. G. Hamilton's Form 3971.

They took their places, Pope at his table, Darren and Jaywalker at theirs, the Kingston family in the spectator section. Justice Davidoff entered from his robing room, through a side door, and called for the jury to be brought in.

There are a lot of superstitions and old wives' tales about "reading" juries. Jaywalker had his own, and it would always prove infallible. As the jurors come back into the courtroom from deliberating, if they make eye contact with his client and him, it's a good sign. If they don't, it's trouble.

Not one of them looked his way.

Jaywalker recognized the taste of blood even before realizing that he'd been biting the inside of his cheek.

Justice Davidoff examined the note. "The court," he said after a long moment, "has received a request from the foreman of the jury. It reads as follows. 'Will you accept a verdict of guilty with a recommendation of mercy?'"

Jaywalker felt as though he'd been hit by a locomotive. He placed a hand on Darren's shoulder, as much for himself as for Darren. He only half heard the judge telling the jury that sentencing was his concern, not theirs, and that their verdict had to be either guilty or not guilty.

The jurors nodded and filed back out.

Darren turned in his seat to face Jaywalker. "What does that mean, Jay?" he asked.

"It means," said Jaywalker, "they're going to convict you." He knew no other way to say it.

It was almost as if someone had transformed Darren into a marionette and then suddenly let go of all the overhead strings. He slumped down in his chair. Jaywalker's hand, still on the young man's shoulder, squeezed harder, as though of its own volition. Jaywalker—the lawyer, the adult—tried hard to fight back the tears.

When finally Darren spoke, it was to say, "Jay, I d-d-d-didn't do it."

"I know," said Jaywalker. And he did. With all of his heart, he knew.

It was twenty past three when the jury came in again. This time, there was no note. The court clerk called the roll, then turned to the foreman of the jury.

THE CLERK: Mr. Foreman, please rise. Has the jury agreed upon a verdict?

THE FOREMAN: Yes, we have.

THE CLERK: How do you find the defendant Darren Kingston as to Count One, Rape in the First Degree of Eleanor Cerami? Guilty, or not guilty?

THE FOREMAN: Guilty.

The clerk read off each of the remaining counts. In response to each, the foreman answered, "Guilty." Darren's wife, Charlene, broke down and had to be helped from the courtroom. As the jurors were polled individually, one of them, a woman in the second row, wept openly. But when it came her turn to answer, she, too, said, "Guilty." Through her tears.

Justice Davidoff thanked the jurors for their service and excused them. He scheduled sentencing for April 9th. And, as a consolation prize, he continued Darren's bail.

Downstairs, Jaywalker struggled to find words of comfort or hope for Darren and his family, but there were none to be found. They'd played by the rules. They'd gone to trial in a system that promised justice. Jaywalker had been their champion, their protector. And he'd failed them.

He drove home and crawled into bed.

Once, as a small boy named Harrison J. Walker, he'd broken a lamp in his parents' living room. The thing had probably cost twenty bucks, but to him it had seemed priceless. When he'd awakened the following morning, his first thought was that it had been a dream. He'd lain awake, relieved that it hadn't really happened. It was only later, when he'd ventured into the living room and seen the shattered pieces, that he'd known it really had.

It was like that when he woke up the morning after Darren Kingston's conviction. For just a moment he allowed himself to think it hadn't happened. But then the awareness came, and with it, the pain.

He would awaken like that for weeks.

20

IN THIS HEART OF MINE

Two days after the verdict, Jaywalker called Darren and had him come down to the office. He seemed to have recovered from the shock and was actually in pretty good spirits, considering everything. It frightened Jaywalker, in a way. Here was a young man who'd just learned he was going to spend the next ten or twenty years of his life in prison for crimes he hadn't committed, *and he was coping with it.* Some people can adjust to anything, Jaywalker concluded. Had it been him, he would have been climbing the walls, screaming his lungs out.

They talked about what came next. Jaywalker confessed that other than an appeal, he was pretty much out of ideas. One of the few suggestions he made was another try at a polygraph test. John McCarthy, the investigator, recommended an examiner named Cleve Bryant. Jaywalker told Darren that it was a long shot at best, but that he was willing to set it up if Darren was interested. He *was* interested. He was willing to try anything, he said, no matter how long the odds.

Before calling Bryant, Jaywalker phoned Pope to let him

know what they were thinking of doing. It wasn't that he needed Pope's approval, but Jaywalker was still feeling a bit defensive over the way Pope had known about the tests with Dick Arledge's office without Jaywalker having told him.

Pope's reaction was negative. His office had recently had some sort of a problem with Bryant, and he said that even in the event of a positive finding—that Darren was telling the truth—he wouldn't be able to recommend any action on the basis of it. In the years to follow, Jaywalker would learn that there was nothing unusual about Pope's reaction. Polygraphists, it seems, went in and out of favor with prosecutors. One day a particular examiner was their darling; the next day his word was worthless.

Based on his conversation with Pope, Jaywalker put off calling Bryant for a day or two. When he finally did call him, he was told he was out of town and wouldn't be back for a week or two.

The following Wednesday, Darren came down to the office again, this time to pick up a letter Jaywalker had written him for his job. It was their hope to keep Darren working at the post office during his appeal. This time, Darren had a suggestion of his own.

"Jay," he said, "what about t-t-truth serum?"

Not exactly the kind of idea a guilty man would come up with, was it? And a new one for Jaywalker. He'd always regarded truth serum as right up there with crystal balls and tarot cards, the stuff of cheap novels and grade-B movies. But, like Darren, he was willing to try just about anything.

The problem was, you couldn't simply go to the yellow pages and let your fingers do the walking until they came to Truth Serum. Or even Serum, Truth, for that matter. So

Jaywalker put in a call to a psychologist friend, George Goldman, on whose couch Jaywalker himself had spent more than a few hours. Goldman came up with the names of two psychiatrists—they were talking about drugs here, so a physician would be needed—who'd worked with sodium amytol, a refinement of sodium pentathol, popularly known as truth serum.

The first of the two psychiatrists Jaywalker contacted wasn't interested; he evidently fit the mold of most doctors when it came to matters involving lawyers and court cases. The second, a man named Herbert Spraigue, seemed genuinely intrigued with the problem, but said that lately he was working less with sodium amytol and more with hypnosis. When Jaywalker asked him why, Spraigue explained that he'd come to put more stock in it and found it safer to work with. Those struck Jaywalker as two pretty sound reasons, and he took the first available appointment. Then, remembering he was only the lawyer, he phoned Darren to ask for his approval.

He got it.

A couple of days later, Charlene went into labor and gave birth to a baby girl, whom she and Darren named Angela. Inez called Jaywalker with the news. He couldn't help thinking that what should have been a wonderful moment for the entire family had its bittersweet edge, with Darren living on borrowed time, looking at a long prison sentence.

April 1st, 1980

Jaywalker had to wonder if it was only fitting that their appointment with a hypnotist fell on April Fools' Day.

Which, along with Halloween, was as close to Jaywalker's national holiday as anything.

He arrived at Dr. Spraigue's office early, ahead of Darren. Spraigue immediately struck him as a strange-looking man of great intensity. His totally bald head and thin body made him seem absolutely ageless. Jaywalker wouldn't have been surprised to hear he was forty or seventy, or anywhere in between. Months later he would learn that Spraigue had lately been focusing on criminal matters, particularly the area of false confessions. He would go on to earn a reputation as one of the foremost forensic hypnotists in the world. But for the moment, at least to Jaywalker, he was nothing but a weird-looking character who might somehow be able to help Darren.

They spoke for about fifteen minutes, with Jaywalker filling Spraigue in on the basics of the case. Whenever the doctor interrupted to make a comment or ask a question, it was in a deep, resonant, almost melodious voice. Jaywalker didn't quite know what to make of it at first, particularly because of the way it contrasted with Spraigue's physical person. But then it hit him: it was the quintessential voice of a hypnotist. From that moment on, Jaywalker found himself unconsciously breaking off eye contact from time to time, as though he were afraid of falling under Spraigue's spell.

Jaywalker explained that he was looking for two things. The first was some sort of verification that Darren was telling the truth when he denied having any involvement with the rapes. The second was anything in the nature of an alibi that might be unearthed from Darren's subconscious while he was under hypnosis. Dr. Spraigue nodded thoughtfully. The first thing he would have to do, he said, was to determine whether or not Darren was a fit subject for hypnosis. "Not everyone is, you know."

Jaywalker confessed that he hadn't known. This was all uncharted territory for him. Up until that moment, he'd tended to regard hypnosis as something between a parlor trick and a magic act. That, and the subject of fiction. *The Manchurian Candidate* came to mind.

But Spraigue assured him that hypnosis was very real. And if they were lucky, and Darren in fact proved to be a fit subject, then they would attempt a "time regression" with him, taking him back to earlier moments of his life. Jaywalker nodded, trying to put on a hopeful face. But who was he kidding? This was a kid who couldn't be poly-graphed, so what made him think he could be *hypnotized?*

By that time, Darren had arrived, accompanied, as always, by his cousin Delroid. Jaywalker's instructions to the Kingston family were still in place. He was hoping that the real Castle Hill rapist might strike again, and if he did, Jaywalker wanted to have someone besides Darren himself to account for his whereabouts.

Leaving Delroid in the waiting room, Jaywalker brought Darren in and introduced him to Dr. Spraigue. Then, recalling the polygraph sessions, he made a move toward the door, assuming that his continued presence might prove a distraction. But the doctor assured him that he could stay without interfering.

Dr. Spraigue seated Darren in a comfortable leather chair directly opposite the one in which he himself sat. He spoke with Darren for a while, explaining what it was he proposed to do, checking to see if it was okay with Darren, and pointing out how it might help. Somewhere during the conversation, Spraigue's voice changed slightly, though it was hard to pinpoint the exact moment when it happened. But there came a time when Jaywalker was aware that although the doctor's voice was still deep and resonant, he was now speaking in an exaggerated monotone, almost without modulation. Darren appeared to be listening with complete attention and said he was anxious to try whatever might work.

"Now," said Spraigue, "put your arms on the arms of the chair. Lean your head back. Look up, way up into the top of your head. Keep looking up. That's good. Now close your eyes. Keep looking up. Take a deep breath. Close, close, deep breath. Aaaaaaahhh. Exhale. Eyes relaxed. Body floating. Now, as you feel yourself floating, you're going into a very deep state of relaxation. Deep, deep relaxation."

Spraigue caught Jaywalker's eye and nodded. Jaywalker looked at Darren. Could it be that he was actually hypnotized? Jaywalker had been waiting for swinging pocket watches and magical incantations.

"Okay, Darren," Spraigue was saying in his monotone. "We're going to test you out. We're going to let you see for yourself how deep a trance you're in. In a while, I'm going to stroke your left arm. After I do, it will become as stiff and rigid as an iron pipe. So stiff and rigid that no matter how hard you try, you won't be able to bend it. Ready."

Spraigue leaned forward and stroked Darren's left arm up and down several times. As he did so, he lifted the arm and extended it in front of Darren. When he stopped stroking it, the arm remained in midair. It struck Jaywalker as a fairly unnatural and uncomfortable position, certainly one that couldn't be maintained for long.

"Now," said Spraigue, "your arm is going to stay in this position, even after I give you the signal to come out of the trance state. You'll notice that the harder you try to bend your elbow, the stiffer it will become. But sometime after that, when I touch your left shoulder, your usual sensation and control will return to your left arm and hand, and you'll find it a very relieving experience.

"Now I'm going to count backward. When I get to two, your eyes will try to open, but they won't be able to. When I get to one, they'll open slowly. Ready. Three, two and one."

Darren's eyes opened slowly. Jaywalker watched in amazement, fighting back the urge to laugh out loud. Darren stared at his own left arm, extended strangely in front of him.

"What in the world is going on?" asked Spraigue. The monotone was gone, replaced by a friendly, conversational cadence.

"I don't know," said Darren.

"What happens if you try to bend it?"

"C-c-can't."

"Has that ever happened to you before?"

"No."

"Let me test it out and see." Spraigue leaned forward and pushed down against the arm. It didn't bend. "If you saw that in someone else," he asked, "would you believe it?"

"I definitely wouldn't."

"Does it frighten you?"

"A little bit."

"All right," said Spraigue. "I'll tell you what. You concentrate on your fist. You try your very hardest to pull it toward you. Go ahead. *Pull!*"

Darren pulled. The arm didn't move. Spraigue stood up and moved to the side of Darren's chair. Unobtrusively, he touched Darren's left shoulder. As if by magic, the arm suddenly moved. Darren bent it back and forth. He smiled, then laughed easily. Jaywalker could do nothing but shake his head. He was suddenly ready to believe in witchcraft, reincarnation, ESP and UFOs. Bring them all on!

Apparently satisfied that his subject was open to hypnosis, Dr. Spraigue proceeded to put Darren through a series of time regressions by putting him under hypnosis, taking him back to an earlier time in his life and waking him up to relive that time. He selected birthdays, explaining to Jaywalker afterward that those tended to be easily remembered.

Red letter days, Justice Davidoff might have called them.

First Spraigue took Darren back to his tenth birthday. Then he woke him from the trance and interviewed him. In a noticeably younger voice, Darren talked about school and his teacher, Miss Curio. When asked the name of the president, Darren proudly answered, "Nixon." Spraigue pointed at Jaywalker and asked if Darren knew who he was.

"No," said Darren.

Taken back to his fourth birthday, Darren spoke in monosyllables. Asked to read from a book, he couldn't. Soon he became frightened and began whimpering for his mother.

At his first birthday, Darren didn't speak at all. Instead, he cried like the baby he was, stopping only when Dr. Spraigue handed him a rubber toy.

The hour was almost finished. Spraigue put Darren back into the trance and brought him up to the present.

Darren woke up on command. Spraigue sent him to the waiting room, so that he and Jaywalker could make arrangements for a second session. Jaywalker wanted Darren brought back to the specific dates of the rapes and woken up at the times they were committed, so they could see where he'd been and whom, if anyone, he'd been with. Spraigue wasn't sure the technique would work on random dates, but he was willing to try. After all, he said, Darren was as good a candidate as he'd seen in a long time. He'd known that as soon as he'd seen how far Darren could roll back the pupils of his eyes, which he'd discovered was a foolproof test.

They set up an appointment for Wednesday evening, and Jaywalker was getting ready to leave, when Delroid suddenly burst into the room, dragging Darren by one arm.

"Something's wrong," said Delroid. "He's acting funny. He doesn't know why he's here or anything."

Jaywalker looked at Darren, who certainly did seem disoriented. Jaywalker froze. Spraigue had said he preferred hypnosis to truth serum because it was safer, and now *this*. All Jaywalker could imagine was an emergency trip to Bellevue, lights flashing, sirens wailing. Darren stuck in a permanent trance, brain damage, coma…

But if Delroid was alarmed, Darren disoriented and Jaywalker panicked, Spraigue never flinched. Calmly, he began to question Darren, whose responses quickly made it clear that he knew nothing of any rape charges, trial or verdict. Nor did he have any idea why he was in a strange doctor's office. He recognized Jaywalker, but only as his lawyer from two years earlier, after he'd gotten into some trouble with a couple of friends. Asked the date, he said

August 1979, and admitted being stumped as to why he was wearing a heavy leather jacket in the middle of summer.

Even as Jaywalker's panic increased, Spraigue understood the problem. Instead of waking up in the present, Darren had somehow misheard or misunderstood Spraigue's commands and had woken up back in August. So Spraigue put him back into the trance, brought him forward to the present and woke him again. This time Darren was familiar with his surroundings and aware of what everyone was doing there. Jaywalker breathed deeply and caught Delroid doing the same. If Herbert Spraigue had had a scary moment of his own, he never once showed it.

And Jaywalker was more of a believer than ever.

Outside, in the cold April air, Darren asked what had happened. Jaywalker explained that Dr. Spraigue had hypnotized him and wanted to do it again Wednesday. Darren reacted with disbelief, insisting there was no way he'd been hypnotized. Jaywalker smiled and assured him that he had been. But Darren still wasn't buying it.

"Who was your fourth-grade teacher?" Jaywalker asked him.

Darren thought a moment. "I d-d-don't know," he said.

"How about Miss Curio?"

It was as though his lawyer had just developed X-ray vision and could suddenly read his mind better than Darren himself could. *"Wow!"* was all he could say, though he did manage to say it several times. Delroid, who'd also been one of Miss Curio's victims, was equally impressed. Converts all, they made arrangements to meet again at Spraigue's office on Wednesday.

Later that afternoon, Jaywalker called Jacob Pope. He described what had happened and invited him to attend Wednesday's session. Pope expressed interest and said he would try to be there. Jaywalker told him that he was planning on tape-recording it, so Pope would be able to listen to it if he couldn't make it. Pope said that was a good idea, but that he would be there in person if possible.

Waiting for Wednesday became increasingly difficult. For the first time since the jury had crushed them with its verdict, Jaywalker dared to be hopeful. As skeptical as he'd originally been about the notion of truth serum and hypnosis, he'd walked out of Dr. Spraigue's office completely won over. If that strange-looking man with the deep voice had been able to take Darren back to the time he was a year old, surely he could take him back to last August. In fact, hadn't he already done precisely that, if only by accident?

This was going to work, Jaywalker told himself. They were going to discover something, someone Darren had seen at or near his home around the time one of the rapes was taking place in Castle Hill. And if Darren had seen someone, it meant that person had seen Darren. Perhaps Darren was going to remember someone he'd spoken to on the phone, some neighbor who'd stopped by, or some repairman who'd been working in the building. Because all of it had to be there in his memory, just beyond his reach. Like Miss Curio's name, it was all waiting to be unlocked by Herbert Spraigue's magic. So what if Jaywalker wasn't going to be the one to find it? All that mattered was that *someone* was going to. And if that someone turned out to be a baldheaded shrink with an otherwordly voice, who cared? This was going to work.

It had to.

* * *

Wednesday came.

Pope didn't.

Darren, Delroid and Jaywalker met at Dr. Spraigue's office at 6:30 in the evening. Delroid took his spot in the waiting room as Darren and Jaywalker went inside for the session. Jaywalker set up his tape recorder, an old reel-to-reel contraption that weighed about fifty pounds and these days would belong in an attic, or perhaps a museum. He pressed the red button that said Record, took a seat and waited for the magic to begin.

Spraigue arranged Darren and himself in the same facing leather chairs as at the earlier session. He began speaking in his practiced, deliberate monotone. He told Darren what he wanted to do this time. He asked Darren if he was agreeable, and Darren said he was. Again Spraigue had Darren place his arms on those of the chair, look upward and close his eyes. It wasn't long before Darren was back in the same trance state he'd been in two days earlier.

Spraigue set up a slightly different test to measure the trance this time. Jaywalker had the feeling the doctor might be showing off for his benefit, but he didn't care. Spraigue told Darren that once he awoke, he would be unable to cross his legs until the word *ankle* was spoken aloud. Then he brought Darren out of the trance, and instructed him to relax and cross his legs. Darren struggled visibly, but was unable to do it.

"Just put one leg over the other," Spraigue suggested.

Nothing happened.

"Put the right foot over the left one."

Nothing.

"Put the left foot over the right one."

Still nothing.

"Try putting the right ankle over the left—"

Darren crossed his legs.

Satisfied, Spraigue put Darren back into the trance. He took him back again to his tenth birthday, woke him and interviewed him. Once again, Darren the ten-year-old materialized before their eyes.

"Now," said Spraigue, "you're growing up. You're getting older. You're twelve years old. You're fourteen years old. You're eighteen years old. You're getting older. You're now coming to a specific day. You're coming up to August sixteenth, nineteen-seventy-nine. It's a Thursday. It's noontime on Thursday, August sixteenth, nineteen-seventy-nine. It's between noon and twelve-thirty, actually. In a short time, I'm going to touch the sides of your eyes, and when I do, you'll be able to open your eyes and tell me what you're doing. Ready…"

Spraigue touched his hands to the outer sides of Darren's eyes. Darren opened them slowly, as though awakening from sleep. He rubbed his face. Jaywalker looked down at his tape recorder, where the reels were moving slowly.

"Hi," said Spraigue.

"Hi," said Darren sleepily.

"What's going on?"

Darren looked around uncertainly.

"What's the date today?" Spraigue asked him.

Jaywalker held his breath while Darren appeared to think for a moment. Then he answered, "August sixteenth."

"What time is it?"

"Twelve-thirty."

"What year is it?"

"Nineteen-seventy-nine."

Jaywalker resumed breathing. It was working. Not even Dr. Spraigue had been sure it would. But it was.

"What were you doing?" Spraigue asked Darren.

"I dunno. Sleeping."

"Sleeping? At twelve-thirty in the afternoon?"

"I w-w-worked last night." Darren yawned.

"Where did you work?"

"Post office."

Jaywalker got Spraigue's attention, and the doctor invited him to join in the questioning.

"Where are you now?" Jaywalker asked.

But Darren had nodded off.

"Even though you're asleep," said Spraigue, "you'll be able to answer our questions. Where are you now, Darren?"

"Home."

"Who's here with you?"

"N-n-nobody."

"What's the address here?"

Darren recited his address.

"Where's your wife?"

"She's at work."

"Darren," Jaywalker asked, "where'd you go when you got off from work this morning?"

"I stopped at the store. Food City."

"What did you buy? Do you remember?"

"B-b-bought some milk," said Darren. "We had no milk."

"And then where'd you go?" Jaywalker asked.

"Home."

"What did you do when you got home?"

"I watched a little TV."

"Do you remember what you watched?"

"Andy Griffith."

"What was it about?" Jaywalker asked.

"Barney was helping Andy look for crooks. And Gomer was helping them. They let the crooks escape outta jail, and Andy came and had to put 'em back in..."

"What else did you watch this morning?"

"Lucy."

"Do you remember what that was about?"

"No," said Darren. "I was d-d-d-dozing off."

Jaywalker signaled Spraigue to move on to the time of the second rape.

"All right," said Spraigue. "The time is passing now. It's getting to one o'clock. It's one-thirty. It's still Thursday, August sixteenth, nineteen-seventy-nine. Now it's quarter to two on Thursday afternoon. In a while, I'm going to touch the sides of your eyes, and you'll be able to open your eyes and talk with us. Ready..."

Darren responded as before. They found him sleeping again, only this time he was a bit agitated, expressing concern that he had to call Charlene at work.

"Where are you?" Jaywalker asked.

"Home."

"Do you know what date it is?"

"August sixteenth."

"What year?"

"Nineteen-seventy-nine."

"Do you know what time it is?"

"'Bout two o'clock."

"Darren, did you see anybody on your way home this morning? Anybody you know?"

"Yeah. The porter from my building."

"What's his name?"

"I don't know him by name. Just 'Hello' and 'Good-bye.'"

"Did anything unusual happen between you and him today?"

"No."

"Did you see anybody else?"

"I seen the lady next door. Elderly lady."

"Did you speak with her?"

"I held the door for her."

"Did she have packages?"

"No. She has trouble w-w-walking, so I open the door for her when I see her."

"Anybody else? Did you see anybody else you know at all?"

"No."

Shit, thought Jaywalker, painfully aware that despite all the drama, nothing useful had been unearthed. He yielded to Spraigue.

"Listen, Darren," he began. "There are a couple of women here who say that you had a little monkey business with them. Know anything about that?"

"What women?" Darren asked. He seemed genuinely confused.

"One's named Eleanor Cerami, and the other's Joanne Kenarden."

"I don't know them," said Darren.

"Well," said Spraigue, "they seem to know you. They say you had a knife and you had sex with them."

"No." Darren shook his head from side to side. "That's not true."

"They say it is."

"No," said Darren. It was more a matter-of-fact statement than a defensive denial. "When?" he asked.

"Just now," said Spraigue. "Just this afternoon."

"No," Darren repeated. "Not me."

"Where's your knife?" Spraigue asked suddenly.

"I don't have a knife."

"Well," Spraigue insisted, "you *had* a knife. And you held it against them, and you made them go down on you. Right?"

"No," said Darren. "Not me."

"Did you ever do anything like that? Hold a knife against someone and make her go down on you?"

"No." Darren shook his head.

"Why should they be saying that about you?"

"I don't know," said Darren. "Tell them to stop lying. I didn't do anything like that. I'm sleepy."

Darren dozed off. Spraigue brought him forward to the following afternoon, August 17th, the day of the attack against Tania Maldonado. As he had before, he touched the sides of Darren's head, near his eyes. This time, when Darren opened them, he was fully awake.

"Hi," said Spraigue.

"Hi."

"Do you know what date it is today?"

"August seventeenth?"

"Right. What year?"

"Nineteen-seventy-nine."

"What are you doing?"

"Writing a song."

"A song?"

"Yeah."

"What kind of a song?"

"A love song," Darren explained.

"How does it go?"

Darren proceeded to half sing, half recite, the words.

> *I want to show what I know*
> *Is in this heart of mine.*
> *Why I live is to give*
> *What's in this heart of mine.*

The tune seemed vaguely familiar to Jaywalker. He had the sense that he'd heard it before, but he couldn't quite place it.

"That's as far as I got," said Darren.

Again, Darren reported that he'd worked at the post office the night before. He'd come straight home, arriving about 9:00 or 9:30 a.m. He'd seen nobody he knew. He'd played some records, a Smokey Robinson album and one by a group called Plantation. He'd slept a bit, but had awakened because it had been so hot. So he'd worked on the song. He hadn't gone out at all. Jaywalker asked him if he'd been up at the Castle Hill Houses yesterday or today.

"No," said Darren.

"Who's Pooh?" Jaywalker asked.

"M-m-my son. That's what we call our son. Pooh."

"Who's Angela?"

"Angela? I don't know. I don't know any Angela."

Angela was the name of Darren and Charlene's daughter, born shortly after the trial. But in August of 1979, the name would indeed have been meaningless to Darren.

Once again, Dr. Spraigue put Darren into the trance state. This time he brought him forward to the afternoon of September 5th and the time of the attack against Elvira Caldwell, the fourth victim. Darren was drowsy but awake. He said he'd just woken up a few minutes ago and was about to take a shower. Once again he was home alone.

"Do you know where the Castle Hill project is?" Spraigue asked him.

"Yeah," said Darren. "It's up past the Korvettes store."

"You ever been there?"

"Yeah, I've been there."

"When was the last time?"

"I don't know," said Darren. "I haven't been there in ages."

"How about last month? Were you there last month?"

"No."

"What month was last month?"

"August," said Darren.

"You weren't there today?"

"No."

"You sure?"

"I'm positive."

Jaywalker asked Darren what he'd done after he'd gotten off from work that morning. Except for a stop to pick up a pack of Kools and some Juicy Fruit gum, he'd come straight home. Again, he'd seen nobody who would remember having seen him. Had they come this far, Jaywalker wondered, only to end up right where they'd been before, with no alibi, nothing to check out? He looked down at the tape recorder. The take-up reel was filling up, turning more slowly now than the other one. But there was nothing on it yet that was going to save them.

Spraigue brought Darren forward to the afternoon of September 17th. Darren was awake, this time at his parents' house. He said he'd spent the morning going down to his job, with Delroid. He'd seen Andrew Emmons, George Riley, P. G. Hamilton and a few others. From there, he and Delroid had come straight home. He hadn't been anywhere near Castle Hill.

"What about this case?" Jaywalker asked him, knowing that by now, Darren would be aware of it. "These four girls who say you attacked them?"

"Jay, I know I didn't do it. I know I couldn't do anything like that."

"They're sure it's you. Every one of them."

"Either they've been b-b-brainwashed into thinking it's me or I've got a double out there. Either way, I didn't do it. I know it's not me. They'll never convince me of that. I know it's not me, Jay."

"Well," said Jaywalker, "you know what happened at the trial, don't you?"

"The trial? That's coming up. I'm trying to prepare myself for it. It's—it's—it's—it's hard to go to trial for something you know you didn't do, you know?"

"Yes," said Jaywalker. "I know."

It was sometime that evening that it hit Jaywalker. The song Darren had sung for them. It was the same one he'd been humming in Dick Arledge's office, on the day of the first polygraph session with Gene Sandusky.

> *I want to show what I know*
> *Is in this heart of mine.*

Jaywalker found himself humming the tune as he rinsed the dinner dishes that night, repeating the words as he took the garbage out. What *was* in Darren's heart? he wondered. This case was torture enough for Jaywalker. What was it like for Darren? How does an innocent young man cope with the prospect of going to prison for someone else's crimes? Jaywalker had no answer for those questions, nothing but Darren Kingston's simple melody and plaintive words to repeat over and over again. They filled his head all evening. He put himself to sleep with them that night, and woke up to them the next morning.

Jaywalker delivered a copy of the tape to Jacob Pope. He told him it was fascinating stuff, which he hoped Pope would find convincing. But when pressed, he was forced to concede that the session had failed to produce an alibi or anything similar. Nevertheless, Pope expressed interest and promised to listen to the tape.

Darren's sentencing date was by that time only five days away. Jaywalker asked Pope if he had any objection to postponing it. He wanted more time, a lot more time, though he didn't put it quite that way. Pope said he wouldn't object.

They appeared before Justice Davidoff on April 9th. Jaywalker made his application for a postponement, basing it on the fact that he was pursuing several leads. Pope, true to his word, voiced no objection. The judge put the sentencing over to May 15th. Six weeks.

Pope returned the tape to Jaywalker. He'd found it interesting, he'd said, but hardly the kind of stuff he could act upon.

Jaywalker tried without success to locate a doctor willing to inject Darren with truth serum. He began studying docket sheets and court calendars for defendants accused of rape or other sexual assaults. Whenever he came across one, he pulled the court file, telling a clerk that the family had expressed interest in retaining him. He looked for a mug shot, if there was one. He studied physical descriptions and arrest records. He checked the complaint to see if the facts matched those of the Castle Hill attacks.

He combed newspapers for articles about rapes and rapists, hoping the real perpetrator would somehow emerge from the print.

Once again, he discovered that his old VW couldn't make it from Manhattan to New Jersey without veering off to the right and taking the Cross Bronx Expressway to Castle Hill. He became a regular in the projects, spending three, four, sometimes five afternoons a week there, staying until it was too dark to see any longer. He fantasized about spotting Darren's look-alike, confronting him, chasing him, running him down, tackling him and dragging him to the nearest precinct. Sometimes he caught him; sometimes he got away.

He tried not to think about the knife.

At work, his desk piled up with paperwork and his other cases went neglected. At home, his wife complained, and his daughter became a stranger to him.

But still he went back.

He was offered drugs by dealers and sex by prostitutes.

He got tickets for parking illegally and a Housing Authority summons for loitering.

But still he went back.

He simply didn't know what else to do, and the idea of doing nothing was unthinkable.

Yet no look-alike appeared.

The only shred of good news came from the post office. Darren had taken an unpaid leave of absence when the trial had begun. With the guilty verdict had come an automatic administrative suspension. Now, largely through the efforts of P. G. Hamilton, he had been reinstated and was back at work. In the great scheme of things, it wasn't much. But it was something.

May 15th came. They appeared again before Justice Davidoff. Jaywalker pleaded for another postponement of sentencing. Pope didn't object, but he did express concern that it should be the last one. The judge put the case over to June 19th, and said that sentencing would take place on that date, no matter what.

Six more weeks.

21

MURDER BURGERS

Toward the end of May, Jaywalker finally located a doctor who was willing to conduct a sodium amytol interview of Darren. Stephen Corman, a psychiatrist with credentials nearly as impressive as those of Herbert Spraigue, agreed to meet with them. Jaywalker checked with Darren, who was as willing as ever. Again Jaywalker invited Jacob Pope to attend. Again he said he'd try. Jaywalker invested in another tape. Again Pope didn't show up.

On May 29th, Jaywalker met up with Darren and his faithful sidekick Delroid at Dr. Corman's office. As before, Delroid stayed in the waiting room while Darren and Jaywalker went inside.

Stephen Corman had a lot more hair than Herbert Spraigue, but he, too, was intense in his manner. He seemed a bit less sure of himself than Spraigue had, but he'd worked extensively with sodium amytol, and had come highly recommended. He'd explained to Jaywalker on the phone the day before that the drug, which was actually a short-lived barbiturate, had a marked relaxing effect, which made it very difficult for the subject to control his responses to questions. Still, he'd cautioned, there was no guarantee that it would produce absolute truth-telling. Now, however, as he spoke to Darren, he made no such qualification. Apparently it was his intent to let Darren believe that once he was under the influence of the drug, he would be physically incapable of lying. It reminded Jaywalker of the technique used by Gene Sandusky, when he'd assured Darren that the polygraph machine would be able to pick up any lie, however minor.

Corman conducted a preliminary interview of Darren, questioning him about family, friends, his job, any use of drugs and his sexual experiences. Darren admitted to the occasional use of alcohol, but denied ever having tried marijuana or other illegal drugs.

Then Corman had Darren roll up a sleeve. He inserted a needle, found a vein and pulled back until blood appeared. Around that point, Jaywalker averted his eyes. There'd been a time when he'd thought seriously about following in a favorite uncle's footsteps and applying to medical school. He'd even put on a gown, mask and gloves, and watched as his uncle had performed surgery. At the first cut of the scalpel, Jaywalker had grown light-headed. The next thing he was aware of, he was lying on a gurney, having the back of his head stitched up. So much for medicine. In law, he would learn over the years, you bled every bit as much, but it was a slow bleeding—a drop here, a drop there. The problem was, there were no transfusions available. What you lost never seemed to get replenished, and if you kept at it long enough and tried enough cases—at least the way Jaywalker tried them— eventually you would run dry.

Almost immediately, Darren reported feeling "very light." Dr. Corman instructed him to sit back and begin counting backward from one hundred. With obvious difficulty, Darren tried. His speech was slow and thick. He fought to keep his eyes open, and lost.

With the drug at its most potent level in Darren's bloodstream, Corman began to question him about his whereabouts in the early afternoon hours of last August 16th. Darren said he'd been home, asleep. Corman asked him to describe the women in his family. Darren characterized his wife as "pretty" and his mother as "nice." He spoke about his sister in detached terms.

Corman asked him about knives. "When's the last time you carried one, Darren?"

"When I was about t-t-ten," said Darren. "I had a knife. I used to throw it against trees."

"Did you get pretty good at it?"

"No." Darren laughed.

And Jaywalker, fool that he was, took heart. What young man, after all, would admit that even with practice, he never mastered the art of sticking the point of a knife into a tree trunk from five or ten paces? Only a man compelled to tell the absolute truth, that's who. And as he had with the polygraphs and the hypnosis, Jaywalker once again dared to believe. That little vial of truth serum, their last chance at magic, was somehow going to come to their rescue.

It turned out that Darren's confession to his inexpertise with knives would be the last word out of him for a good five minutes. The full impact of the barbiturate hit him, and he succumbed as one might to a general anaesthetic. Dr. Corman called his name repeatedly and tried to rouse him several times, before giving up and explaining that they would simply have to wait a while. As he had when Dr. Spraigue had brought Darren out of a trance on the wrong date, Jaywalker could only envision total disaster. Was this what Spraigue had meant when he'd said that hypnosis was safer to work with than sodium amytol? At the moment, death by overdose seemed by far the likeliest outcome to Jaywalker, followed closely by massive brain damage and permanent, drooling confinement to a wheelchair. He wondered how he was going to go about explaining any of that to the Kingston family.

But Darren finally came around, and eventually he reached the point where he was able to respond once again. Dr. Corman questioned him at length about his sexual experiences and fantasies. For a while it seemed to Jaywalker that he was overdoing it. Wasn't an hour a pretty short time to practice Freudian techniques? But then Corman connected the subject to the rape accusations. Darren had described a number of experiences. Many had been erotic, some were humorous. All were embarrassing enough to have kept private, and as he'd listened, Jaywalker had once again felt like a voyeur. But when it came to the rapes, Darren was steadfast in his denial that he'd had anything to do with them.

Jaywalker took a turn at the questioning and asked Darren when he'd last been up to Castle Hill.

"The White Castle?" he asked.

"No." The White Castle was a hamburger joint, a poor man's McDonald's, and one of Jaywalker's personal favorites. The hamburgers were wafer-thin squares with holes punched in them. *Murder burgers,* they used to call them. They were the best. "No," Jaywalker repeated, "the Castle Hill Houses, in the Bronx."

"Long time," said Darren. "No," he corrected himself, "not so long ago."

Out of the corner of his eye, Jaywalker could sense Dr. Corman's sudden interest. "When was that?" the doctor asked.

Jaywalker couldn't tell whether Corman was hoping that the drug had caused Darren to slip up or was merely following up with the next logical question. But Jaywalker himself had no cause for worry. By this time, he knew the answer every bit as well as Darren did.

"Me an' McCarthy was up there," said Darren, before explaining that except for that visit, he hadn't been in the area for four or five years.

No, Darren wasn't going to slip. Not hooked up to a polygraph machine, not on cross-examination, not under hypnosis, not under a drug powerful enough to render him unconscious. You could break this kid's bones, Jaywalker knew. You could pull his fingernails off one by one. And you were still going to get the same answers. Because those answers were true. Because, when you came right down to it, Darren really was as innocent of those crimes as Jaywalker himself was. He cursed the jury for not having seen that, cursed himself for not having been able to *make* them see it.

"How about these young women, Darren?" Jaywalker asked him, not for himself any longer, but for the tape recorder, and for Jacob Pope, if he found the time to listen to it. "How about these young women who swear you raped them and made them go down on you?"

"They're lying," Darren slurred. "Or they been c-c-conditioned to think it's me. But they're wrong."

"When's the first time you saw Joanne Kenarden?" Jaywalker asked him.

"At the arraignment. She was the one who c-c-came to the arraignment. Right?"

"Right," said Jaywalker, surprised by the tears in his eyes. He suddenly felt tremendous pride in Darren. He knew he could question him for the rest of his life. So could Jacob Pope and Herbert Spraigue and Stephen Corman, Gene Sandusky and Dick Arledge and Lou Paulson. It didn't matter what questions they asked, or how they asked them, how many times they asked them, or what they did to him before asking them. The answers were always going to be the same. They were going to be the answers of an innocent man.

"How about Eleanor Cerami?" Jaywalker asked. "When's the first time you saw her?"

"At the hearing," said Darren. "Right?"

"Right," said Jaywalker, the tears overflowing.

The following day, Jaywalker brought a copy of the tape to Pope's office. Pope said he had an hour, so Jaywalker set it up and played it, and they listened to it together. Pope's reaction was pretty much the same as it had been to the Spraigue tape. He was impressed by Darren's consistency, but he felt that nothing new had been discovered to change things.

What, Jaywalker was forced to ask himself, if there simply *was* nothing new to be discovered?

But the very next day, May 31st, something new *was* discovered. Deep within its pages, the *New York Post* reported that a young man named Richard Timmons had been arrested and charged with rape. It wasn't the first newspaper lead Jaywalker would pursue, and it wouldn't be the last. An avid *Times* reader, he'd taken to buying the *Post* and the *Daily News* on a regular basis. He told his wife it was for their extended sports coverage, but he knew better, and she probably did, too. The *Times* simply didn't consider every rape arrest fit to print.

This particular article held out more promise than most, though. There had been a series of rapes; they'd taken place in the Bronx; the accused was a young black man; and the arraignment was to take place that very day.

Jaywalker dropped what he was doing and drove to the Bronx Criminal Courthouse, the same old building where Darren had first been taken following his arrest. He hung around all day, waiting to get a glimpse of Richard Timmons. But he never did. Timmons's case was adjourned without his ever being brought into the courtroom. Jaywalker made a note of the new date, June 13th, and circled it in his calendar. Then, figuring he was already in the Bronx and there were several hours of daylight left, he drove north and east once more, to Castle Hill.

As the spring days were getting longer, so was the weather turning warmer. Jaywalker's self-appointed vigil no longer meant frozen toes and chapped lips. And as the temperature rose and leaves began appearing on the trees, more and more people ventured out into the courtyards and onto the walkways of the project. And each new person, Jaywalker told himself, could be the one he was looking for. After all, it had been mid-August when the rapist had struck, mid-August and early September. Surely it was warm enough for him to surface again.

But a new problem worried Jaywalker now, the problem of time. With each passing day, he realized that his mission was turning into an obsession and beginning to take on a distinct Don Quixote aspect. He knew that after all this time, it was becoming less and less likely that he would spot the real rapist or recognize him if he did. And how could he possibly expect the victims to remember what the man really looked like? They'd seen him for fifteen or twenty minutes, nine months ago. Since then, they'd seen Darren's photograph and picked it out from among seventeen others. They'd seen him in person in court, for hours at a time, and had pointed directly to him. They'd said they were absolutely certain he was the man. And twelve jurors had adopted their certainty and made it their own. Even if Jaywalker were somehow able to spot the real rapist, subdue him and dump him in front of the victims, they would shake their heads and say no, it had been Darren Kingston who'd raped them. What had once been mere certainty was by now carved in stone.

The shadows lengthened that afternoon in Castle Hill, and the walkways gradually emptied. Jaywalker got back into his VW and turned it toward home, knowing he would still go back. It was better than sitting in his office and doing nothing, or staying home and feeling guilty.

And he *did* go back, again and again. And he combed the newspapers. And spoke with detectives and prosecutors, defense attorneys and court officers, asking about any rape cases they might have heard of. And he watched the days grow fewer as Darren's sentencing date drew nearer and nearer.

On June 13th, Jaywalker was back in Bronx Criminal Court to get a look at Richard Timmons, the defendant he'd missed earlier. This time, he got to see him. His case was called, and he was led out of the pen area to be taken before the judge. Jaywalker got up from his seat in the audience and headed for the pen. As he passed by Timmons, he was able to get a glimpse of him, but only a glimpse. He was pretty close to Darren's height of five-eight or five-nine, and of similar complexion. Jaywalker already knew Timmons's age; he'd stolen a look at the court papers, which listed him as twenty. Darren had been twenty-two when the victims had first picked out his photo. But the photo had been taken when he, too, had been twenty.

Jaywalker needed to get a better look at Timmons. He flashed his ID card and was admitted to the pen area. Instead of continuing, he stopped just inside the door, the door Timmons would be coming back through in a minute or so. A corrections officer asked if he could help him.

"No, thanks," said Jaywalker.

The door leading to the courtroom suddenly swung open, and Jaywalker found himself face-to-face with Richard Timmons. He was a baby. He might have been twenty, but he looked more like fourteen or fifteen. The Castle Hill victims had all described a man who looked like he was between twenty-five and thirty.

"Excuse us, counselor," a court officer was saying.

Jaywalker stepped aside.

"Fuckin' lawyers," said another court officer. "Nuthin' better to do than stand around, collectin' taxpayers' money."

22

A NEW YEAR'S TOAST

Darren Kingston was sentenced on June 19th, 1980.

Jaywalker met the Kingstons outside Part 16, the same courtroom in which Darren had been tried and convicted three months earlier. With Darren were Charlene, Inez, Marlin and a half-dozen other members of the family. They knew they were out of postponements.

Any defendant will literally beg you to bail him out. Jail is a horrible place, more horrible by a factor of ten than you can possibly imagine. Jaywalker himself had found that out the hard way in his younger years. Being out on bail becomes pure heaven. But everything changes come sentencing day. Suddenly the defendant in jail is the lucky one, for whom the event is just one more bump in the road. The defendant out on bail becomes the big loser. He has to walk through the courthouse door of his own free will, knowing he won't be walking out. He has to kiss his wife or girlfriend goodbye, tell his kids to grow up right, and know from the look on his mother's face that he might just as well have stabbed her through the heart.

The legal term for what he's doing, that bailed-out defendant, happens to be the same as the military term. He's *surrendering.* Some can't bring themselves to do it. They abscond; they jump bail. Some do so elaborately, staging their deaths, moving away, changing their identities, altering their appearances. Others do it more simply, as if biding their time while waiting for the inevitable to catch up with them. Still others commit new crimes, figuring they're going away anyway.

Of the out-on-bail defendants who *can* bring themselves to surrender, there are those who work out and bulk up as the day of reckoning approaches, knowing they'll need to be tough. There are those who shave their heads, figuring *looking* tough is the next best thing. Jaywalker had one client who'd gone to the dentist the day before and had a gold tooth pulled, because he didn't want another inmate knocking it out of his mouth without the benefit of Novocain.

Darren Kingston did none of these things. Just as he had long felt that his innocence would be established at some point, he now believed that before they put him back in jail, something would happen, something would intervene to prevent it, or at least postpone it once again. Only this time, he had at least a semirational basis for his belief.

Jaywalker hadn't exactly been idle over the past three months, what with arranging, attending and taping two hypnosis sessions and one sodium amytol interview; running down half a dozen leads from newspaper items and other sources; working on a motion to set aside the verdict; and spending literally hundreds of hours hanging around the Castle Hill Houses.

In addition to those chores, Jaywalker had made half a dozen trips to the Bronx County Courthouse with a single purpose in mind. He wanted to keep Darren out of jail after his sentencing. The vehicle for doing that was an appeal bond. It worked the same way a regular bail bond did, except that it covered the period from sentencing through the decision on an appeal, a period that could cover months and sometimes even several years.

The public can hardly be blamed for harboring a misconception about the frequency with which appeal bonds are granted. Open the newspaper or turn on the news, and before too long you'll come across someone who's out on appeal, even though he's already been sentenced to, say, five years in prison. But look again. That someone, it usually turns out, is a former public official, an entertainer, a sports figure or a celebrity of some other stripe. He's out because the same visibility that made him newsworthy in the first place will continue to make him newsworthy, and therefore available, to the criminal justice system, should someone go looking for him. And because his crime—larceny by signature, typically, or driving under the influence—is the sort of transgression that a lot of judges can relate to, sometimes even muttering into their robes, *"There but for the grace of God…"*

Rapists need not apply.

Especially black, knife-wielding, *serial* rapists.

The truth is that only a minuscule number of defendants are granted appeal bonds, a tiny fraction of a single percentage point. Defendants sentenced on crimes of violence are among the least likely candidates, as are those convicted of serious sex offenses, or those with multiple victims, or those who've used weapons in the commission of their crimes. Darren, of course, qualified as all of the above.

But in spite of the jury's verdict, there were still some

positive things to say about Darren. He was gentle, polite and soft-spoken. He came from a good family, had a wife and now two kids, and held down a decent job. All his roots and connections were right there in the Bronx. He had no passport, no driver's license, no place to flee to, even had he chosen to flee. Granted bail following his arrest, he'd never missed or been late for a single court appearance. All those things counted. But there was one thing that counted more. There was the vague, unspoken notion that maybe, just maybe, just possibly, Darren Kingston was completely innocent. By now, Jacob Pope had to have that notion, somewhere deep in his gut. Jaywalker had seen to that. And over the three months since the verdict, Jaywalker had made enlisting Pope's help on an appeal bond a crusade of sorts, second only to finding the real rapist.

He hoped to do better on this one than he'd so far done on the other.

He'd begun with the suggestion of yet another polygraph, but Pope had been cool to the mention of Cleve Bryant's name. Then Jaywalker had invited Pope to Herbert Spraigue's hypnosis regression, and Stephen Corman's sodium amytol interview. When Pope hadn't shown, whether by distraction or design, Jaywalker had brought him the tapes, even listening to one of them with him. And in the past month, Jaywalker had put his cards squarely on the table.

"I'm going to ask Davidoff to continue bail," he'd told Pope. "And I want you to join me in the application. You can say whatever you want. Tell him the corroboration issue is an intriguing one, or the rebuttal witnesses raise a good question of law. Tell him you think his rulings were right, but it'll be interesting to see what an appellate court says."

In the end, as Jaywalker had fully expected, Pope wouldn't go along it with. But he did the next best thing: he agreed not to oppose the application, so long as Davidoff didn't push him to take a position one way or the other.

"Because if the judge presses me," Pope explained, "I'm going to have to say my office opposes bail."

A week after that conversation, Jaywalker had happened to bump in to Max Davidoff. It might have had something to do with the fact that Jaywalker had been waiting outside the judge's courtroom for forty-five minutes. But Davidoff had no way of knowing that.

"How's that young man doing?" the judge asked. "Kingston."

It was about as much as either of them was ethically permitted to say, in the absence of Jacob Pope or someone else from the D.A.'s office. And no doubt Davidoff expected to hear an equally circumspect answer, something like, "Not so good," or "He's hanging in there."

Instead, Jaywalker took his shot. "Actually, he's feeling pretty relieved right now. I just told him that Mr. Pope's going to take no position on an appeal bond. He took it like a reprieve from the governor."

Davidoff, completely thrown off guard, could only raise one bushy white eyebrow, mutter something unintelligible and walk off. But at least whatever he'd muttered hadn't sounded like "No." He'd had his chance to object, and he hadn't taken it.

Knowing Davidoff was likely to ask Pope about the matter, Jaywalker hurried to beat him to the punch. He made a beeline for Pope's office.

"I just happened to run in to Justice Davidoff," he said. "He asked me what was new." It was a stretch, but not much of one for Jaywalker. "So I told him about our conversation. I hope that's okay with you. He kind of caught me by surprise."

Pope didn't seem overjoyed by the development, but he didn't go ballistic. So now he'd had his chance to object, too, and he hadn't.

And the seed had been planted.

The American system of justice is an adversarial one, pitting one lawyer against another, with a supposedly impartial judge placed between them to resolve any disputes. When one of the lawyers says he doesn't oppose what the other one's asking for, it's the functional equivalent of saying, "Go ahead, I don't care one way or the other." At that point, the judge is off the hook, indemnified from after-the-fact criticism. Or, in plainer language, his ass is covered.

Ten days later, as fate would have it, Jaywalker bumped in to Davidoff again.

"Did Pope really say he has no objection to continuing bail?" he asked.

"Scout's honor," said Jaywalker. It was close enough, especially for someone who'd never been a Scout and deemed honor a vastly overrated virtue. "He's going to take no position. He said just don't press him too hard to come right out and say he's okay with it."

"Protecting his boss?" Davidoff asked.

"There was a time," waxed Jaywalker, "when the boss didn't need protecting." That time, he didn't need to add, was when Max Davidoff had been district attorney.

And so the seed took root and sprouted.

By the time they assembled for sentencing, the Kingstons knew that however much time Justice Davidoff was going to give Darren—and it could be as much as fifty years—there was a very good chance he was going to let him stay out pending his appeal. Although even a very good chance may provide cold comfort indeed at such times.

THE CLERK: Number Six on the sentence calendar, Darren Kingston. Ready for sentence?

JAYWALKER: Yes, we are.

THE CLERK: Darren Kingston, is that your name?

DARREN: Y-y-yes.

Jacob Pope spoke first. He recommended that the court, in imposing sentence on the Cerami and Kenarden rapes, "cover" the Maldonado and Caldwell attempted rapes. This was either a rather generous move on Pope's part— since it meant that there wouldn't have to be a second, and perhaps even a third, trial—or yet another indication that by this time Pope himself harbored some nagging doubt about Darren's guilt and had lost the stomach for prosecuting him further.

Beyond that, he observed that the court was very familiar with the facts of the case and stated that he had no particular recommendation for length of sentence. This, too, was something of a concession on Pope's part. An assistant district attorney who's won a conviction after trial on a pair of knifepoint rapes typically urges the judge to impose the maximum sentence allowed by law and occasionally even more than that. The fact that Jacob Pope was urging nothing at all spoke volumes. As he had with his take-no-position stance on continuing bail, Pope was now telling Justice Davidoff that any sentence he chose to impose was okay with the prosecution.

Jaywalker spoke much longer. He began by thanking Pope for his professionalism. Then he moved to set aside the verdict, citing many of the same issues he'd raised at trial—the racially unrepresentative jury panel, the insufficient corroboration, the improper rebuttal case and the discrepancies between the man described by the victims and the one convicted by the jury. Predictably, Davidoff denied the motion.

Next Jaywalker talked about the polygraphs Darren had taken, the hypnosis sessions and the sodium amytol interview. Strictly speaking, none of those matters bore any relevance to sentencing, but Jaywalker wanted to get them into the record anyway. Months from now, a panel of appellate judges was going to have to read the transcript, and Jaywalker didn't want to allow them the luxury of skimming through it as just another case. He wanted them to see how passionately he believed in Darren's innocence, and to know that he wasn't alone in his belief. He wanted, in other words, to make it as hard as he possibly could for them to affirm the conviction. He wanted them to read his words and choke on them.

Jaywalker pointed to Darren's work record, noting that the post office had seen fit to take him back despite the conviction. He mentioned the lack of any prior conviction—indeed, any prior arrest for a sex crime of any sort. He pointed, literally, to Darren's family. It had been his intention to name them, one by one. But now, as he turned to them, he saw Inez, Marlin and Charlene sitting together, their hands intertwined, and the sight overwhelmed him. All his pain and frustration and anger boiled over. All the interviews and sessions and tests they'd been through came back to him, all the freezing afternoons he'd spent in Castle Hill. His eyes filled with tears, and as he looked back down at his notes, the words blurred and disappeared from view. As he continued to speak, the tears rolled freely down his face, and his voice cracked like a schoolboy's.

JAYWALKER: I believe this case is one that has troubled the district attorney's office. I believe it is a case that has troubled Your Honor. I hope each of you has doubts as to the defendant's guilt on these charges, regardless of the jury's verdict. I myself have no doubt whatsoever. I know that the man standing next to me is as innocent of these charges as you and I are.

They were the last words he could get out.

THE CLERK: Mr. Kingston, have you anything to say on your own behalf before the court imposes sentence?

DARREN: Y-y-yes. Your Honor, I'd just like to say that I'm as innocent of these charges as any man in the c-c-c-courtroom. I went along with the court system 'cause I had nothing t-t-to hide. I came here with the truth. I made no alibis, no excuses. I came here with the truth b-b-because I knew I was innocent.

I don't believe that anybody who's listened to

this case can say that they b-b-believe I'm guilty. I think anybody who's related to this c-case must feel inside that I'm innocent. And I just hope that th-th-this moral obligation I hope they have frees me from this conviction.

Justice Davidoff began by saying that every case disturbed him. He noted that the law allowed him to impose a sentence of as much as twenty-five years on each charge, and to run the terms consecutively. Normally, he said, he would do just that, and set a minimum term, as well as a maximum. But, having read the probation report, and having considered the defendant's background and other matters, he'd decided against doing either of those things.

THE COURT: But the jury has spoken, and I do have an obligation. I must impose a term of imprisonment in this case. The jury had a basis to make their determination. They had a duty to evaluate the evidence. They were here. You disagree with their verdict. But nevertheless, based upon the testimony, they had a right to find as they did. That was their privilege, and that was their obligation. The defendant, having been convicted of Rape in the First Degree, is sentenced to a term of imprisonment not to exceed ten years.

The judge went on to impose an additional ten-year sentence on the remaining rape and sodomy counts, as well as a one-year term on the weapon charge. But he directed that all of the sentences run concurrently. The result was a single ten-year sentence, with no required minimum. It was as good as Jaywalker could have hoped for, probably much better. But it was still ten years.

THE COURT: Furthermore, because of several in-teresting legal questions that arose during the course of the trial, unless the People have an objection, I am prepared to continue the defendant's present bail conditions pending the outcome of any appeal. Mr. Pope?

POPE: The People have no objection.

Downstairs, Jaywalker huddled with the Kingstons, as he had so many times before. As always, they thanked him. And they conceded that things could have turned out worse. Even Pope, Inez mentioned, had been reasonable.

"It would all have been reasonable," Marlin observed, "if my son was guilty."

They said their goodbyes. Jaywalker found his car, a parking ticket beneath one windshield wiper. He cursed whoever had given it to him, cursed the jury who'd made him come back to court, cursed his profession. Then, because it was still early in the day and he had nothing better to do, he drove to Castle Hill.

The next day, Jaywalker got a call from somebody named Ed Kirkbride. He said he was a reporter for the *Daily News*. He'd heard about the Kingston case, probably from a court officer or someone else at the courthouse, who might or might not have pocketed a twenty-dollar bill for passing along the word. Kirkbride was interested in doing a piece for the upcoming Sunday edition. He thought some publicity might help, or so he said. Pointedly, he mentioned that his paper had the largest daily circulation in the world.

"Interested?" he asked.

For Jaywalker, this marked a first. Over the years to come, he would handle more than his share of high-profile cases, and his answer to the interview requests that came with them would always be pretty much the same: "Thanks, but we'll try our case in court."

Then he thought of Darren, and his willingness to try anything, no matter how untraditional, expensive or personally inconvenient.

"I'm interested," said Jaywalker.

Kirkbride showed up the following day to interview Darren and Jaywalker. He brought along a photographer, who took several shots of them.

The story, and one of the photos, filled all of Page 5 of June 23rd's Sunday *News*.

CITED IN 4 RAPES, CONVICTED IN 2, BUT DOUBTS LINGER

Jaywalker read the article. It was straightforward stuff, drawn heavily from what he'd told Kirkbride about the case. He sat back, waiting for the phone to ring. Would the real rapist come forward to correct the injustice? Would one of the victims reconsider and admit her mistake? Would the photo bring leads to a look-alike?

The very next day, a woman from Bayside called to say

she'd read the story and was impressed with Jaywalker's diligence. Did he by any chance handle divorces?

Other than that, the phone didn't ring.

On July 10th, Jaywalker appeared in court to have papers signed for Darren's appeal bond. The surety company's agent had insisted on rewriting the bond, requiring Marlin to pay a second—sizeable—premium. By that time he'd paid Jaywalker's fee in full, the two bail-bond premiums, John McCarthy's fee, the private polygraph cost, and the fees of Herbert Spraigue and Stephen Corman. In addition to all of that, he'd put up his home and every dollar he had or could borrow as collateral for the bonds. Now he asked Jaywalker to handle Darren's appeal, explaining that he could borrow the money from his pension plan at the Transit Authority.

Jaywalker had by that time given a great deal of thought to the appeal. It would entail researching the case law even more exhaustively than he already had, putting together a written brief, preparing and defending an oral argument, and then doing it all over again if the state's highest court was interested in reviewing the case. A reasonable fee would be right up there with the five thousand dollars Marlin had already paid for the trial. And Jaywalker could certainly use the money. He had a wife and a child at home to support, a mortgage and a growing stack of overdue bills. And his obsession with Darren's case had pretty much driven the rest of his practice into the ground.

Yet there was no way Jaywalker could take more money from the Kingstons. He told Marlin he would file a notice of appeal for Darren, but that he wasn't enough of an appellate lawyer to handle the appeal himself. Before going into private practice, Jaywalker had worked for the Legal

Aid Society, and he knew they had a very good appeals division. Moreover, they were free. Now he told Marlin that he wanted them to handle it. He promised to work hand-in-hand with them on the brief, and even to argue the case orally if they would let him. But they were the experts, and Darren needed all the help he could get.

"Don't worry about the money, Jay," said Marlin. "I can get the money. I want you to keep working for my son."

"I'll keep working for your son," Jaywalker assured him. He wanted to add that it wasn't just an idle promise on his part, that by this time it would be constitutionally impossible for him to *stop* working for Darren. Instead, he came up with a more rational excuse for bringing Legal Aid in.

"Suppose, after reading the trial transcript, they decide that I messed up? I'd want them to feel free to say so, and to ask for a new trial because of incompetence of counsel."

"Incompetence of counsel? Like, you didn't do your job?" Marlin laughed out loud. "You know how much I love my son, Jay?"

"I think so."

"You know how much I believe he's innocent?"

Jaywalker nodded.

"Jay," said Marlin, "I seen you fight for my son like a tiger, and I seen you cry for him like a baby. I'd tell my son to serve every day of those ten years before I'd let anyone say you didn't do your job."

Jaywalker was tempted to debate the issue. A lawyer could do his job and still end up providing what the courts termed *inadequate assistance of counsel*. But he knew Marlin didn't want to hear nuances, so he simply said, "Thank you," and left it at that. But he continued to be firm about bringing in reinforcements. Jaywalker had lived with the case for the better part of a year by now. He'd done his best, and his best hadn't been good enough. Nothing he'd done had worked—before, during or after the trial. It was time to get help.

He served and filed the notice of appeal, including in it a statement that Darren was without funds and would need counsel appointed to represent him on the appeal. And then, perhaps because his symbolic abandonment of Darren caused him to feel guilty, however irrationally, he cranked the starter on his VW and headed once more for Castle Hill.

Late that July, as a result of his conviction and sentence, Darren Kingston was indefinitely suspended without pay by the post office. His supervisor, P. G. Hamilton, received an official reprimand from headquarters in Washington for having permitted Darren to return to work.

Out of a job, Darren became depressed and, after a time, nearly despondent. Prior to his arrest, both he and his wife had been working, and between their two salaries, they'd been self-sufficient. They'd maintained their own apartment, supported their son, and had even been saving money in anticipation of the arrival of their second child. Following Darren's arrest, they'd moved back in with his parents. Now, with a new baby at home, Charlene had been forced to stop working, and with the loss of his job, Darren's ability to support his wife and children ended abruptly. Reluctantly, he applied for public assistance. In a family where both the men and women were accustomed to working regularly, it was one more humiliation in a never-ending series. And it couldn't have been made any easier by the fact that Darren's mother worked for the same Welfare Department that would now be issuing his checks.

August 19th, 1980

More than a year had passed since the rapes. Jaywalker found himself in a fourth-floor courtroom at 100 Centre Street, the Manhattan Criminal Courthouse. He'd walked into the pen area to conduct an interview. Another lawyer was speaking with a client down at one end of the steel bars. A third prisoner urinated noisily into an open toilet.

Jaywalker muttered a greeting to the corrections officers on duty. One of them commented on the weather. Probably that it was hot.

Jaywalker can no longer recall the name of the client he interviewed that day, or what he was charged with, or what he had to say about those charges. He can recall only that at some point in the conversation he became aware that he'd tuned the man out and was listening instead to the voices coming from the other end of the pen.

"So altogether, Mr. Jackson," the lawyer was saying, "you're charged with three rapes, as well as possession of the knife you had on you when they picked you up."

Jaywalker moved to a spot where he could get a look at this Mr. Jackson. The man he saw was a dead ringer for Darren. A black man of medium complexion, twenty-five years old or so. Same height, but a bit heavier-looking. Multiple rape charges. Even a knife. Jaywalker felt his heart pounding wildly. Totally ignoring his own client, he listened to the rest of the conversation. Back out in the courtroom, he waited until the case had been called and adjourned. Then he checked the court calendar.

JACKSON, Otis (27)
Rape, Poss. Of Weapon

That evening, he fought the impulse to call Darren. He simply didn't have enough to go on yet, and given how depressed Darren was, he didn't want to raise his hopes only to destroy them. But that night he lay awake for hours, feeling the adrenaline pump and the hope build.

The adrenaline pumped and the hope built until three o'clock the following afternoon, when Jaywalker was able to steal a look at Otis Jackson's court papers. Otis was a twenty-seven-year-old black male. He stood five foot nine and weighed 175 pounds, the same weight the Castle Hill victims had estimated for their attacker. And the weapon he'd been arrested with was described as a "kitchen knife, approx. 10 inches in overall length, with a thin, shiney [*sic*] blade approx. 5 inches in length."

But according to Otis's fingerprint sheet, he'd spent all of August of 1979, and most of September, as a guest of the House of Detention for Men on Rikers Island, awaiting disposition of a burglary charge.

In September, Jaywalker learned that the Legal Aid Society had in fact been appointed to represent Darren Kingston on his appeal. He phoned Will Hellerman, the head of their appeals division and the man who'd been instrumental in landing Jaywalker a job with Legal Aid four years earlier. He told Will about the case, and about how strongly he believed in Darren's innocence. He offered him whatever help he could use. Hellerman said he would see to it that one of the senior members of his staff got assigned to the case.

September gave way to October, and October to November. The days grew shorter and colder. It had been well over a year now since Darren's arrest, eight months since his conviction. Jaywalker continued to comb the newspapers and follow up on any leads he spotted. He kept scanning court calendars, checking out defendants accused of rape. And still he made his trips to Castle Hill. But he knew he was only fooling himself. Too much time had passed. The real rapist had moved on or been arrested, maybe even died, or had taken up some new perversion, leaving Darren to face his prison sentence and Jaywalker to chase shadows in the Bronx.

He slowly came to realize that Darren's only hope lay in the appeal. A totally innocent man stood wrongly convicted of horrendous crimes, and now the only thing standing between him and state prison was the appellate process. But that process, Jaywalker knew, was a cold one, a bloodless one. If Darren was to be saved by it, it wouldn't be because he was the wrong man, but because of some legal technicality, some procedural error that had nothing to do with guilt or innocence.

But so be it. If the appeal was Darren's only chance, then the appeal it would be. A win was a win, after all. And they *had* to win. In criminal law, there are no trophies handed out for second place, no honorable mentions. You won it all, or you went off and did your time.

Jaywalker phoned Legal Aid Appeals for the twentieth time. For the twentieth time, the secretary, with whom he was by this time on a first-name basis, told him they still hadn't received the transcript of Darren's trial, and therefore no staff member had yet been assigned to the case. For the twentieth time, Jaywalker left instructions asking to be called as soon as someone was assigned. The secretary assured him that she would see to it. No, she didn't need his phone number. She knew it by heart.

Winter came.

Jaywalker cut down on his trips to Castle Hill. He tried other cases, some of them involving defendants who'd done pretty much what they'd been accused of. He won them all. With each acquittal, he asked himself what he'd done wrong in Darren's case, and came up with plenty of answers. Had he become too personally involved in it, like the doctor who treats a member of his own family? Should he have kept Darren off the stand? Should he have cross-examined Tania Maldonado and Elvira Caldwell more fully? He second-guessed his voir dire of the jury panel, his opening statement, his summation and everything in between. He cursed himself for not having called John McCarthy to the stand, for not putting Marlin on. He wondered how Justice Davidoff would have decided the case, had Jaywalker decided to go nonjury.

The list was endless, the possibilities maddening.

He saw little of Darren and spoke to him only infrequently. It seemed to Jaywalker that the stutter had grown worse than ever. He'd taken to speaking to Charlene to find out how Darren was doing. Or she would call him whenever she came across a newspaper item about a rape case. On the rare occasion when Jaywalker hadn't already seen it himself, he would check it out. Invariably, some similarity would appear and he would feel a sudden flicker of hope. But then something would end up wrong with it. The suspect would turn out to be white or Hispanic, or too young or too old, too tall or too short, or in jail at the time of the Castle Hill rapes. Jaywalker would report back to

Charlene and give her the news. She would say she'd figured as much and apologize for having bothered him. Jaywalker would assure her it hadn't been any bother. And he would tell her in the most positive voice he could muster that one of these days, one of her leads was going to check out. He was quite sure that neither of them believed it anymore. Yet still they continued to repeat their little ritual each time, going through the motions, playing the game, putting on their brave faces, saying all the right things.

Because to do otherwise would have been to give up and admit defeat. And neither of them, it seemed, knew how to do that.

Christmas approached.

Jaywalker and his family neither flew to Florida nor went skiing this time around. There simply wasn't the money. As they wrapped presents and decorated for the holidays, Jaywalker tried to imagine the scene at the Kingston household. Afraid that his voice on the phone would do nothing but remind them of Darren's troubles, he convinced himself that it was best not to call them. That was nonsense, of course. The truth was, he simply couldn't bring himself to dial the phone. Still, the day before Christmas, a greeting card arrived in the mail, signed by all of them, warmly thanking him for everything. It made Jaywalker feel ashamed for not having called and for failing them, and guilty over his own good fortune.

The year drew to an end, and at a friend's New Year's Eve gathering, it came Jaywalker's turn to make a toast. As he raised his glass, he caught sight of someone pouring from a bottle of Seagram's V.O. He fled from the room and locked himself in the bathroom. There he lay on the floor, doubled over in pain, sobbing uncontrollably, the water running full force in the sink to mask the sound. When he finally emerged, he apologized for having had too much to drink.

He didn't know what else to say.

23

NO PLACE TO BE

In late January, Jaywalker received a phone call. The young woman on the other end introduced herself as Carolyn Oates. She was a lawyer with the appeals division of the Legal Aid Society, she explained, and she'd been assigned the case of *The People of the State of New York v. Darren Kingston*. She'd just finished reading the transcript of the trial and had come across an envelope inserted among the pages. Opening it up, she'd found twenty message slips requesting that Jaywalker be called.

They arranged to meet.

The fact that Darren's appeal would finally be moving forward was both good news and bad. Good, because the appeal had come to represent their last real hope to change the outcome of the trial. Bad, because it meant the clock had begun running again. Within a few short months, the briefs would be written, the oral argument heard and a decision handed down. If that decision went against them and the state's highest court were to decline to consider the case further—as it does ninety-nine percent of the time—it meant there would be nothing left to prevent Darren from going to prison to begin serving his sentence.

They met a few days later, over grilled cheese sandwiches in the luncheonette on the ground floor of Jaywalker's office building. Carolyn Oates struck him as young, too young to be one of the senior staff members. Will Hellerman had promised he would assign someone experienced to handle the appeal. But she seemed smart, knowledgeable and interested in the case. What impressed Jaywalker even more was that fact that she'd already reached out to Darren and Charlene, and arranged to meet them. Because appellate lawyers are notorious for their reluctance to get involved with their clients on a personal level, Carolyn's overture to the Kingstons immediately won Jaywalker over.

He felt the most important thing he could contribute at that point was to convince her of Darren's innocence. Even though the appeal would dance around that issue and never confront it head-on, Jaywalker wanted to turn Carolyn into as much a believer as he himself was. And as the hour passed and the grilled cheese disappeared, he felt he was able to do just that. It seemed, in fact, that he could convince just about everyone. Everyone, that was, except the twelve people who'd mattered.

They discussed some of the legal issues in the case. Carolyn believed, as did Jaywalker, that Justice Davidoff's permitting the rebuttal testimony of Tania Maldonado and Elvira Caldwell had been wrong. And she shared his belief that the corroboration issue was fertile ground. But even as they fed off each other's optimism, they were both keenly aware of the reality of appellate practice. Only a small percentage of convictions get reversed. And asking a court to upset a guilty verdict in an armed, multiple rape case was asking a lot. Beyond that, they knew there was a major obstacle they had to contend with on the corroboration issue. Under pressure from women's groups, the legislature had relaxed the corroboration requirement since the time of the Castle Hill rapes. In their brief, Carolyn Oates and Jaywalker would be trying to persuade the court to throw out a conviction that met the standards of the law now in effect. That meant their plea would hardly be the kind of stuff that cries out for justice.

Winter gave way to spring.

Jaywalker took a ride up to Ossining one afternoon, in order to get a look at an inmate at Sing Sing Prison who'd recently been convicted of a rape committed in the South Bronx. But his face bore obvious burn scars from a childhood accident.

Jaywalker began aiming his VW for the Castle Hill Houses again, though not on as regular a basis as before. But still he went. Old habits die hard.

He kept in touch with Carolyn Oates. They agreed to limit the brief to their three best points. They both felt that the inclusion of weaker points would only cost them credibility in the long run and detract from the final product.

In April, Charlene called to say she and Darren had received notification from the Housing Authority that the City of New York was moving to evict them because of Darren's conviction. Although they were living with his parents, they had continued to pay the modest rent on their own apartment, digging into whatever savings they had left. It served as a place to go when the pressure became too much. More importantly, Jaywalker suspected, it represented hope. It was their apartment, their home. It was the place they would return to once Darren was vindicated. Now the city was threatening to take it away from them.

Jaywalker told Charlene to send him the notice, that he would help them fight it if he could. When it arrived in the mail, he studied the specifications.

> On or about September 12, 1979, you, Darren Kingston, did unlawfully force a project tenant to engage in sexual intercourse against her will.
>
> Further, you, Darren Kingston, did unlawfully possess a weapon, to wit, a knife.
>
> By virtue of the above, your continued occupancy constitutes a detriment to the health, safety and/or morals of your neighbors and the community; an adverse influence upon sound family and community life; and a source of danger to the peaceful occupation of other tenants.

Leaving for another day the fact that they'd gotten the date wrong, Jaywalker sent off a letter to the Housing Authority's legal department, informing them that an appeal was pending in the case and requesting that they hold off until it had been decided.

Several days later, he got a call from one of their lawyers. He was willing to grant a postponement of the proceedings, but only a short one. A hearing would have to be held within the next few weeks.

In early May, Darren showed up at Jaywalker's office to report an interesting development. He'd gone into a candy store in the Bronx to buy cigarettes. He'd recognized the young woman behind the cash register as Tania Maldonado, the third of the four victims. What struck him, and Jaywalker, as significant was the fact that Tania Maldonado hadn't recognized *him*. Or if she had, she'd done a wonderful job of pretending not to.

Together, Jaywalker and Carolyn pondered what possible use they might make of the incident. They decided that Darren should visit the store again—several times, if necessary—although never alone. They would keep a detailed written record of the dates and times of his visits. Then, if Darren continued to be unrecognized, they would consider approaching Miss Maldonado or Jacob Pope, or both of them, with the fact that, in a neutral situation, at least one of the victims had completely failed to recognize Darren as her attacker.

In the third week of May, Jaywalker received word from the Housing Authority that a hearing on Darren and Charlene's apartment had been scheduled for early June. He checked with Carolyn Oates, who reported that she expected to submit her brief sometime in August, and estimated that the oral argument would be scheduled for November or December. That meant no decision on the appeal would be likely until early next year. Jaywalker knew there was no way they were going to be able to buy that much time with the Housing Authority. He decided their best bet would be to go forward with the hearing and then try to convince the examiner to put off making a decision for as long as possible. He even allowed himself the fantasy that the hearing might turn up a new lead of some sort.

* * *

Jaywalker met Darren at the Housing Authority's administrative offices on the afternoon of June 5th. He located Kenneth Metzger, the lawyer who would be representing the authority. Metzger explained that he had no "live" witnesses present, that all he intended to do was submit a certified copy of Darren's conviction.

So much for new leads.

Metzger asked if Jaywalker planned on contesting the truth of the document. Jaywalker assured him that he didn't. Together, they went into the hearing room. A printed sign on the door proclaimed

MILES MICHAEL
IMPARTIAL HEARING EXAMINER

The first thing Jaywalker did was to ask if all of the hearing examiners were impartial, or if it had just been their good luck to get one that was. His question drew a smile from Miles Michael, an athletic-looking black man who turned out to be every bit as impartial as his title claimed.

Jaywalker explained that he was prepared to concede the fact of the conviction, and was only asking that Mr. Michael reserve decision on Darren and Charlene's tenancy until the appeal had been decided. When Kenneth Metzger voiced no objection, Mr. Michael agreed.

It was a small victory, but in a war that had been marked with pretty much nothing but defeats, it was a welcome one. And although Jaywalker would never tell his colleagues that he'd stooped to appear on such a lowly administrative matter, he understood its importance to Darren and Charlene. Sometimes being a criminal defense lawyer meant going before the Housing Authority or the Motor Vehicle Department, even the Taxi and Limousine Commission. Sometimes it meant visiting an inmate whose family couldn't afford the bus fare upstate. Sometimes it meant bringing along a book for that inmate to read, or a warm blanket to help him get through the winter. Whatever it was, you did it, and then you went home and thanked your lucky stars that you were fortunate enough to be on the giving end, instead of the receiving one.

The finishing touches were put on the appeal brief by the middle of August. The argument ran twenty-eight pages, and represented the combined efforts of Carolyn Oates and Jaywalker. The final wording was hers, and it was good. Jaywalker had to temper his excitement at reading it by reminding himself how few appeals were successful, and how, to the judges who read it, it would discuss just another rape conviction.

The brief was served upon the district attorney's office and filed with the Appellate Division that governs the Bronx and Manhattan. The next order of business was to sit back and wait for the D.A.'s brief in opposition. But sitting back and waiting was something that Jaywalker found impossible to do. So once again he aimed his old Volkswagen for the Bronx, to Castle Hill.

It had been almost two years since his first trip to the project, and things had been changing, bit by bit. Whereas at first he had been able to pretty much blend in, by now his face was just about the only white one in sight. On this particular day, he spotted only one other, an elderly, ruddy-faced woman whom he took to be Irish, though he had no real way of knowing. She peered out from behind the drapes of a second-floor window. At one point they locked eyes, and she wagged a bony finger back and forth in his direction, her way of warning him that for a person like him, it was no place to be.

24

JAMMED UP PRETTY GOOD

September 12th, 1981

Two years to the day since Darren's arrest.

Jaywalker and Carolyn Oates were still waiting for the district attorney's brief. They'd heard that the appeals bureau was overworked and backed up, and that it would be another month at least before they should expect it. Jaywalker regarded that as good news, a reprieve of sorts.

That was what they were down to.

Jaywalker's wife's sister and her husband had come over to the house to play bridge. Not the younger sister, who still worked at the Welfare Department with Inez Kingston, but the older one, a special-ed teacher from Brooklyn. She and her husband had brought bagels and lox, cream cheese with chives, and that day's *New York Post* and *Daily News*—all items hard to find in New Jersey back then.

Jaywalker was in the process of underplaying a hand he'd overbid. His partner at that particular moment, his sister-in-law, had laid down her hand and assumed the role of dummy. Either bored or exasperated at the number of tricks Jaywalker was managing to lose, she picked up one of the newspapers and began leafing through it.

"Hey, Jay," he heard her say. "Another rapist for you to check out."

By now, Jaywalker and his crusade had become something of a family joke. Not that any of them came right out and ridiculed him to his face. But he'd caught a look or two here and a comment there, and pretty much knew they all thought he'd slipped off the tracks some time ago.

He finished losing the hand before taking a look at what his sister-in-law had spotted. It was a tiny item in the *Daily News,* buried deep in the middle pages, about a Bronx man who'd been charged with a number of rapes in various housing projects. Jaywalker searched for some mention of the Castle Hill Houses, but it was missing from the list. Just their luck. He tore out the article anyway, figuring he would check it out when he got a chance. If nothing else, it would give him something to do and make waiting for the D.A.'s brief a little easier.

Less than an hour later, Charlene Kingston phoned. Jaywalker laughed as soon as he heard her voice. Without giving her a chance to explain why she'd called, he said, "I saw it."

They both laughed, something neither of them had been doing much of lately. Jaywalker promised he would look into it first chance he got.

* * *

On Monday, word came from the D.A.'s office that they were asking for an extension to get their brief in. It's customary to consent to such requests, particularly when the defendant's out on bail. In Darren's case, the request came as music to their ears. Carolyn Oates told them to take as much time as they needed. They could have months if they wanted. Years.

Jaywalker reached into his pocket for something and felt a piece of paper. He took it out and looked at it. The newspaper clipping. The man's name was Joseph Sperling. No age, no race, no physical description. Not much to go on. He phoned the Bronx D.A.'s office. They couldn't help him, other than to tell him that Sperling was due to appear in court on September 25th. Jaywalker made a note of the date and resolved to be there.

He couldn't be.

He was on trial in Manhattan. He tried to get hold of a photo of Sperling but had to settle for a description relayed over the phone by an obliging court officer. Black, medium height, medium build. How many times had Jaywalker been down this road? Far too many to count. But in spite of the odds, he felt the old excitement beginning to build once more.

He asked the officer about Sperling's next court appearance and was told it was October 14th. Jaywalker smiled to himself. The date was his own half-birthday.

He drove his daughter to a farm stand to buy a pumpkin for Halloween. This time, she didn't insist on the biggest one they had. Instead, she wanted two.

"Why two?" he asked her.

"So I can carve two faces," she explained. "One happy and one sad. Like you, Daddy."

It took his breath away and made him resolve to smile more, though it soon went the way of most of his resolutions.

Jaywalker managed to make it to the Bronx on October 14th, but Joseph Sperling didn't. There'd been a mix-up of some sort, and he was never produced. Prisoners aren't just brought to court; they're *produced*.

It was becoming clear to Jaywalker that if he wanted to get a look at Joseph Sperling, he was going to have to do it the hard way. He called the Department of Corrections and learned that Sperling was being held on Rikers Island. Because Jaywalker wasn't his lawyer, he wasn't entitled to a counsel visit with him. He toyed with the idea of contacting Sperling's lawyer—he was someone Jaywalker knew, but not at all well—and working through him. It would certainly be the ethical way of going about it. But would Sperling's lawyer permit Jaywalker access to his client? Jaywalker certainly wouldn't have, had the roles been reversed. So he decided to be devious. In the greater scheme of things, he told himself, what could possibly be more ethical than bending the rules on behalf of a wrongly convicted man? And if that rationalization led to a slippery slope, well, Jaywalker was no stranger to the slopes. And at that point, he was far less interested in ethics than he was in results.

So he drew up papers requesting a special one-day pass, swearing falsely that Sperling was a witness in an upcoming trial. *People v. Esperanza,* he called the nonexistent case. Spanish for *hope*. Jaywalker realized he could land in deep shit if either Sperling or his lawyer decided to make a complaint against him, but it was a chance he was willing to take.

Then, before he could make it out to Rikers Island, he got caught on trial again. Joseph Sperling, the rapist, would have to wait while Jaywalker defended Dwayne Pittman, the robber. Pittman was as guilty as they came. He and an accomplice had attempted a "push-in" robbery, trying to force their way into the apartment of a woman who'd just come home from the supermarket, but her screams had frightened them off. The accomplice had fled to the roof and gotten away. Pittman had run down the stairs and into the arms of the arriving police officers. In spite of that fact, Pittman was acquitted. After the trial, the jurors confided in Jaywalker that they were pretty sure his client was guilty but they hadn't quite been convinced beyond a reasonable doubt.

Two thoughts immediately came to Jaywalker. First, he must be getting better at what he did for a living. And second, where had these jurors been when he'd really needed them?

It was raining the day he finally drove out to Rikers Island. He'd altered the date on his one-day pass, but it got him through the first checkpoint anyway. He crossed the bridge that separates the real world from the redbrick compounds that dot the island. He squeezed his VW into half a parking spot and caught the corrections bus to HDM, the House of Detention for Men. He surrendered his pass, showed his identification and was buzzed into a secure area. At a set of steel bars, he hollered his loudest "On the gate!" and was admitted to the counsel room.

He had spent a lot of hours, awake and asleep, wondering what the real rapist would look like. Because his faith in eyewitness identification was so minimal, each time he'd made one of his forays to Castle Hill, he'd known better than to expect to find a doppelgänger, a perfect double for Darren. He knew that, Yvette Monroe's experience notwithstanding, the resemblance between Darren and the actual perpetrator might turn out to be rather slight. But when Joseph Sperling walked into the room, nobody had to point him out to Jaywalker.

Even from thirty feet away, Jaywalker was immediately struck by two things. First, Sperling looked like Darren. Second, he looked exactly like the man described by the victims. His height, complexion and hair were the same as Darren's. But he looked older and heavier than Darren, precisely as the victims had initially described their attacker.

Jaywalker walked over to him. "Joseph Sperling?" he asked.

The man turned his way and nodded, but said nothing.

"My name is Jaywalker."

They walked to one of the interview cubicles, a small enclosure with a table that separated two matching chairs, both of them bolted to the floor. On the table was a plastic ashtray. In 1981 it was still okay to smoke.

They sat down.

Jaywalker opened his mouth to say something. He'd had all morning to rehearse his speech. Or more than two full years, if you wanted to look at it that way. Yet no words would come out. He could only sit there, frozen, his mouth open, his eyes wide.

There are moments in life that stay with us forever, moments that, years later, when we shut our eyes, we can relive as vividly as if the event were happening all over again. Sitting there in the counsel room, Jaywalker suddenly found himself in the midst of such a moment.

He was looking into a pair of maroon eyes.

Afterward, he would have no idea how long he stared at the man. It might have been ten seconds, or it might have been ten minutes; he truly didn't know. He would know only that somehow he must have managed to get hold of himself, because at some point he found himself speaking.

He asked Sperling to listen to what he had to say before responding. He told him exactly who he was, and why he was there. He told him he was free to speak with him or not, as he pleased. He did all those things not to be fair to Sperling, but to make Joseph Sperling *think* he was being fair to him.

Sperling said he'd speak with him.

"I hear you're jammed up pretty good," said Jaywalker, lapsing into street talk from his DEA days.

Sperling nodded and said, "You could say that."

They discussed his situation. Sperling did most of the talking, Jaywalker most of the listening. In a soft voice, he described the chain of events that had led him to where he was.

If he was to be believed, Joseph Sperling had been a bright and talented teenager. He'd won a track scholarship to a well-known university in the south. There he'd fallen in love with a white woman. They'd moved into an apartment off campus. Before long, a disapproving neighbor had complained to the police. One thing had led to another, and Sperling had been expelled from school and run out of town. He'd ended up in New York. A year or two later, he'd been arrested for a minor sex offense with another white woman, in Manhattan. He'd been tried and convicted—unjustly, he claimed. He came away bitter, and his bitterness festered and ripened into an obsession. He began prowling various housing projects, mostly in the Bronx, committing rapes that in his mind he'd already been punished for. His victims were always young, always pretty and always white. Eventually he'd been caught. Relieved that the ordeal was over, he'd quickly confessed.

"How about my client's rapes?" Jaywalker asked him. "Castle Hill. August and September, nineteen-seventy-nine."

"No," he said, "I didn't do those. But I did make the phone call."

Phone call?

Sperling said that shortly after Darren's trial, he'd seen the article in the *Daily News*. "I picked up the phone and called the D.A.," he said. "I told them they had the wrong man. I sorta made it sound like I did those rapes. But I didn't."

If true, this was an incredible piece of news. No one had ever reported such a call to Jaywalker. But this was no time to wonder why. He needed to press on.

"So why did you call?" he asked.

Sperling shrugged absently. "I felt sorry for your man, I guess. I knew what it felt like to be framed. But there's no way I did those rapes. I was working then, and that was before I started."

"Where were you working?"

"The telephone company," said Sperling. Then, when he saw Jaywalker staring at him, he added, "You can check it out if you want to."

But Jaywalker didn't want to. He was staring not

because he doubted Sperling's employment, but because it struck him that his having worked for the telephone company wasn't all that different from Darren's having worked at the post office. Here were two young men who not only looked alike but whose lives, at least up to a point, hadn't been so different. Now those two lives were on a collision course, with Jaywalker at the intersection. And because he still couldn't get over Sperling's maroon eyes.

"Were you working nights?" Jaywalker asked.

"Yeah."

"Are you by any chance circumcised?"

That drew a strange look from Sperling, but he said, "Yes."

"Are you right-handed or left-handed?" Jaywalker asked him.

"Right-handed."

"The girls," said Jaywalker. "Ever hurt any of them?"

"No," said Sperling. "Well, one of them tried to grab the knife and cut her hand."

Jaywalker tried to conceal his reaction, but it was hard. Not only had there been a knife involved, but he was also listening to an account of the Tania Maldonado incident. Only Sperling had changed the story around a bit, making it Miss Maldonado who'd been cut, rather than Sperling himself. Jaywalker wondered if Sperling still had a scar to show from it. Darren certainly didn't.

"How old was the oldest?" he asked.

"Thirtyish."

"The youngest?"

"Twelve," said Sperling. "But I let her go. One thing I'm not is a child molester."

Maria Sanchez, the fourteen-year-old who'd lied about

her age to escape, and whose parents later refused to allow her to cooperate in the investigation.

Jaywalker spent the next full hour doing everything he could think of to convince Joseph Sperling to admit to the Castle Hill rapes. He tried to show him how doing so couldn't possibly make things any worse for him. In fact, Jaywalker suggested, it would demonstrate his decency and his compassion for someone who'd been falsely convicted. Jaywalker offered to go to court and make a statement on Sperling's behalf at his sentencing. He told him that he could help arrange for a psychiatric evaluation and follow-up care.

He did those things and more, because by now Jaywalker no longer had the slightest bit of doubt. Joseph Sperling was the Castle Hill rapist. It was that simple. The problem was that without Sperling's confession—indeed, with his continuing denial—Jaywalker knew he still didn't have enough to convince anyone else. Jacob Pope would shrug his shoulders, stroke his mustache and say it was interesting, but not enough to act upon.

There came a point during the hour when Sperling, while still maintaining his innocence of the Castle Hill rapes, offered to lie and say he'd committed them. That wasn't good enough, Jaywalker told him. He had to be telling the truth when he said he'd done them. That he couldn't do, said Sperling, shaking his head and telling Jaywalker how terribly sorry he was that he couldn't help him.

Jaywalker left Rikers Island with his head spinning. He'd come so close, only to end up empty-handed. And he knew he might not get another chance. No doubt

Sperling would tell his lawyer about the meeting. Jay-walker could expect a complaint and a reprimand of some sort. That was okay. He was a big boy, and he could handle it. What he couldn't handle was being ordered to stay away from Joseph Sperling.

He phoned Jacob Pope, only to learn that Pope had left the district attorney's office two weeks earlier to take a job as an assistant attorney general in North Carolina. Jay-walker asked who'd taken over Pope's cases, but nobody seemed to know. He demanded to speak to a supervisor and was finally put through to a man named Paul Garner. Garner headed up the Major Offense Bureau, the unit Pope had worked in.

Garner knew about the Kingston case, and about Joseph Sperling. While Jaywalker waited on his end of the phone, Garner pulled Sperling's file and read from it. Sperling had been indicted for eighteen rapes committed over a period beginning in November of 1980 and ending with his arrest in September of 1981. He'd admitted seventeen of them. He'd also admitted calling the D.A.'s office when he'd seen the *Daily News* article and telling them they had the wrong man.

"Why was I never told about that?" Jaywalker wanted to know. It had been a serious breach of ethics, if not an actual violation of the law. As Jaywalker, no stranger to breaching ethics or violating the law, knew only too well.

"He hung up without identifying himself," said Garner. "Hey, come on. Some guy calls to say we've got the wrong guy. For all we know, it's the defendant's brother calling us."

That was a lame answer, Jaywalker told him. "You still notify the guy's lawyer," he said, "and let *him* wonder if the information's worth anything." He pressed Garner to investigate. "Take a look at the photos," he said. "Check Sperling's record to see if he was in jail or out on the street during the 1979 rapes. Have somebody dig up the partial fingerprint lifted from one of the lightbulbs, the one of no value. Do *something,* for God's sake."

Garner said he would ask around and do what he could. But Jaywalker could tell a brush-off when he heard one.

He called Darren and Charlene, and told them that he'd finally gotten around to checking the lead, and that it looked somewhat promising. He wanted to give them hope—by that time, he felt Darren needed something to keep him going—but not too much hope. They'd been down too many roads already, and so far all of them had come to dead ends.

He lied and cheated and scrounged, got another special one-day pass, and drove out to Rikers Island again. He was armed with new arguments, new tactics, new strategies. He was determined to get a confession this time, if it killed him.

Joseph Sperling refused to see him.

A wet snow was falling as Jaywalker climbed back into his VW and headed home. He couldn't believe that after all this time he'd come so close, only to end up feeling farther away than ever.

The snow was beginning to stick on the Cross Bronx Expressway, making driving even more hazardous than usual. In addition to the typical array of potholes and hub-caps, now there were skidding cars and jackknifing trucks to contend with.

Through the snow, Jaywalker spotted the sign for the

Jerome Avenue exit. Reflexively, he pulled the wheel hard to the right, swerving around a gypsy cab and almost sliding into a concrete pillar. But he made the turn. He headed down to 161st Street and parked in a bus stop. In Manhattan, they towed. In the Bronx, they only ticketed.

He caught Paul Garner with his overcoat on, getting ready to leave for the day. He took the coat off, and the two of them spoke for the better part of an hour. Jaywalker described in detail his one meeting with Joseph Sperling. He did everything he possibly could to try to convince Garner that, despite Sperling's denial, he had to be responsible for the Castle Hill rapes.

Garner listened patiently. He was sympathetic but skeptical. He explained that he had four victims and twelve jurors who were absolutely certain that Darren Kingston was the right man. "I'd love to help you, Jay, but I can't. I just don't have enough."

Jacob Pope couldn't have said it any better. Only Pope was gone. This was his boss, and this was where the buck finally stopped.

The awful silence was broken by the ringing of a telephone. Garner excused himself to answer it, something he'd generously refrained from doing for the past hour. Jaywalker could tell he was being dismissed.

So he'd struck out once more.

Try as he had, he'd been unable to get Joseph Sperling to own up to the Castle Hill rapes. Now he'd tried to convince the only person who mattered that it made no difference, that he already had enough to go on, even without Sperling's confession. And he'd failed at that, too.

He wandered over to the window. Down toward River Avenue, the snow was falling on Yankee Stadium. Streetlamps lit up the crosswalks. Cars were inching along, bumper to bumper. People filled the sidewalks. They were all heading home, leaving their work in their offices. As Jaywalker should have been doing. Only his work wouldn't stay in his office. It kept following him around, wherever he went, and it seemed it always would.

Somewhere behind him, he became aware of a voice. It took him a moment to realize it was Paul Garner's. Jaywalker turned to face him, to say goodbye. Garner's hand was still on the phone he'd just cradled, and he was looking directly at Jaywalker.

"We have enough," he said softly. "That was Detective Squitieri, from the latent unit. The fingerprint on the light-bulb is Joseph Sperling's."

Nearly thirty years have passed, but Jaywalker can still recall the moment as though it's happening to him today. His tears catch him by surprise, and his first impulse is to fight them back, to be an adult. Then he gives in to them and lets them come. Two years of battling to keep a young man out of prison because he knew in his heart he didn't belong there. Two years of nothing but frustration, failure and defeat. And now in one instant, in one split second that means nothing to the rest of the universe, the nightmare is suddenly over. He feels the tears well up, spill over and flow freely down his cheeks. Garner stares at him as though he's lost his mind. But Jaywalker couldn't care less. He's earned these tears; he's entitled to them. Darren is free. They've won. It's all over, just like that. He feels his knees begin to shake and buckle. He reaches out behind him and grabs the windowsill for support.

25

THE NICEST THANK-YOU

On December 16th, 1981, twenty-eight months to the day after the rapes of Eleanor Cerami and Joanne Kenarden, Darren Kingston's conviction was set aside, and the indictment dismissed. For one last time Jaywalker stood beside him at the defense table in Part 16.

For Max Davidoff, the event marked his last act as a Supreme Court Justice, the end of a distinguished career as lawyer, prosecutor and judge. He had reached mandatory retirement age and was stepping down from the bench that very day.

The press was assembled, including representatives from all the city's newspapers and television stations. Some of the detectives who'd worked on Joseph Sperling's case had shown up.

As had, as always, Darren's family.

Jaywalker and Paul Garner had submitted papers, citing the body of evidence supporting Darren's innocence: the fingerprint, the hypnosis, the sodium amytol—and the myriad other things that everyone, with hindsight, now agreed pointed away from Darren and directly at Joseph Sperling. Now Garner rose and moved to vacate the judgment, Jaywalker joined in the motion, and Justice Davidoff granted it. What had taken two years to accomplish took two minutes to wrap up.

Outside the courtroom, a shy Darren Kingston faced the lights and cameras, and thanked his family and his lawyer for standing by him. As Jaywalker watched from a distance, he felt a hand come to rest on his arm. He turned to see Marlin.

"Jay," he said, "I got to thank you."

Jaywalker caught him even as he reached for his wallet. "No, you don't," he said. "Not this time."

For once, Marlin yielded. He wrapped both his strong arms around Jaywalker, pulled him close and embraced him, the same way Jaywalker had seen him embrace his wife the morning following their son's arrest, some twenty-seven months ago. The stubble of his beard felt like wet sandpaper against Jaywalker's face.

"Jay," he said, between sobs, "you gave me back my son."

It was the nicest thank-you Jaywalker would ever hear.

26

ELEVEN POINTS

The fingerprint that exonerated Darren Kingston turned out to be the original cellophane tape "lift" taken from the lightbulb in the stairwell where fourteen-year-old Maria Sanchez had been attacked. A photo of the lift had proved worthless. Even the lift itself had been of no value until the known prints of Joseph Sperling had been available. And even then, it had taken Detective Vincent Squitieri more than six hours, hunched over a microscope, to find eleven *points,* or matching characteristics, more than enough to make a positive comparison.

Contacted in North Carolina, Jacob Pope conceded that if it had been Sperling who'd attacked Miss Sanchez, then it only stood to reason that he'd attacked the other four victims, as well.

The victims themselves reacted with a certain amount of bitterness to the final turn of events. To this day, they no doubt continue to believe that Darren Kingston is the man who attacked them. Given the absolute certainty of their identifications of him, for them to suddenly believe otherwise and be forced to confront the fact that they'd been instrumental in convicting an innocent man would be nearly humanly impossible.

The post office took Darren back the same day his conviction was set aside.

Joseph Sperling's lawyer gave Jaywalker hell but never filed a formal complaint.

Jaywalker sent off a letter to Miles Michael, the Housing Authority examiner, requesting that he withdraw the specifications and permit Darren and Charlene to keep their apartment. Michael phoned Jaywalker to say he'd seen them on the evening news and had already done so on his own.

Jaywalker sent off another letter, this one to the New York Police Department, asking that Darren's fingerprint cards and mug shots from both his arrests be returned to him, so that they wouldn't remain in the drawer of some precinct, waiting to be picked out by some future victim. It took almost a year, but on November 17, 1982, a letter arrived, informing Jaywalker that the prints and photos were ready to be picked up.

For a while Jaywalker got calls and letters from people who'd seen his name in the newspaper and thought he could save them, too. None had the money to hire a lawyer, even a young one who worked at modest rates and was looking to rebuild his practice. Almost all were crazy.

Joseph Sperling was sentenced to serve twelve to twenty-five years in state prison.

Jaywalker kept in touch with Darren and the Kingston family for several years. But Jaywalker tends to be a poor custodian of friendships, and eventually they lost contact. To Jaywalker's way of thinking, that was probably for the best. To the Kingstons, he would always be a reminder of a terrible chapter in their lives. It was time for all of them to move on and try to forget.

That said, after his wife would lose her struggle against cancer, Jaywalker would continue to stay in touch with both her sisters, the younger one, who'd brought him Darren's case the first time, and the older one, who'd brought him the newspaper that would ultimately set Darren free.

The last Jaywalker heard of Carolyn Oates, she'd moved out west and written a couple of mystery novels. Jaywalker learned that not too long after he began running from the law and hiding out behind a typewriter himself. It seemed they'd ended up with the same editor, these two lawyers who'd briefly shared a client, thereafter to be separated by a continent.

Among the many other ironies of the case is the fact that had Darren Kingston been arrested ten or twenty years later, a simple DNA test would have cleared him in a matter of days or weeks, just as it eventually would have established with astronomical certainty that Joseph Sperling was the man responsible for the Castle Hill rapes. But largely overlooked in the DNA revolution is the impact that the tool *should* have on the public's understanding of eyewitness identification and confessions but has so far failed to. Long considered the sacrosanct pillars of criminal trial evidence, both cry out for reexamination. Behind every conviction of an innocent man lies a faulty eyewitness identification, a false confession, or both. According to one conservative estimate, there are today upwards of ten thousand individuals serving time in prisons across the country for crimes committed by others.

* * *

Jaywalker's ancient Volkswagen finally gave out some years back, and he's yet to find a suitable replacement. He's been holding out for something special, say a 1970 Gremlin or a '59 Studebaker Lark. Still, not long ago, he took one last trip up to Castle Hill. It was a bright weekday morning in March, a Friday. His daughter supplied the car and did the driving. Now in her early thirties, what little she knew of the case had come from having had an absentee father for two years of her life, and from hearing him mention it now and then over the years. Now Jaywalker wanted to show her the area, wanted to point out the spot where he'd come so many afternoons to stand for endless hours in the cold, searching for a man he knew had to exist. And he wanted to see for himself what the passage of a quarter of a century had done to the place.

He'd expected to find that urban blight and decay had completely taken over the project, much the same way the jungle has a way of reclaiming clearings left uncared for. He'd expected to see huge mounds of trash piled up and blowing everywhere; endless carcasses of cars stripped, torched and left for dead; roaming packs of feral dogs, their ribs showing beneath their flanks.

Instead, he found the tall redbrick buildings cleaner than ever. There was almost no trash in sight, no broken glass, no boarded-over windows. The streets were clean, the playgrounds well kept, the lawns raked and neatly trimmed. Brightly colored row houses marked the way to the southeast, toward the water.

The population in evidence that morning was largely Hispanic, with a distinct black minority. Make that African-American. But to Jaywalker's surprise, there were some whites, too, as well as some interracial couples and families. Mothers were walking their children to school-bus stops, pausing to greet blue-uniformed crossing guards. Men were leaving for work. Trucks were making deliveries to stores along Havemeyer Avenue.

Jaywalker had his daughter circle the blocks and read off the names of streets and avenues long forgotten but still familiar. Randall, Turnbull, Seward, Lacombe, Pugsley. She made a turn onto Stickball Boulevard and drove up Olmstead Avenue, where Darren's uncle Samuel had once lived. The improbable Roman names were still there. Homer, Cicero and Cincinnatus Avenues. Caesar and Virgil Places. Lafayette was there, too.

"It's not such a bad area," his daughter remarked at one point. "I expected much worse."

"Me, too," said Jaywalker.

Sometimes, in the early morning hours, before he climbs out of bed to get ready to go to court, Jaywalker lies awake alone and listens to the sparrows, and wonders how he ever lost the trial in the first place. But then he reminds himself that had he not, he never would have learned what he did from it, or grown into the lawyer he ultimately became.

There are those who believe that everything that happens in our lives happens for a reason. Perhaps they're right. Who's to say?

AUTHOR'S NOTE

Any resemblance between the characters and events depicted in this book with real people and actual occurrences is purely understandable. That's because it all happened, every last bit of it. I know, because many years ago, I was the young lawyer who lived through it.

That said, I've gone to some lengths in an endeavor to make it difficult for you to look the case up. In the interest of protecting individual privacy, I've changed the names of the people involved, and have even shifted the events so that they take place in different years from those in which they actually transpired. Beyond that, in an attempt to make the reading a bit easier, I've edited a word or two of the testimony, though only a word or two. The rest is lifted verbatim from the pages of the official court transcripts.

The locations all remain the same. There is indeed a Castle Hill in the Bronx, and I've kept it exactly as I found it and left it, just as I have with the story itself. It's my firm belief that, for the most part, truth really is far more compelling than fiction. And there are some things that happen in this life that are simply too extraordinary to change in the telling.

ACKNOWLEDGMENTS

I've had the exceedingly good fortune throughout my writing efforts to have been aided and abetted by Bob Diforio, whom I count as literary agent, business manager, advisor, fan and friend. Not long ago he had the wisdom to put me together with Leslie Wainger at MIRA. Not only is Leslie as smart and gifted an editor as I've ever come across, but she puts up with all—well, most of—my quirks and idiosyncrasies. Above all, she makes me laugh, an attribute far more important to me than all the rules of spelling, syntax and sentence structure combined.

My wife, Sandy, continues to be not only my love but my first and toughest reader, and in the end my most ardent supporter. My kids, my sister Tillie, my uncle Joe and my sister-in-law Carol are never far behind. And now that my granddaughters are all of reading age, I'm sure it won't be long before they, too, will be chiming in with suggestions and criticisms of their own. Darcy, the oldest of the four, has already proclaimed this book "pretty good," a comment that for some unfathomable reason MIRA has elected to omit from the front cover.

Finally, I'm indebted to the real people who played

roles in this story. I may have supplied fictitious names to Darren Kingston, his family and all the others who went to bat for him. But I know who they are, and so do they.

If you've enjoyed this Jaywalker novel,
turn the page for a look at
DEPRAVED INDIFFERENCE,
Joseph Teller's next Jaywalker case,
available November 2009
only from
MIRA Books.

And visit www.jaywalkercases.com
for news about
future cases.

A VERY BAD D.W.I.

"So," she said, raising herself onto one elbow, just high enough off the bed to reveal a single nipple, still visibly hard. "What do you do for a living, when you're not busy knocking people down?"

She was Amanda. At least that was as much of a name as he'd gotten out of her over the hour and twenty minutes since he'd literally knocked her to the ground by being overly aggressive with a sticking revolving door at the 42nd Street Public Library. Not that all their time together since that moment had been devoted to small talk. Or any other kind of talk, for that matter. Certainly not the last twenty minutes, anyway.

"I'm a lawyer," said Jaywalker. "Sort of."

"Sort of?"

"I'm not practicing these days," he explained.

"What happened?" she asked. "You get burned out?"

"No," he said. "More like *thrown* out. I'm serving a three-year suspension."

"What for?"

"Oh, various things. Cutting corners. Breaking silly rules. Taking risks. Pissing off stupid judges. The usual stuff."

"They suspend you for those things?"

"It seems so." He left it at that. He didn't feel any particular need to tell her about the juiciest charge of all, that he'd managed to get caught by a security camera in one of the stairwells of the courthouse, accepting—or at least not exactly fending off—an impromptu expression of heartfelt thanks from an accused prostitute for whom he'd just won a hard-fought acquittal.

"What did you say your name was?" she asked.

"I didn't. But it's Jaywalker."

It wasn't just a case of tit for tat, withholding part of his name because she had. The single name was all he had, actually. Harrison J. Walker had years ago elided into Harrison Jaywalker, and not too long after that, the Harrison part had disappeared altogether. So for years now, he'd been known to just about everyone simply as Jaywalker.

"You're that guy!" exclaimed Amanda, suddenly and self-consciously covering up her wayward nipple with a pillow, or perhaps it was a corner of her quilt. "I *knew* you looked familiar. I saw you on Page Six. You were dating that…that *billionaire heiress murderer!"*

Jaywalker winced painfully. Three years ago, had someone asked him to describe his own personal vision of what hell might be like, he might well have replied, "Showing up on the Entertainment Channel," or "Landing on Page Six of the *New York Post.*" But thanks to a brief, torrid, and not-so-discreet romance with a client named Samara Tannenbaum, he'd managed to accomplish not one but *both* of those distinctions, and in the short space of a single week.

"Yup," he acknowledged meekly now, "that would be me."

Amanda threw her head back and laughed out loud, her stylishly short blond hair framing her face in what could easily have been a fashion model's style. In the process, both her breasts came completely free of the sheets, causing a decided swelling in Jaywalker's appreciation of her.

"So tell me, mister famous lawyer man," she said. "How much do you charge for a drunk driving case?"

"I don't," said Jaywalker. "I'm suspended, remember?"

"Right, but for how much longer?"

Jaywalker shrugged. "I don't know. Seven months, maybe eight." The fact was, he hadn't exactly been counting the days. If anything, he'd lately been giving some serious consideration to *re-upping* for another three years. Although even as he'd been enjoying his estrangement from the legal profession, his checking account balance was rapidly approaching zero, making such a choice problematic.

"And if you *weren't* suspended?"

He shrugged again. "I don't know. I used to get twenty-five hundred, thirty-five hundred, something like that." And in spite of everything, he found himself already contemplating the variables, just as he used to do. First of all, it would depend on whether they were talking about a plea or a trial. After that, where the case was. A D.W.I. in Manhattan, the Bronx or Brooklyn was no big deal. If there'd been a blood alcohol test and Amanda's reading hadn't been too high, there was a good chance he could plead her down to driving while impaired. A couple of appearances, and the case would be done. Queens and Staten Island tended to be a bit tougher. And as you worked your way out into the neighboring counties—Westchester, Nassau and Suffolk, where there was a lower volume of cases—the D.A.s got noticeably more hard-assed and could afford to insist on a plea to the full charge. Not that it mattered all that much, though. What they were talking about here was a fine, a license suspension, or at very worst a revocation, a court-ordered one-day safe driving course and a substantial increase in her insurance premiums. In other words, a slap on the wrist and a smack on the wallet.

"Where were you arrested?" he asked her. "And did you take a test?" He couldn't help himself. He had to ask.

"Oh, no," said Amanda, shaking her head from side to side, with the inevitable ripple effect it caused to the, uh, rest of her. "It's not me."

"Oh?" said Jaywalker. "So who are we talking about?"

"My husband."

Jaywalker sat up, reflexively reaching around for his pants. His level of appreciation had suddenly shrunk dramatically. Funny how that happened.

"Don't worry," said Amanda. "It's not like he's about to walk in on us or anything."

"How do you know?"

"Because he's in jail on five million dollars bail. That's how."

Jaywalker relaxed ever so slightly. "Five million dollars," he echoed. "It must have been a very bad D.W.I."

"It was," said Amanda. "Nine people died."

NEW YORK TIMES
BESTSELLING AUTHOR

CARLA NEGGERS

A red velvet bag holding
ten sparkling gems.

A woman who must
confront their legacy
of deceit, scandal and murder.

Rebecca Blackburn caught a glimpse of the famed
Jupiter Stones as a small child. Unaware of their
significance, she forgot about them—until a
seemingly innocent photograph reignites one man's
simmering desire for vengeance.

Rebecca turns to Jared Sloan, the love she lost to
tragedy and scandal, his own life changed forever
by the secrets buried deep in their two families.
Their relentless quest for the truth will dredge up
bitter memories...and they will stop at nothing to
expose a cold-blooded killer.

BETRAYALS

Available wherever books are sold!

MIRA®

New York Times **bestselling author**

STELLA CAMERON

Lust is in the air.

Roche Savage is a talented psychiatrist with an insatiable, some might say kinky, sex drive. As a result, he's always avoided gentle, reserved women. Unfortunately, he's attracted to reticent Bleu Labeau, a young widow who has come to Toussaint to start a new school.

So is murder.

The school has unleashed another passion, as well. When a man is killed in St. Cecil's church, the local sheriff and the townspeople must fend for themselves. Taking the lead, Roche and Bleu race to unravel the mystery. But a shocking revelation indicates that they may not be looking for a stranger.

Cypress Nights

Available March 31, 2009,
wherever books are sold!

MIRA®

NEW YORK TIMES BESTSELLING AUTHOR

SHARON
SALA

Each scar tells a story....

John Nightwalker, a rugged Native American soldier, has
seen many battles. While hunting down an old enemy, he
meets Alicia Ponte. On the run from her father, an arms
manufacturer, Alicia seeks to expose her father's crimes
of selling weapons to Iraq. But Richard Ponte will do
anything to stay below the radar…even kill his own daughter.

John feels compelled to protect Alicia. They travel through
the beautiful yet brutal Arizona desert to uncover deadly
truths and bring her father to justice. But their journey
is about to take an unexpected turn…one that goes
deep into the past.

THE
WARRIOR

Available wherever books are sold.

REQUEST YOUR FREE BOOKS!

2 FREE NOVELS
FROM THE ROMANCE/SUSPENSE
COLLECTION PLUS 2 FREE GIFTS!

YES! Please send me 2 FREE novels from the Romance/Suspense Collection and my 2 FREE gifts (gifts are worth about $10). After receiving them, if I don't wish to receive any more books, I can return the shipping statement marked "cancel." If I don't cancel, I will receive 4 brand-new novels every month and be billed just $5.49 per book in the U.S. or $5.99 per book in Canada, plus 25¢ shipping and handling per book plus applicable taxes, if any*. That's a savings of at least 20% off the cover price! I understand that accepting the 2 free books and gifts places me under no obligation to buy anything. I can always return a shipment and cancel at any time. Even if I never buy another book from the Reader Service, the two free books and gifts are mine to keep forever.

185 MDN EF5Y 385 MDN EF6C

Name	(PLEASE PRINT)	
Address		Apt. #
City	State/Prov.	Zip/Postal Code

Signature (if under 18, a parent or guardian must sign)

Mail to **The Reader Service:**
IN U.S.A.: P.O. Box 1867, Buffalo, NY 14240-1867
IN CANADA: P.O. Box 609, Fort Erie, Ontario L2A 5X3

Not valid to current subscribers to the Romance Collection,
the Suspense Collection or the Romance/Suspense Collection.

Want to try two free books from another line?
Call 1-800-873-8635 or visit www.morefreebooks.com.

* Terms and prices subject to change without notice. N.Y. residents add applicable sales tax. Canadian residents will be charged applicable provincial taxes and GST. Offer not valid in Quebec. This offer is limited to one order per household. All orders subject to approval. Credit or debit balances in a customer's account(s) may be offset by any other outstanding balance owed by or to the customer. Please allow 4 to 6 weeks for delivery. Offer available while quantities last.

Your Privacy: Harlequin is committed to protecting your privacy. Our Privacy Policy is available online at www.eHarlequin.com or upon request from the Reader Service. From time to time we make our lists of customers available to reputable third parties who may have a product or service of interest to you. If you would prefer we not share your name and address, please check here. ☐

BOB08R

JOSEPH TELLER

32605 THE TENTH CASE   ___ $7.99 U.S. ___ $7.99 CAN.

(limited quantities available)

TOTAL AMOUNT $ _____
POSTAGE & HANDLING $ _____
($1.00 FOR 1 BOOK, 50¢ for each additional)
APPLICABLE TAXES* $ _____
TOTAL PAYABLE $ _____

(check or money order—please do not send cash)

To order, complete this form and send it, along with a check or money order for the total above, payable to MIRA Books, to: **In the U.S.:** 3010 Walden Avenue, P.O. Box 9077, Buffalo, NY 14269-9077; **In Canada:** P.O. Box 636, Fort Erie, Ontario, L2A 5X3.

Name: _____
Address: _____ City: _____
State/Prov.: _____ Zip/Postal Code: _____
Account Number (if applicable): _____

075 CSAS

*New York residents remit applicable sales taxes.
*Canadian residents remit applicable GST and provincial taxes.

MIRA®
www.MIRABooks.com

MJT0409BL